Relations

Pamela D. Beverly

abbott press®
A DIVISION OF WRITER'S DIGEST

Relations

ISBN: 978-1-4582-0379-3 (sc)
ISBN: 978-1-4582-0380-9 (e)
ISBN: 978-1-4582-0381-6 (hc)

Library of Congress Control Number: 2012908461

Abbott Press books may be ordered through booksellers or by contacting:

Abbott Press
1663 Liberty Drive
Bloomington, IN 47403
www.abbottpress.com
Phone: 1-866-697-5310

Printed in the United States of America

Abbott Press rev. date: 05/31/12

To Mom and those who believed

Acknowledgments

I acknowledge the Lord, who, through thick and thin, has always had me return to my first love—writing.

Second, I thank Andre Hill for giving me the inspiration for the fishing scene.

Third, I must acknowledge the front desk personnel at the Hampton Inn, Savannah, Georgia, for their hospitality—especially telling me where all of the good watering holes were. They made me feel right at home during my brief stay. Guest service agent Lavernitra Roberson and concierge Mary Hurn were very helpful, vividly painting the color, history, and exuberance of the city. If it just hadn't been so hot!

And finally, you've got to hand it to cities like Savannah and its sister city, New Orleans. Any place that allows you to walk down the street with an alcoholic drink in your hand doesn't take itself too seriously, except when it comes to having fun. Let the good times roll.

I hope to visit again someday soon—but maybe during the winter months.

Chapter One

The eloquence was not in the words Frank Ellis spoke but the way in which he spoke them. His audience listened with rapt attention; only in their subconscious were they incredulous at being fascinated by a topic so dreaded as to border on the macabre—life insurance.

Nevertheless, they continued to sit, on chairs jammed into a meeting space just short of being in violation of the city's fire code, hanging on to his every word. The world just outside of the downtown Atlanta ballroom where Frank was conducting his seminar was forgotten, at least for a little while.

Frank allowed the silence of their enchantment to wash over him for a moment before he resumed speaking. It was almost intoxicating, the sensation of having so many eyes upon him, waiting to hear what words he would utter next. He strolled with a casual but confident air in front of the group as he spoke. His was a striking presence; the fabric of his well-tailored dark-blue suit moved against the muscles of his body in a sensuous way. He was handsome but not overly so, with dark-chocolate brown skin, a mustache that framed his full, expressive mouth, and deep-brown eyes that focused on each person with laser-sharp intensity. His baritone voice, athletic figure, and smooth movements caused all eyes in the room to be riveted on him.

"Death comes to meet and greet each and every one of us—eventually. You may say, 'I don't concern myself with something I can't control.'" Frank paused, milking the moment. "But, ladies and gentlemen, you do have control over one aspect of it. You control that aspect of financial planning that will give your loved ones a secure life—a comfortable life—even as yours has ended.

"Do that for them."

There was silence, and then the audience burst into thunderous applause.

THE NEXT MORNING OF THE seminar dawned sunny but with a decidedly sharp bite in the early April air. Frank went into his presentation that day with his characteristic understated intensity. Financial planning and estate planning weren't exactly topics that would have the average listener hanging on to every word. Yet Frank had a way of relaying information that made the listener want to hear more about it. The subject matter almost didn't matter, although he made sure that his material was always relevant for the times. Being successfully self-employed as a financial consultant depended on it.

"If anyone has any questions, feel free to ask them. I'll entertain them all."

A kind-faced older woman popped up from the sea of people. "I'm interested in mutual funds, but the interest rate isn't really generating much growth."

Frank launched into the pros of entering into the world of mutual funds versus the even more negligible returns she would accrue in a regular savings account. "How comfortable are you with risk, and how far are you from retirement?"

"I've been retired for two years now," she answered, batting her eyelids, flattered at his assumption that she was a younger woman and not a retiree.

He coaxed from the woman the information he needed to give an informed opinion in less than two minutes. By the time the lively banter between Frank and the woman was over, the crowd was in a tizzy. Hands flew up left and right. He smiled with appreciation, almost shyly.

"I need to take a fifteen-minute break," he announced, his low voice cracking like an adolescent boy's, almost as if on cue. It sent the large audience comprised of almost all women into gales of laughter.

"Okay, okay, so I'm not as old as I look. Back in fifteen."

After relieving himself, he went outside and had a quick smoke. Once back inside, he resumed answering their questions. As he viewed the crowd, one face kept capturing his attention.

The young woman stood and spoke, her eye-catching reddish-blonde tousled curls and greenish eyes a departure, even in the highly diversified audience. She was dressed in a gold sweater and cream-colored slacks. They hugged her curves like a second skin but not in a vulgar way. To Frank, they hugged her just right.

"Could you talk a little more about life insurance, Mr. Ellis?" she asked in a soft southern accent. "What should those of us in our thirties be looking for when purchasing life insurance?"

"I surely can. However, it depends." He paused. "Are you married?"

There were a few murmurs and giggles by the women in the audience at his remark. Frank exuded a masculinity that made each of them feel special, as if he were speaking only to them.

Despite their comments, her gaze was unwavering, and she did not giggle. "No."

He dived into the debate about whether single people needed life insurance in the first place, ending with, "If you have assets, say, property or an art collection that you want to bequeath to someone, you need a living will or living trust more so than life insurance. Does that answer your question?"

"Yes, it does. Thank you."

"You're entirely welcome."

The woman sat down and Frank continued, but as he scanned the audience to select those with questions, his eyes kept straying to the area where the young southern woman was sitting. He couldn't help himself. Her eyes mesmerized him from across the room, along with her other physical attributes. He had to force his thoughts back to the task at hand.

AFTER THE SEMINAR, FRANK WAS bombarded, as many of the audience members swarmed around him, continuing to pepper him with inquiries. He was flattered because he gauged his audience's receptiveness by the amount of questions and feedback he received. This was the last day of his seminar, and although he had provided them with his e-mail address and cell phone number, he spent nearly another hour answering their questions. Most of the attendees wanted to order copies of Frank's estate-planning or retirement kits. Some wanted both.

He finished packing his laptop and program materials and then left the ballroom. He was glad that he had only to head upstairs to go to his room. He was exhilarated but drained.

After dropping off his equipment, Frank headed back downstairs, through the hotel lobby, to the hotel bar. It was a little past six, but happy hour was alive and well.

He loosened his tie a bit. "Gin and orange juice," he informed the bartender once he caught his attention. "Make it a double."

Upon receiving the drink, he drained most of it in one gulp. Something caught his eye, and he turned to his right. The shapely young woman with the coppery-blonde hair stood across the room. There were three men and another woman from the seminar surrounding her. She spoke with them for a few more minutes and then threaded her way through the crowded space to where Frank stood at the bar.

"Hello there," she said as she approached Frank.

"Hello." He drained the rest of his drink and indicated her nearly empty glass. "Anything for you?"

"One's my limit," she replied, her voice silk against his ears in a room full of loud music, laughter, and talk.

He summoned the bartender. "I think I'll have another. Gin and orange juice. Double."

"Very interesting presentation, Mr. Ellis."

"Call me Frank." He set his empty glass down and reached for the fresh one. "And you are Miss …?"

"I'll tell you. Now don't laugh." She cast her eyes downward for a moment—but only for a moment. "Delilah. Delilah Carpenter."

"Now why would I laugh at your name? It suits you," Frank said before he took a healthy swallow from his drink.

"Stop teasing me. Most people I meet give me grief about it being old-fashioned, but there's not much I can do about it now, is there?" Delilah asked as she touched his arm and laughed. Her laugh reminded Frank of tinkling bells.

"I think it's the epitome of a southern name for a southern belle—makes me think of Spanish moss and sweet tea."

She looked at him. "That's very sweet. You look at things a lot deeper than most, Frank."

He shrugged and put his empty glass back on the bar. "I call 'em as I see 'em. I think I need one more for the road. Hey, bartender!" His head was swimming a little. He hadn't eaten much all day, and he was feeling the effects of it.

Delilah noticed. "How about dinner?"

Frank drained it in one gulp and tossed several bills on the counter. "I was just about to suggest that." He staggered a little. "Hotel restaurants are notorious for having lousy food, but I don't think I should drive in my condition." He attempted to stifle a belch without success and chuckled.

"I could drive," Delilah said as she reached for his arm.

With clumsiness, they weaved their way through the crowd and toward the bar exit.

"Nope, 'cause I don't think I'd make it." He slipped his arm around her shoulder. "Let's just go to one of the hotel's restaurants."

After reaching the restaurant, they waited a while to be seated and then again to be waited upon. The restaurant was beginning to fill with patrons. Soft music and delectable aromas wafted through the restaurant's tasteful décor.

"I'm starting to lose my appetite," Frank proclaimed in a loud voice. Everyone within earshot turned to look. As if on cue, a harried-looking waiter appeared.

They gave him their orders. Delilah smiled an apology at him, and the young man disappeared.

"I'm glad you liked my presentation, Delilah."

"Call me Dee."

He waved his hand, shaking his head. "Oh no, don't do that. Don't shorten it. I like it just the way it is. Delilah. Full of southern charm." He sipped his water.

"That's one way of looking at it."

"Are you from here, Delilah? Atlanta, I mean?"

"No. I do live in Georgia, but I'm from Savannah. And I know that you're not, judging by your accent."

He smiled. "My accent?"

Delilah smiled in return. She loved Frank's urbane demeanor. He was confident, almost cocky, and it was understandable, since there was no doubt that he was used to having all eyes upon him. Yet he gave her his undivided attention. She didn't know what to make of him. The fact that he was African American hardly factored into it, although she had to admit to herself that it intrigued her. It was the first time a black man had ever shown interest in her. They looked and sometimes verbalized their appreciation in passing but never approached her. When she thought about it, she realized she was the one who had actually approached Frank.

"Sure, you have one," she replied. "I can't place it although I know it's from somewhere in the Northeast. It's very subtle, but it's the way you pronounce some of your vowels."

"Really? I figured you only knew that because I had my address posted on the easel in the front of the ballroom." He nodded his head, as if for emphasis. His temples throbbed, but he ignored it.

"It's true, I did see your address, but most folks have some type of dialect or accent, which is usually only noticed by those who aren't from the same area."

"True that." Frank continued to gaze at her through his water glass. "But yours is very attractive. In fact, you're very attractive." He set down his glass, knocking it over in the process. Water sloshed onto the white tablecloth as it hit the table with a loud clatter, but he paid it no mind in his awkward attempt to take hold of her hand.

"And you're a little drunk, aren't you?" Although quite flattered by his compliments, she was not sure they weren't fueled somewhat by the alcohol.

Using swift but calm movements, Delilah mopped up the water on the tablecloth with a small package of tissues she had in her purse.

Their food arrived. The waiter gave Frank a quick glare as he served them and then stalked over to the next table. Frank failed to notice, and he took a few bites of his steak while Delilah ate her meal with gusto.

"Gotta love a woman who's not afraid to eat."

She swallowed a mouthful of mashed potatoes, dabbing at her mouth with her napkin. The meal was hot and tasty. "Should I be?"

"Not at all. I like that in a woman. You know, a man can tell a lot about a woman by how she eats."

"Is that right? Seems like you like a lot of things, Mr. Ellis." *Probably has a girl in every city he's visited*, she thought.

"It's Frank, remember?" He took a bite of salad, and then put down his fork. "I know this much—I know I like you."

"That's nice. I like you too." She looked up from her plate at him. "You aren't eating."

"I've had enough, but don't you stop. Take your time." He reached for her free hand.

His large hand was warm but firm, his fingers thick. Although he had spilled the water earlier, she knew he was graceful and capable. Watching him during his presentations over the past few days, she could tell that he was not normally a clumsy man. It felt comforting, but it stirred her too. Although he had been a bit rude with the wait staff and more than a little flirtatious during their meal, she chose to blame it on his alcohol consumption and the quick attempt to relax after his speaking engagement.

"You need to eat more than that—"

Her response was interrupted with the loud clanging of dishes and silverware as his head hit the table.

TOGETHER, DELILAH AND A BELLBOY managed to get Frank to his suite on the tenth floor. They led him over to the bed, and he flopped down upon it.

"Ma'am, I'd rather not leave you alone in here with him."

"He's not feeling well," Delilah said as she removed Frank's suit jacket. "I just want to make sure that he's okay." From the bellboy's remark and wrinkled brow, she was sure that he thought Frank was drunk and therefore might be unpredictable.

"Okay, ma'am," the bellboy replied with a shrug and left the suite.

Delilah went to the kitchen area, ripped a handful of paper towels from the roll, and wet them under the faucet. Hurrying back to where Frank lay on the king-sized bed, she wiped his perspiration-slicked forehead, plucking the bits of salad from his closely-cropped hair.

He slid his arm around her waist and pulled her toward him, self-assured even in his semiconscious state. He smelled of cigarette smoke, alcohol, and a fresh-scent cologne, which played with her senses.

"Mmm, you feel real good ..."

Delilah pulled out of his embrace. "No, no, no." She pulled off his shoes and threw the blanket over him. Even through his aggressive behavior, his vulnerability shone as brightly as sunlight on snow. She felt no threat from him, only a growing attraction.

She turned out the lamp on the nearby nightstand. "Good night, Frank," she whispered as she tiptoed out the door.

THE NEXT MORNING, FRANK AWOKE to the sound of jackhammers.

"What the hell—oh wait, that's not outside—that's inside my skull," he mumbled, groping along the nightstand for what he hoped was a pack of cigarettes. Not finding them there, he swung his feet off the bed, sitting there for a moment. Hoping the cacophony inside his head would subside, he swore to himself when it did not and stumbled over to his suit jacket that was slung over a chair. Rummaging around the inside pocket, he yanked out the pack and a tiny lighter. Ignoring the no-smoking policy and lighting up, he took a deep drag and headed for the bathroom. His head still hurt, but now it hurt with more clarity.

As he showered and smoked, keeping his cigarette out of the shower spray, Frank played the previous night's events back in his head with dread. *I was drunk off my ass. Did I pass out? How'd I get to my room?*

Delilah's face emerged from the murkiness of his brain. *Damn, she was here, watching me make a fool of myself. And I didn't even get her number.*

He dried himself off and fastened the towel around his taut waist. Although he smoke and drank, he worked out as often as his scheduled permitted and it showed. He applied deodorant and cologne and then brushed his hair.

Making his way to the large chest, he grabbed a pair of underwear and socks, and then moved to the closet. He glanced over at the bedside clock. He was lucky. He had awakened from his drunken slumber in time to catch his one-thirty flight.

While dressing, he called the front desk. "Would you please connect me to Miss Carpenter's room?"

There was a wait of several minutes and then, "I'm sorry, Mr. Ellis but Miss Carpenter has already checked out."

"Okay. Well, thanks for checking," he replied and hung up. *Damn!*

Well, no doubt, I put my worst foot forward in her case, he thought, packing up the few items still lying around the suite.

He quickly perused his hotel bill while he brushed his teeth. Afterward, he grabbed his belongings and his coat and headed out the door.

Grabbing a to-go breakfast bag before leaving the hotel, Frank rushed to his rental vehicle and zoomed onto the interstate toward the bane of his traveling existence: the Hartsfield-Jackson Atlanta International Airport. He munched on a blueberry muffin as he drove and arrived at the rental car agency, just outside the terminal, with time to spare.

"Have a good day, sir."

Frank acknowledged the greeting with a nod as he handed the keys to a member of the rental car staff. He glanced at his watch and picked up his garment bag. Rolling his computer bag behind him, he headed toward the terminal entrance. In the dim light of the parking garage, a familiar figure several yards ahead caught his attention.

"Delilah!" he called out.

The woman turned around. Although she wore a navy knit hat that covered most of her hair, what was visible was unmistakable. Upon recognizing who was calling her, she smiled and waited for him to catch up.

"Listen, Delilah, I want to apologize to you for last night." Frank shook his head as he said, "I know it's an excuse, but I had too much to drink and hadn't eaten lunch—"

"No need to explain, Frank. It happens to the best of us."

"Yes, there is." He shifted the garment bag he had slung over his shoulder. "Are you taking a flight?"

"No, I gave one of the women who attended the lecture a ride to the airport." She pushed a curly lock of hair out of her eyes. "I drove my car to your seminar."

"Lucky you."

Delilah gazed at him, curious about his comment. "Why do you say that? You don't like flying?"

"Baby, *that* is an understatement. Sorry, baby—I, mean, Delilah. Bad habit of mine, calling women that." He checked his watch again. "I don't have a lot of time, but I'd like to buy you a cup of coffee, if you'll let me."

She smiled. "Sure."

They hurried inside the terminal to what appeared to be an endless row of ticket counters that ran along the wall. Luck was with him as he stepped to the counter; the man in front of him had just finished. He skirted past Frank and the vinyl-strapped walk-through as headed toward the vast gate area beyond. Delilah waited while Frank quickly checked his garment bag.

She pointed to his computer bag. "What about that?" she asked.

"I never check my equipment. This is my traveling office, and we all know how luggage can get lost on flights." They began walking briskly, and Frank pointed to a nearby sandwich shop. "It's lunchtime. Would you like something to eat?"

"Just sweet tea. That is, if you have time."

"Great. I owe you that much since you got stuck with the bill from our last meal. How much was it, anyway?" Frank asked, and gave the young man behind the counter their drink orders.

She waved away his question as they waited. "It's no big deal, Frank."

They threaded their way through the folks coming and going through the terminal to an empty table and two chairs outside the sandwich shop. Once they sat down, they talked for a little while about superficial subjects. Both were trying to keep it light after what had happened the previous night.

All too soon, Frank had to leave. He had just under an hour before he had to board his plane. Since he hated waiting in airports, especially one the size of Hartsfield, Frank had perfected getting through the checkpoints and to the gate with a minimum amount of time remaining before his flight, although he was pressing it now. He didn't care. He wasn't about to leave without talking to Delilah. They exchanged numbers before he sprang to his feet and pulled her chair out for her. "I've got to run, and I mean that literally. I'm glad I got a chance to see you—with me in a better light."

"I am too."

"I haven't forgiven you yet, though." His voice grew even deeper with his teasing. "You were going to just leave town without a word. I didn't have your number. Are you on Facebook?"

"Sorry, I'm not really into Facebook or Twitter." She pointed to her purse. "Anyway, you forget; I did have your cell phone number. You gave it to us during the seminar, remember?"

Frank felt his face grow warm, but he remained cool. "Right. But that's not to say you would've used it."

"True. I might not have." She turned the teasing back on him.

"But I will. It was a pleasure meeting you, Delilah. I'll talk to you later." He held out his arms. "Can I get a hug before I go?"

She went into them, and his arms encircled her. Her face brushed against his nubby wool coat, and she breathed in his fresh scent. He was a strange man in some ways. She still didn't know what to make of him. But she did know that she wanted to know more about him.

DELILAH MADE HER WAY HOME to Savannah before nightfall. She was grateful that the weather was nice, and she had an uneventful drive.

As usual, it was as if her sister, Clementine, had eyes upon her house; she had the uncanny ability to call the moment Delilah set foot across the threshold.

She rooted around in her shoulder bag and dug out her cell phone. "Hello, Clemmie," she replied without bothering to glance at the number displayed on it. Clementine Zimmerman was Delilah's older sister. She and her husband Scott also lived in Savannah, about ten miles away.

"How was the seminar?"

Delilah dropped her suitcase at the door and idly sorted through the mail she had picked up from the mailbox on the way in. "It was stimulating, very stimulating."

"So, who was he?" Clementine asked in a knowing tone.

Delilah turned out the light in the foyer as she walked up the stairs to her bedroom. Once upstairs, Delilah plopped upon the plump mattresses and sighed with contentment. "What do you mean?"

"You know exactly what I mean. Any time life insurance is described as 'stimulating,' there's got to be a man behind it."

Delilah shook her head. She was incredible. "Are you part witch?"

"Nope." She chuckled. "I just know you, little sister."

You can say that again, Delilah thought. Aloud, she said, "The *speaker* was stimulating. His name is Frank Ellis."

"Uh-huh."

"He's just a very talented speaker." Delilah stretched out on the bed and cradled the cell phone against her ear. "He could make talking about dust interesting."

"Wow."

"He lives in Washington, DC."

"A Yankee, huh?"

"Yep." She knew they were heading into dangerous territory, because her sister was going to want to know all about him. Feigning a yawn, she remarked, "Girl, I am tuckered out. You mind if we continue this discussion later?"

"Not at all. Get some rest, Dee."

"I will." She hung up and lay there a while. As the room slowly grew dark, she thought, *I wonder how you'd take it if you knew Mr. Ellis was black.*

THE DRIVING RAIN MADE IT difficult for Frank to see where he was going on the gloomy, wet streets on the outskirts of Washington, DC. Save for a few poor, careless folks running hither and yon to escape the watery deluge, no one was on the road. He continued on his drive, peering between the fast-moving windshield wipers as he listened to jazz on satellite radio.

After what seemed an eternity, Frank arrived home to his condo on the penthouse floor. While hanging up his coat and dispensing with his other dripping paraphernalia, his thoughts traveled to Delilah. He had enjoyed being with her. *And from what I see, she's got a helluva body. Even the freckles on her nose are cute.* He shook his head in disbelief at his own sophomoric thoughts. *She makes me feel like a damn teenager*, he finally admitted to himself.

He changed into a pair of black-and-blue-checked lounging pajama bottoms and, along with the sleeveless undershirt he already wore, slipped his feet into leather slippers and scuffed his way to his updated kitchen. Whenever he was in his condo, his haven, Frank worked on becoming a gourmet cook. He knew that he had above-average culinary skills, but when he cooked for any of his female companions, judging by their expressions he wasn't sure if they felt the same.

Cracking eggs and shredding a hunk of cheddar he had found in the refrigerator and deemed salvageable, he set about making a cheese omelet. He quickly hacked up a portion of a chorizo sausage link in a small frying pan to add to it.

"Let's hear it for cholesterol!" he crowed.

While the food was cooking, he wiped his hands. Snatching the cordless phone from its charger, he dialed the digits that he had already committed to memory.

"Hello?" The female voice sounded tentative.

"Good evening, Delilah," Frank sang, cradling the phone between his ear and shoulder. "Did I wake you?"

"Oh, hey there, Frank. No, you didn't."

There it was: swaying on a swing porch in the sultry summer sun. Basking in the image her voice conjured up for him, he threw a stale slice of bread into the toaster.

"What's that sound?"

"Am I making too much noise? Sorry. I'm putting the finishing touches on my omelet."

"Uh-huh."

Spreading a little butter on the toast, Frank threw it on the plate and shoveled his egg creation beside it. It wasn't exactly an Emeril Lagasse-esque presentation, but he was starving. "I wanted your company while I ate. Is that all right?"

"Yes, it's fine." Delilah laughed. "You are the most peculiar man—"

"But I'm pretty sure that's good." Frank was silent for a moment while he blessed his food. "Isn't it?"

"It is." Her laughter reduced to a chuckle. "I think."

"Don't worry, it is. So, how was your trip home?" He began to eat his omelet.

"Fine. Luckily I didn't run into too much traffic, and the weather was beautiful. And your trip?"

He swallowed. "Kind of long and the weather here is lousy. Noah would pass on coming out in this mess. But I survived."

"That's good. How's your omelet?"

"Great, if I do say so myself. Hey, I hope I'm not smacking in your ear or anything, but this is the only way I can have your company while I'm eating."

That tinkling laugh again. "You're not smacking."

"Good. Although this omelet would be even better if we were here together."

"Okay …"

Frank could hear the trepidation in her voice. "For a *visit*, Delilah. Or I could visit you. Look, I travel a lot, and I've got frequent-flyer miles out the wazoo. I could send you a ticket, and you could meet me somewhere. Or come here." He thought for a second. "I'll only be here a week, and then I'm on the road again. I want to see you—"

"Frank, you're moving kind of fast—"

He set his fork down and wiped his mouth with a napkin. "In all seriousness, Delilah, I do travel a lot, and I'd like to get to know you. I guess I should ask you—would you like to get to know me?"

"Yes I would, but—"

"But what?" He got up from the table. He had been ignoring the nagging thought that had been in the back of his mind since they met, but now it pushed its way to the front. *Go ahead and ask it.* "What is it? You don't like African American men?"

"It's not that. I'm not prejudiced, if that's what you mean."

"What is it, then?"

"Frank, I'm very close to my family. And I'm not sure that my family isn't, among other things."

He placed the dirty dishes in the dishwasher and slammed it shut, smiling to himself. Aloud, he said, "We'll cross that bridge if and when we come to it."

Chapter Two

Once on the airplane, Frank baby-stepped his way through the cramped aisle with a number of other passengers until he found his aisle seat midplane. He sat down in it with reluctance. As soon as the plane's engines began their familiar high-pitched whine, he began his silent countdown until the flight attendant would be taking his drink order.

Finally. Drink time.

"Would you like something to drink?" asked the flight attendant, tossing a lock of blonde hair over her shoulder, an invitation in her eyes.

His smile was brief but the telltale sign of his distress was the death grip he had on the outer armrest. "Gin and orange juice, please."

Frank downed his drink in two gulps and then waited for what seemed an eternity for the attendant to cover her portion of the cabin so he could order another. Later he noticed a slip of paper peeking out from under the napkin as she placed another drink down for him. He lifted a corner of it and pulled out the paper. He smiled as he read the phone number and the name above it. *Rita.* After consuming his second drink, he endured the rest of the flight with an uneasy buzz.

"Frank! Hey, Frank!"

Frank pulled his garment bag from the metal carousel in baggage claim before looking in the direction from which his name was called. He noticed a familiar dirty-blond head of hair bobbing toward him through the throng. It was his best friend, Andy Maxwell, looking like he belonged on a beach somewhere. He had just finished speaking at a training class on Friday, and they would soon be speaking at the same conference in

Las Vegas. With his Keith Urban shaggy hair and boundless exuberance, Andy appeared younger than his thirty-two years.

"Hey, Andy. How'd it go in Utah?"

"Excellent!" He was electrified. "I haven't had a chance to look at the evals, but I think this class was my best yet. Everybody was pumped, the energy was incredible—anyway, how about you?"

"I'm ready," Frank said.

They headed toward the rental car area. They had each rented cars for the week. "You don't sound like it."

"I'm okay. I'm just a little tired. Hey, where's your car parked?"

"On the P2 level. I've got my keys already." Andy shook his head. "You're probably tired because you smoke like a chimney. You need to leave those cigarettes alone."

"Yeah, I know. Look, why don't we meet up at the hotel later?"

"All right. Catch you later," Andy said as he remained on the elevator that would take him to P2.

Frank huffed his way through the double doors on the lower level of the airport where the rental car agencies were located. After standing in line for what seemed like an eternity, he picked up the keys to his rental car for the half-hour drive to the hotel.

HE WAS POETRY IN MOTION. With fluid movements and his compelling voice, he almost hypnotized his listeners into compliance on a satiny carpet of mellifluousness. It wasn't so much sexiness as it was the sincerity in his voice. Both men and women loved his presentations on personal financial management, so he had no shortage of engagements as well as private consultations. Frank loved talking about the subject and could speak on it endlessly, but he always tempered his urge to go on and on, preferring that age-old credo: less is more.

"You ready?" It was Andy, calling on his cell from downstairs in the hotel bar late the next evening.

"Yeah." Frank hung a hanger draped with a pair of slacks in the tiny closet. "I'll be right down."

Within minutes, they were sitting at the richly paneled mahogany bar of their hotel in the midst of the smoke-filled din, enjoying their drinks. Dinner was virtually forgotten. "You didn't bring your girl with you?" Frank inquired.

"Nope. Twyla couldn't get away from her job."

"That's messed up."

"Well, you know, the kids are still in school. And the school that she drives the bus for is short on drivers as it is, so she didn't want to take off right now. Man, I tell you, if this group is anything like that one I had in Utah—" He left the statement unfinished, still basking in the hot and glorious rays of his achievement.

"That's always nice. I like a receptive crowd."

"It was practically orgasmic."

Frank laughed. "Dude, you've been without your woman too long."

"Maybe." A cloud of contemplation crossed his sun-kissed features. "I really miss that girl."

Frank cast an envious glance at his friend. Andy had someone waiting for him at home. He squashed the sensation like an annoying fly in midflight. Single life was great, but sometimes it left a lot to be desired. He felt that more and more of late. He squinted through the smoke to take a long drag from his cigarette and then hold it for a few moments before he sent it billowing into the air.

Andy waved his hand through the air, attempting to diffuse it. "Damn, I wish y'all could contain that stuff. Indoor air pollution."

"Yeah, yeah. Not all of us can subsist on bee pollen and steamed vegetables. Anyway, that drink's not exactly healthful, in and of itself." He signaled to the bartender.

"I'll buy that, but my drinking is pretty much a social pursuit. You, I'm willing to bet, pursue your indulgence solitarily as well as socially. I mean, look at this. You even search out these smoke-filled, death-trap hotels that still allow smoking. That's the reason you like Las Vegas, because they still allow smoking indoors when most states don't. I mean, it's the twenty-first century for Pete's sake. Give it up, and come on over to the other side where the fresh air is." Andy shook his head. "Vegas—the last of the holdouts."

"Vegas." Frank smiled at the attractive older woman who sat on the bar stool on the other side of him and gave her a wink. "My kind of town."

Andy glanced around at an elderly woman as she ambled past him. True to form, she didn't head for the bar but for the row of battered slot machines beyond it. "What the—? Slots in a bar? Vegas—where you can get fleeced every day of the week."

Frank answered his friend with a series of smoke rings.

"Aww, c'mon. I don't know why I even associate with your ass."

Frank affected a heavy Asian accent as he quipped, "Little grasshopper come to sit at the feet of the master. Gain much wisdom."

"Humph." Andy pushed the half-filled ashtray closer to his friend. "More like gain lung cancer."

Frank stubbed out the smoky remains of his cigarette.

"One down." Andy scanned the crowded bar; most of the patrons were smoking. "And about fifteen more to go."

Frank stared at the amber liquid in his glass but remained silent.

Andy glanced sideways at his best friend. Sometimes he couldn't figure him out. He had the world by the tail. He was his own boss and well paid for his speaking engagements. He was enormously self-confident and poised, stiff sometimes, but he had a good sense of humor and could also laugh at himself. He was smooth without even trying, and the women went crazy for him. Although he was in his midthirties, Frank was one of those lucky guys who, on a good day, appeared years younger than his actual age. Anyway, it didn't really matter. His entire package worked with women aged twenty to eighty—and with his strong jaw and good looks, it always would. Of that, Andy was certain. Frank's powerful voice accentuated his features by captivating most who heard it. It was one of the reasons why he was so successful as a public speaker. The refreshing thing was that Frank seemed unaware of it. Most of the time, anyway. Now he seemed circumspect.

"What the hell is it?" Andy asked.

"What is 'what'?" Frank never looked up.

"What is with you, man?" Andy half laughed. "I'm not gay or anything, but you're a reasonably good-looking guy—"

"Thanks."

"I mean it. You don't do anything for me, but I saw you this morning in the ballroom. You've got that 'Quiet Storm' after-dark voice that drives the women crazy. I've even seen Twyla check you out when she thought I wasn't looking, and she told me a long time ago that she only digs 'Cauruthers' now."

At this unfamiliar term, Frank finally emerged from the depths of his glass. "Cauruthers?"

Andy gave him his lopsided grin. "Her word for Caucasian brothers. Me."

Frank threw his head back and let go a hearty laugh. "Sure she did. You are *stupid*, man. But you're my brother, and I love you."

"I love you too man. But seriously, Frank, I'm kinda worried about you. You smoke too much. And lately, you've been drinking too much—"

Frank slammed his glass down on the bar, startling everyone within earshot. "You're the one who asked me to meet you here, in the bar—"

"I know, but that's just because I know that's where you want to go before we go anywhere else. C'mon, Frank, chill. I just wanna know what's wrong." In his eyes, Frank could see the sincere regard Andy had for him. He was truly the younger brother he never had. "What's happening?"

Frank was silent for a long time before he finally spoke. "Hell, Andy, I don't even know. My gig is going okay; I can do this standing on one leg, but the rest of it—"

"The rest of *what*?" Andy was still looking at him with a perplexed expression.

Frank shook some peanuts from the glass bowl on the bar into his hand and tossed them into his mouth. "The rest of my life just ain't happening anymore."

"*What*? Hell, you're your own boss. I still have to report to the office and a boss. And with all of the women you have lined up from coast to coast?"

"Yeah," Frank mumbled, continuing to munch on peanuts.

Chapter Three

❖◆×◆❖

"**M**iss Carpenter? *Miss Carpenter!*"

Delilah stared at a large hand waving in front of her face. "Wha—?"

"Are you finished with those reports yet?" It was Mr. McDermott, her supervisor. He was old school. Although everyone in the Acquisitions Branch where she worked knew that his first name was Steve, no one was allowed to call him that. If a new employee made that mistake, Mr. McDermott would verbally berate that person, ensuring that it never happened again. It was rumored that he was once a drill sergeant at Parris Island and carried that demeanor over into civilian life. He didn't look like a typical drill sergeant, but he could verbally cut a person up like one.

"Uh, yes, sir. They're right here, Mr. McDermott."

"I've been waiting for them for a half hour." He stood behind her, his chest pressed against the back of her chair, his face so close to Delilah's that she smelled the sour odor of coffee he had consumed earlier. He was not an old man, only in his forties, but he had an old-fashioned air about him when it came to supervising his employees. He glanced at his watch and with his long, well-manicured fingers, snatched the stapled sheaf of papers from her hand. "The meeting's in ten minutes."

With that, he threaded his way through the cubicles and was gone.

She heard snickering on the other side of the cubicle, and her face grew warm. *That damned Agnes Wylie.* She couldn't stand her nosy coworker. Not that she had to eavesdrop. With cubicles, everything was in the open in their office, but she was always the first one to spread a rumor.

Delilah typed a task she had nearly forgotten about into her online calendar. *I've got to keep my mind focused on my work,* she silently chided

20

herself. Persistent thoughts rammed themselves into her consciousness, like the sound of Frank's laugh when they last spoke. He had invited her to visit him. She had refused, saying that it was too soon.

And she hadn't spoken to him in the three weeks since then.

The warmth of his closeness when he brushed against her as they hurried inside the airport on the day after the seminar ...

Well, you were the one who wanted to slow things down, she thought.

The way his dark eyes probed hers before they said good-bye ...

You do have his number, her thoughts insisted.

"You going to lunch or what?" Vivian, her coworker and friend, asked, shattering her fragile reverie. A high-energy woman of thirty-three or so, she seemed out of place in their office. She belonged in the movies of the 1950s or in the old sitcom *Married With Children*, wearing stiletto heels and capri pants. Divorced for two years, her rather poufy bleached-blonde hair and snappy black eyes went along with the gum she occasionally popped when she was not in earshot of Mr. McDermott; she was always funny and direct. She now stood with a hand on her hip, not even bothering to disguise her impatience. Had she been standing there long?

Delilah extracted her purse from its confines of her desk drawer. "Come on, let's go."

AFTER WORK, DELILAH RAN TO the supermarket to pick up a few items. She picked up an angel-food cake and a bottle of white wine to take to her sister Clementine's house. She was having dinner with her and her brother-in-law, Scott.

After dinner, they sat on the porch, Delilah fingering the slim cell phone she clutched in her sweaty palm.

Fireflies glowed intermittently in the growing electric-blue dusk. Delilah and Clementine swayed to-and-fro on the porch swing while Scott tinkered with his beloved pick-up truck. The muffled metallic clinking of tools could be heard beyond the closed garage door. The fruity perfume of the climbing roses on the trellis several yards away intermingled with the heavy fragrance of jasmine shrubbery from the backyard. Although it had been a somewhat chilly spring, it was now early May, and the promise of a hot summer lay just ahead.

"I swear, Dee, will you come out with it?"

"Out with what?" She continued to clutch the cell phone as though it were a lucky charm.

"What's got you all quiet and jumpy?"

"Nothing. Is there anymore wine?"

"I don't know. There might be." It was becoming difficult to see her, but Delilah could hear her sister's shrewd tone. "But don't change the subject. What is it?"

"I thought he would've called by now," she admitted in a tiny voice. She was glad that it was almost dark; Clementine couldn't see her face, which she felt grow warm with self-consciousness.

"Who? You mean that guy at the seminar?"

The silence was more than loud.

"Why haven't you called *him*?"

She sighed. "You know what mama always said—"

"'Never call a man first. Let him make the first move.' I know, I know. But this is not 1950 or even 1960. These days, a woman can call a man."

"Ha! Did you call Scotty first, or did he call you after you two first met?" Delilah demanded.

Another pregnant pause; this time it was on Clementine's side.

"Let me guess, Clemmie: *he* did."

They glanced and each other and laughed.

BACK AT HIS CONDO, FRANK flung out a hand, swearing as he banged it against the side of the nightstand when he heard his cell phone ringing. Eyes still closed, he captured his cell phone in his hand, fingering it until he found the location of the talk button.

"Yes?" he hissed.

"Good morning, sugar." Priscilla's satiny voice filled his ear. He felt himself stir down below.

"If you say so." He spoke underneath the comforting cocoon of the silk sheet he had pulled over his head. "What time is it?"

"Eleven thirty."

He burrowed his head deeper into the pillow. "Middle of the night," he mumbled.

Like cool water against his skin on a hot summer afternoon, she whispered, "I'll be your wake-up call."

"Priscilla—"

"I'll be there in twenty minutes."

When he opened the door, she was on him like a tigress, nearly knocking him down. The door slammed shut behind her. Priscilla had skin the color of hot cocoa and black hair that hung down her back like a curtain. She was petite but had curves in all the right places. To Frank, her voice brought Eartha Kitt to mind—catlike, yet commanding. Her black eyes, Asian in their shape, were inherited from her great-grandmother and helped cement her feline characteristics. Although she was a small woman, she was strong and wore her sex appeal like a fragrance: applied liberally and pleasing yet overpowering. She snatched down his boxer briefs, and they tumbled to the bright-red, shag area rug in the middle of the floor. It was good that it was there, as he bore the brunt of the collision once they landed, and it was a concrete floor.

The floor-to-ceiling windows were uncovered, as Frank had not powered the shades closed when he arrived home the night before. It was obvious that Priscilla didn't care.

"You're an exhibitionist," he managed to say.

"Wake up," she sing-songed against his ear.

Oh, he was awake, all right, and he gave himself over to her expert touch. He was no shrinking violet however, and he made sure that he gave as good as he got.

Her joyful cries echoed throughout the loft.

In a little over an hour, Frank sent her on her way, wearing a Cheshire-cat grin.

Although she relieved tension of one type, she exacerbated another—he hadn't had time to put on a condom. She had always been on the pill when they got together, but Priscilla was unpredictable, one of the qualities he always liked best about her.

A wild thought crossed his mind: *You'd better hope she looks the same next month as she does today.*

Chapter Four

Frank could not believe it. *Another* search? He had taken a flight from Baltimore/Washington International Thurgood Marshall Airport to Hartsfield-Jackson Atlanta International Airport, which he detested. Why was this airport so big? He had been singled out for a random search in addition to passing through the metal detection devices that all passengers had to pass through. Now he was running late for his flight to Jacksonville and would probably have to rent a car and drive the rest of the way. Not only did he have to unbuckle his belt and the waistband of his slacks and submit to the hand-held device, but TSA was looking through his bins and hand-inspecting his shoes.

Aw, come on!

As Frank collected his laptop and other belongings, he heard a man's voice over the airport loudspeaker, "Due to a line of severe thunderstorms passing through northern Florida at this time, flight 1120 to Jacksonville will be delayed for approximately ninety minutes."

He made his way past other travelers to a row of seats where several people were putting on their shoes; he sat down to don his own.

No need to rush now, he thought.

"SCOTTY SAYS HE'S A GREAT guy," Clementine had said of Thomas Young, a coworker of her husband. "What can it hurt? It's better than pining over that Frank guy."

Although she hated blind dates, Delilah had finally agreed to go out with him.

So here they sat at a so-so restaurant that Thomas had selected in downtown Savannah. They ate dinner while Thomas, a husky man with pleasant-looking features and short sandy-colored hair, talked about all things mechanical. "It ain't easy rebuilding an engine or, for that matter, working on cars in general these days. They all got those computers in them, you know, and that's why they cost so much to fix. It's more fun to work on the older models, say the models from the 70s on back. Of course, the parts are harder to get. For example, carburetors. Did you know ..."

Delilah was bored stiff. He wouldn't let her get a word in edgewise. By the time they left the restaurant, she knew more than she ever wanted to know about cars.

That evening, she was delivered to her front door just past the three-hour mark. "Baby, you never looked so good," she told it.

At the word *baby*, her thoughts drifted back to Frank Ellis and their conversation at the airport.

I guess he took me at my word when I told him that he was moving kind of fast, she thought to herself, stamping her foot. *Me and my big mouth.*

MOTHER'S DAY WAS COMING, ONE of the hardest days Frank had to get through each year. He had acquired several "adopted" mothers over the years—Twyla's mother, ZiZi, and Andy's mother, Teresa, being among them. He sent all of them cards and most of them flowers or some small gift. If he was able to visit them, he did that as well. It helped a little. Whenever he was in or around New Jersey, he made a stop to place flowers on his mother's grave and have a "conversation" with her. That helped too. But nothing ever took the place of that empty spot in his heart.

Frank had spoken at a three-day conference in Hartford, Connecticut. On his way home on Friday afternoon, he stopped at the cemetery in Trenton where his mother was buried.

The grounds were meticulous and serene. Many of the tombstones had newly laid bouquets of flowers on them in anticipation of Mother's Day that weekend. At that moment, however, he was the only person there.

"Hey, Mamacita," he greeted her small marble headstone as he laid the bouquet of white roses before it. Looking at his mother's headstone always took him back to when he had purchased it. He had been twenty-two, and it was years after she had died, but he hadn't been able to afford it until then. He had been proud when it was placed but also sad because of all of the years she had gone without one.

Today he ran his hand along the top of the cool, black stone and said, "Happy Mother's Day. I love you, lady. I want to talk to you." He paced back and forth for a little while.

"There's a girl—or should I say, woman—who I met last month," he began. "Her name is Delilah Carpenter. I wish you could meet her. Damn, I wish you could meet her. She's Caucasian, but I know you wouldn't care. At least, I don't think you would. I know you'd just want me to be happy."

He stopped and looked toward the soon-to-be-setting sun. It had been a beautiful day, and the drive had been uneventful so far, just the way he liked it. He took off his shades and ran a hand over his eyes. He was tired, but he would be home soon, in his own bed.

"I've had my share of women. Look, Mama, I'm thirty-five now, after all. I've only met one other woman who I can actually say I loved and—" He let go a deep sigh. "Like you, she was taken from this world much too soon." Frank was silent for a moment as painful memories rushed in. He knew that the tender ache in his heart would subside in time, but it always caught him off guard whenever he thought about Monica.

"Yeah, Mom, I know. I just met Delilah. I'll admit, it was quick, but I want to see her again. She thought I was going too fast too, so I gave her the space she asked for."

He closed his eyes for a moment, soaking in the peaceful surroundings and communing with her. Some people thought cemeteries were creepy, no doubt as a result of the proliferation of horror movies over the years with them as the backdrop. Frank didn't feel that way at all. This is where he felt his mother could hear him, although it filled him with a profound sadness every time he came.

"I haven't heard from her since, but I felt a real strong connection—it may sound corny, but it's true. And although she wanted to take it slow, I know she felt it also." He chuckled. "When I was little, you used to say that patience wasn't my strong suit. And I agree. But the way she makes me feel ... aw, I can't even describe it. It just ain't the same with anyone else."

The sky was now a brilliant orange. A helicopter passed overhead.

The warmth of the May day was just about to fade. "I feel very blessed to have Delilah in my life, and I'm sure I'll see her again. Guess I'll just have to be patient." He gazed once more into the sky. "I gotta say, my life's been interesting, to say the least."

"Well, I just wanted to stop by and see you. I've got to head on down the road now." He ran his hand along the top of the headstone again as he said, "I love you, Mama. I'll see you again real soon."

DELILAH FELT HER EXCITEMENT GROWING. She had broken down at last and was sending Frank a text: *How's it going, stranger?* Although it had been two months since the seminar in Atlanta, she could not get him off of her mind.

"Here goes nothing," she told herself and pressed send.

Meanwhile, Frank had been slogging wearily through an endless succession of airports. His thoughts were drifting as they sometimes did, and he wondered if it was worth it.

Except for the exceptional cities like San Francisco, New York City, and San Diego, they're all beginning to look alike, he thought.

He was returning from Jacksonville, when he heard his cell phone's text notification.

He ignored it as he found his car keys and headed for the multilevel parking garage at BWI airport.

Back at his condo, he unpacked and then finally checked his phone. Delilah's name stood out, a neon beacon among the otherwise sundry messages. It was late now, so he texted back instead of calling: *Nothing special. Just trying to make a living. I'm glad 2 hear from you. I figured you lost my number.*

Turning on the TV, he settled on ESPN and lit a cigarette.

Another text message from Delilah: *Now why would I do that?*

The television forgotten, Frank and Delilah texted well into the night.

AFTER THAT FIRST NIGHT, FRANK and Delilah found themselves falling into a routine of one or the other calling or texting each other first thing in the morning or last thing at night.

"What have you got on?" Frank asked during a phone call one Friday evening as he was about to turn off his computer after finishing some work.

"My pajamas," Delilah replied in a coy tone. She had tied a scarf around her hair and she was headed out of the bathroom. Dressed in a light-pink nightie, she kicked off her fluffy slippers and hopped into bed.

"Let me see," Frank commanded, his voice thick with desire. "You've got a laptop, don't you? Turn on your webcam. I want to see you." He lay in bed, but he was still fully dressed in jeans and a gray sleeveless undershirt, and he sat with his laptop on his lap, waiting.

"You're kidding, right?"

"No, I'm not. C'mon, Delilah. Let me see what you've got on."

"Frank—" Delilah started to protest. Instead, she thought, *Why not?*

She rushed into her guest bedroom, which also served as her office and flicked on the overhead light. Whirling around to drop her cell phone on the nearby bed, Delilah turned to the desk and scooped up the laptop. Placing it on the bed, she sat on the side of the bed for a few moments while she snatched off the silk scarf with which she had tied up her hair, She then dashed into the master bathroom to reapply a coat of pale pink lipstick and lip gloss that she had wiped off before brushing her teeth. She plugged in the wireless router and powered up her laptop while she attempted to power down her own heartbeat. She dabbed away the light sheen of perspiration on her forehead with tissues she snatched from the small box on the nightstand, before retrieving her cell phone. "All set? Here I come."

Frank smiled to himself since he could hear some of the commotion in the background as he waited but his lips broke into a full-fledged grin when Delilah came onto the screen. He clicked off his phone as did she. She sat back against her pillows so that he could see her better and struck a pose. The light pink baby-doll creation she wore, comprised of an opaque shortie nightgown with a low-cut neckline and see-through flowing wrap, harkened back to the Marilyn Monroe days. Her curvaceous figure was visible yet at the same time, hidden. But it left Frank with his mouth hanging open.

"Wow, baby. That was worth waiting for."

Delilah felt a warm blush course throughout her body to her face and was glad she was far enough away from her computer for it not to be visible to him.

"Why thank you. I don't dress like this all the time, you understand. For some reason, I just felt like doing it tonight—"

"For me, right?" Frank teased. *Damn, I wish she was lying here next to me.*

"Well ..." She stopped. She knew that he knew.

"Hey, I almost forgot to tell you. I'm going to be in Beaufort, South Carolina, from the first of next week until Thursday. After that, I'll be on my way back to DC. I'd like to stop by and see you, if that's okay." He laughed as he said, "Don't worry. I'll be getting a hotel room."

"I'd love it," Delilah said as she pulled her laptop onto her lap.

"Good. While I'm in Beaufort, I'll make my hotel reservations for Savannah. I'll see you Thursday evening, and we'll have dinner and have some fun, all right? Give me your address."

Delilah gave him her address, and they continued to talk until almost one in the morning.

"I'll talk to you tomorrow night, or should I say tonight. Now that I know what you wear to bed—" Frank stifled the urge to lick his lips; he smiled instead.

She laughed. "Honey, you are so bad. But I'll talk to you later." She waved at the screen. "Good night, Frank."

"Good night, Delilah." After powering down, Frank made a beeline to the bathroom to take a cold shower.

AROUND SEVEN THIRTY NEXT THURSDAY night, there was a knock at the door. Delilah took one last look in the bathroom mirror to fluff her hair before she clattered down the stairs to answer it.

"Hi, Frank," she said.

He wore a dark-gray suit and white shirt with a subtle silver stripe running through it, yellow-and-white-striped tie, and a sexy smile. He brought the hand he held behind his back forward with a flourish.

"For you, Delilah, although they don't do you justice."

In his hand was a large bouquet of delicate tulips in a beautiful dusty-rose shade.

"Frank, they're beautiful! Oh my gosh! Please, come in." Delilah stepped aside to allow Frank to enter. She closed the door behind him, breathing in the seductive scent of the cologne he wore. "Let me get a vase for these."

Frank watched with unmasked desire as Delilah sashayed past, the heady combination of the fragrance in her hair and the perfume she wore stoking his passion even more. Wearing a short-sleeved dress in a floral print, it brushed the tops of her thighs in a flirty fashion, while the top of it fit snug against her breasts, with just enough cleavage to make it interesting. Her gold, strappy, high-heeled sandals clicked upon the wooden floor in the parlor as she headed for the kitchen. He followed, enjoying the view her sexy legs provided.

"I hope you don't mind, but I made reservations at a nice restaurant that I know you'll like," Delilah said as she knelt down in front of a lower cabinet in the cheery kitchen. The room was painted in a vibrant apricot hue. She selected a tall but simple vase to showcase the beautiful flowers. "A steakhouse, to make up for the meal you missed the night of your, um, mishap."

Watching as the hem of her dress slid upward, Frank managed to catch what she said. "Hey, that wasn't your fault. Baby, that's fine. But don't forget that I've got this. I'm taking *you* out."

She turned just in time to catch Frank's gaze travel upward to her eyes and couldn't help but smile. *Men.* Aloud, she said, "I'm not forgetting."

Since they didn't want to be late for their reservations, Delilah thought a tour of her place could wait. Frank opened the passenger door of his rental vehicle for her, and with Delilah's directions, he whisked them in the warm night air toward the restaurant. The restaurant was busy, still full of patrons enjoying their meals. The hostess, exhibiting the haughty air that seemed to be a requirement of those employed in the more upscale restaurants, expertly wove them through tables beautifully draped in pale-gray table linens to one located next to a row of windows that faced the Savannah River. It shimmered in the darkness outside.

"She deserves a tip just for getting us through that maze without causing anyone to wind up snorting their drinks," Frank said, after she presented them with large black menus and left as quickly and obtrusively as she got them there.

"I've never been here, but I've heard nothing but great things about it," Delilah replied.

Mouth-watering aromas drifted from the kitchen area. Before Frank had a chance to respond to her remark, their waiter arrived. "I am John and will be your server tonight. Would you like to start with something to drink?"

"What would you like, Delilah?" Frank asked. They both ordered red wine, and John, who looked and sounded like a very charming version of a cowboy plucked right off the range, departed to put in their drink orders, giving them time to peruse the large menus the hostess had given them. Frank scanned the extensive selection and decided on a sirloin steak with a loaded baked potato and green beans. "I never did finish the one I ordered that night in Atlanta."

They laughed. "I'm glad you can make light of that night," Delilah said.

Frank shrugged as he laid down his menu. "I'm still kind of embarrassed about it. I'm just glad that you finally gave me another chance to make it up to you. So, what are you getting?"

She decided on a steak as well, along with a side salad and whipped sweet potatoes.

"You work hard. I can tell you play hard as well." She felt the intensity of his gaze as he spoke. Although what they were talking about wasn't very titillating, the way he looked first into her eyes, then at her mouth, and then back again was a bit disconcerting. She waved away the thought in her mind and tried to concentrate on what he was saying.

John the waiter returned with their drinks. Frank gave him their orders and handed him their menus. He took a sip of his water and then said, "Tell me more about yourself, Delilah. What kind of work do you do?"

"I fill the orders for furniture and the more expensive items for the agency I work for." A wrinkle formed in her brow for a moment. "It's not exciting like your job, but it pays the bills."

Frank shook his head. "They can't all be 'exciting' as you put it, but they're necessary. As long as you enjoy doing it, that's all that counts. Believe me; being self-employed is difficult. Right now, I schedule all of my bookings and handle my own bookkeeping. I hardly have time to consult with clients anymore. I'm going to have to hire someone one of these days to assist me. But I do like traveling and meeting people."

"It sounds fun." Delilah sipped her wine. "As for myself, I'm kind of on the fence right now about my job."

"So, is that why you attended my seminar?" Frank joked. "Because I can tell you right now that you're much too young to retire." The waiter returned with a basket of warm, crusty rolls and other types of bread, along with whipped butter.

"No. But I do feel that it's never too early to make sure you have all of your ducks in a row."

"That's true." Frank tore a roll in two and began to butter it.

Delilah couldn't suppress a grin as she added, "Besides, the person who was originally supposed to go got sick, so I took her place."

After having a chuckle at that, Frank said, "That means I might never have met you if your coworker hadn't gotten sick. Although she doesn't know it, we have her to thank for that."

"That's right."

They continued to talk about all types of subjects, munching on bread, and before they knew it, the waiter was back with their orders. Delilah was enjoying herself. This time Frank was very engaging and not as aggressive.

Frank watched as Delilah began to eat her salad. "How is it?" he asked. He couldn't stop looking at her mouth. He forced himself.

"Great. I don't know how they make their house dressing, but it is fabulous." They paid little attention to anything beyond the table where they sat. The dining room had a distinctly masculine feel, juxtaposed with a feminine flair. Flowing sheer white draperies flanked each tall window, and delicate light fixtures made of silver ran along walls that were covered in a pewter-toned fabric reminiscent of a well-dressed man's suit. The lighting was strategically placed, just enough for diners to enjoy a romantic evening.

"What a beautiful view."

"It sure is," he replied. "You did very well. But it's got nothing on the view I've got of the woman sitting across the table from me."

"Thank you, Frank." She basked in the compliment and knew it was heartfelt, judging by the look on his face.

They ended up being the last couple to leave the restaurant. Frank placed the check and several bills in the dark-blue leather holder but handed their waiter a substantial tip. "Thanks, John, for your level of service as well as the hanging in there with us for half the night."

"It was my pleasure, sir," John replied, and they shook hands. "Y'all come back soon."

They left the restaurant, taking their time to enjoy the walk back to their car. Once they were inside, Frank said, "I know that it is getting late, and you have to get up early tomorrow for work."

"Yes, I do, I must admit. Frank, dinner was fantastic."

He gave her a smile before returning his attention to the road. "Which is why we will continue this tomorrow evening. That is, if you're not busy tomorrow."

"Consider my calendar clear for this weekend," Delilah replied, giving his free hand a squeeze. His hand was warm but firm, not clammy like the time he had grabbed hers at the restaurant in Atlanta.

He threaded his way through the nighttime traffic. The streets still held a lot of vehicles and pedestrians, mostly tourists enjoying their vacations.

They arrived at her home a short time later. Frank parked at the curb in front and walked her to the door. As Delilah unlocked the door, he followed her in. Before she had a chance to turn on the foyer light, he gently turned her to face him in the semidarkness. "I'll see you tomorrow, around seven." He kissed her cheek and walked out of the still-open door.

She closed the door and leaned against it, whispering, "Tomorrow."

The next evening, Frank arrived at the appointed hour as promised and spirited Delilah off to a jazz club recommended by a young but savvy parking attendant at the hotel where he was staying. There they enjoyed drinks and a tasty assortment of hot hors d'oeuvres while listening to several local up-and-coming jazz ensembles well into the wee hours of the morning.

"Are you still hungry?" Frank asked as they left the club and retrieved the rental car from the valet. He began to drive. "You know better than me what's open around here."

"I couldn't eat another thing," Delilah replied, watching Frank pop several breath mints into his mouth, which she now knew to be a habit with him. She knew he smoked, although curiously enough, he avoided doing so in her presence. "I'm still stuffed from what we ate in the club."

"C'mon, then. Let's go walk some of that off." Frank clicked on the car's overhead light and glanced down at her high-heeled evening sandals. "Wait a minute—you can't walk in those things."

With a giggle, she reached into the tote bag she had brought with her in addition to her purse, extracting a pair of thick-soled flip-flops. "I came prepared." She removed her high heels and with a contented sigh, put them on.

Frank found a place to park and pulled over to the curb on West Bay Street. They got out and ran across the street to walk down the steep and ancient steps that led to River Street. After descending the steps, they carefully made their way to the moonlit river and peeked in some of the shops, restaurants, and bars that lined it. Frank took Delilah's hand, and they strolled along the now more navigable brick walkway, continuing to relish the night that neither wanted to end.

When the moon slid behind the clouds in the night sky and refused to emerge, Frank and Delilah finally headed back to the car.

Saturday would be Frank's last day in Savannah. He came for Delilah at noon, and they spent the day walking through many of the picturesque and shady tree-lined squares filled with monuments reflecting the history of Savannah. The weather had been perfect that weekend—sunny and hot but not too humid. Sometimes they just sat on a bench, eating ice cream cones they purchased from one of the nearby shops, people watching, and continuing to get to know one another. Late that afternoon, Frank drove them back to Delilah's house.

Once inside, Frank took her hand. "I've got to take off for the airport to catch my flight tonight. Delilah, I've really enjoyed spending this weekend with you." He hated leaving her. No woman had made him feel this way in a long time.

"So have I," Delilah replied and smiled.

"So, would you say I've redeemed myself for … before?"

"Absolutely." Her demeanor became teasing. "You've been a perfect gentleman."

"Good." With that, Frank pulled her into his arms and kissed her the way he had been wanting to ever since they met, long and hard. He wanted to make sure that she remembered it. Delilah did not try to pull away but returned the kiss with gentleness. She didn't fool him, however. Frank knew the passion was there, but smoldering, so he took his cue from her. He resisted the powerful urge to just scoop her up and head up the stairs to her bedroom; instead, pulled his lips from hers and said, "I'll talk to you later."

Her eyes shone under the light of the foyer. "You have a safe trip, Frank." She opened the door for him, and he left, closing the door behind him.

After it closed but unbeknownst to each other, they both stood on either side of it and let out a quiet, "Whew!"

A DAY LATER, ON SUNDAY afternoon, Delilah was working in her front yard pulling weeds when she heard the phone ringing through an open window. Happy for a break from the already humid temperatures, she clopped through the cool, dark foyer, walking out of her garden clogs and enjoying the feel of wooden floor beneath her hot feet. She removed her gardening gloves, dropping them on the floor beside her clogs before picking up the phone.

"Hello, Clemmie."

"*Hello, Clemmie?* Girl, I thought I was going to have to send out a posse for you! Every time I called your cell, it went to voice mail. Where have you been?"

"I'm sorry, Clemmie, I haven't been home for most of the weekend."

"Obviously," Clementine replied with a laugh

Delilah joined in. "I meant I've been out on what you could call a three-day date. I didn't even know that the battery in my cell phone had died. We had so much fun—"

"Three-day date? Sure. Come on. Out with it." Clementine paused. "Ah ha, let me guess—Mr. Public Speaker?"

"It wasn't like that. And I *did* come back home afterward, and I *didn't* go to his hotel room." Her tone softened. "I'm sorry, Clemmie. I didn't mean to snap at you."

There was silence on the line for a moment and then, "Wait a minute.

35

What are we talking about here? What happened with Thomas? You never did tell me how your first date with him went."

"My first and last date with him, you mean." Delilah held the phone in the crook of her neck as she walked through the foyer and into the kitchen, picking up her gardening gloves and throwing them into the basket of small gardening tools she kept in a corner by the refrigerator. "I didn't want to tell you or Scotty, but Thomas was a little bit boring—a nice guy, but boring. He didn't seem to care about anything except cars. Hey, how about having supper with me tonight?" she suggested. "I'll tell you more about my date then."

"Okay. Scotty went into work today and won't be home until nine tonight, but I can come."

"Supper's at six. Nothing fancy; I haven't made it to the grocery store this week."

"All right. See you then."

AFTER DINNER, DELILAH STOOD AT the living room window, staring out into the steamy night. She could tell that a storm was on the horizon. She could smell it in the humidity-laden air. Clementine was curled up on the sofa, watching her.

Delilah sat down and told Clementine about her date with Frank at the restaurant on Thursday, the jazz club on Friday, and the historic district on Saturday. After talking, she handed her sister her cell phone. There was a photo on her screensaver of a handsome African American man. He wore a short-sleeved shirt and khaki pants and was standing with riverfront in the background, grinning at the camera.

"Frank Ellis," she said simply. "He's the man I went out with this weekend."

"Mmm. He's cute."

Delilah stared at her. "Well?"

Clementine handed the phone back to her. "Well, what?"

"He's black," she replied, exasperated.

"So?" Clementine laughed. "Tell me something I don't know."

"And it doesn't matter to you?"

"No. Why should it?"

Delilah heaved a sigh of relief. "No reason."

"Because he's black?" She took Delilah's hand. "Come on, Dee, you never heard me talk like that. But you know what? I had a feeling it was something like that. You never described what he looked like."

"I wasn't trying to be secretive or anything. I just didn't know how you were going to take it."

"Why didn't you give me the benefit of the doubt?" Clementine chided, but her voice was gentle as she continued to hold her younger sister's hand. "Have I ever given you reason to think that I was prejudiced?"

"No, and I'm sorry. He's such a nice guy. We really enjoy each other's company. I don't know how Mama and Daddy will take it if we continue to see each other."

"Now that's a horse of a different color," Clementine agreed. "Oops, poor choice of words."

They both giggled.

"Sounds like you had a full weekend. And he didn't stay over?"

Delilah looked up. "Now you know me, Clemmie. Not on the first date. Anyway, a lady doesn't kiss and tell."

"Okay, okay. It's none of my business," she agreed, waving a hand in the air.

"You're right, it's not." Delilah smiled. "But I'm glad you know about him now."

FRANK STOPPED BY ANDY AND Twyla's apartment when he returned to Washington, DC. They lived in a midrise apartment building, which bordered the Washington, DC–Maryland line. It was furnished in an eclectic style, with quirky, colorful artwork that Andy brought back from his travels. These were combined with Twyla's modern outlook—a midsized sofa in tan Ultrasuede with clean lines, a glass coffee table, and matching end tables that held photos of her and Andy's families, slim cut-glass lamps with small black shades, and an African violet with purple blooms. Also part of the décor was a rather large, battered, and ugly dusty-blue recliner that Andy loved. A thirty-two-inch flat screen television, placed atop a black television stand with short metal legs, stood against a wall, strategically placed for his viewing pleasure. Being built close to forty years ago, when many apartments were constructed with larger rooms, the living room had enough space to handle it all.

Fortunately for Twyla and Andy, it had been renovated within the last five.

"Hey, you two," Frank said as Twyla opened the door. Twyla Hayes was Andy's African American girlfriend. She was dressed in a pair of turquoise jogging pants and a white T-shirt and socks; her black hair was styled in a cute bob, which framed her bronze complexion. Frank considered her the little sister he never had. Although she was only twenty-nine, Frank had to admit to himself that she was more mature than either he or Andy.

She gave him a hug. "Hey, Frank." They left the tiny foyer that led into the carpeted living room. "Haven't seen you in a while."

"Haven't been in town for a while, baby girl. I spoke in Beaufort most of last week and then went to see someone down in Savannah."

"So, is she anybody we know?" Andy asked, leaning back in his recliner. They had been watching a movie on TV. Both he and Twyla had met several of Frank's women over the years. Only Andy had met Priscilla.

You want a beer, Frank?" Twyla asked.

"No thanks, Twyla. Thought I'd stop by for a minute. And no, Andrew, you two haven't met her. I met her when I spoke in Atlanta a while back. We had a nice time." Frank sat down on the sofa while Twyla curled her legs under her on the other end.

"Smooth operator," Andy remarked, grinning.

"Not this one, my friend." He sat there thinking about his extended date with Delilah. He tried to wipe the smile off his face but couldn't.

"Look at him, Twyla." Andy laughed. "I wonder what this one looks like."

Twyla waved a hand in Andy's direction. "Aw, leave him alone. I'm glad he met someone who seems to be different from all the rest."

"I love how you two are talking about me like I'm not even here, but thank you, Twyla, for defending me. And don't worry, you will get to meet her someday." He scooted over and kissed Twyla's cheek before he stood up. "I just stopped by to say hello."

"Damn, buddy." Andy stood up as well as he said, "You just got here."

"I've got to get home. I got to mail out some of my financial kits, work on my monthly newsletter, and take care of some other things before I head out of town again. Work is never done, my brother."

"You got that right," Andy agreed as they gave each other the one-armed man hug. "I've got to be in Toledo on Tuesday. See you later, Frank."

"Later." Frank headed down the stairs back to his car and sped away into the night.

"Hi, Daddy," Delilah said a few days later as she watched him stride up the concrete walkway toward where she sat on the porch steps, watching some kids in the neighborhood ride their bikes up and down the streets. Cicadas kept up their continuous shrilling racket in the distance. She patted the front step beside him. "Have a sit down."

Patrick Carpenter sat and slid a beefy arm around her as he kissed her cheek. "I will, as long as you help me up when I leave. My knee's been acting up lately," he replied with a deep chuckle.

She hugged him back. At nearly sixty, with his gray buzz cut, steely blue eyes, and husky, muscular build, he was Superman in her eyes.

"I'm glad you stopped by. How's Mama?" Delilah asked, swatting away a group of tiny gnats.

"Your mother's doin' fine. Out somewhere spending my money." He smiled as he shook his head. "Gotta love her."

"Gotta love her." Delilah agreed as she started to rise. "You want some lemonade?"

"Naw, girl, I'm fine, unless you're going to get yourself some."

"No, I'm good." Delilah sat back down and waved at her neighbors across the street as they arrived home from work. She remained silent but smiled at her father. She was truly a daddy's girl and had been for as long as she could remember. She loved her mother dearly, but she began to tag along behind her father when she was barely able to crawl. And he had let her. Her mother, Hazel, was unable to have any more children after Delilah, and her father had loved her tinkering along with him under the hoods of their car and lawn tractor or accompanying him to rodeos, bull riding, and monster-truck shows. Delilah soaked in every tale he had ever told her and Clementine about his days as a drill sergeant and about the earlier jobs he had held while he was dating their mother. Maybe she served as a sort of surrogate son for him; she didn't know nor had she ever asked. She was just as much a lady as she was a tomboy.

Patrick slipped his arm back around Delilah again once she was seated. "Your sister mentioned you had a date last week. I figured you must've been out on the town somewhere, 'cause I swung by last Friday night, but you were out. Guess I should've called first."

"Yes, I did go out last week. A friend of mine from out of town came to see me. His name's Frank Ellis." Delilah leaned her head against her father's shoulder as they sat and watched the world go by.

"I'm glad you've been getting out and aren't sitting in the house moping over that Victor boy."

Delilah laughed. "Daddy, Victor and I broke up two years ago."

"Between you and Clementine, I'm waiting to see some grandchildren," Patrick continued as if she hadn't spoken but winked at her. "Been waiting for quite a while now. Get you one of those guys from that academy down in Brunswick. Or a corn-fed, milk-drinkin' marine, like me."

Delilah punched him on the arm. "I hear you, Dad."

Chapter Five

Around one forty-five on Thursday morning, Frank lay atop the sheets of his bed, more listening to the encore broadcast of *Anderson Cooper 360* than watching him. He had not yet gone to sleep, attempting to wind down from the week's events. The conference he spoke at in Lexington, Kentucky, had gone off without a hitch, and he had arrived home only a few hours earlier. Frank smiled to himself. He knew that his presentation had surpassed most of the other speakers. He had garnered another speaking request as a result. As he wondered where he would squeeze it in his already full schedule, he felt cell phone vibrate, notifying him of a text message. He reached for where it laid on the bed beside him and with one eye open, glanced at the screen.

Want some company? was the invitation. Priscilla. The woman was as subtle as an avalanche.

Frank grabbed his reading glasses from the gray leather case on top of his nightstand and texted a reply: *Not 2 night, baby. I wouldn't be any good.*

Aloud, he mumbled, "I could've been a politician." He breathed a sigh of relief once he realized that she wasn't texting him to announce that their impromptu rendezvous produced more than just a good time the last time they were together.

The phone vibrated again. Another text: *How about letting me be the judge of that?*

Frank texted back: *Sorry, baby. No can do. Good night, Priscilla,* and he turned off his phone. He knew she would be mad as hell, but he was only partially deceiving her. He *was* tired. Pulling off his glasses and returning them to the nightstand, he thought about Priscilla. They were a lot alike. Aggressive. That was what had attracted him in the first place. They had met in downtown Washington, DC, at a conference where he was speaking about two years ago. Because of their similarities, theirs was a casual thing from the word go—intimate friends.

She's a female playa and hates the word no. As that thought crossed his mind, without rhyme or reason Delilah's face drifted before him and that curvaceous body of hers. *Mmm.* A beautiful, ripe fruit hanging from a tree, just within his reach.

With his eyes closed again and an even wider smile, he returned his auditory attention back to the TV and Anderson—and his thoughts to Delilah.

JULY BEGAN MAKING ITS PRESENCE felt with classic, sweltering heat in Washington, DC. Cedar Rapids, where Frank had been speaking at a four-day conference, wasn't quite as hot. However, it was Friday, and Frank had done his time in Iowa and was ready to travel again.

"I should've asked you this sooner, but what are you doing for the fourth?" Frank asked Delilah over the phone as he put the finishing touches on his packing. He had a late checkout.

"Oh, my dad's hosting a cookout for the family and a few friends."

"Hmm. You don't know it yet, but I love cookouts."

There was silence on the line and then, "Oh? That's nice. You know, Frank—"

"I was going to go home, but then I thought I'd like to see you. And since you're going to the cookout ... well, how 'bout it?"

"Frank—"

"Or would you rather I just go on home? They're holding a room for me in Savannah at the hotel I stayed at when I came down to see you last month. But I'm not trying to pressure you or anything. You can always say no. Of course, I hope that you don't. Say the word, and I'll change my flight instead of heading back to DC. But you've got to let me know something now, baby, 'cause I'm about to head to the airport in a few minutes." He couldn't help but smile to himself at his underhandedness. He zipped up his garment bag.

"Of course they won't mind if I bring someone. But you sure are forcing my hand," Delilah replied in a resigned tone.

"I know, Delilah, but I'm only doing it because I can tell from our nightly conversations that it's hard for you. You aren't sure how your family will react to me. From what you've told me about Clementine, she seems cool. But look, I want to see you again. And hey, we live a thousand miles from each other. The only way I want to continue seeing you is if it's out in the open. I'm not going to sneak around as if we've got something to be ashamed of. I enjoyed being with you during our date last month, and I know you did too. So, what's the alternative? The holiday's coming up next week, which would be a great time for me to come down and see you again. So, may I come?"

"Yes, Frank. I'd love to see you, and you're right—we've got nothing to be ashamed of."

"Move over, Sidney Poitier. Guess who's coming to the cookout?" Frank announced, laughing.

FRANK FLEW FROM CEDAR RAPIDS, Iowa, to Savannah, Georgia, on Friday night. He felt a sense of déjà vu as he checked into the hotel. He hoped that the great way their extended date had turned out last month would be repeated this weekend. Just getting Delilah to invite him to her parents' cookout was a major coup in Frank's book. Truth be told, he did invite himself. He couldn't wait to see her, and he was glad that she wanted to see him too.

Her eyes were huge and her smile heart-stopping when she opened the door to greet him the next day. He wished he had thought to snap a picture with his cell phone. Nevertheless, Frank knew that he would replay that moment in time in his mind many times over.

"Frank! It's so good to see you, but I didn't think I'd see you until tomorrow at the earliest," Delilah cried, throwing her arms around his neck and giving him a hug.

He buried his face in her neck for a moment. "I'm glad you still feel that way. I know I kinda bum-rushed you on the phone yesterday. Anyway, I wanted to see you before the cookout, so I thought I'd surprise you," he whispered. "Because if you're not busy this weekend, I don't have to go back out until next Wednesday."

"The government will actually observe the Fourth of July holiday on the fifth this year. And since I haven't taken any annual leave since last Christmas, I had already put in a leave slip for Tuesday, so I don't have to be back until Wednesday, either."

"Great. We've got until then. I figure we'd make the best of any time we've got alone with each other."

He was about to kiss her when she said, "Only we aren't alone. Frank, I want you to meet my older sister, Clementine Zimmerman. Clemmie!"

There were footsteps, and then Clementine stepped into the foyer.

"Hello, Frank." She was a taller, statuesque version of her younger sister, with shoulder-length blonde hair and an easy smile.

"Hello … Clementine, is it? Wow, your parents really had a thing for unforgettable names, didn't they?"

Her smile grew wider. "You could say that. Or else they watched too many old movies."

They all laughed. "Nice to meet you, Clementine."

"Most folks just call me Clemmie."

"Do you mind if I call you Clementine?" Frank asked as they went into the parlor. It was decorated simply but very warmly in pale blues, greens, and whites. It was more of a beach motif and although the floor was dark wood, somehow it worked.

"He likes names like ours," Delilah explained.

"Or maybe I like the ladies who come with the names," he replied as he took her hand in his.

They settled into the parlor, exchanging lighthearted stories of Savannah, travel, and the upcoming cookout.

Later, as Clemmie was leaving, Delilah walked her to the front door.

Clementine whispered in her ear, "Dee, nothing against my Scotty, but that voice of Frank's could make butter boil!"

SAVANNAH WAS FULL OF BEAUTIFUL, stately old homes, although Delilah's home was not quite as old or stately. To say the property where Patrick and Hazel Carpenter lived was picturesque would be an understatement. Black, wrought-iron balconies decorated with elaborate scrollwork wrapped themselves around the fronts and sides of the first and second stories of the house, which was clad in white wood siding. There were beautiful sprays of flowers in the flowerbeds throughout the well-manicured lawn.

Delilah cruised down the long driveway Sunday afternoon, parking behind one of what must have been more than a dozen other vehicles that lined both sides of it. Clementine emerged from the house, and after making her way down the front steps carrying a large bowl, joined her husband, Scott, who stood nearby, waiting for her.

What the hell—? Frank thought to himself as he sat in the passenger seat and noticed the number of parked cars. At the car trunk, after helping Delilah with the cooler they brought with them containing bottles of wine and a tossed salad, Frank pulled her to him. "How many people are going to be at this 'cookout'?"

"I don't know. About fifty or so." She shrugged. "Why?"

"*Fifty?*"

Delilah grinned. "You invited yourself, didn't you?"

"I did, didn't I?" Frank rubbed his hand across his mustache. "Should've kept my big mouth shut."

She giggled, and he rolled the cooler behind them. They stopped when they reached Clementine and Scott. "Frank, this is Clemmie's husband, Scott. Scott, this is my date, Frank Ellis. And you and Clemmie have already met."

"Hello again, Clementine," Frank said. He turned to Scott and extended his hand. "Nice to meet you, Scott."

Scott shook it without hesitation. "Same here," he replied, with a wide grin, and the two couples headed to the backyard with the food and drink.

The backyard was just as huge as the front and framed by numerous shade trees. As Delilah had said, about fifty adults and children milled about, eating, drinking, playing horseshoes and other games, and socializing. As Frank guessed, he was the only African American face that he saw on the property.

I wonder if there are any folk who look like me in the kitchen, he silently mused, grimacing at the thought.

They continued to weave their way through the yard, with Delilah greeting friends who she hadn't seen for a while and then telling Frank a little about them. Her family's next-door neighbor from years ago, Isabel Brooks, was there with her family, looking almost the same as when Delilah left home and moved into her first apartment at the age of nineteen. Delilah's Uncle Jack, her mother brother, was famous for playing practical jokes on anyone unsuspecting; tall, but now stout and totally bald, he still had a booming laugh that never failed to make any child within earshot laugh too. Many other folks said hello and stopped to talk, some of them relatives and some not. They finally reached a powerfully built, drill sergeant of a man, complete with a marine-style haircut, manning several smoky barbecue grills and a smoker.

Delilah threw her arms around him.

"Hi, Daddy!"

He gripped her in a one-arm embrace, while turning over a slab of ribs with the tongs he held in his free hand. "Hey there, baby girl."

"Daddy, I want you to meet someone." She took his hand and led him over to where Frank stood, smiling. "Daddy, this is my date, Frank Ellis. Frank, this is my dad, Patrick Carpenter."

Patrick's eyes narrowed ever so slightly.

"Nice to meet you, sir," Frank said, offering his hand. The older man shook it, but afterward, wiped his hand on his chef's apron.

"Been cooking most of the day. Sweaty."

Frank's gaze was steady. "Uh-huh."

The tension between the two men was almost as thick as the Georgia humidity. Thicker, in fact, since it was actually slightly cooler at the Carpenter house, which was located not far from the beach.

"Uh, Daddy, where's Mama?"

"She went to the house, but she'll be back directly. Everything's ready. Just help yourself. There's sweet tea, lemonade … well, you know."

"I know, and we brought some stuff too. Thanks, Daddy."

Long tables draped with brightly colored tablecloths were lined with benches and stretched end to end across the large backyard. The tables were loaded with all types of food and drink: platters of fried chicken, county-style pork ribs, catfish, crab legs, corn on the cob, and bowls of potato salad, macaroni salad, and other delectable items. Clementine added a bowl of potato chips to what was already there. Large coolers were stationed next to the end of each table. Delilah placed the bottles of red and white wine in two of the coolers and the large bowl of salad on the table where Clementine and Scott sat, which was the table designated, albeit unofficially, for the immediate family.

Before they had headed into the backyard, Frank had donned his sunglasses. Now he tried not to notice the various heads that turned and followed them, watching longer than necessary in his estimation, as he and Delilah emptied the contents of the cooler they had brought. Instinctively, his teeth began to clench. He willed himself to relax and keep an open mind. *I could be wrong*, he thought.

Scott indicated the two empty picnic tables reserved to the immediate family. "Sit down, Frank. There's a lot of food, so just dig in. We don't stand on ceremony here."

He and Delilah sat on one bench, while Scott and Clementine took seats across the table from them.

"You ever get told you've got a voice for radio?" Scott asked as he handed the both of them paper plates and utensils.

Frank laughed. "All the time."

Scott pointed to a cooler. "Crack open that six-pack, will ya, hon?"

"We brought wine," Delilah announced.

"Like I said, crack open that six-pack."

They all laughed, and Scott handed a bottle to Frank, which he accepted.

The camaraderie was genuine and instantaneous. When Delilah and Clementine's mother, Hazel, arrived, both sisters sprang to their feet to hug and kiss her. She was a petite woman, with a white-blonde bob and a genteel manner.

"Mama, I want you to meet someone. This is Frank Ellis, my date. Frank, this is my mama, Hazel Carpenter."

Frank stood and strode over to shake her hand. He almost laughed out loud. Hazel's eyes widened, but she recovered almost immediately.

Still, he noticed.

"Nice to meet you, ma'am," he said, the epitome of graciousness. He had had years of practice. And he had to give it to her—at least she didn't wipe her hands on her clothes afterward.

"Nice to meet you too, Frank." She looked around. "Dee, is your daddy still over there cooking?"

"You know Dad," Scott laughed and took a swig of beer before he went on. "He's like the captain of a ship with those grills and that smoker. Doesn't want anybody else to touch 'em."

Everyone laughed, and Hazel went to retrieve her husband so that he could get a bite of food. After a few minutes, she emerged, with Patrick in tow. "I managed to get him to let cousin Yancy take the helm."

"I can't believe it!" both Clementine and Scott exclaimed.

Frank munched on a rib and contemplated Patrick behind his sunglasses. Everyone continued to talk and eat, but Frank felt the tension across the table as he watched Patrick watching him. Frank had to give it to him, the man made excellent ribs, fall-off-the-bone tender, with just the right amount of smoky, tangy spiciness that stood up to the meatiness of the pork. No where's-the-meat spareribs here. In fact, Frank had to admit that they were the best ribs he had ever eaten, bar none. But he withheld his compliments to the chef. Only moments before, when Patrick had asked for the salt and Frank passed it to him, Patrick had snatched it from Frank's hand without so much as a thank you and continued to talk to Scott, who sat next to him looking dumbfounded.

At one point in the conversation, Hazel asked, "What type of work do you do, Frank?" She took a sip of iced tea.

"I was once an instructor, teaching mostly for the government, but now I own my own financial consulting company. In addition to consulting, I conduct speaking engagements regarding human resource and financial issues. For example, life insurance, retirement, et cetera."

"That's how we met," Delilah added, glancing at him and touching his hand.

From behind his sunglasses, Frank looked over at Patrick to see if he had seen what had just transpired. He had.

"I noticed you clear across the room, baby," he replied, hearing the term of endearment as it left his lips. Again, he looked across the table. This time, they all were watching.

Delilah started talking rapidly, while Scott and Clementine exchanged bemused looks. Hazel resumed eating, a nervous look crossing her features.

Frank knew by the way he was clenching his fork and now glaring at him that Patrick was seething inside.

Both he and Frank continued to stare at one another. Finally, Frank looked away.

But he continued to smile on the inside. He had managed to maintain his cool.

"So, what would you like to do today?" Frank was asking.

Delilah clutched a plump pillow in one arm with the phone against her ear, while she lay in bed and listened to Frank's sexy wake-up call the next morning. She was puzzled. She had observed some of the vehement glances and actual stare downs between Frank and her father at the cookout. She had never seen her father act that way toward any of her friends before. As far as she could see, Frank hadn't done anything to warrant such behavior. Her smile faded. She refused to believe the reason was simply because he was black.

She pushed her thoughts forward to the present. "I need to hold off on planning anything just yet. My dad's coming over. And I'm pretty sure I know why."

Frank's languid tone vanished, became one of concern. "Do you want me to come over? For moral support?"

"No, I don't think that would be wise," she quickly replied, and threw the covers off her body. Her father would be arriving at noon. It was already half past nine now. "I need to see him alone."

"I understand."

"I know you do. I'll call you afterward."

"You do that. I guess I'll just lie here and go back to sleep, then."

"Thanks a lot. You're killing me, Frank."

"Am I, baby?"

Whew! "I'm getting off this phone," she laughed in return and hung up. Getting up, she ran to the bathroom to jump in the shower.

She no sooner opened the door with a "Hi, Daddy," than her father burst through it and slammed it behind him.

"What the *hell* do you think you're doing?" Patrick bellowed as he followed his daughter into the kitchen.

She whirled around. He had never used profanity toward her. "M-maybe we should go into another room. Too many sharp objects in here." She willed her hands to stop shaking as she poured him a glass of iced tea from the pitcher that stood on the concrete countertop.

"This is no joking matter, Missy."

"I'm a grown woman, Daddy," she replied, handing him the glass.

He took it and without taking a drink, set it down on the nearby table.

"I know that." He took a deep breath and then exhaled in an explosion. "Whatever possessed you to take up with a—"

"*Don't say it.*" The cloak of trepidation fell away, replaced with white-hot anger, and for a moment, she felt as if she was looking at the world through Frank's eyes. It was not a view she enjoyed.

"Frank is a human being, Dad. A man. A man who happens to be black."

"Yes." His eyes blazed. "Black."

She turned away from him to gaze out of the window into the bright sunshine. Her entire body began to shake. Frank was capable of taking care of himself, but at this moment, she was filled with a feeling of protectiveness so powerful, it scared her. "His name is *Frank*."

"Darlin', there are just too many differences between black and white people for these things to work."

"Such as?"

"I didn't come here to talk to your back, young lady!"

She took her time turning to face him. "Such as?"

"The history between the two races, the cultures—"

"The *cultures?* Are you kidding?" She shook her head, as much as in an attempt to curb the anger she was feeling toward her father as well as from incredulity. "Take a look around. There are interracial couples all over the United States. Heck, all over the world!"

Her father raked a hand through his thick hair, causing it to stand on end in a comical way. "And they have a lot of problems too."

"Mostly due to outside influences, not because they are of different races."

They were silent for a while, and then he said, "And you couldn't find a decent white man to date from here in the state of Georgia? Aw, never mind."

"Nothing's wrong with them, Dad," Delilah replied. "There are plenty of good men around here, both black and white. But I want you to tell me what's wrong with Frank." She stood there waiting, still not believing what she had just heard come out of her father's mouth. He had always been a right-wing, flag-waving American, full of patriotism as well as the pride of his ancestors. But prejudiced? Had he always been this way?

Patrick snorted and said, "He's uppity, for one thing."

"Uppity?" Delilah laughed, but there was no jocularity in it. "Come on, you can do better than that! You're holding it against the man because he's self-employed? Or is it his command of the English language? I have heard it all. Face it, Dad, you're grasping at straws."

"Look, I just don't believe in race mixing. There are too many differences between ..."

Delilah failed to hear the rest of her father's response as she thought about the other remark he had just made. She remembered her father telling her once about her great-grandfather having been a member of the Ku Klux Klan. She had listened with shame and disbelief, and although she never knew the man, it colored the way she remembered him from that point on. Never in her wildest dreams had she thought that her own father subscribed to that way of life or thinking. The words hurt her throat and heart but she asked them anyway. "Daddy, I'm sorry that I have to ask you this, but—are you a member of the Klan?"

He stalked over to the paper-towel dispenser. Tearing off a sheet, he wiped his reddening face as he barked, "No, I am not." He swung around and waved a finger at her. "You need to give this a lot of thought."

All of a sudden, she was emotionally exhausted. "Sure, Dad." She gave him a kiss. "We'll talk again soon."

LATER, FRANK JOINED DELILAH AT her place. The wind was picking up; a storm was brewing. Thunder rumbled in the distance. She was sitting on the porch swing, staring into space.

"You shouldn't be sitting out here with a storm coming up," he announced as he walked up the porch stairs toward her.

Delilah hoped she didn't look as gloomy as she felt. She plastered on what she hoped was a convincing smile and patted the space beside her. "Just for a little while. The breeze feels so good."

Frank sat down on the swing, turning to face her. They swung for several minutes before he asked, "How did it go?"

Although it was darker than usual because of the approaching storm, through flashes of lightning she could see the sympathy expressed on his face, and she could hear it in his voice.

"About how you probably expected it to," she replied, sighing. "I never really thought about it. I didn't know. My daddy is prejudiced."

"You've never dated a black man before."

"True, but I brought friends home—Latino, Chinese. He just tolerated them, I guess."

"There's a difference between friends visiting and your baby girl spending time with a man, especially one of another race."

She tried to laugh but choked on it. "What's this? Are you siding with him?"

"Nope. Just trying to see things from his point of view."

"It was horrible, Frank. He thinks that people of different races and cultures have nothing in common, so they're doomed to fail from the start."

"And what do you think?" His voice was quiet but strong against the breeze that had shifted into stiff gusts of wind.

She could barely see him now although he sat less than an arm's length away. She felt for his face in the darkness and felt the warmth of his cheek and the strong line of his jaw. "I don't agree. He's from a different generation, and that's what he was raised to think in his family. That's his right, I guess. But it's not how I want to live."

A jagged spear of lightning sliced through the sky beyond the trees that stood like swaying sentries behind her house, startling them both. Moments later, there was the thunderous boom. "I think we'd better go inside," Frank advised as he reached up and clasped the hand she held against his face in his own.

They made their way to the front door a few yards away. Delilah felt him searching her hand, and she gave him the keys. It was still too early for the porch light to come on, so it was difficult to see the locks.

He fumbled for several moments as he determined which key fit which lock and then opened the door. Delilah felt his hand take hold of hers, and she followed him inside.

"I'll see you tomorrow," Frank said.

Delilah flipped on the switch to the light in the foyer. It flickered as the storm began to intensify and the rain began to pelt the sides of the house and roof. She turned to face him. "I don't want you to go."

She went to him, sliding her arms around his waist and snuggling against him, feeling his heart beat hard against her cheek. She looked up and saw the naked desire in his gaze that he was unable to conceal. Her own heart was pounding just as hard.

"Are you sure?"

"Yes."

"I don't have anything with me."

She smiled. "I'm on the pill, but there's a Walgreen's a few miles away—"

"I saw it on my way here." He touched her cheek. "I'll be right back." He left the house and hurried in the pounding rain to his rental vehicle. He wasted no time in getting to the store and back.

Delilah opened the door, and Frank handed her the plastic bag. She took his hand and led the way to her bedroom. Halfway up the stairs, the power went out as did the foyer light, and they stumbled the rest of the way.

Once there, they bumped and banged their way through the darkness; Delilah made her way to her nightstand, emptying the contents of the bag Frank had given her onto it. She tore open a box and slid her hand around until she felt the hard, sharp edges of a foil-wrapped envelope. She could smell and feel Frank's nearness.

"Here," she whispered, thrusting out her hand and handing one to him.

She heard Frank as he tossed it onto the top of the nightstand. "Not yet."

Delilah exhaled as he pulled her roughly into his arms, crushing her lips with his. She pushed him over to her queen-sized sleigh bed in the lightning's fleeting glare, falling on top of him.

Frank's strong arms gripped her around the waist. He slid one hand around and upward to unbutton the tiny buttons of her blouse. "I wish I could see you," Frank rumbled against her ear. The draperies had been closed against the daytime summer heat, but now darkness had fallen.

"See me with your hands."

She pulled the soaking wet T-shirt he wore over his head. She ran her hands over the smooth, damp hairs of his chest, followed by her lips.

He groaned. "Oh my goodness."

With one hand, Delilah grappled on top of the nightstand until she found the condom envelope Frank had thrown on top of it and pressed it into his hand.

"Get ready," he whispered.

They wrestled for a while with their clothes and each other, until finally Frank ripped open the condom package.

"Here," he said, his breathing fast and ragged as he slid the condom into her hand. "You do it, baby." She took it from his grasp and felt downward to place it on his growing stiffness.

"You're killing me," he groaned weakly.

Delilah chuckled, remembering not more than a day before when she had uttered those same words. "Tough."

In response, Frank flipped her over and moved on top of her.

Time seemed to stand still while they explored each other in the darkness, with only glimpses of light here and there from the raging storm. Words were not needed as their bodies did the talking. Delilah marveled at his strong yet tender touch as he caressed her almost as a blind man would, and she did the same to him. She wanted to know all she could about what excited him, what delighted him.

Delilah gasped as Frank pounded deep inside her. She knew that he had wanted her and had held himself in check for a while. She attempted to match Frank's movements with her own, running her hands up and down his back.

"Delilah," he growled, thrusting once more as shudders overtook him.

She reached up, wiping the sweat from his brow as they kissed. Her heart hammered in her chest as he collapsed on top of her.

They fell asleep that way.

FRANK AWOKE AS DAWN WAS breaking. Weak sunlight shone around the edges of the draperies and through the slight opening of one. It was enough for him to watch Delilah as she slept, her head to one side and one arm partially around his waist, the other flung against the mattress.

A slight smile played upon her lips.

He watched the rise and fall of her breasts and stomach, down to where they were both still joined. Bracing himself on one arm, he used his other hand to gently trace the curvature of her neck and brush the hair off the side of her face. She was a wonder to him, a mixture of southern warmth and genteelness, not unlike her mother, yet with an exciting womanliness that Frank was having fun learning more about as time went on.

Delilah stirred, turning her head and looking up into his eyes.

"I'm sorry, baby. I was trying not to wake you." Frank leaned forward and kissed her with tenderness. "Good morning."

"Good morning to you, too." The way she said it, with her soft accent, sent a pleasurable sensation through him.

"Any regrets?" he asked.

"None."

He lifted himself from her and rolled over so that he could continue to look at her. He ran a hand along her belly, watching her shiver at his touch.

"Good. I like how you said that, with no hesitation. And since we didn't get to do much yesterday—"

They both smiled at the thought as they lay there after their first night together.

"You know what I mean," he said with a chuckle. "Anyway, I thought we'd go to the beach, if that's okay with you."

"That sounds good." But the way she was looking at him was giving him other ideas.

He pulled her on top of him. "First things first ..."

They drove to Hilton Head, where once again, Frank was in the minority. This time he didn't care because he was focused on Delilah and nothing else.

They set up her beach umbrella and spread out the blanket beneath it.

"Will you rub this on me?" she asked, indicating the bottle of sunblock she held in her hand.

"Oh, yeah." Frank squeezed a generous amount of the cream in his hand and then set about massaging it into her neck and shoulders.

"On my back too." She untied the straps to her bikini, holding the top against her breasts.

"But of course." He moved his hands down her back to where her bikini bottom began and up again several times until it glistened.

"You've got great hands," she whispered.

He could see that she was clearly enjoying his ministrations. He lifted her hair, planted kisses along her neck, and then moved around to her face to kiss her lips.

"Frank! Honey, you've got to stop this, or we'll get thrown off the beach!"

"Mmm? Okay. I'm sorry. But I gotta tell you: you look luscious, baby. Good enough to eat ..."

"Frank, stop!"

"Is this man bothering you?" A lifeguard passing by asked loudly, throwing cold water on their scintillating interlude.

"Of course not," Delilah replied, quickly tying the straps of her bikini top.

"Look, this is none of your business," Frank said between clenched teeth, "so go be about your business."

"Look, we don't go in for lewd and lascivious acts on the beach," the lifeguard shot back.

"I'm fine," Delilah replied. "He's my boyfriend!"

He gave Frank a quick once-over. "Yeah, well, you're judged by the company you keep."

Frank's blood was beginning to boil. "I think you better get the hell out of my face before your colleagues see you get your ass beat up and down this beach."

The lifeguard gave them both a look of disdain before he walked away. Fast.

Frank used all of the self-control he could muster to lower his blood pressure before he turned to smile at Delilah. "Let's go take a dip."

Delilah was looking at him closely. "Honey, are you okay?"

"I'm fine. I'm not going to let that jackass spoil my day with you." He took her hand. "Come on, let's go."

He helped her up, and they ran toward the shining ocean waves.

THEY ARRIVED BACK AT DELILAH'S house later that evening.

"I know you've got to go to work tomorrow, and I've got to head on to my next speaking engagement, so I won't keep you too long," Frank said as they walked to the parlor.

"I had such a great time." Despite the sunblock, Delilah had a little bit of a tan. It was very becoming with her eyes and coppery hair.

"Me too. I sure hate to leave you."

"Before you leave, I have one request." She slipped her arms around his neck.

He nuzzled hers. "Name it."

"Let's go take a shower together."

"Come on, let's go!"

She ran, laughing, up the stairs, and he followed.

Chapter Six

July was now in full swing, and the dog days of summer had grown into full-blown, bloodthirsty hounds. From the east coast to the west, Frank ran into unrelenting hot weather. Oppressively humid, wet heat was in the east and south, and dry heat was in the west and desert regions. In any case, it was hot.

"Man, I am sick of this hot weather," Andy remarked one evening to Frank when they both happened to be on the same coast at the same time. They were sitting in front of the TV in Andy and Twyla's apartment, drinking beer.

"It's getting monotonous, that's for sure." Frank tipped his bottle and savored the cool liquid as it rolled down his throat.

"It's past monotonous. It's two and a half hells hot out there. But I've got a great idea."

Frank toyed with him a little, not answering right away.

"You're supposed to say, 'What?' jackass," Andy retorted.

Frank stifled his laughter and then echoed, "What, jackass?"

"Very funny. But listen, my friend Ozzie Rollins knows about a great place in West Virginia. He wants to go camping and do a little fishing up in the mountains this weekend. He's already made reservations, so the more the merrier. All you have to bring with you are clothes. Ozzie's got the gear. You wanna go?"

"Camping?" Frank gave a slight snort. "I haven't been camping since never."

"So come with us, man," Andy suggested, his excitement apparent. "Anyway, it's likely to be cooler. We can relax and get away from it all. You got anything else planned?"

"Not really."

"Me either." Andy gave a contented burp. "And Twyla went up to Philly yesterday to visit her mother."

Frank set his empty bottle down on the coffee table in front of them. "So you're on the loose?"

Andy grinned. "I'm on the loose."

"*Sure* you are. Okay, I'm game. When do we leave?"

"Well, since we're both off on Friday and Ozzie's taking the day off, what say we meet here about four o'clock?"

"Maybe that's the reason I've never been camping." Frank got up and stretched before heading for the bathroom. "Gotta get up too early."

"What do you care?" Andy asked as he got up to get more beer. "You're like New York City, except you're the man that never sleeps."

"Doesn't mean I like it," Frank called out and closed the bathroom door.

A DAY LATER, THEY WERE heading down the Shenandoah Valley and then up through the Shenandoah Mountains to Ozzie's favorite camping area. It took them less than three hours, but as they weaved their way through the mountains, it was as if they were a world away from civilization. It was still warm but not as warm as it was in the city, and the air was fresher. The vista went on for miles and miles.

A quiet, good-natured man in his early forties, Ozzie was an expert when it came to camping. Within a half hour, they had their tents up, kindling for the campfire in a pile, and he was handing Andy and Frank each a fishing pole.

"You got anything to wear that you don't mind getting wet?" he asked Frank as he stared at the jeans Frank wore. "Some hip waders?"

"Some hip what-ers?" Frank asked, giving him a perplexed look.

"Waterproof pants."

"Nope."

Andy stifled a laugh. "How about boots?"

"Yep, I brought a pair besides the ones I've got on."

"Although it's summer, the river can be cold," Ozzie explained. "We're going to try our luck at fly-fishing, since Andy here says he's tired of the heat. It should cool the two of you off."

They made their way to the Shenandoah River, and Ozzie instructed the others on how to cast their lines. After a while, both Andy and Frank got into the rhythm of it. Frank lit a cigarette and proceeded to cast away in the midday quiet. The river seemed alive, rushing but not frantic—beautiful, with the sun shining down upon its waves. It was hypnotic to him, and the cool wetness of it against the area above his boots where the water lapped was refreshing. He didn't even mind his feet getting wet.

Ozzie was a lanky country boy with country instincts. While Frank and Andy were fly-fishing, he made his way down to a calmer portion of the river and caught a couple of bass and trout for their dinner. Spoon bread, baked beans, and bottles of beer completed the meal.

"Man, Ozzie, you're a good cook!" Andy exclaimed as he grabbed another hunk of bread, shoving some of it into his mouth.

"A very good cook," Frank echoed as he finished his second helping of fried fish.

"Thanks." A faint hint of the Appalachians leached out.

"With you around, who needs a wife?" Andy remarked, wiping his hands on his jeans.

They laughed.

After dinner, they sat around the campfire, telling stories as night fell. Ozzie had a storehouse of them, and Frank and Andy tried their hands at telling a few. They talked and joked well into the night.

They kept spraying themselves liberally with insect repellent, but Andy and Frank still were bitten by mosquitoes. Ozzie seemed immune.

"They don't like my flavor," he announced, and added more wood to the fire.

The moon appeared huge to Frank as it hung low behind the trees. He felt as if he could reach out and pull it to him. He couldn't believe how peaceful it was: frogs croaking in the distance and the smell of the woodlands and the wood from the fire. He didn't even miss not being able to use his cell phone. Except, that is, when it came to one person.

"Damn, I miss the hell out of you," he whispered later into the night as he lay in his sleeping bag. He and Andy were sharing a tent.

Andy stirred. "Wha'd you say?"

"Nothing."

The next day they got in a good morning's worth of fishing and afterward ran into a few other men in the woods hiking. Although he was the only person of color he had seen since they arrived in the mountains, Frank felt completely at ease. Ozzie invited the other men to join them at their campsite, and they spent hours playing poker and drinking beer. One of the men who was not playing cards broke out a harmonica, and the music was a nice accompaniment, capping a guys-only weekend.

Sunday morning they awoke to thunder booming through the mountains and a cat-drowning downpour. They quickly dismantled the tents and packed their gear in the car, zigzagging their way back down the mountain.

"So, LET'S JUST LEAVE FROM here on Friday afternoon and head straight for the theatre," Vivian was saying on Tuesday as she and Delilah headed back indoors from lunch. "Afterward, we can grab something to eat. We should get our tickets online 'cause they might be sold out when we reach the theatre."

"That's sounds good. The lines will probably be long too, since that's the day of its release."

"I'll get them, and you can just pay me later. I can't wait. I just love George Clooney." Vivian pretended to swoon, and they snickered as they headed to their respective cubicles.

Right then, Mr. McDermott appeared from around a corner. "Delilah, I would like a word with you." They walked to her cubicle. His arm continuously brushed against hers, and she edged away. "I need you to stay late this Friday evening as well as come in on Saturday morning. We will be getting new carpeting installed here in the office, and the installers will need access. They will also need to be escorted into the building. There will be a supervisor with them so you won't have anything to worry about. Put in for compensatory time. I'll approve it. If they're fast, you won't have to come in on Sunday." His cold gray eyes probed hers, as if waiting for her to challenge him.

Delilah fumed inside. *It would've been nice to have been asked*, she thought. Aloud she just said, "I had plans, Mr. McDermott, but I will cancel them." She thought she saw a glimmer of triumph in his eyes before he pivoted on his heel and walked away.

She was glad that Agnes wasn't there that day to snicker. She dropped her handbag on the desk and dialed Vivian's extension. "Don't purchase any tickets yet, Viv. I've got to hang around here this weekend. The carpet installers will be coming to put in new carpet."

"Oh no! Is that what Mr. McDermott wanted to talk to you about?"

"Yes. We'll have to play it by ear until Sunday. Hopefully they'll finish on Saturday. If you really want to go this weekend, you might want to ask your boyfriend to go with you instead."

"No way, Dee! I want us to go together, so that we can *ooh* and *ahh* to our hearts' content. Xion, my boyfriend, rolls his eyes whenever I go on about George Clooney. He can't understand why I do, when I have what he calls 'my own Japanese-Korean sex symbol'—him. He always asks, 'What does George Clooney have that I don't?' Dee, I haven't the heart to tell him."

They laughed, and then Delilah said, "Well, I'll have to let you know. I should hear something one way or another by Saturday afternoon. 'Bye, Viv." Delilah hung up and shoved her bag into her desk drawer as she got back to work, still wondering what that gleam in Mr. McDermott's eyes really meant.

Chapter Seven

"Andy, are you traveling next week?" Twyla asked as they gathered their dirty clothes to take to the laundry room at the end of the hall on the floor of their apartment.

He found a mate-less sock under his side of the bed and rammed it into the laundry bag reserved for the colored clothes. "Nope, I'm free as a bird, baby. What's up?"

"Momma wants to have one of her Sunday dinners for the family members on the East Coast. Those who can make it, come. Those who can't come, she'll see another time."

"Sure, let's go. We haven't been out of town together at all lately with my crazy schedule."

"Let's leave on Friday. Make a weekend of it." She set the jugs of detergent and fabric softener by the front door. "Have you seen the bleach?"

He came up behind her and kissed the back of her neck. "It's in the bathroom, I think. Tell your momma we'll be there with bells on."

TWYLA'S MOTHER, ZIZI HAYES, LIVED in an old, narrow brick row house, typical of Philadelphia's older neighborhoods. That's where the characteristic aspects of her home ended. Inside, her living and dining room resembled a museum with all of the photographs she had taken and curios she had picked up during her travels in Mexico and all over the United States; they were showcased against a backdrop of gold-painted walls.

Twyla and Andy took a train up and a taxi from Penn Station. Andy sighed with contentment. "Love not spending an hour looking for parking." He grabbed their small suitcase, and they headed for ZiZi's front door.

She whipped open the door before Andy could set the suitcase down. "Hi, babies. Come on in." ZiZi was ageless. Chronologically she was in her early fifties, but she did not subscribe to labels. She was tall, her dark-brown skin the color of semisweet chocolate, her short-cropped natural hair bleached blonde. She was a take-charge woman, yet warm and gregarious—one big human puzzle, which somehow worked.

"Hi, Momma ZiZi," Andy sang, giving her a kiss and a hug.

Twyla followed suit, then stood back and watched the two of them interact. She laughed. "You take after my mother more than I do."

"I love her," he announced. He said it with such earnestness that the two women laughed.

"And I love you too, Andy. Are you two staying here this weekend?" ZiZi swooped around the narrow yet spacious living room, showing them whatever changes she had made since their last visit, which for Twyla had been several months ago and for Andy, nearly a year.

Andy looked swiftly at Twyla, who gave him a subtle wink. Although Twyla knew he loved her mother, they both wanted to make the most of their brief out-of-town rendezvous. "We'd love to, Momma ZiZi, but ... ah, well, you know ..."

"Gotcha. You want your privacy." She swept them into her smallish kitchen, from where delectable smells emanated. She wore a grape-hued voluminous and flowing caftan, just a shade short of eggplant, with long, loose sleeves—a throwback to the dashiki dresses and caftans of the sixties. It, along with her dangling earrings and clanging bracelets, suited her. "Staying for dinner?"

"Sure, Momma, if you're sure you have enough."

"Sweetie, if I didn't have enough," ZiZi said, "I wouldn't be inviting you two."

At dinner, they talked incessantly. That is, ZiZi and Andy talked while Twyla listened, basking in the warmth of their exuberance with life in general and with one another in particular. The seafood stew was delicious and gave them all the perfect excuse to linger over their meal while they exchanged the latest family news. Andy regaled them with his father's misdeed—betting on the latest Boston Red Sox game with him but making the mistake of mentioning it when his mother could overhear. His mother did not like gambling.

The feelings she felt whenever she and Andy visited her mother were a restorative tonic to Twyla. Her parents had divorced when she was a child; her only sibling was her brother, Tyler, who was now a soldier stationed in the demilitarized zone in South Korea. Twyla knew her mother missed him terribly. With Tyler gone, Andy infused the house with a masculine presence. Not that ZiZi's house was ever empty for long. Although she worked from home as a freelance writer, she had a constant stream of male and female visitors, more often than not.

They stayed until nightfall and obtained lodging at a hotel downtown. If the desk clerk thought anything strange regarding their union, he was professional enough not to show it.

Andy threw their luggage onto a sofa in the suite. Twyla clicked on the television and stifled a yawn. She noticed a look of alarm in his eyes and smiled to herself.

"Wanna take a shower together?" she asked.

At that suggestion, he began to rip his shirt off, sprinting to the bathroom to turn on the shower.

Twyla grabbed her toiletry bag and followed.

Andy seemed nervous as he helped her remove her clothing. He dived inside the shower.

"Come on in, baby."

She grabbed a bottle of shampoo and conditioner from the bag, along with a deliciously scented bar of soap. Placing the soap in the wall inset, she turned to him and pushed him under the stream of warm water. Setting down the bottle of conditioner, she squeezed a stream of shampoo into her palm.

"Come here, baby. I want to wash your hair."

Andy bent his head forward to kiss her and give her access to his longish blond locks. "Mmm. It's been a long time since you've washed my hair."

"You know why that is." Her voice was quiet but not disapproving.

"I know, baby, I know." He took her face in his hands. "Twyla, I know that I joke a lot. But whenever you're not with me, I miss you so much. You know that, don't you?"

"Yes I do, Andy." She showered his face with feathery kisses. "Turn around."

He did so, leaning back so she could scrub his hair with her expert touch. "Man, that feels so good."

After she rinsed his hair, Twyla added the conditioner. "I'm glad you enjoy your job. I love that. I love mine too. Mine's not as flexible, though. I wish I could go with you more, but don't think that I hold it against you."

"Oh, I know that you don't." Andy smiled. "Thanks, honey." He grabbed the cake of soap and a washcloth and began to wash every inch of her body.

Twyla closed her eyes, taking time to savor the feel of his free hand as well, which traced the movements of the hand he was using to wash her. She ran her hands through his hair as she lifted her lips to his. "You know that I love you, right?"

"I know."

She pushed him under the stream of water once more to rinse the conditioner from his hair. She then took her turn to wash him, enjoying the hard, masculine feel of his body.

Andy gently shoved her against the cold, hard wall tiles. The steamy water magnified their desire as he kissed her. They held each other almost in desperation as their lovemaking flowed as freely as the water cascading down their bodies. "Your hair's getting wet, baby," he whispered, nibbling her ear.

"Hell wit' it," she gasped, and she pressed herself even closer to him.

They finally emerged from the shower, making love into the wee hours of the morning. Andy was normally an adventurous lover. However, this time he was more thoughtful, yet strong and tender. Spent, they fell asleep. Before dawn broke, Twyla awoke with a start.

Andy stirred as well. "Baby, what's wrong?" His voice was soft in the velvety-black darkness.

"We ... we didn't use any backup."

He pulled her back into his warm embrace. "Would it be so bad?" he asked, the sleepiness evident in his husky voice. "Having a baby with me?"

She was glad he fell asleep again before she had to answer.

SUNDAY ARRIVED, RAINY AND COOL for the beginning of August. Andy was feeling even more affectionate than usual toward Twyla. He was enjoying their time away together.

They helped ZiZi put the finishing touches on dinner preparation in the little kitchen as the other family members and their significant others began to arrive. Earlier she had Andy install the extra leaves in her cinnamon-colored dining room table.

Not long after, it was time to eat. Andy pulled out ZiZi's and Twyla's chairs and then sat down next to Twyla.

Uncle Jimmy, ZiZi's brother, a tall, slim, and sly-looking man in his midfifties, who was sitting on the other side of Andy, winked at him. They had met at a ZiZi-hosted dinner the previous year. "How's it going, Andy?"

"Never better," he replied.

"Hey, Brother Andy. How you doin'?" Diane, Twyla's cousin—pretty and "pleasingly plump" in her own estimation and a vivacious woman of forty—asked as she took a seat across from Andy. They had met at a cookout several summers ago and now considered themselves to be old friends.

"I'm doing great, Miss Diane. How are you?"

The banter was lively and loud. Andy felt right at home with Twyla's relatives. Racially he was in the minority, with the exception of Uncle Jimmy's current girlfriend, Lena Li, who was Chinese, yet they always made him feel welcome. Andy reached over into Twyla's lap and squeezed her hand. Although she was engaged in conversation with her grandfather at the head of the table, she returned the squeeze without missing a beat.

They ate and talked well into the evening. After several futile attempts to help clear the dishes and clean up the kitchen, they hugged ZiZi and those relatives who had not left yet and accepted a ride from Diane and her husband, Montgomery, back to Penn Station.

Not long after they took their seats on the chilly train, Andy felt Twyla's head fall lightly against his shoulder. He hugged her to him as she dozed, and the city limits whirred past them in the darkness.

Chapter Eight

*O*kay, *it's your turn. Come for a weekend. I'll send you a ticket. Let me know when.*

Delilah read the text message she received from Frank as she soaked in a bubble bath one night. Her workweek had been long and tedious, with the exception of Mr. McDermott. She couldn't figure him out. He was hot one minute–finding something to call her to his office about— but cold the next, as once she got there, it was usually much ado about nothing, and he would just sit across the desk, staring through her. He sometimes looked at her as if she were an alien.

Time to forget about Mr. McDermott. She smiled to herself, *Yes, Mr. Ellis, it is time for me to come visit you for a change. That's probably what I need anyway, a change of scenery.*

Once the water had cooled, she toweled herself dry, applied lotion, and padded to the bedroom to throw on panties and an oversized T-shirt. Afterward, she texted: *I'll give my supervisor a leave slip for Wednesday, the week after next, returning on Sunday, if that's okay with you. Let me know if it isn't. Book me an early flight. I can't wait 2 see u. Work day 2-morrow. Good night, sweetie.*

FRANK WAITED INSIDE HIS CAR at BWI airport on Wednesday morning. He resisted the powerful urge to light up. It wouldn't be long; he had pulled up within minutes of the flight on which Delilah was scheduled to arrive. The police wouldn't allow any more time than what it took for travelers to disembark from vehicles or be picked up by drivers.

Just when he was thinking about pulling off and finding a parking spot in the nearby multilevel parking garage, he spotted a familiar figure stepping outside the automated doors of the terminal and looking around. He jumped out of the car and ran to her.

"Delilah." They stood face-to-face. "How was your flight?"

"It was just fine. Short." She started to grab the strap of her large colorful duffle bag, but Frank took it from her.

"Let me get those for you." His hand brushed against hers, and he allowed it to linger there for a moment. He slipped a quick kiss along the back of her neck.

Damn, she always smells so good! he thought to himself.

"Thank you, honey."

Frank ushered Delilah to his car as he noticed a member of the airport transit police giving him the evil eye. "C'mon baby, let's get out of here."

About forty minutes later, he pulled into the parking lot of his condo building, which was surrounded by a tall, black, wrought-iron fence. The complex consisted of three tan-and-red twelve-story brick high-rises nestled amid small groupings of birch trees and beautiful landscaping.

"Welcome to my home," he announced.

He opened the door to the lobby area; the clicking of Delilah's shoes echoed through the lobby, which was elegantly done in blue-veined white Carrara marble. They passed the alcove where the bank of metal mailboxes were located and headed toward elevators with copper doors polished to a brilliant shine.

Frank's condo was located on the penthouse level, constructed architecturally in a loft style with high ceilings and decorated in a masculine vibe with two black sofas made of butter-soft leather grouped in the living area, maximizing one's view of the city as well as the slate fireplace that stood in one corner. Large ceramic pots, some with what looked to be African-style prints and others of various patterns, stood on graceful metal stands flanking the entry door. They were full of lush, dark-green palms and bright-green, lanky bamboo. A wall of windows led to a substantial balcony. The gray fabric shades were powered all the way up, showcasing the eye-catching view and filling the massive room with light. A delicate white-and-pink orchid stood in a simple but stunning Asian vase on the huge black wood coffee table. Gaily colored African prints hung on the walls behind the sofas that were bordered by simple glass end tables. Three stark black-and-white lithographs of women's naked silhouettes lined one wall of the dining room. The living room

69

was painted in a cool gray, reminiscent of the steakhouse they dined at in Savannah; the dining room was painted a relaxing slate blue. The rooms were spacious yet contained intimate settings. He glanced at her.

"This looks like you—full of contradictions."

"Is that good, baby?" Frank asked.

Delilah smiled. "In your case, yes."

"I'm going to take it as a compliment. Come over here and check out the view," he replied as he set her bags down on one of the sofas.

They walked over to the huge wall of floor-length windows, where an incredible view of the city stretched out in front of them in the distance. The sun was high in the nearly cloudless sky and the other two high-rises, which stood like guards on either side of the building Frank lived in, formed a formidable brick arc.

"What a stunning view."

"It's what attracted me to this condo in the first place." He was standing behind Delilah. "It has a calming effect on me."

She swung around to face him with a warm smile. "Calming effect? You? Honey, you look like *Mr. Suave and Debonair* out there on that lecture circuit: calm, cool, and collected."

"My turmoil's on the inside," he replied, surprising himself. He didn't know where that remark came from. Without even trying, she made him reveal personal things about himself. "What I meant was, don't take what you see here as all that I am. I only just got to the place where I can afford to enjoy some of the finer things in life. Trust me, I always put some away for a rainy day. I never forget my hungry days. Come on, let me show you around, and then we can eat."

His bedroom was dark and cool. Frank picked up the remote from the bedside table and the gray fabric shades lifted to reveal an equally spectacular a view of the city beyond but from a different angle. The room resembled one found in an upscale hotel—dark-wood furnishings with clean lines, neutral linens on the king-sized bed, and a restful gray paint on the walls. A mixed bouquet of flowers stood in a simple glass vase on the bureau.

"You've outdone yourself, Frank. It's beautiful."

"Thanks. I travel so much that I decided to decorate my place in the style of a nice hotel. Whatever you need, you just let me know." He gently took her hands and looked into her eyes. "My home is your home."

She gave him a quick kiss on the lips. "I need you to show me the culinary skills you've boasted about so many times on the phone."

He led her back through the condo to the kitchen and sat her down at the granite-topped breakfast bar.

"What's your pleasure, ma'am? It's lunchtime, but if you want eggs or a waffle, that's good too."

"Oh, I don't know." Her tone was teasing. "Surprise me."

Frank washed his hands and snatched a dish towel out of a drawer underneath it. He tucked it into the waistband of his jeans, letting it serve as a makeshift apron. He looked up in time to see Delilah stifle a laugh, and he pretended to be hurt. "*Oh ho*, you doubt my skills? Well, come on then. You can act as my sous-chef."

"Somebody's been watching a little too much Food Network," Delilah mumbled as she rose from her stool and headed around the bar toward him.

"What's that?"

"Nothing."

After several more minutes of good-natured bickering, they decided on grilled salmon and a garden salad with bleu-cheese dressing. Although the kitchen was spacious, they kept bumping into each other, most times on purpose. Each time his hands weren't full, Frank made it his business to slip his arms around her, his fingers lingering.

He finally announced, "Lunch is ready, so let's eat."

After lunch, Frank began to clear the table, and Delilah followed suit. "You probably want to rest, so—"

"No, I had a nap on the plane. What did you want to do?"

"The question is, what do you want to do?" He placed the leftovers in the refrigerator and the dirty dishes in the dishwasher.

"I've never been to Washington, DC, before. I'd like to see some of the city."

"Then that's what we'll do."

They toured the Lincoln and Jefferson memorials and checked out the Newseum, which took the rest of the afternoon. Afterward, as evening was descending on the city, they went back to Frank's place.

Delilah dozed in the car, and once they arrived back at the complex, Frank gently shook her awake. Without a word, she followed him to the condo lobby and into the elevator. He had planned to prepare dinner for the two of them. But upon noticing that her pretty eyes still looked sleepy, he gently sent her to his bedroom. She obeyed without protest.

Not long after, he followed suit.

DELILAH AWOKE THE NEXT MORNING to the tantalizing smell of bacon frying. Her stomach growled in response. She was starving!

After rummaging around in her duffle bag, she threw on her robe and mules and hurried to the kitchen. She stopped abruptly when she saw Frank at the stove, shirtless, in his pajama bottoms, removing bacon from the frying pan. His muscles rippled along his dark-brown shoulders and arms as he moved about, unaware of her presence.

"Lord have mercy," she murmured. When had he gotten up? Better yet, when had he gone to bed? She had slept like a stone.

He turned around at the sound of her voice. "Good morning," he rumbled, and her heart fluttered. "It's only nine fifteen. I thought you'd be sleeping a little while longer. I was going to bring it to you—serve you breakfast in bed." His dark eyes held the promise of much more.

"I smelled bacon and realized how hungry I was. I didn't have any dinner last night."

"Neither did I. But everything's ready so go ahead and sit down. Breakfast bar or table?"

"Table."

"Back with you in a minute. I'm going to put on a T-shirt."

"Oh, don't do so on my account," she quickly remarked.

He flashed a smile at her but left anyway. When he returned, they set the table and sat down. Frank had prepared bacon, eggs, and waffles. He poured orange juice for the both of them. "I don't drink coffee much, but I have some, if you want. Or would you like milk?"

"No, this is fine, Frank. I declare, I am going to gain a ton eating like this!" Delilah cried, waving a hand in protest.

"Delilah, you have nothing to worry about," he replied before taking a bite of his food. Sliding her slipper off with his foot, he played footsie with her under the table.

Desire surged through her as she returned the foot-play exchange. Breakfast was delicious, but all of a sudden she didn't notice what she was eating. The only thing in the room that mattered was this incredible sexy man sitting across the table from her, looking at her in a way that made her dizzy.

"Why is a phenomenal woman like you still single?" was the question Frank was asking, his voice full of wonder.

She stared into her orange juice. "My last relationship just didn't work out. In the end, we wanted different things." She looked up, their eyes meeting. "How about you?"

"I don't know. I guess I never really wanted to get married." His gaze did not waver.

Neither did hers. "And now?"

"Well, the idea is not so foreign to me now."

THEY SPENT THE DAY CONTINUING to take in the sights. Delilah was amazed at the history that Washington, DC, and the surrounding area had to offer. After their tour of "The Wall" of the Vietnam Veterans Memorial, the heavens opened up and drenched them both. They ran to the car, laughing and cursing the elements, for neither had thought to bring an umbrella.

Frank swore and Delilah looked over, startled, but began to laugh when she realized what he held up for her review was exactly that. "A fat lot of good this did us, back here in the car!" he remarked before joining in. He hurried to the trunk and extracted a roll of paper towels with which they attempted to mop themselves dry.

Other residents of the condo gave them looks of mild amusement as they tramped through the lobby some time later, waterlogged and bedraggled, toward the elevators. It was August and the rain had been warm, but once inside the air-conditioned building, Delilah began to shiver.

"Go take a shower," Frank said, once they were upstairs. "I'll get a fire going."

She laughed. "A fire? In August?"

"Sure. It's chilly in here." He walked over to the coffee table in front of one of the leather sofas, picked up a remote, and aimed it at the fireplace across from him. It ignited in an instant. "I wouldn't want you to catch cold while you're in my care."

Delilah noticed the change in his demeanor; it was almost as fast as he had switched on the fireplace, but not so fast as not to be noticed by her. The interplay of emotions on his face transitioned from one of jocularity to one of tenderness, which was so powerful that she felt it across the room. At a loss for words, she sped from the room.

When she returned to the living room, she found Frank on the balcony. She could see the tip of his cigarette glowing in the growing darkness. "Isn't it raining out there?"

He stamped out the remnants and returned to the living room. "Ah, you caught me. I planned on being finished by the time you got out of the shower. One sec."

Frank left the room, and moments later, she heard him gargling. After a short while, he emerged from the bathroom. "Fresh and clean," he announced, popping a few breath mints.

"I must admit, I never see you do it. Or hardly smell it, for that matter."

He sat down on the rug where she already sat with her legs curled under her. "That's because I know you don't like it." He touched her cheek. "You warm enough?"

"Very." Frank's touch emanated more heat than the fireplace. "Thanks."

"I hope you enjoyed yourself today."

"Oh yes, it was fun." Lightning lit up the room for a moment, and they both jumped and then laughed. The storm had given them a brief respite, but now it was raging again. "What about you? Aren't you going to shower or change your clothes?"

"I'm okay. Fire took the chill off." A soft grunt escaped his lips.

"I heard that. Tired?"

"Not really." Frank leaned back against the huge coffee table. He pulled her next to him and closed his eyes. "That was my 'I need to do this more often' grunt."

"Oh." They were both quiet for a while, deep in their own thoughts. Delilah closed her eyes as well. It was so relaxing, here with Frank, with the sound of the rain and wind pounding the windows. Yet at the same time, she was hungry for him. The more she discovered about him, the more she wanted to know. His bare arm pressed against hers, the warmth of his body seeping into hers, along with the warmth of the fire. She felt his hand close over hers in the darkness.

The next evening, unbeknownst to Delilah, Frank had made plans for them. When she went to the refrigerator to get bottled water for the both of them, she saw a pile of raw steaks on a platter, seasoned and wrapped in plastic. He followed her into the kitchen and began to wash his hands.

"What's this?" she asked, indicating the steaks.

"We're having a cookout," he replied, then headed for the balcony to fire up the barbecue grill. "I invited a few friends over. You'll like them."

"Do you want me to do anything?" she asked.

"You can get out the cooler on the floor in the hall closet and the bag of ice in the freezer," he called out as he checked the propane tank behind the grill.

"Is this shindig formal?" she asked, lugging the cooler and ice out to the balcony where Frank stood scraping the grill with a wire brush.

"No, whatever you'd normally wear to a cookout is fine. But we are going out later."

"Alrighty then," she replied. "I can't wait to meet them."

A few hours later, they arrived at the condo. Andy looked even more the beachcomber in a Hawaiian shirt, long shorts, and sandals. Twyla wore an orange sundress, which accentuated her deep bronze complexion.

"Hi, I'm Delilah," Delilah announced as Frank joined them at the door.

"Delilah, this is 'the boy who never grew up,' Andy Maxwell, and his girlfriend, Twyla Hayes, Frank announced.

"We brought some refreshments," Andy said, indicating the six-pack of beer he carried in one hand. Twyla carried a box.

"And lemon cake," she chimed in.

"'Cause I'm not sure brother man can cook," Andy joked as they walked to the balcony.

Frank picked up a platter and began pulling the steaks off the grill.

"Andrew, I was throwing down on the grill before you were drinking your first cold one."

"Yeah, yeah." Andy plopped himself down upon the nearest of the two colorful chaise lounges.

Frank walked over and kissed Twyla on the cheek. "Hey, Twyla. I don't know why you go around with this young 'un."

"Hi, Frank," she said with a smile.

"So tell us more about this beautiful young lady who answered the door," said Andy, cracking open the beer he held in his hand and looking in Delilah's direction.

"She's the guest of honor, Delilah Carpenter." After setting down the platter, Frank walked over and placed his arm around her waist.

"We've heard *a lot* about you," Andy replied before he took a swallow.

"Good things," Twyla added as she helped Delilah with the food. "It's so nice to finally meet you."

"Yep, 'cause we've been waiting for a while. I was just asking him the other day when we were going to finally meet this elusive lady he's always talking about."

Frank shook his head. "Shut up, Andy."

Twyla gave Delilah a sympathetic glance. "They're like this all the time, fussing like brothers."

"Brothers from two other mothers." Andy grinned. "You know, you have a sexy southern accent, Dee."

"Boy, I will knock you into next week if you start flirting with her," Twyla announced, getting in on the good-natured ribbing.

Andy pretended to be afraid. "And she will too."

"Come on, everybody; let's eat," said Frank.

After dinner, they talked until the sun sank. Andy and Twyla then went home to change and later met up with Frank and Delilah again at the nightclub L'Elegance.

When Twyla went with Delilah to the ladies' room, Frank turned to Andy. "Well?"

"Now I see why you kept her to yourself. She is fine."

"This is the first time she's been up to visit me. And yeah, I like her," Frank admitted.

"Go on, don't give me that! You're crazy about her."

"I am." The music pounded around them, but Frank barely noticed. "I don't know what to do about it, though."

"What do you mean?" Andy demanded. "You just keep on seeing her."

"I know that she likes me, otherwise, she wouldn't be here. She's got that southern family-value thing happening, which I'm cool with. But like I said, she's from the South, so we don't know how *that's* going to play out."

"And you won't know how it's going to play out, until it plays out." Andy took a sip of his drink. "You know racism ain't only in the South."

"Tell me something I don't know. But I already got a taste of it at her house on the Fourth of July."

When the women returned, the men pretended as if they had been discussing sports. A slow number came on, and Frank held out his hand. "May I have this dance, Delilah?"

"Yes, you may." She took his hand, and they threaded their way through the crowd to a tiny spot on the dance floor.

Frank slid his arms around her and breathed in the scent of her. *Yep, she's mine*, he thought as they slow danced. He felt Delilah's arms around his neck, and he pressed himself even closer to her. She did not resist, and her silent acquiescence proved his point. He felt her movements matching his own, conveying their feelings for one another in a tribal ritual as old as history itself.

Back at the table, Andy turned his attention to Twyla. "Ain't love grand?" he asked with a wink.

EIGHT O'CLOCK THE NEXT MORNING, Delilah headed toward the kitchen, rested despite an amorous night with Frank and determined to be the one to prepare breakfast this time. As usual, Frank's side of the bed had been empty, and he was already up and in the kitchen, placing cooked link sausages on a napkin-draped platter. She stopped in her tracks for a moment, but he had heard her just the same.

"Good morning. I was just about to call you."

"I swear, Frank, do you *ever* sleep?" she asked, attempting to steady her pulse after the greeting and heart-stopping look he was now giving her. "I never manage to get up earlier than you."

He gave a slight chuckle. "That's partly because I'm an early riser when I'm motivated enough and partly because I'm an insomniac. It's no problem, so don't worry about it."

Delilah walked over to Frank and took the platter from his hand, setting it on the nearby breakfast bar. "Come sit down." Then she took his hand and led him to the kitchen table. They both sat down. She continued to hold his hand in hers. "Frank, I've enjoyed the time I've spent with you so much. I see why you enjoy living here. But I need you to do something for me."

"Anything."

"Just relax with me. *Be* with me." She gave his hand a slight squeeze and smiled into his eyes. "We don't have to do something every second of the day. And let me do for you sometimes."

"I hear you." A sheepish look crossed his features.

"Don't, Frank. I don't want you to feel embarrassed. I'll admit it; it feels great being spoiled by you. I hope you know that I appreciate it. But you don't have to, sweetie. I'm not a high-maintenance woman."

Reaching out with his free hand, Frank clasped her hand in both of his. "I know. You just make it easy for a man to spoil you."

Delilah smiled and looked away. "Come on, let's finish cooking."

Frank and Delilah saw Andy and Twyla later that evening when they went to the movies together at White Flint Mall, a mall frequented by a diverse but primarily white population.

They enjoyed the movie, a comedy with an up-and-coming comedian, and were still laughing when they made their way out of the cool air-conditioned movieplex into the hot and muggy night. As they passed a group of African American teenagers and twenty-somethings, one in the group of young men stepped in front of the two couples.

"Look at this," he spat. "A checkerboard."

The group of young men laughed. "More like chess!" another boy remarked.

"Step out of my way, son," Frank demanded in a quiet tone of voice.

"*Son!* He called you 'son,' Orlando!" someone in the crowd yelled.

"I ain't your son, man," Orlando retorted.

"I wouldn't have to call you 'son' if you weren't acting so ignorant," Frank said. "*So back up off me.*"

"I say punch 'im in his face!" yelled another person in the group. By this time, a crowd was gathering.

Frank attempted to lead Delilah and the others past the unruly young men when Orlando pushed him. "I guarantee you won't do that again," Frank hissed. He was quickly losing his patience.

"He's a punk!" someone else from Orlando's posse cried.

"Why don't you guys just move on?" Andy suggested, stepping next to Frank.

"You need to close your mouth, white boy!"

"Maybe I need to check out what Oreo here sees in this here white girl—"

Orlando reached out to touch Delilah's hair when Frank blocked him with his body.

"Touch her, and you'll answer to me," he growled, the hands he held at his sides forming fists.

The onlookers were shoved to opposite sides of the sidewalk as two policemen barreled their way through them. "All right, what's going on here?"

"We're just trying to go on our merry way, Officer," Andy replied, "when these young 'uns accosted us."

"Well, break it up, or we'll take you all in and figure it out at the station," the policeman announced. Tall and broad-shouldered, he cut an imposing figure, towering over everyone there.

"If anyone needs to go to the station, it's them," Frank said.

The officer cast a sidelong glance at him.

For all of the noise they were making just moments ago, the young troublemakers were now silent.

"Just get out of here, all of you."

Delilah stood there, stock-still and wide-eyed, clearly in a state of shock. Twyla nudged her, and the four of them resumed walking toward Frank's car.

"Break it up," chimed in the second policeman. "Nothing to see here."

THE MOOD WAS SUBDUED AS Andy drove them to Frank's place.

"So what do you think, bro?" he was asking Frank, who sat beside him. The women sat in the backseat, talking among themselves.

"I think I'm still pissed off, that's what I think," Frank seethed.

"That's not what I was talking about," Andy calmly replied.

"Well, that's what I was thinking about." He stared out of the passenger window. "Did you see the way that cop looked at me? Like I was one of those simple-assed teenagers!"

"Yeah, I saw."

"Yeah, well, I'm sick to death of that look."

The next morning was Sunday, and Delilah awoke with every intention of making Frank breakfast for a change. She would be flying home later that day. His side of the bed was empty, the bedclothes barely disturbed. *He beat me to the punch again*, she thought with a smile. When she walked down the hallway and rounded the corner, she was startled to find him standing at the balcony window in the same clothes he had worn the night before, staring out at the early morning sunrise. It was obvious to her that he had never gone to bed.

"Frank! What in the world—"

"Good morning," he greeted her. His manner was subdued. But the veins in his arms were straining, visible to her naked eye in the short-sleeved shirt he wore, and his fists were clenched. He stood at the window, almost in a boxer's stance.

"Oh, Frank!" Her eyes began to sting and fill with tears as she rushed to him, embracing him from behind. He stiffened further at her touch but only for an instant.

"Yes, Delilah, I am still angry. Angry that I let those little punks rile me; angry that in this day and age, we still have to deal with that stupid shit. I'm sorry, baby. But most of all, I'm sorry that those sworn to uphold the law still look at me the way that policeman looked at me yesterday, full of suspicion and intolerance for them and for us. Or should I say, us as couples, and me for daring to speak the hell up!"

Tears slid down her cheeks, one by one, and began to wet the back of Frank's shirt. If he noticed, he didn't show it. She felt the tension in him, the searing pain and hatred for the system; she could practically smell it emanating from him. "I wish I could do something—"

He pulled away from her. "*Society* needs to do something."

They both stood silent for a long time while the sun climbed higher in the sky. It was going to be another hot day.

A DEFINITE PALLOR HAD FALLEN over the rest of Delilah's visit. It almost felt as if someone had died. They spent a quiet morning at his home, which was restful, but it was not the comfortable companionship they had experienced in front of the fireplace on the night of the storm.

They rode most of the way to the airport in silence. To Frank, the drive seemed interminable, yet desperately short. There was so much left unsaid. He parked his car in the multilevel parking garage and took her luggage out of the trunk. When Delilah went to grab the handle of her duffle bag, he fixed her with a glare. "I got this."

Once at the terminal, they checked Delilah's baggage curbside, and then stood for a few moments, looking helplessly at one another. Frank shook off the feeling and grabbed her hand. "Come with me."

"My flight—"

He almost yanked her off her feet. "You have plenty of time."

He led her inside, through the throng, and over to a bank of windows where there weren't as many people and they could talk a little more freely. Planes were taking off and landing; people were arriving and departing. Life went on, no matter the circumstances in individuals' lives.

"We're so insignificant, in the scheme of things," Delilah murmured, as if reading his mind.

"We are and we aren't," Frank agreed, turning around to look into her eyes. "Next to those airplanes or Earth, we look like nothing. But in our individual worlds and to the people we care about, we're a lot. Delilah, I know that I'm not expressing myself that great right now—"

"You're doing fine." Her voice sounded mechanical.

He grabbed both of her arms and gave her a slight shake. "Listen to me. Everything was going great this week. I couldn't have asked for better. But then, after that incident with those idiots, it seemed like cold water was thrown on everything. On us."

"It freaked me out, Frank." She gazed at him, and her eyes filled with tears.

"It wasn't exactly a walk in the park for me either, baby, but the difference is, it happens to me on a regular basis when I'm alone or in a crowd like this."

"I'm so sorry about that," she replied, sniffing.

"Thanks, but you have nothing to feel sorry about." He took a deep breath, and then let it out in a slow and measured way. "But that's the thing about racism—it's stupid. There's no rhyme or reason to it. Someone hates you because of the color of your skin. How idiotic is that? Yet it persists."

"I've never experienced it before. I've had black and Latino friends who it's happened to, and I tried to be supportive. But this time—it was aimed at you and me. And I didn't know how to handle it." Her lip trembled. "I felt so powerless."

"It's a bad feeling," he agreed, wiping the tears from her eyes with his thumbs. "And those kids hated the fact that I was out with you. They didn't even know me, but that didn't matter. It's ridiculous."

"At least you spoke up," Delilah replied, her tears gushing anew. "I just stood there like a bump on a log."

"You said it yourself, you're new at it." He tried to stem the flow of tears but was unsuccessful.

She fumbled around in her purse. "I don't have any tissue!" Delilah declared, stamping her foot.

The gesture was so childlike that they both began to laugh. Frank brushed the tendrils of loose curls off of her wet face. "Go to the ladies' room and blow your nose. I'll be here waiting for you."

A few minutes later, she returned; her nose and face somewhat pink from crying, but her eyes now sparkling. "That's it. That's what I want to see," Frank whispered as she walked into his arms. "We're going to deal with this thing. We're not going to let it win, okay?"

He bent his head toward her to kiss her good-bye. She slid her arms around his neck and pressed her lips to his as urgently as he was to hers. For a few moments, they both forgot where they were.

At last, Frank pulled away. "They're going to tell us to get a room," he announced as he caught his breath.

Delilah nodded, looking dazed.

"Come on, let's get you on that plane."

BOTH FRANK AND ANDY WERE speaking at a three-day conference in Boise, Idaho, and then Frank would be going on to Los Angeles the following week. He hadn't spoken to Andy or Twyla since their run-in with the young hoodlums five days before. He could barely speak to Andy when they parted that afternoon.

"Hey, buddy," Andy greeted Frank when they crossed paths in the Boise hotel.

"Hey."

"All right, Frank, are you still mad at me?" Confusion was evident on his face. "Explain it to me. What the *hell* did I do?"

"Look, let's take this stuff upstairs and get something to eat. I'll tell you then."

They found a great steakhouse a few blocks from the hotel where they were staying. Frank waited for the waitress to take their orders and leave before he spoke.

"I'm not mad at you, Andy. It just puzzles me how you were able to shake off what happened to us so quickly. By the time we were in the car, you seemed to be over it."

Andy took a sip of his Bloody Mary and shrugged. "What more could we do? Short of throwin' down and ending up in jail."

"True. But it's not that easy for me. In places like this, and even in big cities like New York City, I usually get some type of slight. Either I'm treated as if I'm not even there, or I'm the object of interest, like an art exhibit. I'm not whining, you understand, just stating a fact."

"I know, bro. And that's what's so messed up about it."

Contrary to his look as a guy who would eat only alfalfa sprouts and drink only carrot juice, Andy attacked his porterhouse steak with gusto. Frank followed suit.

But before he did, he said, "I'm telling you, man, I don't know how much more of it I can take."

Chapter Nine

After Boise, Idaho, Frank went to his next speaking engagement, a conference in Los Angeles, and then on to his condo in Washington, DC. He exorcised the frustration he had been feeling of late through his presentations. Drained but satisfied, he concluded to thunderous applause at each venue.

"Never thought I'd enjoy doing laundry," he muttered to himself later that evening as he threw a load of underwear and socks into the washer and strolled to the living room, "but it's sure nice to be home."

He stretched out on the sofa and was in the midst of a catnap when his intercom buzzed.

"Hello?" He didn't bother to look at the caller ID when he got up to answer it.

"Frank, I'm downstairs." It was Priscilla, and she wasn't purring this time. The icy hand of dread slapped him full in the face, and in an instant, he was wide-awake. "Let me in."

He had hardly buzzed her in when she was knocking on his door. A bead of sweat began to form on his forehead. *Calm down*, he silently chanted as he opened the door.

She pushed past him in a form-fitting cardinal-red dress and four-inch heels, with blood in her eye. The way she was looking, he kept his eyes on her purse, just in case she reached inside it and pulled out a handgun.

"Hello, Priscilla. To what do I owe the pleasure?"

"Oh, shut up!"

He stared at her. "Excuse you?"

"I saw her."

"Saw who?" Frank breathed a sigh of relief. She wasn't there to make the dreaded announcement he thought she might make.

"Sally Sue or whatever her name is." She flung herself upon one of the sofas.

"Make yourself at home."

"Shut up!"

"That's the second time you've told me to shut up in my own house." He walked over to the coffee table, picking up his half-full bottle of beer and taking a swig. "But I'm not going to let it go a third time."

She glared up at him without saying a word.

"That's better." He indicated the beer. "You want one?"

"I can't believe you! A white girl?"

"So what? You know that you and I have always just been friends with benefits. And I don't know the nationalities of the other guys you mess with."

Priscilla sat silently, clearly still stewing.

"I take it you came by when she was in town." Frank laughed. "I keep telling you to call first. I always called before I came to your place, didn't I?"

"I was in the neighborhood, sweetie, and I thought I'd stop by. I was about to get out of my car and who do I see you escorting into the building? A white girl. You two sure looked cozy too—"

"Stop. I don't want to hear it, all right? She's a human being, first and foremost." Like a cold blast of wind, the fight left him just as suddenly as it had appeared. "Baby, we've got to get past this skin-color thing. I'm convinced that's why we've got so many problems in the world today. They're not even for any valid reasons—just because one person calls God *Allah* and the other uses the word *Buddha*. Who cares? Look, Priscilla, you live where you live, and I live where I live, so how in the world am I affecting you?"

"Brothers and sisters have got to stick together," she retorted.

"C'mon, don't go there. I am sick of hearing that." He sat down beside her. "I've never dated a white woman before, but I've heard that line so many times. Do you think if you met a great guy and he just happened to be Italian, you should just drop him while you wait for that 'good black man'? I say love the one you're with, because tomorrow's not a given."

"That's true." Priscilla nodded her head, but she still looked confused.

With two fingers, Frank lifted her chin and forced her to look him in the eye. "Don't get me wrong, baby, I love black women. Love y'all. But when I see a sister with a man of another race, I don't look at it as a knock against me or black men as a whole. I look at it as a woman looking at another option, another avenue that just happened to open up to her. Hell, I'd rather see her happy with him than unhappy and fighting with a brother."

"You know, that makes sense. I never looked at it that way before." Priscilla was quiet for a moment. "Frank, how come we never tried to make it together? I mean, as a couple?"

"You're asking *me*?" he asked, chuckling. "We're like thunder and lightning. Good for a lot of fireworks and explosions but only for a short time."

"You're right about explosions," she agreed, joining in the laughter. "We had plenty of those. Good ones. So, I'm not complaining."

"Neither am I. I enjoyed being with you. And I don't mind telling you this—you are unforgettable."

She stood up, grasping his hands and pulling him up with her. There was the glimmer of unshed tears in her eyes. "She's a lucky woman, Frank. You're a great guy—"

"All right now, stop it," he protested good-naturedly. He gave her hands a squeeze and then pulled her into an embrace. "So, are we good now?"

"We're good." She smiled.

At the door, she turned to him, tugging gently on the neckline of his undershirt. Despite the high-heels, she only stood about five feet five. She brought his face down to hers and kissed him, hard and lingering, on the mouth. "One for the road," she replied, winking.

His smile grew wider as he watched her spin on her heel and strut down the hall toward the elevator, jiggling in all the right places. "Bye, baby."

FRANK'S NEXT SPEAKING ENGAGEMENT WAS at a college in Boston. It was his first time in that city, and even though it was somewhat of a hassle navigating by automobile once he left the airport, he enjoyed the old vibe of the place. He received a cool reception when he entered the auditorium, but by the second hour of his presentation, *Generation Indebtedness*, he had them eating them out of his hand. A few of the guys and girls even invited him to go out with them to a nearby pub, which he accepted. One of the students rode with him to show him the way. He was glad he had chosen to dress casually in distressed black jeans, a pale-green long-sleeved polo shirt, and black boots instead of his usual lecturing attire.

"I really enjoyed your presentation, Mr. Ellis. I mean, you're wicked good. Not stiff and dry like those banker types." The announcement came from one of the guys, a husky, dark-haired young man around twenty-one years old named Mick, his voice flavored with a strong Bostonian accent. He was one of the two in their group of six who wasn't actually playing darts. He stood near Frank with his beer, watching. He reminded Frank of a bouncer with his hulking physique. He half-expected Mick to grab a guy or two by the collar and toss them out of the establishment if things got too lively.

"It's Frank, okay? You guys made it easy." Frank imitated what Penny, the girl who threw her dart before him, had done since he had never played darts before. He spent a few moments more than she had lining up his dart in the cozily lit pub. He threw it hard but with a precise aim. It landed about an inch and a half short of the bull's-eye, eliciting a cheer from the group and from other onlookers in the already loud and raucous establishment. He figured those in his group were trying to be charitable; the other onlookers were probably just intoxicated.

"Pretty good," said Penny, the slender brunette who had gone before him.

He grinned. "Sure."

The players took their turns until it was evident that Penny had won the round. Only after another member of the group was crowned the champ, winning four games out of five, did they finally crowd around the only battered dark-wood booth available and hoist a few more beers along with the nonplayers. Frank tried a craft beer, which he had to admit wasn't bad. He sat on one side of the booth with Mick across from him and Penny beside him; she was one of the two women in their group. They shared an exceptionally good extra-large pizza, more beer, and killer buffalo wings, while Frank regaled them with some of his exploits on the road.

Later, Frank checked his watch. "I've got an early flight tomorrow, or should I say today, so I'm going to head back to my hotel." He shook hands all around. "Thanks for giving me a taste of Boston." He slid out of the booth and headed toward the restroom.

When he emerged, Mick was standing outside the restroom entrance. "Thought I'd walk with you to your car. I need some air."

Frank grinned at him in the moody darkness of the corridor. "I know what you mean. Come on." They walked up the side streets in the cool and fresh early-September night toward his rental car, which was parked on a main street. For Frank, it was a welcome respite anytime he could escape the stifling heat still in full force further south. He was happy that autumn was just around the corner. "I don't know how you and the others get up in the morning to go to class after drinking half the night."

"We manage," Mick said, a grin shattering his usual stoic demeanor, making him appear more like a cuddly teddy bear than a bouncer. He lit a cigarette and held out the pack. "Want one?"

"No thanks." Frank popped a breath strip in his mouth. They reached his rental car within a matter of minutes. "Take it easy, Mick." Frank clicked the remote to unlock the door and began to walk to the driver's side."

"Uh ... wait, Frank." Mick's voice sounded urgent.

He turned quickly. When he did, Mick was standing close, uncomfortably close, close enough to smell beer and the cigarette he was smoking on his breath. That's when the knowledge hit Frank squarely in the face. *Damn*, he thought. *My radar let me down on this one.* He tried to make his voice sound light and casual although he now knew what Mick wanted. "Yeah, man, what's up?" He tried to make his backing up seem random and not because of Mick's spatial proximity.

"I wanted to give you my cell number. I know you travel a lot, but we could hang out whenever you're in town. Or maybe I could come see you in DC sometime." Mick laughed, and nervousness tinged the edges of it. "I know I don't look like what you'd expect."

"Hey, Mick, I'm ... um, flattered that you like me." Frank wanted to be delicate. He remembered their handshake. *He could probably break me in half without really trying if he doesn't like what I say—although I sure as hell will give him a run for his money if I have to*, he thought. *I just hope I don't have to. He's a nice guy.*

Aloud Frank said, "And I like you too—just not in that way. I like women, man. Sure, we could have a drink if I'm in town, but, uh—"

"Gotcha. I understand." Mick crumpled the piece of paper in his fist, dropped it, and shrugged. "You can't blame a guy for trying." He held out his hand. "Well, have a good flight."

Frank held his out and shook it. Just as he remembered, Mick had a viselike grip. "Thanks, Mick. Hey, what position do you play?"

Mick grinned. "*Used* to play. Linebacker."

"I figured as much." Frank walked over to the driver's side, clicking the door open again since it had relocked itself moments earlier. "Later, Mick."

As he pulled away from the curb and drove away, he could see Mick's silhouette as he continued to stand there on the sidewalk in the darkness, watching.

FRANK DITCHED THE THOUGHT of sleeping since he only had time to shower, change, settle his hotel bill, and head to the airport. While on the airplane, his throat grew scratchy. Once off the plane, he dialed Delilah's number.

"Hi, sweetie," she greeted him. To him, it was almost as if she had her arms around him. He whisked his garment bag from the baggage claim and let the feeling wash over him. "How was Boston?"

"It was great. I wish you'd been there with me."

"What's up with your voice? You don't sound good."

He headed through the crowd and to the parking garage. "Aww, really? I thought it made me sound kind of sexy."

"You've got to be pulling my leg. Your voice was already sexy, along with the rest of you."

Frank loved when she talked about what she liked about him. It made him want to just scoop her up in his arms and have his way with her. It reassured him, knowing this powerful attraction wasn't one-sided. "Thanks. I think I had a little too much nightlife last night. Some of the students who attended my seminar took me to a pub and taught me how to play darts. And I haven't gone to bed yet, so I guess it's catching up with me. But I'm going to gargle when I get home."

"You'd better do more than that." Concern had overridden flirtation with Delilah, and he could hear that plainly. "Take some aspirin and make some hot tea. If you feel up to it, stop off at the store and buy some lemon to put in it. And put some brandy in it too, if you have it."

"Yes, ma'am."

"I'll call you later, to check on you." Her voice softened. "I'm glad you're home, Frank."

He threw his bags in his car and climbed inside. "So am I."

Later that night, Frank dreamt he was trapped in a forest that was on fire. He awoke, thrashing in tangled sheets, his skin dripping with perspiration.

Staggering to the bathroom, he found a bottle of expired aspirin and struggled to open the top. After finally managing to open it, he took two and choked on the water he drank with them. His throat felt as if he had gargled with ground glass, and his lungs hurt with every breath. *What the hell is wrong with me?* he thought.

He called Andy.

"What's up, partner? It's a little late to conversate."

"I … need you to … call Delilah for me later—"

"Damn, man, what's wrong with you? You sound terrible."

"Yeah, I know—I sound terrible." Every breath was a struggle. "And no, I have no idea what it is. Listen. I may need you to cancel a flight for me—I'm supposed to travel later this … Look, I'm sick."

"No problem." Frank heard some muffled sounds in the background for a few seconds, and then Andy came back on the line. "Sorry. That was Twyla. She sends her love. Hey, I can be over there in fifteen minutes to—"

"No, I—" He coughed, and it took his breath away at how painful it was to do so. "Andy, I'm gonna go on to the hospital. Look, I've got to go."

He hung up and threw a shirt over his undershirt and jeans over his boxer briefs. His head throbbed as he grabbed his keys and wallet from his bedside table and stumbled out the door.

"I NEED SOME HELP."

In the midst of the noise and chaos of the emergency room, a resident who was walking by heard the man with surprising clarity. The ill man stood at the security station where he nearly collapsed.

"Get me a wheelchair," she yelled to the nearest person, which was a security guard, a large, muscular man. The resident held Frank against her body until the guard returned. There were no empty chairs in the emergency room, and no one bothered to offer one. They all had their own problems.

Frank managed to choke out his information while he was placed next in triage behind a gunshot victim. He went through a spate of coughing and hacking while seated in the triage area, which made many of the other people and staff there and in the adjoining waiting room look in his direction with concern or undisguised disdain. A few people placed tissues or handkerchiefs up to their faces. Some, who already sat with respiratory masks on, touched them reassuringly.

About an hour later, Andy rounded the corner to where a staff member directed him and where Frank waited and did a double-take. He couldn't believe how bad his friend looked. He had been with him at the conference in Boise about ten days ago, and he had been the picture of health.

"What the hell—? Frank!"

"I told you ... not to come—"

"Shut up, man. What did you think I was going to do?"

"Yeah, I know." He grabbed Andy's arm. "Look, call Delilah for me."

He handed him his cell phone.

"Frank! Frank, how are you?" Delilah yelled into the phone, after springing up in bed like a jack-in-the-box.

"It's not Frank, Dee."

A chilled crawled up her spine. "Andy! Where's Frank? Wha—"

"Calm down, Delilah. Frank wanted me to call you. He's at the hospital, in the emergency room."

"Oh. Well, I'm glad he went." She heard a quiver worm its way into her voice but didn't care. "He's gotten worse, I take it."

"Yes. They're doing tests now, but—they think he has pneumonia."

"Pneumonia? Oh my goodness! No!"

"Yes. But he's getting checked out, which is good."

Delilah rocked back and forth as she sat in bed, talking to Andy. "I'm just glad you were there to take him to the emergency room."

She heard him sigh, "No, I wasn't. He drove himself."

"*What?* Oh my God, he could've passed out behind the wheel or something!"

"I know, Dee, I know. I wanted to drive him, but he didn't wait. That might've been a good thing, actually."

"Well, why didn't he take a cab?"

There was silence for a moment and then, "You know why." Andy was very quiet when he replied, "He can't always get a cab."

At this, a sob escaped her throat and it tightened. Delilah felt as if she were channeling Frank, and how he had been feeling, and how he probably felt at that moment. "Poor Frank."

"Dee, just sit tight. I'll let you know what the doctors say—"

"You do that. But I'll be on a plane later today."

"Delilah, I don't think—"

"Later today." She softened her tone. "Thank you for calling, Andy."

"No problem. Well then, I'll see you later."

She hung up and lay down but did not go back to sleep for the rest of the night.

"WHAT IS IT, MISS CARPENTER? It's six fifteen in the morning—"

"I know, Mr. McDermott, and I apologize for disturbing you. I know you're probably getting ready for work—"

"What is it, Miss Carpenter?"

She bit back a nasty retort and instead, adopted a businesslike tone. "I need to take leave for a few days."

"A few days?" He exhaled a sigh of exasperation. "Miss Carpenter, you know that—"

"I know that it's short notice, but my boyfriend is very ill and in the hospital.

The sneer in his voice was unmistakable. "Your *boyfriend?*"

"Yes, Mr. McDermott. As I said, he's very ill."

"Delilah, you took leave in August—"

"I know, Mr. McDermott. But it's September, and I haven't taken any leave this year besides those three days last month and a dentist appointment in April. As it is, I will have 'use or lose' at the end of this year." She attempted to rein in the volume of her voice and stay calm. How she had managed to work for this male-chauvinist tyrant for the past four years was beyond her. *What more does he want from me?* Aloud, she said, "I know it's short notice, but it couldn't be helped. His illness came on suddenly. Anyway, it's been slow in the office for a while, so I'm about to head for the airport—"

"The airport? Doesn't he live in town?"

"No, he doesn't. I don't know how long it will be. I'm taking my laptop to submit my leave slip, and if anything—"

"Okay, Miss Carpenter, okay." This time his tone was dismissive. "Just send me your leave slip as soon as you can."

She wished she had one of the older model phones so she could slam the receiver in his ear. "I will, Mr. McDermott. Thanks."

DELILAH HAD THE TAXI DRIVER take her directly from the airport to the hospital. It cost a small fortune, but that was the least of her worries, and she practically threw the money at him.

"I'm sorry, sir. Thank you so much." She snatched her laptop bag and small suitcase and raced toward the hospital entrance.

After navigating the confusing corridors and directions, she was suddenly standing in the area of the Intensive Care Unit. She walked over to the lone man sitting outside the bank of rooms.

"Andy?" she whispered.

He stood up, stifling a yawn. Without a word, they embraced. Unlike the effervescent and mischievous man she had spent time with during her visit with Frank, the man who stood before her appeared to have aged ten years since then. He had about two days' worth of blond stubble on his face, his clothes were wrinkled, and his eyes looked tired. It was clear he had spent most of the night in the hospital. But to Delilah, he was a friendly port in an angry storm. "Hello, bright eyes."

"Hey, Andy. How's Frank?"

"It took a while for them to stabilize him." He rubbed an eye and then ran a hand through his disheveled locks. "He's in there."

He led her to a door with a small window, and she peered inside. Her blood froze. "What's that on his face?"

"His lungs are so filled with fluid that he can't breathe on his own. It's an oxygen mask."

"Oh my—"

"They won't let us see him just yet. They don't want to disturb him." He yawned again. "I'm sorry. I spent most of the night in the hospital chapel, praying."

"Oh, Andy." Tears sprang to Delilah's eyes.

"Don't you do that, girl. Here, take a seat."

She felt transfixed by the narrow glass window, beyond which Frank lay in the dim room. She felt if she took her eyes off him …

"I know. You're scared to take your eyes off him. But rest is what he needs right now. He had a tough night."

"What about his family?" She sat down on one of the hard chairs, which, although cushioned, was still hard. "Is there anyone we should notify? His mama?"

"I've known Frank for at least seven years, and he's got no family. His mother died years ago, when he was fifteen, and he's never known his old man. So he's been on his own ever since."

Delilah thought about her own comfortable upbringing, and she felt a lump growing in her throat. "Wow," she managed to say.

"I'm glad you're here, Dee. I was going to give this to the nurse to give to you, but now I don't have to. It's from Frank." In his hand, he held an envelope.

She took it and sat there for a moment, staring at it.

Andy cleared his throat. "I've got to go home, grab a shower, and then go into the office. If anything happens—he wakes up or anything—call me."

"Of course I will, Andy."

He patted her cheek. "That's my brother in there," he said, his voice cracking a bit. He gave her his cell phone number and left.

It was another few minutes before Delilah remembered the envelope. She tore it open carefully, and three keys fell into her hand. She read the scribbled letter that accompanied it:

Delilah,

Andy's writing this for me while I wait to be seen. I know that you will be here soon. I don't know when they will let me see you.

I'm not doing too well at the moment. It came on me kind of sudden. Something in the air, I guess, although I'm not sure if a person can catch pneumonia.

Anyway, I hope this doesn't put you in a bind, financially or with your boss. If you haven't made a round-trip, I want you to go to my desk drawer in the kitchen nook, where you'll find an envelope. I've got some frequent-flyer reward letters in there, but I don't know if you'll be able to use them without my authorization. There's also about three or four hundred dollars that I keep for emergencies. It's yours. Use it to make your return flight home, although I'm hoping you won't have to leave too soon.

Delilah, I want you to stay at my place. I've included the keys to the building as well as my front door and mailbox. There should be food enough to last you for a little while, at least. If not, use some of the money to buy whatever you need. Andy and Twyla will help you.

Well, the doctors want me now. I'm touched that two of the three closest people in the world to me have come to check on the old boy—more than I can even express.

I'll try to make it up to you later.
With warmest regards,
Frank

She folded the letter, placed it back in the envelope, and let the tears fall freely.

DELILAH WAS IN THE INTENSIVE Care Unit, watching while the nurses and doctors came and went and other visitors waited to visit their loved ones who were now in Intensive Care as well.

Twyla arrived about four hours into her vigil. They embraced. "Hi, Delilah. How are you?"

"I'm fine." She suppressed a yawn.

Twyla peered through the narrow window on the door. "Have they let you in to see him?"

"No. From the little they've told me, his case is very serious as a result of those damned cigarettes. Oh, don't mind me; I'm just a little tired."

"You've been here all this time?" Twyla sat down beside her.

"Since Andy left."

"I stopped by the cafeteria and picked up some tea for you." She handed Delilah the cup of steaming liquid and several sugar packets.

They chatted for a while as Delilah drank the tea. "How long have you known Frank?" she asked Twyla between cautious sips.

The other woman looked up toward the ceiling, thinking. "Oh, I've been going with Andy for about four years now, so—almost as long as I've known him."

"Four years?" Delilah got up and took their cups to the trash receptacle. "I don't mean to be nosy, but the two of you get along so well. You two never thought about getting married?"

Twyla laughed. Although she wasn't loud, they both looked around at the same time. It sounded a bit incongruous in the area in which they waited. "We've thought about it. But if it ain't broke, don't fix it, I always say. Actually, Andy asked me two years ago, but I wasn't ready."

"What made you two start dating?" Delilah asked as she sat back down beside Twyla. "A white man, I mean. I hope you don't mind me asking."

"I had nothing against black men, if that's what you think," Twyla replied. "It's just that once I met Andy, I didn't want anyone else. Don't tell him I said this, but he was irresistible. I never met a man like him before. He just happened to be white."

"You two live together, right?"

"Uh-huh. It's great. I love Andy; I really do." She sighed.

"I'm sorry, Twyla. I didn't mean to pry—"

"It's okay. I know that if we do get married, Andy's going to want to have kids right away. I love him, I do, but—"

"You're afraid when it comes to the race thing?" Delilah surprised herself, throwing the question out there. By now she considered Twyla a friend, and she could see the pain that now revealed itself in her eyes.

"Yes. I don't know if I could handle the way society still acts toward mixed-race children." She brightened. "Girl, get out of here for a while. I'll let you know if there's any change. Let me guess, you're staying at Frank's place?"

Delilah smiled, feeling a bit self-conscious.

"It won't do him or you any good if you get sick. You're about to fall out of that chair."

The two women hugged again. "Either Andy or I will see you later," Twyla added as she settled into a chair.

"No! I don't believe it! No! Frank!"

Delilah awoke in the early evening, tears streaming down her face and nose running. The room was dark, the shades down. She lay in Frank's bed, in the master bedroom, clutching the sheets. She could smell Frank's presence all over the condo but especially here, in his bed.

The phone on the nightstand was ringing. She snatched it up. "Hello?"

"Hey there, bright eyes—"

"Oh, Andy! Is ... is he dead?"

"Who, Frank? No, no, no! I was calling to tell you that he regained consciousness. If he continues to improve, they're going to move him out of Intensive Care." Silence, then, "Are you over there cryin'?"

"No," she lied. She turned on the lamp and padded over to the master bathroom to blow her nose. "I'll catch a cab and join you."

"No, they're not letting him have any visitors. They only let me see him for a few minutes. Stay there and get some rest." He paused. "He told me to tell you that he sends his love."

In spite of her raw emotions, she felt a warm sensation course through her veins. "Thanks for calling me, Andy. I'm just so glad that he's doing better."

"You stop that crying and get some sleep. The nurse told me to go home, that they're sick of looking at me. I thought to put up an argument, but then I thought I'd humor her. I'll come by tomorrow around nine and pick you up, okay?"

"Okay. I'll see you then."

The next day Delilah awoke to rain pitter-pattering on the windows. The sky was overcast, and it promised to be cool for early September. But she barely noticed. To her, the day seemed sunny and bright as she hurried through the breakfast of orange juice and toast that she managed to swallow.

Her hair was not even dry after her shower when Andy called on the intercom. "You ready?"

"I'll be right down."

Andy fought his way through the rain, construction zones, and horrendous rush-hour traffic to arrive at the hospital almost an hour later. They hurried to the Intensive Care Unit, only to discover that Frank had been moved to another room.

Right outside the room, Andy suddenly stopped and pulled Delilah's arm. She glanced back. "What is it?" Impatience tainted her voice.

"I was just going to say you go on in. I'll wait out here." He looked so boyish and apologetic with his lopsided smile that her impatience evaporated as swiftly as it had appeared, and she threw her arms around him, giving him a quick hug. "I'm sorry, Andy, and thanks."

She pushed the door open and without making a sound, stepped into the room; it was lit only by the weak daylight that leaked around the sides of the closed blinds.

"Come," Frank managed to say. He reached over to where the nurse had left a pad and pen on the metal nightstand. An IV pierced his left arm, and there was a tube down his throat. He made signs with his hands for her to come closer and then held one out for her to clasp. His grip was not as strong as the other times they had held hands, but to Delilah, it felt good, and she couldn't believe how much she had missed this simple expression of endearment.

With his right hand, he wrote on the pad and then gave it to her. He had written, *I missed you.*

"Sweetie, you took the words right out of my mouth," she whispered and tears sprang to her eyes. "Damn it!"

His eyes widened, and she recalled that she had never cursed in front of him. He shook his head in a playful way and indicated the hard plastic chair beside the bed.

Instead, she snaked her way past it and inched closer to him. Bending down, she kissed him lightly on the lips. "Frank, we were so scared. Oh my goodness, I can't tell you how scared I was."

He crossed out what he had written before and scribbled underneath it. He turned it to her. *I was afraid I'd never see you again.*

She sat on the bed, facing him, still holding his other hand. It was cold. "Would you like some water?"

He nodded, and she finally released his hand so she could reach the plastic pitcher and cup on top of the crowded bedside table. She held the straw to his lips, and he swallowed with difficulty. Once he indicated that he'd had enough, she placed it back on the tray and sat back down on the bed.

Her lips trembled as she thought about what he had written.

Frank reached out and gently brushed the back of his hand across her cheek, as if to say, Don't cry, baby.

"I'll try not to." Although Delilah was the only one speaking, it was as though they were talking nonstop. Yet they knew what hadn't been said. And they purposely left it that way. He had been knocking at heaven's door, and he still wasn't out of the woods yet.

Frank was gazing at her with tenderness. He scribbled, *I'm so glad you're here, Delilah.*

"Me too." She took a deep breath. The hospital atmosphere gave her the creeps, but she kept telling herself that the staff there had saved his life. That was all that mattered. "Nothing could have kept me away."

She scooted back into his arms. With clumsiness, they slipped their arms around each other, being careful of the IV tube and pole and any other medical apparatus. They kissed around the breathing tube.

"Andy's waiting in the hall," she announced, after they pulled away from each other. Her heart pounded as she caressed his five o'clock shadow. "I'll see you later, okay? Take care, sweetie."

"Good-bye, baby," he rasped.

"Hey, buddy," Andy said as he walked in after Delilah left.

Frank indicated the window blinds and then wrote, *It's like a morgue in here.*

"No joke." After opening them, Andy maneuvered back over to the bed and sat down on the chair beside it. "Twyla sends her love."

Frank smiled his acknowledgment.

"Don't scare us like that anymore, man." Andy shook his head. "Hell, you scared about a year's growth off of me."

Frank shrugged, his arms outstretched as if to say, *I'm sorry. I didn't mean to.*

"You know, I don't care if you want to hear this or not but you have *got* to stop smoking."

Frank scribbled on the pad, *It's a hard habit to break. Not that I'm able to smoke in here.*

"Good," Andy said without sympathy. "I don't know how Dee handles it."

Frank looked over at the rain dripping down the window and did not respond. *What can I say?* he thought. Then he wrote, *You'd have to ask her.* After that, he wrote, *It's kind of cold in here. Help me pull up this blanket.*

As Andy moved the bed tray and bedpan to adjust the thin blanket and fluff Frank's pillows, he laughed. "How do you use this thing, hooked to all these wires and tubes like you are?" He pointed to the bedpan.

Frank wrote on the pad and then turned it to face his friend. He had written, *Don't ask. Let's just say that I'll have to have some help.*

"Well, don't ask me. I draw the line at bedpans." Andy placed the items back on his bed tray within easy reach and then sat down.

Frank scribbled, *I haven't had to use it yet. While I was out of it, they must've had me attached to a catheter.*

In an instant, Andy's mood changed. "I'm sorry, partner. I know the last two days have been rough for you. If you need me to, I'll help you in any way I can."

Frank tried not to laugh and almost choked. Once he pulled himself together, he managed to croak out, "Not in that way, bro."

"Have you eaten? How's the food in this cellblock?"

Frank pointed to the IV bag and then wrote, *This has been it so far. Throat's sore, anyway, with this thing in it.* He pointed to the breathing tube.

"Damn, man. You're gonna make me start cryin'."

Frank shook his head no. Andy had said it in a joking tone, but he knew that he was only half joking. They sat there in silence for a while, each man occupied with his own thoughts. Finally, Frank reached over to the bedside table and picked up an envelope. He handed it to his closest friend.

Andy ripped it open.

Andy,

I can't really talk right now with this breathing tube down my throat. But I want you to really know how I feel about you. I'm not trying to be mushy, but I think this is the perfect time for me to express myself.

Although my mother didn't give birth to you, I don't consider you any less my brother. I don't give a damn about your color, the fact that you're Catholic, or any of that. I know that I have sometimes taken our friendship or should I say, brotherhood, for granted, as brothers sometimes do. But I don't want you to ever think that the way I feel about you has changed. I have considered you my brother almost from the moment we became friends years ago. Andy, you are my brother.

I am doing better now, but if anything should ever happen to me, in a safe deposit box at my bank is my power of attorney and advance directive. I meant to tell you this a few years ago, but it kept slipping my mind. The key is kept in the desk in the kitchen. Like I said, if anything of a permanent nature should ever happen to me, or if I need some type of treatment, you have my advance directive to speak on my behalf. You can review the documents at any time, or, if you would rather not have this responsibility, let me know now, while you have the chance.
I love you, man.
Frank

Frank happened to stop gazing out of the window at the gray day beyond in time to see Andy look up from the letter. He noticed the glint of tears in his soft blue eyes.

"Wow, my allergies are really acting up today," Andy mumbled in a clumsy attempt to wipe them away.

Frank simply smiled.

Chapter Ten

Frank spent two additional days in Intensive Care until he was able to breathe on his own. He spent another four days in a regular hospital room for observation and further treatment. Andy, Twyla, and Delilah spent hours visiting with him, when they weren't being shooed out by the nurses and doctors to perform one test or another. He still faced several weeks of recovery ahead of him.

"You were a very sick man, Mr. Ellis. As you might have guessed, your smoking history contributed greatly to your condition. You must take it easy for a while and regain your strength, or you *will* relapse," Dr. Stewart announced. He was a very solemn, tall, bespectacled African American man, with an ominous habit of looking at a person as if he had X-ray vision.

"I understand, Doctor."

"I understand that you travel a lot. None of that for a while." He closed the metal clipboard and looked down at Frank with his scary stare. "I'll let you know when it's safe for you to do so."

"Okay, Doctor." He shook the doctor's hand as he was about to leave. "Dr. Stewart, had you ever thought of being an undertaker—before you became a physician?"

Dr. Stewart appeared startled, and then the corner of his eyes crinkled. He warmed a bit as he realized Frank was pulling his leg. "No, Mr. Ellis. When contemplating my residency, I didn't know what I wanted to pursue. I did know what I wanted to confer with patients who were still among the living as opposed to those who had crossed over."

"Touché."

"Let's make sure that you remain on this side, Mr. Ellis." With that, and a slight nod of his head, he was gone.

"Would've made a good one," Frank was muttering as Twyla entered the room.

"What the heck are you talking to yourself about?" she joked as she walked over and gave him a hug and kiss on the cheek. "Do I need to call that doctor back and tell him that you need some psychiatric treatment?"

Frank laughed but stopped short, because it still hurt to do so or to even breathe deeply for that matter. "Nothing, Twyla. What's shaking, baby?"

"*You*, baby. How are you feeling?" She took a seat next to his bed. "You still look like death warmed over, but you sound better."

"I feel like I got a professional beat-down, but I guess I'll live," he replied and reached around the IV stand to fluff his pillows.

"Will you stop? Here, let me do that before you yank that thing out of your arm." Twyla stood up and fluffed them and then adjusted his sheet and blanket.

"Thank you." Frank nuzzled her neck playfully. "Mmm, you smell good."

"You don't. You smell like this hospital, and you look like a pirate. You need a shave."

"You wanna do it?"

She looked around. "You got a razor?"

"Andy brought me one. Poor boy, doesn't he know that brothers don't do Bics? But I'll sacrifice myself."

"That's mighty big of you, Frank."

"I know." He pointed to a plastic bag on the bedside table. "The razor and shaving cream are in that bag there. Do you know how to shave a man?"

Twyla stopped in midstep and turned to look at him. A sly smile played upon her lips. "I know how to do anything that pertains to a man."

"*Excuse me.*" Frank attempted to stifle a laugh and coughed instead.

She found a towel in the adjacent bathroom. She ran hot water over it, wrung it out, and then brought it over and draped it over his head.

"Oww!"

"Place this on your face."

After a few minutes, Twyla snatched the towel from his face. Shaking the can of shaving cream, she sprayed a generous amount into her hand and then plastered it onto his jawline.

"Just watch my mustache. And remember, it ain't quite the same as shaving your man."

"A man's a man."

"I don't know about that." Although he was enjoying their slightly risqué banter, Frank regarded Twyla as the younger sister he never had. "A brother's a brother, and a Cauruther's a Cauruther."

She chuckled. "Andy told you about that?"

"Yep." He wiped the shaving foam off his mouth.

"Big mouth." She cupped his chin in one hand and began to shave with the other.

"Don't be like that. Truth be told, I think he regards it sort of as a badge of honor."

Twyla continued to shave him, but again, a smile tugged at her mouth, this time, one of tenderness. "Really?"

"I kid you not."

"Well, I love him for his own unique qualities, but I have to admit, he could've been a brother."

"I know."

Twyla sloshed the foamy contents into the plastic vomit container that was serving as a substitute sink while she shaved Frank. She turned his face so that she could shave the other side.

"Funny, how we're both dating someone outside our race," she reflected, almost to herself.

Frank gazed at the beautiful blue sky—what he could see of it from his hospital bed vantage point. "The human race is how I like to look at it."

"That's true."

She continued to shave him and he continued to be shaved, both engrossed in their own thoughts.

FRANK HAD BEEN DOZING OFF and on between Twyla's departure and Delilah's arrival. But he sensed her presence rather than heard her arrive. He slowly opened his eyes as he said, "You're a sight for sore eyes. That is, what I can see of you." Her face was half hidden by a large bouquet of flowers. "Flowers? For me?"

"Who's to say that women are the only people who can receive flowers, mister?" she joked, placing them on the crowded bedside table.

"Not me." He held out his arms. "Come over here, and give me some sugar."

"Here I come." After eagerly obliging, she caressed his face. "Mmm, baby soft. You?"

"No, Twyla was here a little while ago."

"Hmm, I'm jealous. Touching my man's face." She pretended to pout.

They continued to joke for a while, when Frank stopped abruptly. Delilah was joking with him, but the laughter wasn't reaching her eyes. "Okay, what's wrong, Delilah?"

She sat down on the bed, facing him, but she averted her face to look at some nonexistent spot on the blanket.

"Don't lie to me, baby. What is it?"

He reached out to hold both of her hands in his own. "You look sad. Come on, tell me. Please."

"I can handle it, Frank."

He continued to look at her pointedly, until she finally met his gaze.

"I was just thinking about my boss. He was obnoxious, as usual."

"About you being here?" His grip on her hands tightened. "Really?"

"Really."

"Aww, I'm sorry."

"It's not your fault. You were, and still are, ill. He just likes to act like that. About everything. I guess I'm not supposed to have a personal life or a significant other, especially one who lives out of town. I probably shouldn't have even told him that, but it *was* kind of sudden, my having to leave town." She shrugged. "You know, I don't even pretend to understand him."

"Excuse me, baby, I want to get up." He stood up and threw on his robe. He moved the IV pole as she got up as well.

"Are you sure?"

"Sure, I'm sure. They want me to get up when I feel up to it. Anyway, don't change the subject, young lady."

She smiled, and this time, it was as if the clouds parted and the sun began to shine. "All right. Look, it's okay. I haven't taken much annual or sick leave this year, and because of the economy, it's been slow in our office. So he really doesn't have a leg to stand on. What annual leave I don't use now, I'll just have to use or forfeit by the end of the year anyway. Here, honey, let me get that for you." She held open the door for him.

"Thanks. That's why I'm glad that I work for myself."

They walked down to the end of the corridor, opposite the bank of elevators and the nurses' station. There was the low hum of activity in the hallway.

"I didn't tell you this, but I'll be here next week too."

"You will?" Frank leaned against the wall and glanced out of the window and down at the busy street below. No noise could be heard through it; the hospital was a self-contained, insulated world of its own. It was, that is, until someone from the outside world stepped inside.

"Of course. You're going to need someone to help you, run errands—Andy told me that he'll be back on the road next week. Anyhow, last year I only took a week off during the summer and a few days at Christmas. My boss just always seems to want to get a rise out of me for some unknown reason, and sometimes he treats me more like his personal secretary than a valued employee. He's a pompous bastard."

"Man, he's really pissed you off, huh?"

"I always knew he was kind of a control freak, but only since I met you have I realized how ridiculous he is. It wouldn't be so bad if he treated everyone like that, but from what I've observed, I'm the only one, and I don't know why. If I ask him, I'll look like a complainer." She tried to smile. "I just deal with it."

"I'm sorry to hear that." He drew her against him and held her close. He could feel the tension in her body and felt partly responsible. "Why don't you try to get out of that place?"

"I'm considering it." She kissed him on the cheek. "Anyway, I don't want to talk about him anymore. I'll be here next week, if you want me."

"That goes without saying," he whispered against her ear, and they headed back to his room.

SATURDAY MORNING FRANK WASHED HIMSELF, and brushed his teeth as he prepared to be discharged. He dressed in jeans and a casual short-sleeved shirt. He noticed with a bit of concern the amount of weight he had lost in the days since his admittance. Although he knew he had been at death's door, he felt impatient to rejoin life outside the hospital walls. He was bouncing on the balls of his feet when the nurse walked in with the discharge papers.

"You about to box somebody, Mr. Ellis?" the nurse who attended him for much of the week joked.

He turned from where he was standing, his hand already outstretched. "No. Just ready to go."

"I should say you are." She recited some of the more important post discharge instructions while Frank perused the forms and signed them.

"Dr. Stewart wants to see you in his office next week."

"I understand, ma'am." He attempted to conceal the impatience in his voice and manner as he handed her the signed forms and stuffed the instructions into the small suitcase Delilah had brought him several days earlier.

"Is anyone driving you home, Mr. Ellis?"

He restrained himself from tapping his foot. "No. I'll be driving myself."

"Come with me." She swished out of the room into the hallway. Grabbing his belongings and the vase of flowers; Frank reluctantly followed.

"You have *got* to be kidding," he remarked, when she indicated the wheelchair.

"No, I am not, Mr. Ellis."

He endured the slow ride through the crowded corridor, past the orderlies and equipment, and past the other patients, until they boarded the elevator and finally arrived at the hospital entrance.

"My car's in the parking garage." He gazed at her with some skepticism. "I can leave now, right?"

"Yes, you're free to leave."

He had to go back into the hospital to validate his parking, and then he headed out of the building. He restrained himself from running in the event that his nurse was standing somewhere nearby, watching. Then he made the long trek to his car.

"Don't you think he's going to be suspicious about why none of us came to the hospital today to see him home?" Delilah asked Andy and Twyla.

Andy shrugged. "He might be pouting, but he'll probably figure that we'll think he needs time to sign out and pack up his stuff. He might wonder about *you* not showing up, but he's so used to traveling alone, I doubt he's even thought much about it."

"And if he thought that much about it, he would have called her by now," Twyla replied, always the pragmatist. "He should be here any minute."

As if on cue, the intercom buzzed. Delilah walked over to the door to answer it. "Yes?"

"Hey, baby, it's me."

"Okay, sweetie. Just a second."

Upon hearing Frank's footfall a few minutes later, she opened the door, and she, Andy, and Twyla yelled, "Welcome home!"

Frank stood there, a look of utter confusion crossing his features and then burst out laughing. It was good to hear. "You got me."

The trio had decorated the dining and living rooms with colorful balloons and streamers.

"Put that stuff down and follow us," Delilah directed, pleased that she had finally managed to surprise him. On the dining room table there was a small cake with one lit candle and the words, 'Welcome home, Frank,' written in blue-and-white icing. "We know you shouldn't really be eating much of this—"

"So I'll eat your share," Andy announced.

Frank stood at the head of the table, gazing at the cake. "I can't believe the three of you did this."

Twyla gave him a little push. "Blow out the candle!"

He did as he was told and then looked up at the three of them.

Delilah handed him a knife. "You cut the first piece."

Frank obliged, sliding his hand on top of hers so that they both cut it. As he removed his hand from hers, he gave her hand a slow caress, handing the small plate with a large slice of cake on it to her. "For you," he replied with a smile. His eyes roamed her body for a moment, revealing exactly what he was in the mood for.

Delilah blushed, knowing from the sly glances now passing between Twyla and Andy that they had witnessed the brief but sexy exchange. And the smile Frank was still giving her was not making her think of cake. "Thank you, sweetie. But why such a big piece—"

"I'll take that," Andy announced, smoothly removing the plate from her and handing her an empty one.

Twyla was shaking her head and laughing. "The boy has no shame."

"Sit down, honey. You look a little tired." Delilah could see that Frank had lost weight. He looked tired around the eyes, and he needed a haircut. Despite it all, she couldn't take her eyes off him.

They sat around, eating cake and ice cream and enjoying each other's company.

Although she had only known Andy and Twyla a short while, Delilah felt as if she had known them for years. She was thankful that although the visit to Washington, DC had started out scary, they now had something to celebrate—Frank's eventual recovery. Andy sent out for Chinese food, with Delilah selecting steamed white rice for Frank. After being fed intravenously for several days and then being on a light diet for the remainder of his hospital stay, he had to be careful. Although she felt bad for him, he said that he did not mind.

"I'm just glad to be out of there," he said later as he ate steamed rice along with chicken broth and applesauce that Delilah had found in the cupboard. He washed it down with hot tea while the others ate Chinese food of a more flavorful variety.

They talked for a while longer when Twyla said, "All right, Andy. We've tortured them with our presence long enough. Let's get out of here."

"Later, you two," said Andy as he clasped his best friend in a brief embrace and kissed Delilah on the cheek. Twyla did the same and they left.

Although it was only half past six, Delilah ushered Frank to the master bedroom. "I'm going to clean up, and I'll see you in a few minutes."

He nodded.

She cleared the table, discarding the debris, stowing the leftover slices of cake, and washing the few dishes. She shivered with delight at the thought of being alone with him, after nearly a month since he came to her in Georgia.

"Frank, I—"

Delilah halted in midsentence as she bounded into the bedroom. She stopped short of the king-sized bed where Frank lay, bare-chested and clad only in boxer shorts, awake and crooking his index finger at her. His face and chest were bathed in the late-afternoon September sunlight that streamed through the large windows. Sexual energy radiated from him. She kicked off the sandals she wore and slipped into the bed beside him, dressed in a yellow sundress.

"I've been waiting all day to do this," he said.

Frank pulled Delilah into his arms. He kissed her, his manner slow and gentle, while running his hands through her hair. He looked at her. "You're an incredible woman, Delilah. What you did for me this week … you went above and beyond what I would've expected." He chuckled. "I knew that you would, though."

"Come on. You know how I feel about you, honey."

Frank nuzzled her neck. "Tell me, baby."

Delilah turned and looked him straight in the eye. Her hair and eyes shone in the wide swath of sunlight, "I care about you so much."

"I know."

She threw a fake punch at him. Frank grabbed her hands, kissing each and laughing. "I swear, you are the most—"

"Lovable, sexy—" He began kissing her neck again, lowering his lips to her shoulders, and untying the straps of her dress with his mouth.

"Smart-alecky man—" Delilah reached over him to grab the window remote that lay on the bed beside them, to keep from crushing it with their bodies. Then she aimed it toward the windows to power down the shades. The room began to darken.

"Who loves you …" Frank took the remote from her and reopened the shades. Sunlight flooded the room. Then he turned over and moved on top of her, continuing his descent down her body.

"Man who loves me …"

LATE THE NEXT DAY, DELILAH found Frank standing at the bank of windows in the living room, dressed in jeans and a short-sleeved shirt. His hair was freshly cut. He was gazing out at the activity below and turned when he heard her footsteps.

"Frank? Why didn't you wake me?" she asked as she tightened the sash of her robe around her.

"Because you obviously needed your sleep. Between worrying about me and running back and forth to the hospital, you probably didn't get much. Not to mention you having your way with me last night."

"That's right, blame it on me." She smiled as she walked toward him. "When did you go out?" she asked, indicating his haircut.

"I did it myself. Shaving the other day was tricky because I was hooked up to stuff."

She touched his face and looked into his eyes." You look a little tense. What is it?"

"I'm fine. Look, would you like breakfast or lunch? It's after twelve so I think—"

"No, you're not, Frank. You think you can read me? Well, I can read you too, mister."

"Oh, you can, can you?" He attempted to soften his tone, but she saw through that.

As he played with the sash of her robe, she noticed his hands were shaking. "Sweetie, your hands are shaking!"

He pulled away. "Forget it."

She stared at him, perplexed. "Why should I? I mean—" Realization began to set in.

"I want a cigarette, all right?" He turned and stalked over to the balcony doors.

She followed. "I don't understand. You were in the hospital all that time, and you never mentioned anything."

"I was a little preoccupied," he snapped. "Now I'm not." He slid open the doors and walked out onto the balcony into the hot and humid summer air.

Delilah stood there, motionless. He had never used that tone with her, with the exception of the time they had a brief, heated discussion about racism at the airport. But she knew he had to go through it alone, and so she walked to the kitchen to prepare lunch.

When she finished, she returned to the sun-drenched living room. He was still out on the balcony, leaning on the railing and staring into space.

"Frank, I fixed some sandwiches. I think your stomach can handle that. I'm going to take a shower."

There was no response from him, so she headed to the master bedroom and the adjoining bathroom. She took her time showering and getting dressed in a T-shirt, jeans, and sneakers. Finally, she returned to the kitchen.

Frank was now sitting at the breakfast bar but had not touched the food. As Delilah walked by, he took hold of her arm and pulled her to him. "I'm sorry, Delilah. I didn't mean to jump down your throat."

She smiled. "I know you didn't. I should've realized that you—"

"No, you shouldn't. It makes sense that you thought I was over it. I *was* there for a while. But it takes longer than eight days to kick that habit." He slid his arms around her and ran his hands up and down her back. "Man, you look good. Mmm, smell good too."

"So do you." Delilah gazed into his eyes. She could see the pain there. He had so much to deal with: the pneumonia, not being able to return to work right away, and now this. "Why don't you try the patch or that nicotine gum they have on the market—"

"I've used them both in the past, but they don't work for me. So I've decided to do this thing cold turkey. You don't know it, but since I met you I haven't smoked as much as I normally do." Frank spread his hands wide. "Look, I've been smoking since I was sixteen. I don't even know how I picked up the habit; the same way most young people start, I guess. I never told you much about my life, huh?" He sat down on a stool at the breakfast bar.

"No, you haven't," Delilah replied, kissing his cheek. "I realized that when Andy told me that you didn't have any family to call."

112

"My mother died when I was fifteen." He sighed. "I tried to maintain the status quo, but the authorities found out and wanted to place me in a group home while they looked for my relatives. Well, it had just been my mom and me for a long as I could remember, and I considered myself the man of the house, so I wasn't having it. I looked a little older than my age and sounded even older, so I cleaned out my mother's bank account, sold most of the furniture, pawned the other stuff, and booked."

"Wow!" Delilah sat down on the stool next to him. "You weren't scared?"

He shrugged. "I didn't have time to be scared. I already had a part-time job at a grocery store, and I used a friend's address for a while and continued working and going to school while staying at a homeless shelter at night. Someone stole some of my clothes there, and the authorities came one day looking for me, so I left and never went back."

"What'd you do, then?"

"Well, when the money ran out, I hung out with several drop-out friends I knew, staying at their houses at night and mooching off of their families. I did that for a few months. Finally, I couldn't take the nightly arguments and left."

Delilah found herself holding her breath. "And after that?"

"I lived on the streets. I stole food and lifted a wallet or purse when the opportunity presented itself. I'm not proud of it, but I did what I had to do to survive."

Delilah's eyes started to water, but she willed the tears away.

"I even did the 'hop a freight train' thing like the hobos did back in the old days." Frank grinned at her and shook his head. "It's not as easy as they make it look in the movies."

He looked tired. She brought him a bottle of water. "You don't have to talk about it anymore if you don't want to."

Frank took a look around the kitchen. He hadn't thought about his early life in a long time. "Yeah, I have been running my mouth nonstop, haven't I?"

Delilah aimed a mock blow at his chin. "I didn't mean it like that. I want you to talk about it. But only if you want to."

He sat for a moment, just drinking his water and looking at the glass in his hand. Finally, he went on. "I guess I started smoking then—the cigarettes I found in the purses I snatched. I'm originally from Newark, New Jersey. When I hopped the freights, I ended up in Pennsylvania and then Ohio. Eventually, I wound up here. I liked the vibe here, so I decided to stay.

"It was hard for a while, because I couldn't find a job. I didn't want to be a bum or illiterate so every chance I got, when I wasn't dodging the police or the juvenile authorities, I ran into a library and escaped for a while.

"One particular night, I was in between places to stay and it was wintertime and cold, so I tried to ride the Metrorail as long as I could until it closed. I think I was around seventeen at the time. Well, I fell asleep and didn't get off at the end of the line, so the conductor ran me off. After that, I kind of walked the streets, just trying to stay awake and stay warm. It was around two in the morning when I heard a woman scream.

"Two men were roughing up this woman. I think they would've raped her if I hadn't shown up. Like a fool, I just charged in and managed to get her away from them, but not before we exchanged some blows, and one of them took a shot at me. It grazed my forehead. You can barely see the scar now."

"Oh, that cute little scar," Delilah murmured. "I thought you got that from playing sports in high school or college."

Frank chuckled. "Not quite." He drained the last of his water. "Anyway, her car was close by, so we ran to it and drove to her place. Well, when I went to walk her upstairs to her apartment, I became really dizzy and passed out on her doorstep. She dragged me in and bandaged my forehead. She probably knew it wasn't life threatening, but no doubt it shook her up a little—considering what we had just escaped and the fact that she didn't know me from Adam."

"I should say so." Delilah leaned against the breakfast bar, transfixed.

"She worked as a bartender in a club and was a little older than me. She nursed me back to health, and after that, we started living together. Her name was Monica—"

"Uh-huh. How old?"

Frank leaned back and gazed up into the air, a mischievous look crossing his features. "Umm, twenty-three."

"*Twenty-three?* That's a six-year age difference. And at that age—"

"Yeah, I know. Most women are more mature than men. But I always handled myself like someone older, so I guess I was all right in her book."

"I see."

"C'mere." He pulled her off the stool where she sat and onto his lap.

She gave him a light push and said, "Go on with your story."

"For a while, I guess you could say I was a 'kept man,' until I finally found a job and was able to bring in a little income. Monica even taught me to drive. Life was easier by then, because I think the authorities lost track of me or had stopped looking for me. I wasn't crazy about her working around a lot of men or the hours she worked, but we got along pretty good. She made good tips, and I was working in a warehouse then, so I wasn't doing too badly. Since Monica worked at night and I didn't, I began to go to night school to get my GED. I never liked the feeling that I had let my mother down by not finishing school. Besides that, I didn't want to be anybody's statistic."

"That's good." Delilah was impressed. "So, what happened? What broke you two up?"

Frank didn't answer her question right away. "One night, when I was nineteen, I had gone to visit a friend and afterward, decided to go to the club and see her. Well, about a block before I reached the club, I notice police cars and flashing lights and crime scene tape."

Her heart skipped a beat. "No!"

Frank coughed, averting his head. After clearing his throat, he said, "I began to run. But when I reached the club, the police wouldn't let me in. I had begun to get loud, when all of a sudden the front doors opened and the paramedics wheeled her out."

"Oh, Frank."

His grip tightened around her waist. "I followed the ambulance in her car. I got to talk to her—just before she died."

"Oh, honey." She was at a loss for words. "I'm sorry."

"Yes, it was senseless. Thugs tried to rob the club, and Monica got shot. For years, I wondered if they were the same men who had tried to rape her the night we met. But I never found out, because to this day, they have never been caught."

Delilah wrapped her arms around his neck, and they hugged each other close.

Chapter Eleven

The next day, Frank and Delilah took in a midday movie. The theatre was virtually empty, and they enjoyed the intimacy of the cool darkness and being in the theatre in the early part of the day while most people were at work. Frank savored the time they spent together because he knew that she would be leaving soon to go back to Savannah.

Later in the afternoon, Twyla took Delilah to her favorite manicurist, and Frank returned to the condo alone.

Alone, that is, with the exception of an unwelcome visitor. He was fighting an all-encompassing headache he had been suffering off-and-on since the day before. Stopping a pack-a-day habit cold-turkey was up there with the most difficult things that Frank had ever had to face. If Delilah had not been visiting, he doubted if he would have had the strength or inclination to even get out of bed.

The fitness center downstairs beckoned but Frank had promised Dr. Stewart that he would not exert himself until he was given the go-ahead. Instead, he sat on the cool silk sheets of his bed and put the finishing touches on the presentation he had been preparing before falling ill. Andy had already made calls for him, cancelling two engagements that week and the week before, along with his airline, hotel, and rental car reservations. Frank perused his online calendar, trying to decide on how to pencil them back into his already hectic schedule. He was already booked past the New Year.

He was still puzzling over it when Delilah returned later that evening. He had managed to kill some time productively, which took his mind off of wanting a cigarette for a while.

"Frank, I'm back," she called out. "Where are you?"

"In the bedroom."

Moments later, she appeared. "You haven't eaten?

"I wasn't really hungry," Frank replied as he logged off and closed his laptop. Twilight was falling, and he turned on one of the bedside lamps. "Did you?"

"Twyla and I grabbed a little something." She sat down on the bed. "Sweetie, you've got to eat to keep up your strength."

"Maybe later." He shoved the laptop in its bag and placed it in the floor against the nightstand. Frank looked at her for a moment without speaking. Never had he enjoyed being with a woman so much—just doing simple things or doing nothing at all. Until yesterday, with the exception of the talk he had with his mother at the cemetery, he hadn't thought of Monica for years. He had loved her, yes, in his young and inexperienced way. She had been his first love. Since then, he hadn't had time for it. The women in his life, like Priscilla, had been pleasant diversions.

With Delilah, it was different. He wanted her body, mind, and soul.

Frank lay back against the pillows and reached out for her. "I'm through with work now."

Delilah smiled. "Okay."

He began to caress her hand. "I told you that I'd make it up to you, you dropping everything to come see me."

Her smile grew wider. "You did, didn't you?"

He pulled her to him. "And I'm a man of my word. I remember you saying to me once that you wanted me to just stand still and be with you."

Her eyes sparkled. "I'm listening."

"Lie down."

"Mmm?"

Frank got out of bed and pulled Delilah's T-shirt over her hair, mussing it and serving only to further excite him, but he held his excitement in check. "I lied—sort of. Let me do this one thing: I want to give you a full-body massage."

"So who's arguing?"

He went to the linen closet and grabbed a large, fluffy towel and then stopped by the master bathroom for a bottle of jasmine-scented oil he kept in a small basket on a shelf under the sink along with other scented oils, lotions, and assorted toiletries. He placed the towel on the bed beside where Delilah lay watching him. "Roll over, baby."

Delilah did as she was told, rolling onto her stomach on the towel Frank had provided. Frank stood for a moment, drinking in the vision of her lovely body, the body he had dreamt of capturing for months before she finally gave into the feelings they both shared. He proceeded to remove the rest of her clothes and her flip-flops, catching a glimpse of her freshly pedicured toes. He poured some of the oil into his palm, warming it between both of his hands, and then slowly worked his way down her neck to her shoulders.

"You truly have the most amazing hands," Delilah gasped with pleasure.

Frank smiled to himself, but with supreme effort, he kept his mind on what he was doing and ignored the effect she was having on him. "I'm here to service you, madam. You tell me what you want me to do, and I'll do my best to accommodate you."

She moaned as his hands traveled with deliberate precision up and down the small of her back toward the base of her spine. "You're doing just fine."

"Oh no, baby, I've just started." With firm yet gentle pressure, Frank kneaded one silken thigh downward to its shapely calf.

"Oh my gosh, Frank, where have you been all my life!" she cried, tenderness and delight wrapped in that single statement.

"Here—waiting for you."

On Wednesday, Frank visited Dr. Stewart for his follow-up examination. After performing a battery of tests, Dr. Stewart logged the resulting information in Frank's online medical record.

"You're coming along, Mr. Ellis. One more week avoiding the travel as well as the working out."

"I hear you, Doctor."

Andy was out of town at a speaking engagement, so Frank took his two favorite girls, Delilah and Twyla, out to eat. He mostly just sat and ate his meal, watching the two interact. They had become fast friends, and he was glad. As he listened to their animated conversation, he kept pushing to the back of his mind how he always enjoyed a cigarette at the end of a meal. The overpowering urge was becoming a little less intense each day.

The next day, Thursday, dawned cool and crisp. Frank and Delilah took advantage of the fall-like weather, spending the day visiting museums and other sights that they had not had a chance to see during Delilah's first visit to Washington, DC. As late afternoon approached, they fought their way through the stop-and-go rush-hour traffic and returned to Frank's place.

Dinner was a hurried affair. After dinner, they went to the master bedroom and packed Delilah's belongings. The mood was solemn. She would be leaving midmorning the next day.

Frank noticed a tube of lipstick on the floor beside the bed and bent to pick it up. As he rose to give it to her, she quickly turned her back to him. Her shoulders were trembling. "Baby, what is it?" he asked, although he already knew. He felt it too.

He hurried to her side and gently turned her around to face him. Lifting her face, he felt her warm tears spill upon his hand.

"I'm sorry—" She dissolved into heartbreaking sobs.

He pulled her into a fierce embrace. "There's nothing to be sorry for. I'll miss the hell out of you too. I know I was close to death when I was in the hospital. But in an odd way, I felt at peace. I knew you would come. And Andy. And Twyla. All the people I care about. And the first time you walked through that door in ICU, although I felt like hell and looked even worse, it was a great moment in my life."

"I knew I would probably cry," she sobbed. "But not like this."

He kissed her forehead. "I'll be down to see you just as soon as I can." He kissed her lips. "And we've still got tonight."

DELILAH ARRIVED AT HER HOME in the late afternoon. She had texted Clementine and Vivian with short bulletins about Frank's status since leaving town, and she had called her mother on her cell phone. When her mother offered to hand the phone over so she could speak to her father, Delilah declined. She wasn't ready for another heated conversation with him yet, especially not over the phone.

Before unpacking, she called and spoke with her mother for a while. Thankfully, her father was not at home. Although she didn't want to talk to him again unless they were face-to-face and they were both in conciliatory moods, she did miss their father/daughter talks.

Afterward, she phoned Clementine.

"Hi, Clemmie."

"So, how are you doing?"

Delilah draped herself onto one of the sofas in her parlor as she replied, "I feel as though I've been around the world in eighty days. Or in my case, two weeks."

They talked briefly about Frank's progress and having dinner with Clementine and Scott on Sunday.

"Well, I won't keep you," Clementine said. "Go get some rest. I'm so glad Frank's doing better. I really like him."

"I'm glad. I'll talk to you later, Clemmie."

She hung up, taking her luggage upstairs to unpack and tackle the laundry.

Saturday arrived and after showering and dressing, Delilah called Frank.

"What's for breakfast?" was her greeting once he was on the line.

"I was thinking about eating some cereal," he replied. "Hey, baby, I thought you were going to call me when you got home yesterday."

She poured herself a glass of orange juice and opened the kitchen curtains to take a look at the gorgeous morning taking shape. "I did. You didn't answer, so I guessed you were busy."

He laughed. "I did take out the trash. That must've been when you called." He checked the log. "Yep. I'm sorry I missed your call. So, why are you up so early on a Saturday? It's only seven fifteen."

Delilah took a sip of her juice and then replied, "I wanted to have breakfast with you."

He laughed. "Trying to be like me, huh?"

"We had breakfast together every day this week. Kind of a hard habit to break." She pulled milk out of the refrigerator and glanced at the expiration date on the plastic jug. "The date's still good on my milk, so I guess I'll have cereal too."

It felt good to be laughing after crying her eyes out just the other day.

"What have you got on, baby? Frank asked. "I want to see you."

121

She laughed and shook her head. "I'm not firing up the webcam just so you can watch me eat. You're insatiable!"

They each sat in their respective kitchens, eating cereal and talking for nearly two hours. It was difficult being apart after seeing each other every day for almost two weeks straight.

"I'm kind of glad that I got home during the weekend. It gives me a few days to try to figure out what Mr. McDermott is going to pull out of his trick bag on Monday. I'm sure he's going to want to see me for one thing or another."

Although rushing to Frank's bedside had been stressful, anytime she was away from Mr. McDermott was a welcome respite.

"You let me know what happens, whatever it is," Frank said.

"I will."

"And try not to worry about it, baby."

Delilah gazed out of the window at the sun continuing its ascent into the nearly cloudless sky. She decided to try to be like the sun and rise, come what may, on Monday. "I'll try not to."

ON MONDAY MORNING, DELILAH STROLLED to her desk, checking her in-box and mailbox before sitting down. As she expected, there wasn't much in either of them because things had been slow in the office overall for the past few months. Money was tight for many agencies, so orders for supplies and big-ticket items had only been trickling in or were nonexistent.

Unfortunately, resident busybody Agnes Wylie arrived about an hour later. Popping her head around the corner of the cubicle, she proclaimed in a loud voice, "Oh, what have we here? Miss Delilah Carpenter has decided to grace us with her presence."

"Stuff it, Agnes," Delilah replied, not even bothering to look in her direction as she listened to the few voicemail messages on her phone.

"I held the fort in your absence," Agnes went on, as if Delilah hadn't spoken. "We must stay the course, as it were."

"I'm on the phone, Agnes, as if you didn't know."

"Pardon *moi*." At last, Agnes's head retreated to the other side of the cubicle.

There is no excuse for you, Delilah thought.

Fifteen minutes later, her intercom buzzed. "Please see me in my office," Mr. McDermott said.

Delilah made her way through the maze of cubicles, her confident and purposeful stride belying the apprehension she felt. *I can handle this,* she thought.

She turned the corner and knocked briskly on the closed oak door. "Come in," was Mr. McDermott's muffled response.

She opened the door and stepped inside the handsome and well-appointed corner office. Their offices were on the seventh floor, so he had an impressive view of downtown Savannah. She walked up to the set of chocolate-brown leather wing chairs that faced Steve McDermott's leather-topped desk and stood there.

"Good morning, Mr. McDermott."

He deflected her greeting and said, "You may be seated, Miss Carpenter." His slate-gray eyes bored into hers as she sat down. "I just wanted to ask you about your boyfriend, Miss Carpenter. He's doing better, I take it?" Something dark flickered in his eyes, although he had finished speaking.

"Yes, he is. Thanks for asking," Delilah replied as she took one of the chairs across from him. She felt funny about discussing Frank with her supervisor, but she had only told him about the situation because of her hasty departure. "He still has a way to go." She noticed another flicker and knew his concern was disingenuous.

"I'm glad to hear that." He continued to stare at her, now looking as if he were at a loss for words. "Welcome back."

"Thank you, sir. Is that all, Mr. McDermott?"

Mr. McDermott's eyes held hers for a moment longer before he looked away to glance at the quartz-wrapped clock on his desk. "Yes, thank you."

Moving swiftly, he hurried from where he had been sitting and knelt in front of Delilah's chair. He clutched both chair arms so that she was held captive where she sat, his face only inches from hers.

"One thing more: If there's anything I can do for you, Dee—anything at all—don't hesitate to ask. There's no reason why we can't put the uh … unpleasantness between us, shall we say, behind us. Don't give me such a hard time, and I'll try my best to help you." He lurched forward and attempted to kiss her.

Shocked and not knowing what to say, Delilah wrenched her face to one side as she threw her hands forward and pushed him as hard as she could in the chest. He fell backward to the floor with a bemused expression, and Delilah scrambled over him as she ran out of the office. On the other side of the closed door, she stood for a moment as realization set in. Confusion collided with it.

Vivian was right, she thought, an invisible cloak of dread short-circuiting her earlier feelings of confidence. *Boyfriend or not, he wants me to go to bed with him.*

Like ghosts haunting her, the disturbing thoughts followed Delilah as she hurried back to her cubicle.

DELILAH NEVER FAILED TO APPRECIATE the cooler lushness of each tree-filled square in downtown Savannah. She and Vivian made their way through one of the geometric wonders to go to lunch that afternoon. They were massive tree-lined tunnels, serving as natural canopies and making the oppressive heat reflected from the buildings and concrete surfaces around them a little more bearable.

"Whew, is it hot out here or what?" Vivian dabbed her face with a wad of tissues she had pulled out of her purse. Summer was in full force in Savannah. "Whose bright idea was it to come out here?"

Delilah grinned. "Yours. You said we should walk. Get away from the office. Help me take my mind off things."

"Me and my big mouth."

Once they reached the sparsely-populated sandwich shop, they both stood for a moment just enjoying the air-conditioned comfort. Most people had more sense than to venture outdoors for lunch on such a stifling day. Even though the tree-lined squares provided some relief, the sweltering heat made it a major endeavor to walk any more than a block. They had walked two.

They gave their orders, sat down, and began to eat.

"So, how was your talk with Mr. McDermott?"

"News travels fast around our office," Delilah replied, taking a sip of lemonade. "That's what I always hated about that place."

"Well, you've got Agnes to thank for that," Vivian announced, offering Delilah a cookie, which she declined. "She's been moving through the office like the pony express, talking about your meeting with Mr. McDermott."

"Don't get me started about that woman." She scooted her chair closer to the table as a couple sat down at the table behind her. "She probably had her ear to the door."

They laughed, and for a moment, Delilah felt the gray cloud begin to lift for the first time since her meeting with McDermott.

Vivian dabbed at her mouth with a napkin. "Maybe she'll retire soon."

"Nah. They'll have to carry her out in a pine box." Delilah shook her head and chuckled. "Wow, that sounded kind of harsh, didn't it?"

"Just a little," Vivian agreed, laughing.

"He asked me about Frank. But you were right, Viv—he likes me. In fact, that's an understatement. And I really think he's jealous of Frank, although he doesn't even know him. You should've seen his face when he had me stay late on the weekend they carpeted the office. I didn't recognize it then, but I did today. It's like he enjoys exerting some kind of control over me, almost as if it's payback for me not giving him the time of day."

"I was half kidding when I made that remark about him liking you. I can't believe it—Mr. McDermott?" Vivian asked. "Ugh."

"I know. I guess that's why he's always been so hot and cold with me and why he singles me out all of the time. I can't say I like the distinction. In fact, it gives me the creeps. Today, he actually grabbed my hand and said that if there was anything he could do for me to just ask. I can't believe it. He even tried to kiss me. The man wants to have sex with me."

They began to clear their tiny table, taking their trash to the nearest receptacle.

"Oh my God! So, what are you going to do about it?"

Delilah spread her hands. "What can I do? Nothing—unless I want to lose my job."

Chapter Twelve

"Where are you going?" Andy asked when he and Frank spoke on the phone Sunday evening.

"Going to San Antone," Frank replied as he pulled out his garment bag. "Yee-hah!"

"All right, bro. You'd better start slow."

Frank smiled at the phone. Andy could be a worrywart sometimes. "All right, Dad."

"I'll come down there and kick your butt if you don't."

"*Okay*, Andy."

He clicked off and went to his closet, trying to decide between several of the suits he had just picked up from the cleaners. He took his time, relishing in the process. He couldn't wait to get back into the thick of it. He had a lingering cough, but he was feeling more and more energetic every day.

Since the seminar would be three days, he selected a navy-blue pinstripe, a lightweight gray, and a tan suit that he didn't wear much.

The next day it was hotter than Hades. The heat slammed into Frank as soon as he got off the plane in San Antonio. He had heard Andy's voice in his head earlier as he took his nerve-calming drink on the plane. But he only had one. On each leg of the flight, that is.

Not everyone was a fan of flying.

Does it ever cool off in Texas? Frank thought as he headed to his hotel.

He called Delilah once he was upstairs in his hotel room.

"Hi, sweetie." Her voice always managed to soothe him. "I hope the flight was okay."

"*Flights*, you mean. Yep. I dealt with them." He performed his ritualistic in-depth search for anything in his room that might be crawling around as they talked. Bedbugs in particular were a problem in many hotels, upscale or not, and he didn't intend on sleeping with any of them. "How 'bout you, baby? Did he call you in his office? What's his name—Mr. McDermott?"

She hesitated and then said, "He did. He asked how you were. He's just strange, Frank. And I'm dealing with it."

"That's my baby." He could not put his finger on it, but he knew that she wasn't giving him the full story. *What was it with that guy?* he thought. But he knew that she would tell him about it when she was ready.

After San Antonio, Frank was home for half a week, and then it was on to a conference in Detroit. The crowd was large, dismaying him somewhat because the area had been hard hit by the recession and the resulting unemployment. He rolled out his newest presentation, *Surviving Financially in the Face of a Recession.*

"Having fun, partner?" Andy asked as Frank ate his dinner in his hotel room later that night.

"I have to tell you, man, it is really an eye-opener, how the recession and unemployment has devastated entire cities. I'm starting to get a lot of requests from agencies with people who are eligible to retire but are afraid to because of the economy—people who have been working all their lives. I feel a little guilty getting paid for speaking at this one."

"Depressing, isn't it?"

"Yes. And next week, I'll be in Buffalo. I drove through there once last year on my way to Rochester, and it was bad then." He clicked his way through channels with the remote as he ate.

"I'm expanding my presentation, *Disaster Preparedness*, to include a block relating to financial disaster preparedness. Hey, I won't be stepping on your toes, will I?" Andy asked.

"Nope. In fact, there's so much ground to cover that I can't cover it all. And I've got an idea. Maybe we could combine our presentations more often."

"Hey, that would be great."

"Yeah." Frank took a drink of water, wiped his mouth, and pushed his plate away. Night had fallen, so he got up, closed the draperies, and turned on another lamp. "Don't make your mind up yet. Take a while and think about it. There's no rush. The demand is there, and even when the economy improves, people will always have questions about their money—and since 9/11, disaster preparedness too. If it ever slows down, I'll finally be able to get my office established so I don't have to handle my scheduling and administrative stuff. I can start taking some clients when I'm in town. Maybe you'll quit your government job and come in and be partners with me. Anyway, we'll talk about it."

"Will do. Take it easy, Frank."

"Talk to you later, man." Frank hung up, sat back down at the desk, and turned up the volume on CNBC.

"I'LL BE AT YOUR PLACE on Friday evening," Frank announced during their Tuesday night phone call, "so drop whatever you might've had planned."

"I tell you—you are the cockiest man I have ever met!" Delilah hugged herself with glee.

"I'll be at your place Friday evening."

Frank arrived at Delilah's on Friday as promised. She barely had the door open when they collided in a passionate embrace. Only after minutes of nonstop kissing and hugging did they finally release each other.

"I missed you," they announced at the same time and laughed.

A gust of wind slammed the front door shut.

"Oops." Frank turned back to the door and locked it. Delilah went with him, since he was holding her hand.

She pushed him against the door and time elapsed once again as they kissed. "I made dinner. Complete with peach cobbler."

"So that's what I smell besides your intoxicating perfume." He slipped an arm around her shoulder, and they headed toward the kitchen.

"That, along with steak and biscuits and—"

"Whoa, baby. You're going to have me spend the next seventy-two hours here eating."

"Not if I have anything to say about it," she said with a wink. "Anyway, you lost weight, so you can afford to put it back on. And I'll just help you burn it back off."

"Alrighty, then."

Frank washed his hands, while Delilah dished up the food. "Beer or wine, sugar?" she asked.

"Neither." He took a seat at the table. "I'll take water."

"Water? Wow."

"Don't make a lot out of it. Wine would probably just put me to sleep. And I'm not ready to do that just yet."

They exchanged knowing smiles.

"But you can make a big deal out of this: no cigarettes for about three weeks now."

Delilah sat across from him. "That's incredible, Frank. Well, actually, I knew you could do it."

"Really? Because I didn't."

She reached for his hand. "I had faith in you."

"I guess you had faith enough for the both of us. But I had to do it alone."

"I know."

"It's a day-by-day thing, baby. I haven't totally lost that craving yet. But I had a lot of inspiration this time."

They ate for a while in silence, enjoying the feeling of being together without any noise or interference from the outside world.

Delilah watched him as he watched her. Her heart was full of contentment as this incredibly strong and sexy man, from a world unlike her own, enjoyed a meal she prepared. They could just as well be sitting there watching paint dry, and she would be just as happy.

"I love you, Frank," she blurted out, surprising herself.

Frank took a drink of water. A broad smile spread across his lips as he set his glass down. He took both of her hands in his. "I know."

"You know? Why, if that don't beat all—"

"You know what I mean, baby." He kissed her hands and gazed into her eyes. She found no conceit there. "You know I've been crazy about you right from the start. I had to wait for you to catch up."

"It has been a bit fast—"

Frank shrugged. "Sometimes I think the stars are aligned or whatever it is—fate. We just happened to be at the right place at the right time. And we've lived a lot of life in six months."

"We sure have." Delilah held his hands as tightly as he was holding hers.

"But we're weathering the storms."

After eating, they straightened up the kitchen, and because the moon was so bright, they took a stroll through the neighborhood. Crickets chirped and frogs croaked in a creek that meandered not far from Delilah's house. The night air was sultry, but the trees' leaves stirred from a gentle breeze.

"I've never been in a long-distance relationship," Delilah replied. She loved holding his hand and the strength yet gentleness she derived from it. "I wasn't sure if it was … if you …"

"Just wanted your body?" Frank asked, his baritone voice soft and low. "I won't lie; I love your body. But more importantly, I enjoy how I feel when I'm with you, Delilah. It's as simple as that." He thought for a moment. "I've never really had a long-distance relationship, either. Never really been interested in having one, to tell you the truth. I've known a lot of women around the country, but I wouldn't call those relationships."

Delilah listened without speaking. She heard the wonder and sincerity in his voice.

"With you, it's different. When I'm with you, I want you. When I'm without you, I want you more. But not just your body. Everything."

Upon their return to the house, Delilah tugged on the cuff of Frank's shirt. "Frank, I'm so glad you're here."

He cupped her chin in his hand, raising her face to his for a kiss. "Me too."

FRANK GOT A CHANCE TO visit with Clementine and Scott that weekend. They were having a cookout in honor of Scott's birthday with a few of Scott's friends and family.

Family that included Scott's father-in-law, Patrick.

"It's good to see you again, buddy," Scott remarked as he shook Frank's hand.

"You too, man. I didn't have a lot of time to think about what to get you, so I got you this." He bent down and picked up a case of beer and handed it to his newest friend.

"A man after my own heart." Scott scooped the case under his arm and clapped Frank on the back.

"Happy birthday, Scotty!" Delilah sang. She kissed him on the cheek.

Scott led the way to the spacious deck attached to the back the Zimmerman's townhouse. Scott's immediate family, his friends, and several coworkers were already there.

Including Patrick.

He stared straight at Frank with undisguised anger.

Frank stared back, plastering a benign smile on his lips.

Almost immediately, Delilah positioned herself between the two of them.

"Stop it, Dad," she said, loud enough for only the three of them to hear.

Frank gently pulled her to his side as he whispered, "Don't worry, baby. There won't be any fighting if I can help it."

Scott introduced Frank and Delilah to everyone, and then Frank stood around for a while with Scott and two of his coworkers, drinking beer and talking. Delilah and Clementine sat at one of the two gaily decorated tables on the deck, talking with Hazel.

Patrick was once again manning the grill and talking with Scott's parents. But his gaze continued to travel to where Frank stood.

They played games in the backyard and then ate and drank until they were stuffed. Music wafted from tiny speakers installed around the deck.

"They're playing our song," Frank said, against her ear.

She stared at him. "We have a song?"

"We have a song. *Love Ballad* by LTD. This song was playing the night Andy and I took you and Twyla to L'Elegance, and we danced for the first time." He shook his head, pretending to be hurt. "I thought women were the ones who remembered things like that."

Those sitting at the table with them laughed.

Nearby, Patrick glowered over his bottle of beer.

Frank stood up and excused himself. Walking over to where Patrick stood, he said, "Hello, Mr. Carpenter."

"Hello, uh—Frank."

"I've got to say that I just don't get it. I don't get you. You don't know jack about me, yet you can't stand me. I can see it in your eyes."

Patrick said nothing for a while. He finally spat out, "You don't know anything about my daughter, either."

"I care about your daughter very much, Mr. Carpenter."

Patrick's eyes narrowed even more. "How could you? Y'all met—what—five or six months ago?"

"That's right. But we've learned a lot about each other in that period of time. We know that we care about each other." Frank's gaze was steady, and he held his temper in check. He wanted to try to understand the older man.

Patrick took a swig from his bottle of beer and *humphed*.

"Well, how long did you know your wife before the two of you got married?"

"Never mind when we got married." His voice rose. "We're not talking about me; we're talking about you and *my daughter!*"

"How long we've known each other isn't the problem anyway," Frank shot back. "We both know what your problem is, Patrick: you are prejudiced."

"Look, this is not the place for this discussion!"

"Where *is* the place, Patrick? If looks could kill, I'd be stone right about now."

"If you really want to know the truth about it, you aren't good enough for my daughter!" Patrick retorted.

"Because I'm black, right?" Frank demanded. "Say it!"

At this point, Hazel rose from where she had been sitting and headed toward them. Delilah had been in the kitchen washing her hands and had just returned to the deck. She rushed over as well. Others, talking in the backyard and sitting at the tables, turned to look.

Hazel reached them first. "Patrick, honey, calm down. Remember your blood pressure—"

He shook off his wife's grasp. "Never mind my blood pressure! This boy's got the nerve to try to analyze me—"

At the word *boy*, Frank's blood ran cold. "Excuse me, Hazel, but to hell with your husband. I am a grown man, not a boy! This is the twenty-first century. He needs to be living in it and not the 1940s!"

Delilah was now standing beside him. "Frank, please—"

Frank fixed his gaze on her. "No!" He spun around and walked over to where Scott and Clementine sat as if rooted to their chairs, bewilderment and embarrassment etched on their faces. "I'm sorry, Scott. I didn't mean to wreck your party. Good-bye, Clementine. Delilah?"

She quickly kissed her parents. "I've got to go," she whispered to them and fled.

"FOR WHAT IT'S WORTH, DELILAH, I saw your father staring a hole in my head, so I went over to talk to him. I'm trying to understand where he's coming from." Frank took her hand in his as he drove the rental vehicle back to her place.

She nodded in the growing darkness.

"He looks at me as if I have no right to even be alive. Or maybe he just thinks that I should've been serving the food at the party and not been a guest."

"Frank, I'm so sorry." Her voice was small and weary.

"Baby, you have absolutely nothing to be sorry about." He withdrew his hand in order to make the last turn to her house and park. "Just don't expect me to go easy on your father. He's a grown man."

Delilah started to unlock the car but Frank did not budge. "Aren't you coming in?" she asked.

"Do you want me to?" His voice was quiet in the early-autumn night.

"What do you think?"

They walked up the porch stairs, and Delilah unlocked the door. In the parlor, she turned on a lamp, and they sank into the plush softness of a nearby sofa.

"Frank, I don't blame you. I know how frustrated you've been, trying to understand my dad." She sighed. "To tell you the truth, I don't understand his stubbornness. He's not even trying to meet you halfway. I've talked to him and told him that I'm going to see you no matter what he thinks."

Frank ran a hand over his eyes. He was tired. "What the hell did we as a people ever do to him or his ancestors to make him hate me and my people the way he does?"

Delilah bowed her head.

He pulled her into his arms. They both lay there quietly, listening to the other's heartbeat.

Neither of them had an answer.

FRANK SPENT THE ENTIRE WEEKEND with Delilah. They spent most of Sunday at her place before he had to leave.

Their time together was enjoyable, but Delilah could see what looked like a mixture of pain and anger on Frank's face at times, although he was attempting to conceal it, without success.

"Honey, I'm going to run to the drugstore for a few minutes. Do you need anything?" she asked as she picked up her car keys from the coffee table.

"You want me to go with you?" Frank asked, and he started to get up from where he sat on the sofa watching a football game.

"No, I won't be long." She walked over to where he sat, her sandals click-clacking on the wood floor. She kissed him on the forehead, deftly slipping out of his reach. "Watch your game."

"I'm going to want more than that when you come back," Frank remarked as she turned and walked away. She winked at him as she left the room.

Delilah picked up a few items at the drugstore and then pulled out of the parking lot, driving in the direction of her parents' house. *I can't face Daddy right now, as angry as I am,* she thought. Instead, at a red light, she dialed her parents' phone number and donned her earpiece.

Her father answered on the second ring. "Hi, doll baby. Where are you?"

"I'm in my car, Daddy. I can't see you right now, because I'm still very angry at you."

"At *me?*" There was a long pause and for a moment, she thought he had hung up on her. "I should've known you'd take his side. I declare, I don't know what it is you see in him—"

"It's not that I'm taking sides." She burned inside. "I'm just doing what's right. And you should be too. Frank's never done a thing to you—"

"Lord, I am sick to death of hearing his name!"

"Well, you're going to be hearing it if you want to see me, Dad."

Patrick lowered his volume but his tone was sinister. "Are you threatening me, girl?"

"I would never do that, Dad." She pulled up in front of her house. "Consider it a promise. Good-bye."

Stepping into the house, she forced gaiety into her voice as she called out, "Who's winning the game, sugar?"

Twyla and Andy invited Frank to dinner when he returned to town.

"Happy belated Rosh Hashanah, my brother," Frank announced as Andy opened the door.

"You need to stop, man," Andy laughed, clapping him on the back as they made their way to the kitchen. Twyla was putting the finishing touches on dinner. "Hey, Twyla, funny man is here."

"Funnier than you?" she quipped, giving Frank a hug and a kiss on the cheek.

Frank glanced back at him with a smirk.

"Touché. Wow, even my girl's got jokes." Andy retrieved a stack of plates and headed for the dining room.

"But we love you, man." Frank handed Twyla a bottle of wine. "Do you need any help?"

"No, Frank, you timed it just right. Everything is done." She took the bottle and put it on ice.

Frank laughed. "See, Andy? She's got jokes for me too."

Andy joined in. "Good. I feel better now."

Frank helped him finish setting the table, and not long after, they all sat down to eat.

"So, how's every little thing?" Andy asked as they ate.

"How's Dee?" Twyla added.

"She's fine." Frank stared off into the distance for a moment. "Her father is giving me the blues though. I tried to have a conversation with him at her brother-in-law's house, and I'm telling you, I thought the man was either going to have a stroke or attack me."

"Good grief! What is he, a psychopath?" Andy asked.

"I don't think so. I'd hate to call Delilah's father a nutcase."

"How's she taking all of this?" Twyla's eyes were full of sympathy.

"I know it's hard on her. She's embarrassed by how he's been acting. I feel for her, but I don't know what to do." Frank ate for a while, reliving the past weekend in his mind.

"Just take it day by day, man," Andy suggested, breaking into his reverie. "As long as you don't disrespect her father, you two should be okay."

"I told him he was prejudiced," Frank replied.

At that, both Andy and Twyla laughed. "'Cause that's what he is," they said in unison.

But he didn't laugh. "I know."

Chapter Thirteen

⬥◦✕◦⬥

Supply orders picked up in Delilah's department, which relieved her of the boredom she felt of late in her office. However, it did nothing for her growing apprehension regarding her supervisor, Mr. McDermott. She avoided him as if he were the H1N1 virus. She was at odds with herself about what to do. She could go to the Equal Employment Office and report him. Although from what she had seen happen to others and from reports she had read regarding other sexual harassment cases, it did not always go well. Even if he was reprimanded or punished, if she wasn't placed in another office or if he wasn't removed from his position, she could wind up a pariah in her own office. She knew that Vivian would be in her corner, but she couldn't be sure about the others in her branch or the other higher ups in the office, especially the men.

Delilah knew that Mr. McDermott was considered a steadfast, reliable member of the executive team. Donning her headphones, Delilah listened to her radio when she could to block out Agnes's incessant chatter. But nothing could block out the voices of her own conscience. She had to figure something out soon.

Yard sales sprang up during the spring and summer in the South. With the advent of autumn, festivals cropped up as well. Delilah tagged along to a fall festival with Clementine and Scott that was being held just outside the city limits. She browsed the booths and stands with Clementine. Scott brought up the rear, pulling a metal laundry cart behind him with the treasures they had acquired so far.

"You talk to Dad lately?" Clementine asked, perusing a beautiful old metal chest.

Scott threw up a hand. "I can't get that in this thing!"

"I know, I know, I'm just looking at it. Hush. I'm talking to Dee."

"Nope," Delilah replied, munching on a bag of boiled peanuts.

"I don't blame you, Dee." Scott stopped walking to wipe his forehead against his bare arm in the sunshine. "Patrick looked like he was about to blow his stack at the party."

"I've never known Dad to be so obstinate about something." Clementine gave the vendor the money for a pair of earrings and waited for her change.

"You mean *someone*, don't you?" Delilah corrected.

"Well, prejudiced in general and Frank in particular. He's got a right to like who he wants to like, but he still needs to treat the man with respect."

"Exactly."

"I gotta admit, I've never seen him act that way," Scott remarked as they resumed making their way through the crowded marketplace teeming with all sorts of interesting wares. "But come to think of it, I don't recall ever seeing him with any black people before Frank."

"Well, I don't plan to stop seeing Frank," Delilah declared, now eyeing a uniquely woven basket. After dickering with the vendor for several minutes, she purchased it for five dollars less than the asking price. She placed it in the cart.

"I don't expect you to, Dee," Clementine replied. "Dad *is* being unfair. I just don't want it to affect your relationship with him."

"Neither do I, but it already has. And Daddy's the one who has to come to grips with the way he's been acting toward him. Till then, I plan on giving him plenty of space."

"That's probably the best thing." Clementine touched Scott's arm. "You know, I really liked that chest. Let's go back. I'll help you carry it to the car, hon."

FRANK WAS STARING IN THE refrigerator, trying to figure out what to have for dinner when he buzzed Twyla into the building. Her voice had sounded strange over the phone, and he wondered what she wanted to talk to him about.

"Hey, Frank."

"To what do I owe the pleasure? Andy not treating you right?" he joked as they embraced. The look on her face quickly told him that she was in no mood for jokes. "I'm sorry. What's going on, baby girl?"

Frank headed back to the kitchen, and Twyla followed. "I was just trying to decide what to fix for dinner. Have you eaten?"

"No."

"Good. Everything's frozen except the bread and cold cuts, so I guess we're having cold cuts."

She remained silent.

"Oh, and I've got these." He snatched an unopened bag of potato chips from one of the cupboards. He held it up. "Barbecue. All right now—speak."

"Andy and I are fine. We went up to see my momma in Philly a while back. Everything was wonderful. They love Andy up there."

"So what's wrong?" He grabbed the mustard and mayonnaise, setting them on the counter.

"I'm on the pill, and I always have Andy wear a condom, for backup."

Frank felt a little uncomfortable, as if he was peeking into his friend's underwear drawer. "Yeah, so? I don't understand—"

"Well, while we were in Philly, he didn't."

The statement yanked Frank back to the day he had slept with Priscilla. He had never heard anything to the contrary from her. Although it had been stupid of him to let Priscilla have sex with him without added protection, especially since he knew there were times they had other partners, he knew he had dodged a bullet. *Thank God for that*, he thought. Aloud, he said, "Aw, you'll be okay. The pill is very—"

"It's not 100 percent, Frank," she replied. "And by the time I thought of going to the drugstore to buy the 'morning-after' pill, it was too late."

He returned to the refrigerator and pulled out pastrami, smoked ham, and Swiss cheese. "You want onions?"

She shook her head.

"Then I won't, either. Hell, Twyla, nothing's 100 percent. Even with a condom on, it could tear." He handed her a plate and knife.

Twyla was still silent. After placing two slices of bread on her plate, she just stood there looking at them.

Frank grabbed her arm and spun her around to face him. In her eyes, the weight of the world was reflected. "I can see you're upset. You're afraid that you're pregnant?"

Tears gathered in Twyla's eyes as she nodded.

He pulled her into his arms and held her for a few minutes.

"I'm all right, Frank." She pulled away from him. "I'm not going to cry."

"Hey, you can cry if you want to—"

"No!" she exclaimed with such vehemence that it stopped him in his tracks. "I'm sorry, Frank. I didn't mean to bite your head off."

"That's okay. You're a little upset. I understand." He chuckled. "Boy, *do* I understand."

Twyla shook her head. "You partly understand. I don't want to cry. If I did cry, it'd be for the thousands of women out there who can't have kids."

She began to prepare her sandwich, and Frank followed suit. He knew that sometimes it was best for a man to just keep his mouth shut when a woman was talking. From eight to eighty, sometimes they just wanted someone to listen to them.

"I need your opinion. If it was Dee who became pregnant, what would you do?"

"I can't speak for anyone else—"

She turned to look at him. "I know that. I just want your opinion. If it was Dee, how would you feel?"

He completed preparing his sandwich without speaking for a moment. The question was simple, yet it blindsided him just the same. He almost felt as if he were Andy standing there talking to Twyla instead of himself. He stared down at his hands as he chose his words carefully.

"Twyla, if Delilah came to me and told me that she was having my baby, I'd be happy. Even if I felt it was the wrong time, because we haven't known each other as long as the two of you have, I would be happy. Look, Twyla, every couple's situation is different. And this is just my opinion—because you asked for it, right—but if she told me that she wanted to have an abortion, I'd be highly upset. But that's just me."

"Really?"

"Really." He returned the cold cuts and other items to the refrigerator and took out two bottles of water. They sat down at the breakfast bar to eat. "But it's her body, so I would have to respect her wishes. Anyway, who can pick the right time to have a baby? They tend to show up at the funniest times. But most people end up keeping them anyway."

They ate in silence for a while. "Thanks, Frank."

"I also have to say that I've seen the way he looks at you, Twyla. If ever a man loved a woman, it's Andy."

He watched as an uneasy smile spread across her lips. "Yes, I know. But do you ever think about bringing a biracial baby into the world?"

"Sure, baby, ever since I started seeing Delilah." He shoved several chips into his mouth.

"And you aren't scared?" She reminded Frank of a young deer; her eyes were so huge.

"Scared, no. Concerned, yes. Not for me but for what the child might face. But I've always looked at people in terms of the human race and not in terms of race. People may think I'm naïve, but, hey, that's how I feel. I'm hoping that one day we'll live in a colorblind society. Will it be in our lifetimes? I doubt it. But I wouldn't let that stop me from having a baby with the woman I love, even if she was of another race." He squeezed her arm and smiled. "Does that help you any?"

She was beginning to smile. "You helped just by talking to me. I know you can see it from my point of view—not as a woman, but as an African American and how we're viewed and how our children are viewed, even those who aren't biracial." She took a bite of her sandwich.

"I'm glad," he replied as he stood up and headed for the refrigerator. "Hey, I think I've got some beer in here. You want one?"

ANDY RETURNED FROM OSHKOSH, WISCONSIN, a few days later on pins and needles. He had been resisting on a daily basis the almost painful urge to ask Twyla about her cycle. He knew that she was on the pill and usually regular. She had even taken a pregnancy test a month after it was supposed to begin, and two weeks after that she had gone to her gynecologist who conducted another pregnancy test. That result had also been negative, and the doctor chalked it up to stress. It had been over two months since the time they made love while visiting her mother in Philadelphia without him wearing his backup. This, according to his calculations, made her way overdue. Andy was nearly over the moon over what that might mean.

Upon his return, he and Frank had gotten together to work on preparing a presentation they could do when their clients and schedules coincided. Their consensus was that the audience would get more bang for their buck, especially in those economically hardest hit communities around the country. And besides that, they worked well together.

Andy knew he had been acting strange and kind of goofy, but he couldn't help himself. He even noticed Frank watching him at times when Frank thought he wasn't looking. Nevertheless, he kept his mouth shut about his feelings, a first for him with his brother friend.

After Frank left, he and Twyla had dinner together. They watched television for a little while, and then had their own private reuniting. Afterward, Andy lay there in the dark, his body molded against hers, listening to Twyla's slow, steady breathing as she slept. He caressed her belly almost reverently, wondering if it contained the beginnings of a life growing within.

The next day when he awoke, Twyla was in the kitchen, making breakfast.

"Aw, baby, I was gonna do that." Andy slid his arms around her and kissed her cheek.

"You were tired." She turned her face to him briefly, giving him a wicked grin, appearing to be her old self again.

Later, they ate bacon and eggs in their bedclothes while playing footsie under the kitchen table.

"How about round two?" he suggested, smiling broadly.

At the same time, the phone rang, and Twyla rose to answer it.

Andy rose as well, placed the dishes in the dishwasher, and then went to the bathroom. As he washed his hands, he noticed a familiar-looking wrapper in the wastebasket. A tampon wrapper.

A wrapper that he hadn't want to see, at least for nine months.

He felt the wind leave his sails. "Damn," he mumbled.

Once Twyla finished her phone call, she went into the bedroom where Andy was now sitting on the side of the bed. "Momma and Granddad send their love."

"That's nice."

She peered at him from the foot of the bed. "Andy, what's wrong?"

"I thought you said you were late," he replied after a while, staring straight ahead.

"I was, but I came on this morning." She buzzed around the room, opening the curtains to the chilly daylight outside. "My doctor was right. I guess I was stressed out, and it threw me off my cycle."

"Stressed out, huh?" he echoed.

"What is it? What's the matter?"

He looked up at her with effort. "It actually stressed you out, the thought of being pregnant." He felt a searing pain in his chest, his heart slowly tearing in two.

The look in her eyes was a mixture of something resembling shame and tenderness. "You're all wrong. I'm just not ready. And besides, I don't want to have a baby out of wedlock. All that 'my baby daddy' nonsense—"

He sprang from the bed and marched over to where she stood. "It wouldn't have to be out of wedlock, if you would marry me!"

"Don't yell at me!" Twyla lowered her voice. "Baby, we're an interracial couple—"

"So tell me something I don't know." He ran a hand over the five o'clock stubble on his jaw. "We've been one for years."

"Listen to me." Her eyes were beseeching. "Bringing a biracial child into the world is a whole different matter."

He stood less than a foot away from her and stared her in the eye. "When I approached you the day we met, I knew what I was doing. I didn't do it as a joke. I wanted to meet you. And when we started dating, I knew the pros and cons of it. The same thing when I proposed to you—I did it because I was in it for the long haul. So the baby would be mixed. So what? I look at it as being a mixture of what our love created—all of the good things."

Twyla shook her head, her eyes brimming with unshed tears. "That's a beautiful but naïve way of looking at it. You've got to be realistic!"

"So, we'll explain to our child and try to prepare him or her for the bigots out there. Hell, we're dealing with it." A sigh escaped from deep within him. "At least I thought we were."

She seemed to crumple then, emotionally as well as physically, and she fell into his arms. "I'm scared," she sobbed.

He held her tight, and strangely enough, her tears were a soothing salve to his ragged heart. He knew now that she wasn't rejecting marriage or having a baby with him, not really. She had been attempting to piece together a solution to their situation, to spare their future children grief. But there were no guarantees in life. One could not insulate one's self from its slings and arrows.

"Hell, I'm scared too sometimes. But life is a crapshoot, baby," Andy replied; and as he stroked her hair, his own eyes burned. "You just gotta roll the dice and take it from there."

"I don't know how!" she cried.

"You know how," he soothed. "You've been doing it all along, with me."

"Hello, Delilah. Were you asleep?" Frank asked.

"I was about to take a shower. I just got in a few minutes ago. I was hanging out with a few girlfriends and Clemmie. It's my birthday. At least it was as of midnight."

"I know. I wanted to be the first to wish you a happy birthday."

"Well, you know because of my birthday being so close to Halloween, it tends to get wrapped up in the festivities of that holiday." Her voice was soft in his ear. "I'm glad you remembered, though."

"I would never forget, and you'll realize that a few hours from now when you receive a special delivery." Frank replied.

"Ooh, let me guess. You, wrapped up in gift wrap?"

"I wish. I wish I was down there. Or you were up here with me." He undressed, threw on a pair of pajama bottoms, and turned out the lamp. Crawling under the cool, Egyptian-cotton sheets, he stretched out with the phone beneath his ear.

"So do I," Delilah announced in a quiet tone. "I miss you, Frank."

"Sure you do, baby," he joked. "So, how many men were at the club?"

"I don't know. A few, I guess. There were Halloween parties going on in town, but the girls took me out for a few drinks." She paused. "Is my sweetie jealous?"

"Yeah, I'm jealous. Jealous that they're down there in close proximity to you, and I'm not." Frank's voice rumbled with pent-up emotion. "I love you, Delilah."

"I know." Delilah sounded close to tears. "I love you too."

"C'mon now—I didn't say that to make you cry. I'm just sorry that I couldn't be down there for your birthday. I hope you had fun and enjoy the rest of your day today."

"Thanks, honey. I did and I will. But—"

Frank smiled in the darkness. "I know."

"Maybe we'll be together to celebrate yours."

"The eleventh of December? I don't know; I'll have to look my schedule." He sighed. "Sometimes I feel about a hundred years old."

"You've held up mighty well, considering." She laughed her tinkly laugh. "Thirty-six is not that old."

"Yeah, I know. I've just packed a lot of living in those years," he replied.

"I'm not that far behind."

"Don't mind me, baby. Hey, I'm glad you had fun."

"Well, honey, I'm going to take a shower and hit the hay. Please try to get some sleep too, okay? Good night."

"Good night, and happy birthday, baby."

Chapter Fourteen

November arrived, and with it, loomed Thanksgiving. Delilah looked forward to it, and at the same time, she dreaded it this year. Although they lived in the same town, she hadn't spoken to her father since Scott's birthday party. She loved her father, but the way he treated Frank was wrong, and she wouldn't stand for it.

She left work late one afternoon, and upon arriving home, Delilah prepared dinner and then phoned Frank. "What are you doing?" she asked.

"I just got to my hotel room. I was tightening up my presentation for tomorrow."

"Oh, I'm sorry. I didn't mean to disturb you." She sat down at the kitchen table with her plate and a steaming mug of hot tea.

"Hey, I can deal with it later. And you are never a disturbance to me, Delilah."

She never tired of the way Frank made her feel when he said her name. "Thanks. I thought I'd like to have dinner with you. I'll even turn on my computer and activate the webcam so you can see me."

"I'd love to," Frank replied. "Haven't ordered room service yet, but I'll sit with you while you eat yours."

She heard his deep chuckle on the other end. "What's funny?" she asked and took a bite of salad.

"Nothing, really. I just like how you adopted my little idiosyncrasy, eating with you."

"Ooh, honey, I love it when you use those big words." Delilah glanced at the growing lavender and apricot-hued sky peeking through the cheery kitchen curtains. "Hold on for a minute." She hurried to her office to retrieve her laptop. She brought it to the kitchen and set it up. "Anyway,

146

I like it, eating while talking to you. It makes being away from you seem a little easier."

"It does, doesn't it?" Frank replied as he did the same, and they hung up their cell phones. "Especially when I get to see you too."

"You probably did this with your old girlfriends, though," she remarked. He looked so attractive to her, dressed in a light-blue dress shirt and dark-blue-and-white polka-dot tie, loosened casually around his neck. He was already watching her eat in that disarming way of his.

"Nope. It was something I thought of that first time I did it with you."

Delilah smiled to herself. "Really?"

"Really. Hey, is everything all right?" he asked.

"Sure, honey." She took a sip of tea. "Um, I was wondering what you were planning to do for Thanksgiving."

"I was wondering about that too. I know that Andy and Twyla will be going to his parents' house." Frank paused. "Aren't you going to yours?"

She finished her dinner and scooted back from the table. "I doubt it. I haven't spoken to my dad since Scotty's birthday party." She felt her heart beat faster at the mere thought she was about to put into words. "So I thought we could have it together—just the two of us."

"Are you serious? Baby, that would be great. But your family—"

"Don't worry about them. I can drop over to the house to see Mama when I know Daddy's not there. And Clemmie and I already had a talk. Frank, I'm serious about you, and it's time my dad learns to accept it. And learns to respect you."

There was silence for a moment. Finally, Frank said, "Delilah, I'm sorry about putting you in the middle of this thing."

She washed the few dishes and straightened up the kitchen before clicking off the light, taking her laptop with her. She strolled through the darkness toward her bedroom. "This 'thing' is *us*. And even if he doesn't accept you, I demand that he respect you. He got to choose my mother. Now he's got to allow me to make my choice."

"Wow, baby. I've got to say that you sound—"

"Like you?" Delilah supplied and laughed.

"Well, I didn't want to be that presumptuous ..."

"Ooh, four syllables this time."

"You are silly!" They both laughed—she in Georgia and he in New Mexico. "But I like it. I always want you to have fun with me, to enjoy being with me."

"I do, honey." She placed her laptop on her bed and after turning on her bedside lamp, pulled it onto her lap. The radiator heat made the room toasty, although it wasn't exactly freezing outside. "I love being with you. And I remember what you said that day in the airport. We have to stick together."

"Yes, we do," Frank replied, very softly.

"Now we have to decide—your place or mine?"

"How about mine? If you don't mind."

"I'd love to," she squealed. "We can eat out or cook—and you have that beautiful kitchen."

"It's a date. You let me know what day and time, and I'll make the arrangements."

"Okay." Delilah began to undress and padded in her bare feet to the bathroom. So Frank could hear, she loudly announced, "I'm going to take a shower."

Frank's voice was low and sexy. "May I join you?"

She laughed once more. "*Now* who's being silly?"

THE WEEK OF THANKSGIVING ARRIVED. Frank had used one of his many frequent-flyer awards to fly Delilah back to Washington, DC. It was cold in the city, but that did nothing to dampen their moods. Delilah was glad to be there to enjoy the holiday weekend with him and get away from Mr. McDermott, while Frank was glad for the break from traveling. As always, both were ecstatic to see one another.

Frank picked her up from the airport. The traffic was light going, however, inside the terminal was frenetic. He was glad he was on the outside looking in for a change.

"Hey, baby," he greeted her in a brief embrace before placing her bag in his car. The airport police were out in full force, and he didn't want his car to get towed. "How was your flight?"

"It was fine. Ooh, I love your goatee," she squealed and caressed his face. "Between that and the glasses you're sporting, you look very jazz musician-like."

"Is that good?" He teased as he opened the car door for her.

Delilah's eyes sparkled, their changeable color made more bewitching under the cute knit cap she wore. "I think so."

"Thanks. Well, you can thank looking at all of those PowerPoint presentations for me having to wear reading glasses now. And you're looking beautiful as always," he replied, stealing a kiss before pulling away from the curb.

When they arrived at the condo, Frank dropped her bag at the door and snatched Delilah up into a bone-crushing embrace.

"Oh my goodness," she gasped. "I gather that you missed me."

"Need you ask?" he whispered against her ear before releasing her.

"No. I missed you too." She threw her arms around his neck and kissed him long and hard.

After he recovered, Frank headed over to the fireplace and flipped the switch.

"Mmm," Delilah purred.

"Instant ambience," Frank growled, gently pulling her back into his arms.

The next day after breakfast, Frank had her double check the items he had purchased two days before at the grocery store. "Did I get everything we need? Is there anything that you'd like that I didn't get?"

"It looks like you got everything. Wait—do you have flour? I'd like to make some rolls. And maybe a pie. And my special eggnog—"

"Okay, we'll make a run to the store, early before the folks working this week get off for the day. Then I can get started on that turkey."

They headed first to the liquor store for brandy. Frank already had an unopened bottle of rum at the condo.

"Rum? And brandy?" he asked her.

She gave him a sly smile. "That's the secret of my eggnog recipe, along with a few other ingredients you already have at your place."

Next they headed to his favorite grocery store. They got a few questioning looks from some of the customers, but none of the frowns and downright hostile stares and comments they sometimes received from people of both races when they were together. Today, the overall mood around town was festive. Frank smiled inwardly, relieved that he didn't have to feel that all-too-familiar tension for the time being.

Afterward, they hurried back to the car with their packages.

"Hoo-wee, it's cold out here!" Delilah declared.

Frank took her gloved hand and squeezed it. "We'll have to do something about that."

Later, as she peeled onions for the stuffing and he cleaned the inside of the turkey, Frank asked Delilah, "How's Clementine? And your mother?"

"Clemmie and Scotty said hi. My mama's doing fine. I expect she's a bit upset because I won't be there for Thanksgiving this year, but she understands. She should. She's lived with my daddy for thirty-five years now."

He remained silent. He didn't really know what to say. "I'm sorry, Delilah. I didn't want things to be like—"

"Stop it, Frank! Just stop! It's not your fault. You didn't do anything."

He stole a look but kept his mouth shut. She didn't seem to be upset about her father but about him constantly revisiting the issue.

"I'm just so tired of talking about it," Delilah replied, confirming his suspicions.

"Fair enough."

They talked nonstop, about everything and nothing. Frank couldn't believe how much he was enjoying himself, with his hand inside a cold wet bird and Delilah by his side.

After she finished chopping the celery and onions for the stuffing, she announced, "Time to make the eggnog. You have to get out."

Frank laughed until he realized she was serious, at which time he laughed even harder. He obliged her by going into the living room and turning on the stereo. Then he stood at the window and watched the sunset and twilight set in. Except for the ever-present knowledge about Delilah being on the outs with her father, he was happy.

"You can come back in now," she called out.

"Smells promising." He took a whiff of the contents in the goblet she handed him.

Delilah took his free hand in hers. "I'm sorry for snapping at you."

Frank shook his head. "No need. I should've left it alone." He took a drink of eggnog and then another.

"You wouldn't ask if you didn't care."

"I love you, is why I ask." He gazed into her eyes. "I want you to be happy."

"I am." She smiled. "Well?"

"I've got to admit, it's really good. And it's got a little kick to it. A little something, something."

"I told you you'd like it." She took a sip of her eggnog.

Frank held out his goblet. "Some more, please?"

Delilah smiled even wider this time. "Well, when you ask me that way …"

THANKSGIVING DAY ARRIVED, COLD, WITH intermittent rain, but nothing could dampen Frank's and Delilah's spirits. They put the finishing touches on their meal; the rest of the time they spent watching football, while Frank taught Delilah the fundamentals of chess.

Finally, they sat down to their Thanksgiving dinner together. Frank couldn't help but smile.

It was not lost on Delilah. "What's that smile all about?" she inquired.

"Oh, I was just thinking to myself how different this Thanksgiving is from last year."

"And how is that?" She took a bite of turkey.

"Well, I spent most of it dodging bad weather in the Midwest. By the time I got home, it was around eleven at night. Thanksgiving Day was over."

"That's so sad," Delilah replied. "So what did you do when you got home?"

Frank wiped his mouth. "I talked to Andy and Twyla for a little while, ate a little something, drank a little, and fell asleep in front of the TV." He shrugged with an air of nonchalance.

She took his hand.

"I've done that more times than not. Some holidays I've spent in hotel rooms or with Twyla and Andy or other friends who invited me to their shindigs. Kind of like when I was younger, only not out of financial necessity." His smile tightened, and his hand underneath hers tensed into a fist.

"I'm glad I'm able to be with you this Thanksgiving," Delilah announced in a soft voice.

"So am I, baby." He resumed eating.

"I can't believe how delicious this turkey is, Frank. It's so moist and full of flavor."

"Why shouldn't it be?" Frank demanded with a grin. "I had a great sous-chef."

Delilah shook her head. "You did most of the work."

"I told you, I like cooking. That is, when I have the time."

"I apologize for laughing when you first told me that." She giggled.

Frank pretended to be hurt. "You're very sincere about it, I see."

"How can I make it up to you?" Delilah asked, her voice dripping promises wrapped in southern charm to a question for which she already knew the answer.

"I'll think of something."

The next day they sought shelter from the cold weather at the movies and afterward returned to the condo to eat Thanksgiving leftovers. They spread the food out on a blanket on the floor in front of the fireplace.

"This is nice," Delilah sighed, before scooping up a dollop of sweet potatoes with her fork. "It's cozy."

"I've never enjoyed eating leftovers more," Frank agreed. He took a drink of eggnog. "No job worries—"

"Ugh. Don't mention it."

"Speaking of which, how is Mr. McDermott?"

"I asked you not to mention it," she remarked, a bit sharply. She took a deep breath. "Oh, Frank, I'm sorry."

"*I'm* sorry. What I should've said was why don't you leave?" He pushed his plate aside.

Delilah gazed at him. "Jobs don't just walk up to you and say, 'Here I am.' And I've got to make a living."

"You could move to DC. There are still jobs here. I know a few people."

She continued to stare at him while he talked. "You mean, move up here?"

"I mean, *move in here*, with me." He moved closer to her.

Delilah pushed her plate out of the way for him, but she looked toward the balcony windows at the approaching nightfall. *Did I just hear what I think I just heard? He wants me to move in with him?*

"Did you just say—"

"You heard right, baby." Frank's voice was quiet but assured as he said,

"Yes, I know, it hasn't been that long since we first met. But we already know that we love each other. We don't have to stand on ceremony; let's do what's right for us. As it is, we can't stand it whenever we're apart."

"I—I don't know." Delilah continued to stare at the beautiful city view.

"I also told you that I'd wait for you to catch up." He was sitting next to her but he did not touch her. "And you did. We feel the same way about each other. Look, Delilah, I'm not trying to rush you into anything. Ultimately, it's up to you."

She finally turned and smiled at him. The flickering flames from the fireplace made his dark eyes very compelling. "Thank you for the offer, honey. Give me a little more time."

"The offer will still be open if and when you're ready."

Sunday afternoon following Thanksgiving, Delilah and Clementine attended the baby shower of a mutual friend. Afterward, Delilah dropped Clementine off at her house and drove home. Later that evening, the doorbell rang. Her father, Patrick, stood on the porch.

Delilah stood at the front door, her mouth agape. He was the last person she expected. As it was, she was not expecting anyone.

"May I come in?" Patrick asked. Although his powerful physique nearly filled the doorway, his voice was pensive in the cool night air.

"S—sure." She stepped aside to allow him to enter. She followed him into the parlor. "Have a seat."

He obliged, slowly sitting down on the nearest sofa. Although his carriage was still ramrod straight, weariness was evident in his voice. "Good evening, daughter."

"It's getting kind of late, Dad," Delilah replied. "What brings you here?" She was at a loss for words with him, which had only happened within the last few months—the months since his altercation with Frank.

"Do I have to have a reason to see my girls?" he asked in a tone bordering on contrition. His eyes, however, still held a challenge.

"Of course not." She began straightening items around the room that didn't need straightening. "You want something to drink? Or eat?"

"I don't want anything to eat, girl." Her father patted the cushion on the sofa next to him. "I just want you to sit down here and talk to me."

Delilah's smile was tentative. "I can do that." She sat down beside her father.

"We missed you at Thanksgiving," he said.

"We haven't talked since the day of Scotty's birthday party. And we both know how that ended," she replied, managing to keep her voice firm.

Patrick sprang from the sofa. "You're not going to continue to hold that against me, are you?"

"What's changed since then?" She took deep breath. "I'm not trying to hold anything against you. But I am seeing Frank, as you know, and you need to treat him with respect."

"He confronted me!" he declared.

Delilah was still seated, but she held her father's angry gaze with one of her own. "You sound like a kid saying that, Dad, and not the mature man I know you are! He confronted you because we are dating. He wants to get to know you, Daddy. But you look at him the way you look at a panhandler: 'Get away from me, boy, you bother me.'"

"You're exaggerating," he mumbled, now pacing back and forth.

"No, I'm not. And that's what is so sad about it." She stood up and walked toward the kitchen. Her temples were beginning to throb. The day had started out so promising and fun.

"I … I just don't want to lose you." His voice cracked a little, but he quickly cleared his throat. "You're my baby girl."

She whirled around to face him. "That might be part of the reason, but it's not the main reason, and you know it. You're not being fair, Dad, and that's all there is to it. I'm not asking you to like him, but you will treat him like a human being. I'm a grown woman, and I'm going to continue to see Frank for as long as I choose, so you need to get used to it. Until then, I think you should stop dropping by to see me."

She bolted to the kitchen, only allowing the bitter, burning tears to fall once she heard the front door close.

Chapter Fifteen

The beginning of the workweek arrived. Delilah was on autopilot, performing her duties in a courteous yet detached fashion.

Vivian noticed. "What's with you, girl?"

Delilah put down the invoice she was perusing and looked up at her coworker and friend. "Hi, Vivian. Did you say something?"

Vivian crooked her index finger. "Come. Walk with me; talk with me."

They headed for the cafeteria on the lobby level of their office building. Vivian purchased a cup of hot chocolate, Delilah, nothing. Afterward, Delilah strode out of the cafeteria, and Vivian followed.

"Nothing's 'up'. I'm just tired. I'm also dealing with some issues with my dad."

"At least McDermott hasn't been here to breathe down your neck." They stopped at an area adjacent to the bank of elevators but out of the way of the other workers who were coming and going.

"Yessiree. Thank God for 'use or lose' leave. I hope he has a lot of it."

"I don't blame you. I can't help looking at him in a different way now, knowing that he's been sexually harassing you. It would bug the hell out of me," Vivian announced before blowing on and sipping the steaming liquid.

Delilah smirked. "Don't think that it doesn't. Especially when he skulks around really quiet. I turn around and there he is, watching me or standing close enough to touch me."

Vivian pretended to shiver. "Creepy."

"Very." They took the elevator up to their office. "And I still don't know what to do about it."

ANDY HAD SEVERAL WEEKS FOLLOWING Thanksgiving when his scheduled slowed dramatically and he remained home in Washington. When Twyla was away at work, he worked on fine-tuning his solo presentations, and he studied. Other times he went grocery shopping or just relaxed.

If I did all of the housework, Twyla would think I was sick or something. Mostly something, he joked one day in a text to Frank.

One evening, he prepared a spaghetti dinner for her. He met her at the door of their apartment with a glass of red wine.

"What's this?" Twyla asked with a growing smile.

Andy reached for her shoulder bag with one hand and handed her the glass of wine with the other. "Can't I give my lovely lady a glass of wine after she has had a hard day at work?"

"Sure you can." She sniffed, "Smells good in here."

"Spaghetti and Bolognese sauce. Oh, and I cleaned out the refrigerator."

"You're so romantic." She put the glass down on an end table to take off her coat, and he eagerly assisted.

"You don't know from romantic," he gaily replied, and then smacked himself in the forehead. "*Oy vey*, I sound like my Jewish grandfather on my mother's side, Joseph." They laughed until the tears ran down their cheeks. Finally, Andy managed to sputter, "Go wash your hands. I'll put the food on the table."

He placed Twyla's coat and bag on a sofa and then hurried to their small kitchen, wiping his eyes on his sleeve as he went. He washed his own hands at the sink. He was actually getting a kick out of doing some of the chores around the apartment.

I'll never enjoy cleaning the bathroom. But I don't think Tywla'll mind doing that, so long as I do some of 'em, he thought as he whistled to himself.

By the time Twyla emerged from the bathroom, Andy had the food on the table. "I'm not exactly dressed for a wine-with-dinner dinner," she remarked, looking down at her sweater and jeans.

"C'mon now, you're pulling my leg. Spaghetti is spaghetti. Dress it up with a fancy wine; dress it down with a beer." He held up her glass, saying, "Let's just say this is a 'not too fancy' wine so it'll go with what you're wearing." He shook his head when he noticed her struggling to keep from laughing.

"Yes, crazy man, I *am* pulling your leg." She grabbed his free hand and pulled him close. "Thank you so much for this."

Andy pulled Twyla's chair out for her, and they sat down at the table. He had prepared spaghetti, tossed salad, and Italian bread.

"You know, more and more lately, I've been hearing the Jewish side of you coming out," Twyla remarked as they ate.

He smiled in that lopsided way of his. "Really? Maybe I'm channeling my grandparents. Can you channel people if they're still alive? I don't know," he replied, answering his own question.

"You are a nut," Twyla laughed, "but this salad is delicious!"

"Thanks." For a few moments, Andy stared into the flames of the candles he had lit before they sat down. "You know, baby, it's funny that you mention that, because I've been studying Judaism for a little while now."

Her eyes widened. "Wow, Andy, I didn't know that."

"Yeah, I know. I've been doing it while I've been on travel. And I've done some studying since I've been home this week. No one knows about it except Frank. I told him to keep quiet about it. He slipped that one time a few months back when we had dinner together, but you didn't catch it. I wasn't going to mention it until I really had a handle on it. It's kind of difficult, doing it on the fly." He ate a forkful of spaghetti before he continued speaking.

"You already know that my mom's Jewish and my dad's Catholic. They met at UC Berkley back in the early 70s. Both of them are from fairly religious backgrounds, but when they were in college, they discovered how liberating it was to dabble in other religions or none at all.

"When they got married, they talked about it—their different backgrounds." Andy laughed. "Actually, they *debated* about it because my mother's from Brooklyn and my father's from Lynn, Massachusetts. As you know, they've got their share of opinions, coming from highly opinionated backgrounds. But they're pretty liberal. When I was born, they decided to raise me as what I call a 'relaxed Catholic.'"

This time, Twyla raised one eyebrow. "I never heard it put that way before."

"That's because I made it up. We went to Mass and things, but my father didn't drill it into my head, nor did he prohibit my mom from talking about her heritage when she placed a menorah on the mantle during the holiday season when I was growing up."

"I guess that's why they didn't bat an eye when you introduced me to them."

"Probably." Andy took a swallow of wine. "They couldn't help but love you the moment they laid their eyes on you—like I did."

"Now I hear the Irish side: you've got the gift of blarney, as they say," she deadpanned.

"Okay, Miss Jokey. That means you've got to kiss me, because I'm Irish—at least part of me is," he replied with a wink.

She did so and without protest.

DECEMBER ROLLED ALONG, WITH BOTH Frank and Delilah avoiding the C word: Christmas. What the devil were they going to do about that holiday?

Both Frank and Andy had a joint presentation in Eugene, Oregon, for three days earlier in the month. Afterward, Frank had one in Newark, New Jersey, for two days, and after that, he would be off until New Year's.

In the evenings while in Oregon, both Frank and Andy scoured the malls and shops for gifts for Delilah and Twyla. Frank found what he wanted and placed it in the bag that held his laptop. He always carried his laptop on board aircraft with him, so he was sure that it would neither get lost nor stolen.

Finally, Frank took the bull by the horns. "What are your plans for Christmas, Delilah?" It was December 20. His presentation had ended the day before, and he would be leaving for the airport soon.

"I don't know," Delilah replied. "I want to spend it with you. The last time I spoke with my daddy, it ended up in a stalemate. We still didn't solve anything."

He was looking out the window of his hotel room at the multitude of roofs of other hotel buildings. It did not have the best views nor give anything near the best hotel service, so he was more than ready to leave the place.

Watching the local weather reports earlier, Frank had been filled with a sense of dread. Vicious snowstorms were systematically paralyzing various regions of the country. Normally he would not have agreed to speak at an engagement that close to the holidays, but they wanted him there and he wanted to pack in as many speaking engagements as he could before the end of the year.

The call-waiting notification beeped as Delilah was speaking. He glanced at the screen on his phone: Southwest Airlines. He already knew what *that* meant. "Hold on, baby. My other line's ringing, and it's the airline."

Frank clicked over and listened, his heart sinking, while the recording notified him of his flight's cancellation. He clicked back over to Delilah's line. "Well, I won't be going anywhere anytime soon."

Her soft Georgia drawl almost felt as if she had reached out and touched him when she replied, "*Oh no!* Your flight was cancelled?"

"My flight was cancelled. I figured it would be, judging by what's going on outside my window." Fat, heavy snowflakes were rapidly amassing on the streets below and had been for most of the morning and part of the previous night. All of the crack-of-dawn flights had been snatched up when Frank inquired earlier, in anticipation of the impending snowstorm. "I should've flown out on the last thing smokin' last night."

"That's a shame. So what are you going to do?"

Frank tore his eyes away from the window. He picked up the remote control from the bedside table and turned on the television. He swore to himself as he attempted in vain to turn up the volume a little. *Damn raggedy old hotel remotes never worked right!* "They could at least have a flat screen in this rat trap," he muttered.

Aloud, he asked, "What *can* I do? I'll just have to wait it out."

"Poor baby."

"Don't worry about it." He folded himself into the chaise lounge adjacent to the bed, thoroughly checking first for any creeping inhabitants. "Anyway, don't change the subject. I want you to spend Christmas with your family."

There was silence on the other end and then, "But my father—"

"But nothing." He softened his tone. "Listen, your family consists of more than just your father. How do you think your mother feels? It's like

159

you're holding it against her too. Guilt by association. And Clementine's cool, but I'm sure she's feeling the same way. Neither one of them will ever tell you, though. I know that too."

"Do you now?" Delilah asked.

"Yep. I'm a pretty good judge of character." He yawned. "Hell, I could've slept in."

"Ha! You?"

"I could have tried," he replied. "I would have tried, if you were here."

"Honey, I miss you."

"I miss you too." Frank clicked the remote to another local news channel. He was sure they would be monopolizing the airwaves reporting about the snowstorm, standing outside in it, as if he and the other viewers couldn't look out their own windows and see it for themselves. He never could understand the logic in that. "But do what I say, okay? Your mother's a nice lady."

He heard her sigh. "I know."

"C'mon, now. I'll see you during the holiday, just not for Christmas dinner. Now get off the phone before your boss hears you."

She chuckled. "I'm in the lady's room where he can't hear me, but you're right. I'll talk to you later."

"Bet on it, baby."

He clicked off and settled in for a day's worth of weather and financial reports.

THE NORTHEAST WAS PUMMELED WITH over two feet of snow in two days. Frank nearly went berserk, having to continue lodging in a lousy hotel with even lousier food, while most of New Jersey as well as neighboring states dug themselves out. He spent an additional two days there while the airlines took care of the passengers stranded in the airports from numerous cancelled flights. He was so bored that he was tempted to help the hotel staff clear the parking lots and sidewalks. Besides watching the news and weather reports, he worked out at the hotel's fitness center, its one saving grace.

Finally, he could not stand it any longer and decided to incur the possible wrath of Southwest Airlines and the extra expense from Avis by driving his rental car to DC instead of returning it to the agency in New Jersey. It would probably cost as much as his flight had in the first place.

"I should've just driven my own car here," Frank muttered later as he sloshed his way through the city streets of New Jersey, toward the interstate. Snow was piled everywhere and a lot of it was already dirty, but at least the main arteries were clear. Buses lumbered past him, throwing clods of heavy, dirty wet snow onto his windshield.

"Dammit, just let me get the hell out of this city!" he roared. It was Christmas Eve, and he wouldn't get to see Delilah until the day after Christmas, but he was determined to see her during the holiday. Once on the road, he noticed that his cell phone wasn't working. *I'm batting a thousand this week*, he thought. Well, it couldn't be helped. At least he was on the same side of the country as she was and not stuck in the middle of nowhere or on the West Coast. The thought warmed him a little.

Once he arrived back in DC, hours later, Frank stopped long enough to drop the rental car off at its sister location and then browbeat a lazy cab driver he saw sitting on the side of the road into taking him home. Once home, he took a shower and packed a bag with a few pair of jeans and other clothes. Frank had planned to book a connecting flight to Savannah but once he began hearing a lot of ominous-sounding forecasts earlier in the week, he figured he would have better chances getting to DC first and trying to find a flight to Georgia later. It was not to be. Due to the holidays and the back up from the snowstorm, there still weren't any flights available.

Frank called both Delilah's cell and home phone numbers using his landline. When he got no answer on either, he left a voice mail on her cell phone: "I'm on my way to you, baby." He only meant to take a quick nap before driving to Georgia, but when he awoke, it was nearly seven pm on Christmas night.

Frank left the warmth of his condo and strode through the parking lot. With a broom, he cleaned off the snow and ice that remained on his parked car in order to retrieve the shovel he carried in his trunk during the winter months. Once Frank was able to start his car, he threw the broom in the trunk. While it warmed up, he used the shovel to clear the now icy and hard-packed snow from the front and sides of his vehicle.

Once on the road, he encountered cold rain but otherwise no other precipitation as he drove nonstop the ten hours to Savannah, Georgia.

It was a quarter to five the next morning when Frank arrived at Delilah's house and rang the doorbell. After several more rings and now chilled to the bone, he noticed a light illuminate the room beyond her bedroom draperies, and soon after, he heard the clatter of her footfall on the wooden floor of the foyer.

"Who is it?" was her muffled question.

"Baby, it's cold outside," he sang.

Delilah threw the door open. "What the—Frank, what are you doing here?"

"You didn't think I was going to spend the holidays with you here and me in DC, did you? I told you I'd be here but not for dinner. You ought to know that I wouldn't let a little thing like cancelled flights or snow stop me. Besides, the highways up north are clear now. I called you before I left DC. I guess you were at your parents' house then." Frank knew he probably looked as blurry-eyed and rumpled as he felt, but none of it mattered right then. And he *knew* it didn't matter by the way she flung herself into his arms.

"Hold on, baby," he replied, his mouth against hers, "I don't want you to catch cold."

Frank ushered her inside and then grabbed his bag and dropped it at the door. He shut the door quickly with one hand and pulled her to him with the other. "Now, come here."

They stood in the foyer, his wool jacket and her robe wrapped around them both. His hands were tangled in her hair; her hands clutched the back of his shoulders. Their mouths spoke a language that words could not.

"Merry Christmas," Frank managed to get out as he attempted to recover his breath and his voice.

"Merry Christmas," Delilah echoed, her arms still around him. "I never got your message. Well, it is Christmas. The cell phone towers are probably really busy. I'll probably get it tomorrow. I called you on your cell phone, but I didn't get an answer either. Clemmie and Scott send their love. I can't believe it! I'm so glad you're here! Let's go upstairs. Hey, are you hungry, honey?"

"I'll show you how hungry." He grabbed her hand, and they took the stairs two at a time.

Although he was dead tired, Frank found renewed strength as they undressed each other and he made love to her. Delilah turned out the lamp, and they rediscovered one another in the darkness before the dawn.

Just as dawn began to break, bodies entwined, they fell asleep.

Delilah awoke, with the heat from Frank's body a human blanket seeping into her. The way he slept was eerie, so quiet that she was tempted to place a mirror underneath his nose to see if he was still breathing. But his chest rose and fell against hers, and she knew that it was just his way.

She unwound herself, slowly extricating herself from underneath him. She threw on her robe and slippers and tip-toed to the master bathroom. Afterward, she headed toward the bedroom door.

"Where are you going?" Frank's voice rumbled.

Her heart actually skipped a beat. "You must be part owl. Go back to sleep. I was about to fix us some breakfast."

"Later, baby." He beckoned to her. The rumpled bedclothes fell away to reveal his slim waist in the daylight streaming between the draperies and across his torso. "I just want to lie here with you."

Delilah obliged, feeling that ever-growing excitement she felt whenever she was near him. She shrugged off her robe and climbed back in bed beside him.

Frank turned on his side, to face her. "That's better."

"Aren't you tired?" She stroked his face.

"I'll live." He kissed her hand. "Wait here. I have something for you." He emerged from the bed stark naked and strolled downstairs. He returned a few minutes later, with his hands behind his back. Delilah turned on the bedside lamp, drinking him in with her eyes. "Oh my," she murmured.

He held out his hands with a flourish. In them, he held a small, slender white box. "I didn't have a chance to wrap it. I thought I would be on a plane, and you know they don't want you bringing anything that's wrapped—"

"Oh, Frank." In the box was a slim gold necklace with a heart-shaped emerald in the center of it. "It's so beautiful."

"It's the closest thing I could find to match the color of your eyes."

"You are so romantic! Here, sweetie, help me with the clasp."

Frank shook his head as he fumbled with it. "Not really. I just say what I feel. You make it easy."

Delilah let down her hair and allowed him a full gaze. She felt her face grow warm as he did so slowly. "Do you like it?"

"Yes." He was gazing unabashedly at her unclothed bosom where the emerald rested.

"I have a gift for you too." She bounded from the bed, snatching up her robe and wrapping herself within it as Frank emitted a knowing chuckle. She definitely had the modesty and manners of a southern lady, along with sweet yet sexy ways. To him, it made for an exciting combination.

Downstairs in the parlor on a table stood a small but beautifully decorated Christmas tree, its fragrance enveloping the room, evoking childhood memories for Delilah every time she entered it. "I'm not a child anymore," she said to herself as she picked up the only wrapped present left underneath it.

Back upstairs, she returned to the bed where Frank still lay, watching her approach with a smile. She was finally getting used to Frank's bold admiration of her body. But he liked her even more in her velour robe and pajamas, with her hair mussed. "Because I get to take them off you," he never failed to reply. She tightened the sash around her waist. He made her tingle the way he looked at her.

"You don't have to do that," he announced, his voice firm but quiet. "You have nothing to be self-conscious about. I love looking at you."

"Thank you, sir." She smiled. "I have something for you." Delilah pulled a small box out of the pocket of her robe. It was wrapped in a beautiful blue foil, with a tiny white bow on top. "For you, sweetie. Merry Christmas."

Frank accepted the box with one hand, pulling her down to his side with the other.

Delilah sat and watched as Frank tore open the wrapping. Inside was a pair of square blue-and-sterling-silver cuff links. "I remembered that blue checkered tie you wore on the day we met—"

The area around his eyes crinkled as his smile grew wider. "That tie must've made a big impression."

"The man wearing it made a big impression." Her heart swelled with the love she felt for him. "Still does."

"That's nice to know."

"Don't act like you don't." She leaned forward and kissed him lightly upon the lips.

"You're right. I won't," he replied, increasing the pressure as they slowly lay down again.

Frank and Delilah got to spend time with Scott and Clementine and even Hazel and Patrick while Frank was in town. "I don't want to disrespect the man in his own house, so I just wanted to come by to pay my respects to your mother," Frank explained out of earshot of anyone but Delilah when they stopped by the Carpenter home.

"Frank, it's so nice to see you. Merry Christmas," Hazel said, giving him a hug and kiss on the cheek. Upon hearing voices in the living room, Patrick barreled into the room and then stopped abruptly, looking uncomfortable when he saw Frank.

"Merry Christmas to you too, Mrs. Carpenter."

She smiled and Frank could clearly see aspects of both Delilah and Clementine in her speech and mannerisms. "Oh, come now. You can certainly call me Hazel."

"Okay, um … Hazel." He turned and extended a hand to Patrick. "Hello, Mr. Carpenter. Merry Christmas."

Slowly Patrick extended his and the men shook hands. "Merry Christmas, Frank."

Delilah admired both men for that. Both women exchanged hopeful glances.

"I have something for you, Hazel," Frank announced. He picked up the two boxes he had placed on the sofa earlier. "I'm not good at gift wrapping so you can thank your daughter for that part." He handed her a long flat box beautifully wrapped in red and silver paper. Inside was a silk scarf in a beautiful shade of mauve.

"Oh, it's beautiful, Frank." She held it up for Delilah and Patrick to see. "Thank you so much."

To Patrick, Frank handed a box wrapped in green Christmas wrapping paper. "For you, Patrick."

Patrick slowly unwrapped the box. In it was a book entitled *Barbecuing with Jack Daniels*. He gazed down at the book, at a loss for words, and finally up at Frank. "Thanks, Frank."

Again, Delilah and Hazel exchanged glances full of optimism. They both hoped this would be the beginning of the two men being civil to one another.

Delilah returned to the office on the Wednesday following Christmas, although Frank would not be heading back to DC until Sunday following New Year's Eve. Coming home from work late Wednesday afternoon, she found him at the house in an undershirt and jogging pants, looking sexy as usual, but something was not right.

"Hi, honey," she sang out as he headed down the stairs to meet her. When she leaned in for a kiss, Frank averted his head.

And let loose with a barrage of phlegm-wrapped coughing.

Delilah gazed at him in horror. "No!"

He waved a hand in the air. "Don't get bent out of shape, baby," he replied with a bit of effort. "Probably the flu."

"Don't tell *me* not to get bent out of shape!" she yelled. She took a deep breath when she noticed the look of disbelief on his face. She dropped her handbag and fled to the nearest bathroom.

Closing and locking the door behind her, she sat on the toilet, rocking back and forth. Sweat dampened the armpit areas beneath her coat and blouse. *Pneumonia? Not again!*

She sat on the closed toilet in the bathroom, staring at the small blue-and-white floor tiles, until she heard a faint tapping on the door. "Are you all right?" Frank asked.

She rose, unlocked the door, and then sat down again. "I'm sorry, Frank. I didn't mean to snap at you."

"You've been stressed out … this situation with your father … and your job …"

"I'll admit, they haven't helped, but that's not why I jumped down your throat." She fingered the emerald necklace around her neck.

"Then what is it?" Frank coughed and sat on the rim of the tub next to her.

"You." Delilah looked at him amid the tears gathering in her eyes. "I don't know if I can handle you being sick again."

"You mean my coughing? Ah, you know, it's the change of weather and all of the running around that I do."

She stared at him silently and crossed her arms against her chest.

"All right, it could be more than that." He shrugged. "What can I say? I've got a history of smoking. I'm liable to always be catching any respiratory ailment that comes down the pike." He coughed again. "Hell, you knew that I smoked when you met me. Even though I've stopped, that doesn't eliminate all risk."

Delilah wiped her eyes, sniffed, and still said nothing. She felt ashamed of herself at being so selfish. It was as he said: he couldn't help being sick. At least he did stop smoking. She wasn't helping, freaking out at his time of need.

Frank stood up. "I'll be in the bedroom," he announced and left the room.

Delilah continued to sit there on the toilet, thinking for a long while. *I'm a fair-weather girlfriend. I'm fine until the chips are down, and then I fall apart.*

No, I'm not, another part of her mind protested. *I was there for him when he had pneumonia. Although I was scared out of my mind at times, I stayed with him the entire time. And as for dealing with Daddy, I've always been in Frank's corner.*

Well, racism's not Frank's fault, either, she had to admit to herself. *And he needs me again, so suck it up and deal. That is, if I want to be with him. If not, then don't.*

With that, she stood up and washed her face and hands. Then she walked to the kitchen, prepared a piece of toast, and waited for the kettle to boil for tea. Once it did, she poured the boiling water into a large mug that she had purchased the last time she visited Frank in DC, along with two teabags, a slice of lemon, and a splash of brandy. After arranging everything on a tray, she carried it upstairs to the bedroom.

Frank lay asleep in bed, his breathing labored and halting. Delilah nudged the bed, the tray in her hands, until his eyes slowly opened.

"Hey," he rasped.

"Sit up, sweetie." Her voice was soft and tender. "I've got something here that'll make you feel better."

Chapter Sixteen

Frank saw a doctor while he was in Savannah, who informed him that he had an acute respiratory infection.

"Oh, Dr. Stewart's going to love seeing this in my record," Frank mumbled.

Dr. Levinson turned from the sink where he was washing his hands. "Dr. Stewart? His name wouldn't happen to be Gary Stewart, would it?"

Frank pulled the sweatshirt over his head and put on his reading glasses. "Huh? Yeah, I think that's his first name. You know him?"

"I think so. We were both interns at Byrn Mawr Hospital in Philadelphia. I'll have to call him sometime, relive old times." He smiled. "Small world."

"Ain't it, though?" He shrugged on his jacket. "Take it easy, Doc."

Dr. Levinson told him the same thing that Dr. Stewart told him when he had pneumonia: He needed to rest and not work so hard. He also wanted Frank to go see Dr. Stewart for further tests and follow-up when he returned home to Washington, DC.

Frank returned to Delilah's just as she was arriving home from work. It was Thursday, two days before New Year's.

"Hi, honey. How are you feeling?" she asked as they stepped inside. "What did the doctor say?"

"That I have a respiratory infection. That I need to rest more. That I need a lot more lovin'." He pushed her gently toward the parlor. Once there, he pulled the handbag from her grip and the coat she wore from her shoulders.

"Did he now?" Delilah's eyes widened.

"Not quite. I did." He could hardly get his jacket off fast enough. It was still somewhat difficult for him to breathe, but at the moment, desire overrode that bit of discomfort. He held her tight. "I'll restrain myself from kissing you, but we at least we can snuggle a little bit. But I think I'll sleep in your spare bedroom for the duration."

"Is it catching?" she asked.

He urged her onto a nearby sofa and then sat next to her. "It is, but I'll be a perfect gentleman, like when we first started dating." He attempted to give her an innocent smile, without success, and they laughed. "Well, I'll try to be one."

FRANK AND DELILAH RANG IN the New Year with sparkling cider since he was still taking medication.

"Happy New Year," they whispered to each other in a toast in Delilah's bed, enjoying their own private celebration.

MEANWHILE, IN DC AND THE surrounding environs, Andy's and Twyla's plates were full. They attended a holiday party given for Twyla and the other school bus drivers at a local hotel. Several days later, they drove up to Philadelphia and partied with Twyla's mother ZiZi and some of their other relatives. They gave ZiZi a beautiful African wood carving that Andy had found while on his travels and hammered silver earrings that Twyla had purchased for her. For her grandfather, they presented a sporty fedora to add to his ever-growing collection. Then they all got to talk to Twyla's brother, Tyler, for a few precious minutes on the telephone. He was unable to come home for Christmas due to the recent hostilities between North and South Korea.

Andy had a new male second cousin who had been born at the end of November. He and Twyla took their holiday visit to his parents as an opportunity to zip over to Brooklyn, where some of his mother's siblings still lived, with a gift for the new arrival.

"It is very commendable of you, Andrew, to want to learn more about your Jewish heritage," his grandfather Joseph remarked. "With you studying Judaism, and my new grandson being given the name of Joseph, after me, this is a very proud moment for me."

Other family members gasped and a few applauded a little upon hearing the news. Andy's mother, Teresa, turned to him, surprise evident in her eyes. "You've been studying Judaism? Oh, Andy!"

"That *is* commendable," his father, Sean, agreed. "Why didn't you tell us?"

"I thought I'd let Grandpa Joe make the announcement," Andy replied, feeling a bit shy as all eyes were now upon him. "Anyway, I didn't want to step on Little Joe's toes."

Everyone laughed. "Don't be silly," Baby Joseph's mother and his cousin, Liza, replied. She grabbed his face and kissed his cheek. "It's wonderful news, although we are not in any way attempting to disparage Christianity or any other religions by any means."

"No offense taken," both Andy's father and Twyla replied as they smiled at each other.

"Not in this family," Andy added. "We've got our own United Nations."

They spent Christmas Day in South Boston with Andy's parents and actually attended Christmas Eve Mass with them. As for accommodations, Twyla slept in the Maxwell's guest room and Andy slept in the family room in the basement. Although they weren't the most religious parents, Andy respected the rule he had grown up abiding—no unmarried couples sleeping together under their roof. He and Twyla had long gotten used to it, which was why they usually stayed at a nearby hotel or motel.

They were snowed in for a day by the same storm that had affected Frank in New Jersey. "I'd like to kiss the man who invented the snow blower," Andy remarked when his father emerged from the garage with his in tow. Mercifully, the snow had finally stopped falling.

"How do you know it wasn't a woman?" Twyla demanded good-naturedly.

To that, Andy shrugged. "Could've been." He rubbed his hands together. He loved anything with an engine. "Let me at it!"

They returned to DC by train two days after Christmas. Twyla set about unpacking their bags, placing their dirty clothes in a laundry bag for the wash the next day. Andy hung their coats in the hall closet and then stood at the bedroom doorway, watching her.

When Twyla finished, Andy placed their luggage in the hall closet as well. Upon returning to the bedroom, he took her hand as she was about to walk past him. He sat her down on the bed. When he was sure he had her attention, he said, "Twyla."

Then he slowly lowered himself to one knee.

"I know I've already said this to you before, but I'm going to do it again. Lately, I've been doing a lot of thinking. I know you may be thinking, 'Yeah, right, Mr. Deep Thinker. The deepest thinking you ever do is decide whether to go to the gym or not.'" He grinned. "But I have my moments."

Twyla nodded with a smile but remained silent.

"And this is one of them. Twyla, I've got to have you. Not just live with you; that's not enough for me anymore. I'm not trying to sound corny or anything—I'm just trying to give it to you straight. And I don't mean in a possessive way, although it might sound that way." He exhaled. "You are my soul mate, baby, is what I mean, and I want you with me on this journey. As my wife. Twyla Maxwell, Twyla Hayes-Maxwell, whatever you want. I just want you to be my wife. Four years plus of you being my girl isn't enough. Hell, this is sounding more like an ultimatum and—"

"Yes, Andy."

"Because I know that you're an independent woman—what did you say?"

"I said, 'Yes, Andy.'"

Andy let out a whoop. "You have the ring I gave you the last time, but we can change it, if you want."

She sat there, as calm as a Sunday morning. "It's perfect just as it is, baby."

He rose and stood before her. He pulled her to her feet, throwing his arms around her and kissing her. He felt unshed tears sting his eyes. "Thank you."

Twyla wiped a tear that escaped and was now rolling down his cheek as well as those staining her own. "No need to thank me, baby. I love you. I guess I never really looked at it from your perspective. I am now."

JANUARY'S ARRIVAL SIGNALED BACK TO work and more hopscotching around the country for both Frank and Andy. They both spoke at a conference in Great Falls, Montana. "I just hope we don't get snowed in up here," Frank remarked. They were working out at the hotel's fitness center after the second day of the conference. It was an impressive, state-of-the-art facility. It had to be, since the town wasn't exactly Times Square.

"So, how were your holidays?" he asked Andy as he put the finishing touches on two hundred push-ups.

"Oh, the usual. Nothing special," Andy puffed as he ran on a treadmill several yards away. "By the way, Twyla and I are engaged."

Frank almost fell on his face when he realized what he had just heard. "I can't believe it! She finally said yes?" He sprang to his feet. "Hey, congrats, man!"

"You don't have to put it that way," Andy replied with a laugh. "Seriously though, I'd like you to be my best man. It's going to be soon too. I'll let you know when to clear your calendar."

"How do you know that?" Frank sidestepped out of the path of a woman on her way to the shelves where the free weights were located. "Twyla's going to need time to plan it."

"Nope." As the treadmill slowed to a stop, Andy stepped down to the floor. Wiping his face with a towel, he walked over to his friend. "We're doing the justice of the peace thang."

"What?" Frank couldn't believe his ears. "Are you serious? And she's going to stand for that?"

"She's the one who suggested it." Andy laughed. "Hell, it would take forever for us to figure out what type of ceremony to have: Jewish, Catholic, or good ole Southern Baptist."

Frank joined him in the laughter as he slapped his friend on the back. "I forgot about that. I guess you two better get married at the courthouse. And you know I'd be honored to be your best man."

Chapter Seventeen

Delilah could not get Frank's suggestion that she move in with him out of her mind. It had been many weeks since he made it, and they hadn't spoken of it since that time. She knew why she was torn, however. Despite her love for him, she could not live with him or any man without being married.

Delilah was at home one rare snowy evening watching an old movie on television when her phone rang. It was Twyla.

"Hey, Twyla. How are you?" she asked, grasping a handful of popcorn from the plastic bowl she held in her lap.

Twyla, usually the epitome of steadfastness, was incomprehensible: "Married …!"

"I didn't understand you. What did you say?"

"Andy and I are getting married!"

Delilah sat upright, spilling the contents of the bowl onto the area rug. "Darn it! Oops, I'm sorry, Twyla—I just dropped a bowl on the floor. Oh my goodness! Congratulations! When did this happen?"

"Two days ago. I had to swear Frank to secrecy, because I wanted to tell you myself. You think women gossip? Humph."

"You're right about that," Delilah said with a laugh as she picked up the debris. "So, what made you accept this time, when you didn't last time?"

Twyla was quiet for a moment. "It was a feeling I got from him. Andy's a great guy as you know, but I wanted him to understand where I was coming from. I'm looking at it from an African American perspective. We both know that Andy takes most things lightly but this isn't a game for me. I think he really understands that now."

"I'm glad." They were a beautiful couple in Delilah's eyes. She rose and took the mess she cleaned up to the kitchen. "So, have you started looking for a dress? When—?"

"Presidents' Day."

"Great. Next year?"

"Next month," Twyla replied.

Delilah took the phone from her ear and just stared at it.

"Are you still there, Dee?"

"Uh, y-yes, I'm still here. *Next month?* How in the world—? Let me guess, you're eloping, right?" She washed and dried the few dishes she had used for dinner and her TV-watching snack.

"No, girl, we're going to the courthouse. My mom's going to be my best woman, and I wanted to make sure that you were there too. That's why we're doing it on a holiday. Just a few family and friends. We'll have a reception later and invite everybody."

"I'm really touched, Twyla, that you want me to be there."

"Hey, you're my friend, and I know you understand and relate. You're going through the same thing with Frank."

"You're right." Delilah returned to her comfy sofa. She found herself superimposing Fred Astaire and Ginger Rogers in the movie classic she had been watching, *Top Hat*, with Twyla's and Andy's faces. She knew exactly what her friend was talking about, but from the flip side. Neither they, nor Frank and her, would have been allowed to dance cheek to cheek back in the thirties.

Or the forties or the fifties.

Although legal, among some people, it was barely accepted in the twenty-first century.

"I hope you didn't have anything planned."

"As a matter of fact, I do," Delilah replied.

"Oh no! What's that?" Twyla sounded concerned.

Delilah took a sip of her soda and smiled. "I'm going to a wedding."

THE NEXT MONTH WAS A busy time for Frank and Delilah and for Twyla and Andy. Bad weather was occurring around most of the country and wreaked havoc with both couples' schedules.

Frank and Delilah had to make do with phone calls, e-mails, texting, and webcams.

A bouquet of flowers arrived at her office on Valentine's Day.

"You got a special delivery, Dee," John, a coworker of hers said, a crystal vase of flowers in tow. "You weren't at your desk, so I signed for them for you."

"Oh, thank you, Johnny. Ooh, they're so pretty!"

The eyes of Agnes Wylie peered around the side of the cubicle.

Nosy! Aloud, Delilah joked, "Do I need to give you a tip?"

The younger man nearly blushed. "Naw, that's okay. Happy Valentine's Day."

Delilah glanced over her shoulder with a dismissive air and then took the vase of pale pink roses and tulips over to her desk. She set them down and pulled the card from the tiny envelope, which read,

Counting the days until I see you again. Happy Valentine's Day.
Love,
Frank

"So am I," she murmured.

She called Frank later, on her way home from work. She had purposely left the bouquet at work, without the card of course. Since Delilah now knew that Mr. McDermott wanted to sleep with her, she wanted them to serve as a damper—like wet leaves kicked onto a smoldering campfire. Nip it in the bud. Now.

"Hi, baby." His smooth, dark-chocolate voice came on the line.

"I got your beautiful flowers. Happy Valentine's Day. Did you get my card, honey?"

"Yes, I did."

"Good. But soon I'll be there in person. I'll catch a flight right after work that Friday evening and return home on Tuesday."

"I'll make the arrangements. And I'll let you know what time I'll be at the airport to pick you up."

Despite the chill in the car, she felt his warmth touch her. "I can't wait. Hey, what do you think I should wear to the wedding?"

"Something courthouse-like. Then put your hair up, pick up some cheap eyeglasses from the drugstore, and wear a trench coat. Mmm ..."

"Frank!" she giggled as she wound her way through rush-hour traffic. "Never mind, I'll figure it out."

"Sure you will," he replied with a sexy chuckle.

DELILAH PULLED THE WINTER-WHITE KNIT cap down on her red-blonde curls and buttoned her matching coat all the way up before she pulled her small bag down from the overhead compartment. Then she headed quickly up the aisle toward the plane's exit. She was becoming quite the seasoned traveler, adjusting to the climate changes between Savannah, Georgia, and Washington, DC. This year, she noticed with dismay that the weather at both locations was a lot more alike than different.

A cold wind managed to creep down the upturned collar of Delilah's long wool coat.

"You look like a snow bunny in all that white," Frank remarked, taking her bag as she stepped out of the terminal.

"*Winter white*, sweetie," she corrected as he placed her bag into the trunk of his car. "No white after Labor Day."

"Oh, excuse me," he kidded, enveloping her in a quick hug before spiriting her inside.

"Unless you're a bride," she replied.

They crawled past the taxicabs, shuttle buses, and pedestrians and out of the terminal area and onto Interstate 295 toward the outskirts of Washington, DC. She saw him glance over at her in the darkness of the car interior and smiled to herself. She was excited to see Frank and to attend their friends' wedding.

"Do you want to stop for something to eat?" he asked when they were halfway to his place.

"No, I'm fine." She squeezed his hand. She just wanted to get to the condo.

Once safely ensconced upstairs in his condo, he dropped her bag, and she turned to him. Wrapping her arms around his neck, Delilah pressed her lips to his.

"Well, hello to you too." Frank pulled the cap from her hair and ran his hands through her tousled curls. He kissed her neck. "You know, my bed feels twice as large and twice as empty when you're gone."

She slid her hands underneath his sweatshirt and played with the hairs on his chest. "It does?"

"Um-hmm. I don't understand it. I used to love lying in my king-sized bed, whether I was alone or not, enjoying the space. Now all I think about is you being there with me, lying next to me, making love to me." Frank suppressed a groan. "I tell you, girl, what you do to me …"

She nibbled on his ear. "What do I do?"

"Drive me crazy, baby." He unbuttoned the buttons of her coat, fumbling in his attempt to remove it as swiftly as he could.

Delilah smiled at his unusual clumsiness. Without a word, she took him by the hand, and they headed for his bedroom.

They both awoke the next morning within minutes of each other. Delilah laughed, her voice soft in the early morning quiet, her body still tired from last night's lovemaking. "I finally managed to wake up the same time as you."

"I'm getting old, I guess." He pulled her to him for a languorous kiss. "I need fuel if I'm going to keep up with you this weekend."

She laughed again. "You're right about that."

Frank's suit was already pressed, but he put the finishing touches on the shirt he was going to wear to the courthouse on Monday. "I can press what you're going to wear too, baby," he volunteered later that afternoon.

"That's sweet, but you don't have to do that. Just leave the ironing board up, and I'll handle it."

"Okay." He hung the shirt on a hanger and placed it beside the suit inside his ultra-organized closet. "I've got some errands to run, and I want to check on Andy. You need anything?"

She shook her head. "No, thanks. I want to take care of this now. And since Twyla's mama is coming down to help her—as well as her soon-to-be mother-in-law—she probably doesn't need a lot of women buzzing around, making her nervous."

He walked over and gave her a kiss and a squeeze. "I doubt if she'd think you were in the way but okay. See you later." With that, he left.

Frank ran a few last-minute errands and then headed over to Ozzie's house where Andy was spending his last days as a bachelor. Twyla and her mother, ZiZi, were sequestered at the couple's apartment.

"What's up, Andy?" Frank asked as he opened the door.

"Nothing, man."

He looked around as they headed into the small kitchen, where Andy had been sitting at the kitchen table, drinking a glass of water. "Where's Ozzie?"

"He had to work today. He'll be back later." He took a drink.

Frank took a look in the refrigerator. "Hey, you want me to order a pizza or something?"

Andy shook his head. "I wouldn't be able to eat it."

Frank took a closer look at his friend. He looked a little tense, which meant he was a lot tense because Andy was an easygoing guy. "Look, knucklehead, you can't last two days without food. You might pass out on Monday."

"All right, bro. I'll eat some cereal or something later."

"Yep, that's good. A good recipe for upchucking." He clasped Andy on the shoulder. "You need anything?"

"What time is it?"

Frank laughed. "You've got your watch on."

"Oh yeah." He didn't look at it, though.

You need anything?"

"Naw, I'm okay."

"You gonna get a haircut?"

At that, Andy smiled, looking like his normal, relaxed self. "Are you kidding? It's what Twyla loves most about me, man. That would be like Samson chopping his hair off."

They laughed. Frank was glad he could do something to help his friend relax. "Okay, okay." He held up his hands. "Just a suggestion."

"Well, I might have Ozzie trim it a little later on tonight." He took another drink. "You've got the ring, right?"

"Yep. It's back at my place and trust me, if I even *think* about forgetting it, Delilah will remind me." He sat down at the table opposite his friend.

Chuckling, Andy replied, "You're right. Women don't forget those kinds of things."

"No, they don't."

MONDAY, THE DAY OF THE wedding, arrived. There was no sign of rain or frozen precipitation, to which all who came to witness the marriage of Andrew Sean Maxwell to Twyla Louise Hayes were grateful.

Andy was rock-star handsome, in a gray pinstripe suit, his shaggy, dirty-blond hair just touching the open collar of his white shirt.

Twyla was a serene vision in a lacy, white dress that just reached the top of her knees. Her jazzy, white headdress was a gift from ZiZi. The sterling-silver necklace and blue pendant were given to her by Delilah. Her soon-to-be mother-in-law, Teresa, contributed an old pale-pink lace handkerchief, and her soon-to-be father-in-law, Sean, tucked a tiny book of Irish poetry into her small clutch bag.

"It classifies as 'borrowed,' doesn't it?" he had announced earlier to his wife and ZiZi, who both responded with bemused shrugs.

Delilah watched as the ceremony began, hardly breathing as the Clerk of the Court spoke. "Now the couple wants to say a few words to each other."

Andy said, "Although this is a civil ceremony, Twyla and I wanted to personalize it a little bit. We wanted to write our own vows. Believe it or not, I couldn't think of a thing to say."

Everyone at the small gathering laughed. He continued. "So we're going to do this thing freestyle."

"What's 'freestyle'?" Andy's mother, Teresa, asked her husband, Sean.

"They're going to wing it," Ozzie said.

Andy took a deep breath. "You ready, baby? I'll go first. Usually only once in a lifetime do we find the one we were meant to spend our lives with. You are that one for me, Twyla." He lifted Twyla's hand to his lips and kissed it as he gazed into her eyes. "I can't even express to you how much I love you. I promise you that I'll spend the rest of my life trying."

After a moment, Twyla said, "Amazing, isn't it—that out of the billions on this planet, we manage to find that one person perfect for us. You are that one for me, Andy." She lifted the small veil for a moment to carefully dab at her eyes with a white lace handkerchief.

Andy went on. "Some spend their entire life searching. I am so glad that I had the sense to know when the search was over. Divine intervention stepped in and said, 'You'll never find another woman that complements your life the way she does.' You tell me when I'm being stupid—but with love. You fulfill me in every way, and I'll try my best to fulfill your every wish, until the end of my days. I love you, Twyla, my wife."

Twyla laughed as she said, "Andy, God truly had a sense of humor when he created you, but in a good way. He whispered to me, 'Twyla, you need a man to add a bit of whimsy to your seriousness and to help you squeeze all of the joy and laughter out of life.' And so he sent me you. I love you, Andy, my husband."

Their words were spoken with such heartfelt emotion that just about everyone in the small group was crying. Delilah watched Frank, exuding a chairman-of-the-board air in his dark-blue suit and blue-and-silver-checkered silk tie as he handed Andy the rings. She blushed as she realized it was the same suit and tie that he wore when they first met at the conference nearly one year ago. Romantic symbolism perfumed the air so thickly that she felt light-headed for a moment.

As the couple kissed, Delilah had the sensation of being watched.

She was being watched. By Frank. His gaze traveled from Andy and Twyla to her.

They gazed at each other with longing. Both felt the forceful tide of their friends' emotions, as well as their own, wash over them.

Then, as if magnets, their gazes returned to the still-kissing couple and those gathered around them clapping. They all followed the couple outside.

They had enough time for Andy's father, Sean, to pop open a bottle of champagne. He managed to sprint to his parked car, bringing back with him a basket, which he had forgotten earlier, containing champagne glasses to toast the couple.

"Dad!" Andy hissed as he glanced around. They were all standing, windblown, on the courthouse steps. "You're going to get us arrested for public intoxication or something!"

"One toast does not public intoxication make!" his father replied as he quickly gave everyone a delicate champagne glass.

Both Frank and Ozzie burst out laughing. The women tittered but looked around as well.

Sean held up his glass. "May the wind always be at your back, Twyla and Andy."

"And may we soon hear the pitter-patter of little feet around the house," ZiZi added.

"Amen to that!" Andy agreed, beaming at his new wife, and then drank his champagne. Afterward, he whipped out his pocket handkerchief, wrapped the glass in it, and after placing it upon the step, stomped on it.

"*Mazel tov!*" everyone cried—even those hurrying up and down the courthouse stairs as they conducted their own business.

"Get going!" Sean ordered with a wink, as he kissed his son and daughter-in-law and then hurried to clean up the glass before any police or sheriffs arrived. Delilah could clearly see where Andy had inherited his mischievous nature.

Hugs, kisses, and handshakes were exchanged in haste before the happy couple bounded down the stairs to the waiting limousine. "St. Thomas or bust!" Andy yelled just before he ducked inside, and the limo pulled away from the curb.

Delilah's eyesight blurred from tears of joy as she watched it slink away through the midday traffic. A pair of firm, warm hands clasped her shoulders.

"Are you okay?" Frank whispered against her ear.

She held her hands against her dress, to prevent the front of it from blowing upward in the blustery breeze. She nodded, without speaking.

"My little sister and my knucklehead brother." Frank's voice sounded small in the wind. The love and pride he felt for his friends gathered in a lump at the base of his throat.

With an air of wistfulness, Delilah continued to gaze down the street even though the limo was gone.

Chapter Eighteen

They played chess on the coffee table at Frank's place, with the fireplace going and a glass of white wine for each of them. Delilah was becoming an adept player, and secretly she was proud of herself. She never thought she had the patience to learn the game; however, Frank was a thorough, straightforward teacher, entertaining her as he taught.

She watched him as he watched her contemplating her next move. She had felt strange ever since the wedding. It had been such a joyous occasion for her, yet sad as well.

"A penny for your thoughts, baby." Frank's voice broke into her reverie.

"Just thinking about Twyla and Andy." She moved a chess piece. "I wonder what they're doing right now."

He laughed. "You *know* what they're doing."

Delilah watched how the lamplight highlighted the pale golden liquid in her wineglass. How could something that came from a vine and essentially dirt could result in something so light and delicate? Life was so mysterious. The more you thought you knew about it, the more you realized how much you had yet to learn. The mere thought made her feel overwhelmed.

"Delilah."

Frank was now standing at the balcony window, watching her. *When did he get up?* she wondered. "I'm sorry, sweetie, what did you say?"

"Is something wrong?"

She shook her head. "No. I was just thinking."

"Have you thought anymore about my—suggestion?"

Maybe this is what I've been feeling strange about. I had a feeling the subject would come up on this visit. Aloud, she replied, "Yes I have. But I can't."

"Why not?" Frank returned to where he had been sitting across from her.

Delilah looked into his eyes. She could see the confusion there. "I just can't, Frank."

His eyes narrowed. "Because of my race, right? And your father—"

She sprang to her feet. "You ought to know better than that. I couldn't live with *any* man. I just wasn't raised that way. I guess I should've told you that the day you asked me."

His gaze was direct but sympathetic. "Well, why didn't you?"

She sighed. "I didn't know it at the time. I mean—I kind of knew. And my job—" She walked over to the sofa and sat down on the area rug, leaning against the sofa and staring at the nighttime view beyond the balcony windows.

Frank sat down beside her and took her hand. "I'm sorry—for bringing up the race thing. Look, I just want you to be happy."

"I know." Delilah closed her eyes. Tomorrow she would be flying back to Savannah, and she wanted their last night to be special. She concentrated on the soothing sax music in the background and tried to relax.

When she awoke a few hours later, in the wee hours of the night, she was undressed and lying in bed beside Frank. She smiled as she thought of him carrying her upstairs, like Rhett Butler did in *Gone with the Wind*, and undressing her tenderly. *Too bad I missed it*, she thought, wistfully. *Another time, I hope.* She turned onto her other side and bumped against his shoulder in the darkness.

He brought his hand backward, found hers, and grasped it as she spooned her body against his.

Then they both went back to sleep.

I CAN'T BELIEVE THAT *I asked Delilah to live with me. What an idiot! With her living in Georgia and me living here in DC, she's used to being self-sufficient. She'd have to have a job first*, Frank pondered in his office at the condo as he sweated over his tax returns. He would be speaking at a community college in Northern Virginia later in the week and figured he would get them out of the way.

He knew she wasn't happy in her job, and he wanted to take her away from that situation, but he had handled it wrong. Granted, they had known each other less than a year. But they could not deny that they already enjoyed an exciting physical relationship, and they knew they loved each other. Still, she had to do what was best for herself and no one else.

Twyla and Andy had returned to town the day before, and it was sickening to watch them. Andy was tanned, nearly Twyla's complexion, and his pale-blue eyes were ethereal whenever he gazed at or spoke of his beloved. Twyla, on the other hand, was serene and beautiful, wearing her Mona Lisa-like smile.

"I hope to hell I don't walk around looking like you two whenever I talk about Delilah," Frank remarked as he listened to his closest friends talk, albeit prudently, about their honeymoon.

They just smiled their beatific smiles at him and went on as though he had said nothing at all.

While thinking about their visit the day before, Frank almost doubled over in pain. It scared him for a few moments until he finally recognized it for what it was—pangs of jealousy.

And he felt ashamed.

Ashamed because he wanted nothing but the best for them and always had, especially since he noticed the two of them becoming closer a few years ago.

Where the hell was this coming from?

Damn.

Frank took off his glasses, rubbed his eyes, and stretched. He strode over to the windows where, unbeknownst to him, a beautiful day had unfolded.

Maybe Delilah was feeling the same way. He sure hoped not.

"Cupid oughta be shot," he mumbled as he turned away from the window and went to make himself some lunch.

Delilah began to watch Mr. McDermott when he wasn't looking. What she used to think was merely dislike or haughtiness toward her, she was now certain was more. *When had it changed?* she wondered. She did not know. Ever since she began working there, she knew Mr. McDermott to be a complex man and very difficult to decipher.

He had always given her that look of disdain whenever he glanced her way. Then, for a while, he seemed to avoid her as much as she did him. Since the delivery of Frank's flowers on Valentine's Day, his actions were less and less hidden, although to Delilah, he had never been able to disguise the most noticeable aspect of himself—the expression in his eyes. She observed one such moment when Mr. McDermott's eyes rested upon the bouquet as he placed several papers on her desk; she stood, unnoticed, across the room. Even from that distance, she observed the look of silent hatred roll across his face. It scared her.

When she returned to work after the wedding, and Mr. McDermott spoke about a project she was working on, he stood behind her chair and rested his hands upon her shoulders, kneading them with his long, bony hands. At that moment, she accidentally-on-purpose pushed her chair backward, forcing him to back up as well. Interspersed with the fear, Delilah felt a growing anger. She didn't know where to turn without possibly causing damage to her reputation if she reported him. Who would they believe?

She received a phone call shortly after arriving home from work one evening in late February. It was her mother. Since Christmas, she and her mother were talking as frequently as they used to, and she and her father had begun to talk more. "Hi, Mama. Is anything wrong?"

"No, sweetie. I just wanted you to know that I was thinking of having a little get-together for your daddy's birthday this year."

Delilah dropped her coat and bag on the nearest sofa. "That's nice, but I thought that Daddy hated surprise parties."

Hazel chuckled. "He does, but he knows about it so it won't be a surprise, now will it? Besides, one doesn't turn sixty every day."

"True," Delilah laughed. She kicked off her pumps and plopped onto the plump cushions. The weeks seemed longer and longer at work. With the tension lessening between her and her father; however, she was looking forward to it.

"You know that his birthday's March twentieth, the first day of spring, so it will be sort of a spring fling. You'll come, won't you?"

"Yes, Mama. I wouldn't miss it."

"Good." Hazel sounded relieved. "And if Frank is in town that week, please tell him that he is welcome too."

"Really?" Delilah sputtered. "By Daddy?"

There was a pause. "Well, maybe not by your father, but maybe the more exposed he is to Frank, the more he'll get used to his presence."

"Great, like being exposed to the mumps or something," Delilah murmured, feeling the heat of indignation scorch her cheeks.

"I didn't mean it like that, sweetie. I just meant—well, we've got to keep hammering at him. That is, if we want to see you."

"That's right, Mama. If *he* wants to see me."

"Hi, sweetie. How's it going?" Delilah asked after she called Frank one evening.

"The usual. Knocking them out with my usual flair," Frank answered, logging off his laptop and stowing everything in the bag he would need for the conference in the morning.

"And with your usual modesty," Delilah laughed.

Frank joined in the laughter. "True." But it wasn't entirely true. For a while that morning, his computer had behaved like a cantankerous old man. The ballroom was as frigid as a meat locker until maintenance was finally corralled and adjusted the thermostat a few degrees in the other direction. But Frank took it all in stride—the first day of a conference or seminar more often than not had a few bugs to work out. He was glad it was over, though. "How's everything with you?"

"Everything's fine. Hey, I wanted to ask you if you'll be down this way next month."

He cleared all of the items off the king-sized bed and lay upon it with a contented sigh. He was tired but pumped about the rest of the conference. "As a matter of fact, I'll be in Garden City, the twenty-second through the twenty-fifth. I'll be coming by to see you the weekend before. So you know what to do." He flicked on the television and clicked to a local news station.

"Well—" Delilah's Georgia accent was even more pronounced when she was attempting to charm her way into his good graces. He had found that out about her through the course of their dating. He did not mind. In fact, he thought it was amusing—even more amusing since he was aware of it, but she didn't know that he was. "My mama's having a birthday dinner for my daddy. It'll probably be at a nice steakhouse. It'll be that Sunday. I wanted to know if you'd like to go with me."

Frank suddenly felt cold—with dread. But he would not lie. "I'd rather not. I think you should go without me."

She was quiet for a moment. "I see."

He pulled the cover over his head as he replied, "Baby, your father can't *stand* me. I'm just putting myself in his place—the last person I'd want to see on my birthday would be someone I hate."

"But Mama *invited* you." Her voice trembled. "She said if you were going to be in town, to be sure to invite you. And the tension between you two seemed to thaw during Christmas."

Frank kicked off his shoes, pulled his feet under the covers with the rest of him, and closed his eyes. Day one of the conference in Oklahoma City was under his belt. The weather was cold, and the uncertainty of a major snowstorm hung in the air. He was hoping that it didn't get any colder and that the occasional snow flurry would hold until he got out of there on Friday. Right now, he was feeling a storm of another kind brewing. "I appreciate your mom's invitation and all that but—I'm trying to give your father a break."

"I know, Frank. But *I* want you to be there."

"Delilah, baby, it's not about us. It's your father's day."

She was silent so he went on.

"I'm still not sure how he feels about me—"

"Okay, okay. I heard you."

"C'mon, baby, don't go all cold on me now." Frank softened his tone. "Do you still want to see me that weekend?"

"What do you think?" She exhaled.

He suppressed a groan. "I don't know; you might not want me to now. C'mon now, don't get all quiet on me. Let's give the man his day. I'll see you down there on Saturday or in the evenings after the conference if you like. Whatever you want. But not at the dinner. I'm sorry, but I won't do that. Maybe one day he'll invite me, instead of your mother. I hope you understand my reasoning."

"I understand."

"Good."

He stifled a yawn. "I'm kind of tired, baby. I got in late last night. I'll call you tomorrow, all right?"

"Okay, honey. Good night."

Soon afterward, Frank fell into a difficult slumber. He knew he was right in insisting that Delilah go to her father's birthday dinner without him, but she wasn't making it easy. As far as Frank was concerned, Patrick hated his insides. Why rub salt in the wound by having him sit there at the table on his birthday? He understood her point of view too. She wanted him to be there, by her side. And he wanted to be there. But he knew best in this case.

Chapter Nineteen

Delilah swept the porch, shook out the sisal area rug, and straightened the furniture before sitting on the porch swing. As she swung back and forth, she watched the sun slowly sink into the horizon behind her neighborhood. There was a gentle breeze stirring the greenery, and every plant that held a bud was bursting out all over. She took a deep breath of it and listened to the birds settling in for the night. She was pleased with the gift she bought her father at the sporting-goods store at the mall—a beautiful new fishing rod. He had used his old one until there was practically nothing left of it. Clementine wouldn't tell her what she and Scott were giving him. But that was okay. That meant it would be a surprise to her, also.

She waved at the neighbors who called out greetings on their way into their house two doors down. She had good neighbors. Since she and Frank began dating, no racist comments had been lobbed their way. In the beginning, she had wondered, watched, and waited.

She swayed back and forth, and her head tilted back as she recalled recent events. Life was topsy-turvy in so many ways now. *When did it happen?* she wondered, her thoughts merging into one big stain, like wet paint on carpet. Her eyelids felt lead heavy, as she tried to remember when she had no worries …

"Delilah."

Her eyes fluttered open.

Frank towered over her in her semiconscious state. "Sorry. I didn't mean to scare you. Baby, you'd better watch falling asleep out here—"

"Oh, Frank. Hi. I didn't mean to." She rubbed an eye, her mind still cloudy. It was now dark, but his body was in silhouette, backlit by the street lamps throwing a wide swath of strange orange-tinged light across the road.

"Come on in the house, woman. And you need to turn your porch light on at night, if you're going to be out here."

"Yes, Daddy," she replied, following him inside.

"I'm sorry, Delilah." He turned and locked the door behind them. "I'm not trying to tell you what to do in your own house. I just worry about you. You may be down south, but crimes occur down here too."

She gazed into his eyes and smiled. "I know. And you're right."

He cupped her chin in his hand. "I love you." He kissed her with tenderness. "You look tired. I know it's early, but let's go to bed. I'll give you a massage."

She did not protest.

The next day, their moods were somber. Delilah prepared breakfast for the two of them, and they decided to go to an early church service at the mostly white Baptist church in the center of town. Neither Delilah nor Frank were regular churchgoers, but they both decided they wanted to go that Sunday morning. They got more than a few curious looks from the older parishioners, which was nothing new. The pastor's smile was indiscriminate as they took their seats.

Afterward, they changed clothes, and Delilah worked for a little while in her flower beds. Frank turned on the television and watched aimlessly. The two-ton elephant in the room was her father's birthday dinner, although neither of them spoke anymore about it.

When she emerged from the garden, she headed to the master bathroom to shower and change. It was two fifteen. She came back downstairs with her fiery curls swept up, dressed in a light-green springtime frock and sandals with a lightweight shawl around her shoulders. She snatched up the keys she had dropped on the coffee table the previous night. On her way out, she glanced at Frank. Her eyes held a hopeful look.

"Have a good time, baby," said Frank. He returned his gaze to the television.

FRANK DOZED OFF IN FRONT of the TV after Delilah left and after about a half hour, awoke with a start. At first he thought he was in a hotel room, but after a few moments, he realized he was at Delilah's place. He was at loose ends at what to do with himself. After making himself a sandwich, he set about washing the breakfast dishes. He unpacked the items he would need for the week, placing his suits and shirts in the closet of her spare bedroom. Afterward, he decided to take the rental car and go for a ride.

FRANK ENTERED THE BRICK-WALLED RESTAURANT, where delicious smoky aromas tantalized his senses. He made his way to the wooden counter where several hostesses were seating a group of patrons. He held a hand up in the air as he replied, "I'm not trying to jump ahead in line; I'm looking for a party that's already here: The Carpenter Party."

The pretty Latina hostess eyed him with appreciation. "They're the big party. I'll show you where—"

"No. I mean, could you page Miss Delilah Carpenter, please?"

"Sure." They returned to the front of the restaurant.

A few minutes later, Delilah made her way to where he stood. Even in the moodily-lit restaurant, he could see the way her face lit up when she saw him. She looked delectable.

"I came to see if you wanted to have a drink or something later on, after your father's dinner. We could go for a drive, if you want."

Her smile seemed tentative. "Sure, I guess. But—"

In the midst of their conversation, a voice rang out above the other voices in the restaurant. "Help!"

Clementine was racing toward the restaurant staff standing at the counter. "I need help!" She noticed Frank and Delilah. "Delilah! It's Dad!"

Frank grabbed Delilah's hand, and they followed Clementine to the large gathering of panic-stricken people.

"He ate a piece of bread and he's choking!" Hazel cried as she and a friend of Patrick's loosened his tie.

Patrick was attempting to cough, with a labored sound.

Frank reached the table first. "Move!" He brushed Patrick's friend out of the way as he shoved other onlookers out of the way as well. He got behind Patrick who half sat, half stood, as he struggled in vain to gasp and breathe.

He yanked Patrick from his chair, stood behind him, and with several swift movements, administered the Heimlich maneuver. On the third thrust, the chunk of bread became dislodged, and Patrick fell backward into his chair, grasping his throat and gasping.

Hazel and his family rushed to his side, along with his friends, several restaurant patrons, and some of the restaurant staff. "Honey, are you all right?"

Patrick nodded. "I—I'm fine. Everybody, please sit down." He was clearly embarrassed by the attention.

"Are you sure, Mr. Carpenter?" The manager hovered, along with several young members of the wait staff.

"Yes, he's okay now," Scott replied. "How about some water, Patrick?"

The older man took the goblet and gulped it with gratitude.

The crowd of people finally dispersed and the party did as well shortly thereafter. No one thought of the presents at that moment; thinking more about the gift of life Patrick almost had slip away from him.

Delilah broke away from the crowd of concerned friends and family and threw her arms around Frank's neck. She buried her face in his shirt. "Thank you, Frank," she said, her voice muffled.

He held her in a one-armed embrace, not saying a word. They stood only a few yards from everyone else, but to Frank, it seemed a chasm.

Frank decided to return to Delilah's house. Delilah followed the family home, to stay with her father a while. "I just want to make sure that he doesn't need any medical attention," she told Frank before they parted.

"I'm all right, I tell you," Patrick bellowed, good-naturedly shooing away their fawning ministrations and plopping himself down in his favorite easy chair once they had all arrived at the Carpenter home.

"Thank God Frank showed up when he did," Hazel replied, wiping away a stray tear. "I didn't even thank him."

"Oh, Lord." His mood darkened in an instant. "Does he have to be thanked for walking down the street?"

"He saved your life!" Delilah cried. She attempted to rein in her emotions. "You could at least give the man credit for knowing what to do!"

"I absolutely froze," Hazel admitted as she handed her daughter the box of tissue from an end table, still dabbing her own eyes. "I didn't know what to do."

He did not reply. Scott and Clementine exchanged nervous glances.

Delilah kissed her father's forehead, speechless. She picked up her purse and said, "Daddy, I'm glad that you're okay. But if that's what you think, I … well, good night everybody."

She ran to the front door, shutting it quietly behind her.

"DELILAH?"

Frank bounded down the stairs as she locked the front door. She tossed her purse and shawl onto a nearby sofa and then walked into his arms. She closed her eyes and breathed in his wonderful, clean scent.

"Is your father okay? Are you okay?" he asked softly.

She nodded.

They stood in the middle of the parlor, holding each other. "I … I'm tired, Frank. Do you mind if we just go to bed? If you're not tired, I can go alone—"

"Let's go to bed, baby."

Frank turned out the lights as she led the way. She shrugged out of her clothes, draping them on the easy chair and kicked off her shoes beside it. On the bedside table, a glass of white wine was waiting. The glass was wet with water droplets. It was obvious that he had been waiting a while.

Frank handed her the glass. "Drink this. It'll relax you."

Delilah did so without a sound. She was at a loss for words, and even if she could find them, she had no strength to utter them. As she drank, she felt Frank's hands firmly kneading her shoulders. It felt so good that she simply hung her head as he continued.

Frank took the now-empty glass from her hand. He put it on the nightstand and continued massaging her shoulders and neck. After some time, he kissed the side of her neck. "Do you want to take a shower? Or a bath?"

She shook her head no. She would probably fall asleep in it and drown, although she was sure Frank would be right by her side to see that she didn't.

Frank went to the closet and emerged with her favorite nightshirt. Delilah wasn't surprised that he did not grab any of her nighties but could not help but be touched by this act of consideration. Tears burned her eyes, but she willed them away.

In the dark, they climbed under the cool, crisp sheets. She felt the warmth of his strong arms as they encircled her waist, his head nestled against her shoulder.

"Good night," she managed to whisper before she was out like a light.

The morning was overcast when Delilah awoke. Typical of Frank, when she did, he was already awake. He slipped out of bed and within a matter of minutes, returned with a glass of orange juice.

"What time is it?" she asked groggily, the veil of slumber still hanging over her. Her throat felt scratchy, and she was beyond tired. Was she catching the flu?

"Almost seven o'clock." He climbed in beside her.

He was lithe and sensuous, like a panther, but Delilah could not summon up an ounce of desire. "Oh, Lordy, I'm supposed to be on my way to work!"

"So call in sick. You don't sound too good. Could be the flu, although I think yesterday just caught up with you."

When Frank mentioned the word 'yesterday,' it all came flooding back. Without hesitation, she called Mr. McDermott's cell phone and spoke quietly but firmly into the phone and then hung up. She could tell by the gleam in Frank's eyes that he was pleased. "What would you like to eat, Delilah?"

"Nothing, actually," she murmured. "I can't believe how exhausted I am."

"Well, just rest, then. I'll feed you later." He kissed her cheek and slid out of bed, closing the door behind him.

She took two sips of juice, which she barely got down, burrowed her face in the pillows and fell asleep.

Her sleep was fraught with disturbing thoughts and images, so much so that she awoke drenched in perspiration, thrashing around on the bed. Frank returned to find her sitting, disheveled, among the tangled bedclothes.

"I heard you out in the hallway. You were having a nightmare." He sat down on the bed and pulled her into his arms. "You ready for some breakfast now?"

"No." Her heart hammered in her chest. She didn't want him to leave, not even for a minute. "Just hold me, okay?"

"All right, baby."

His soothing voice always had a calming influence on her. This time was different, and she knew it. She bit her lip to prevent it from trembling.

She spent the next two days in bed, suffering from a panic attack so severe she was unable to leave the house, overwhelmed to where she was too tired to move. Frank participated in the conference with the other speakers because he wanted to honor his commitment, but he hurried back to Delilah's as soon as his segments were over. He became more and more alarmed about her.

"You don't seem to have a fever or even a temperature," Frank stated on the second afternoon as he had on the first. "Do you want me to take you to the hospital?"

She shook her head a vehement no.

"Then I don't know what to do for you." He picked up the untouched bowl of soup he had brought to her ten minutes earlier. He placed it on the tray, which he retrieved from the easy chair. "Maybe you've just been working too hard. Or is it your boss? That and your father's—"

At the mere mention of her father and Mr. McDermott, Delilah burst into tears and fled to the bathroom. Frank stood in the middle of the bedroom, the tray in his hand, perplexed. It was déjà vu. *This happened when I was down here for the Christmas holiday,* he thought.

He took the tray to the kitchen and when he returned, she was back in the bedroom, standing by a window. "I can't do this anymore, Frank."

"Do what?" he asked although his stomach dropping toward the vicinity of his shoes told him all he had to know. He walked to her.

Her head fell forward as she emitted a shuddering sigh.

Frank resisted the urge to brush the hair from her neck and gently kiss it. "Do what?" he repeated. He wanted to hear her say it.

196

She spun around and her beautiful eyes looked tortured. They sparkled with tears. "I'm being pulled apart! My daddy, my job, you—"

"I pushed you *toward* your father, Delilah." He felt himself growing angry but at the same time, felt her pain, her dilemma. "I only wanted your love. Did I ever bad-mouth him, baby? I only told the truth."

"I know, and it's tearing my heart out. Because he's my father—and you've never done anything but love me." The tears were streaming down her face, but she made no move to wipe them away. "I can't keep doing this to you. I love you too much."

Grabbing her arms, he hissed, "Am I complaining?"

"No. And that's one reason why I can't let you do this."

"*Let* me?" Unconsciously, he tightened his grip on her. "Delilah, I am a man. *I* decide whether I want to do something. I make up my own mind about things. I think I should have a say in this."

She stood silently, the tears continuing to flow.

"I've had kind of a hard life. I told you about it. Harder still is just trying to exist in this world as a black man. Society has so many preconceived notions about 'my kind.' And not just black men—Asians, Mexicans—we're all human. But you wouldn't think so sometimes.

"I helped your father, but he still couldn't bring himself to say thank you." His grip relaxed. "I didn't really expect him to." He sighed. "But how much do the words 'thank you' cost?"

He turned from her then, so that she could not see his own pain. He straightened a few items on the nightstand and picked up her robe, which lay crumpled on the floor.

"I know. I'm so ashamed. But he is my dad. And I don't know what to do."

"Why do *you* feel you have to do something?" Frank returned to Delilah and pulled her into his arms, holding her tightly. He could not determine whose heart was beating faster. He buried his face in her fragrant hair for a moment. "Everybody's got a family member who is … eccentric, you might say: Crazy Aunt Harriet, who still keeps her money under the mattress instead of in a bank. The man down the street who thinks his dog is his dead wife reincarnated—"

At this, she giggled in spite of herself.

"And bigots. That's just the way it is."

She pulled away. "Frank, I … I need some time to deal with my emotions. I can't do it while I'm seeing you. It's just too hard. Watching my daddy act the way he has been toward you rips my heart apart. And my job—dealing with Mr. McDermott—oh, sweetie, I need time to sort it all out." She gazed at him, unblinking. "Can you understand that?"

The room was growing darker with the approaching twilight, although neither made a move to turn on a lamp. "Delilah, I understand you've got to do what's best for you and your peace of mind. But I know there's something that you're not telling me. I don't know why you won't tell me what's happening with you and this Mr. McDermott. Even if you don't want to talk about it with me, you have got to *deal* with it."

He went to the spare room and placed the suits he had already worn into his garment bag, leaving one out to wear in the morning. He removed his tie and took off his suit, swapping it for a pair of jeans and a T-shirt. He had no appetite.

He returned to her bedroom, only to say, "I'll sleep in the spare bedroom tonight and leave tomorrow. Good night, Delilah." He heard a soft "Good night" as he turned and walked away.

Although he was still weary when he awoke, Frank made sure he was up very early the next morning. He moved quietly through the house, going so far as to take a shower in the downstairs bathroom. Although he didn't have a spare key, he made sure the doorknob lock was locked before he left the house.

"Being what I like to call 'chronically unemployed' is not a new phenomenon," Frank began, strolling back and forth upon the colorfully carpeted floor in front of his audience later that morning at the hotel in Garden City. Most of the seats at the white-draped tables in the Amsterdam Ballroom, where the financial-based tracks of the conference were being held, were full. He was the second of four speakers who would be speaking that day. He continued: "But tell that to the man who has a family and can't even afford the gas to get to his job."

Frank surveyed his audience and honed in on a middle-aged woman in the audience who was nodding her head. "Tell that to a woman who is embarrassed when her young son asks her for money to go on a field trip, and she doesn't have it to give." He struggled to smile as a sharp, burning pain seared through his stomach. Nausea threatened to overtake him, but he fought it. The woman's face rippled through waves of pain. He doubled over. "Let's take a break."

The facilitator of the conference, whose name was Jacqueline, and several audience members hurried to where Frank stood. He was still bent over as he attempted to compose himself. Beads of sweat sprouted on his forehead.

"Let's take a fifteen minute break," Jacqueline said to the audience as she took hold of his arm. "Are you okay, Frank? Are you having chest pains? Come on, I think you should take a seat."

She attempted to lead Frank to a seat in the front of the ballroom, but he waved her off.

"No, Jacqueline, it's my stomach, but I'll be all right. I could use a drink of water, though."

A member of the audience, who had rushed to Frank's side, made his way back to where he had been sitting and poured him a glass of water from the pitcher of water on the table. He brought it back to where Frank and the facilitator still stood, along with another presenter and other concerned audience members.

Frank was embarrassed by the attention and now understood what Delilah's father had endured after he performed the Heimlich on him. *Delilah. Why does everything have to remind me of her?* he thought as he slowly caught his breath and the pain began to subside.

"Here, Mr. Ellis." The man handed Frank a plastic cup of water.

Frank took a sip of the cold water and winced as it burned and sizzled in his stomach. "Thanks."

After the break and consuming an entire roll of Ultra-Strength Tums, Frank managed to finish his presentation. He received enthusiastic applause, but he knew it wasn't his best. He figured most of it was given because he was a trooper and epitomized the old adage, "the show must go on." He was glad he had been able to change his reservations and grab a flight later that evening after the conference concluded, instead of staying overnight and leaving Friday evening, as he had originally planned. He couldn't get away from Savannah fast enough.

Later he said his good-byes to the other speakers and made his way through the traffic to the airport.

Once on the plane and against his better judgment, Frank ordered two gin and juices. After tossing them back, he sat there, staring into space, as he waited for the pain in his stomach, heart, and soul to subside.

WHEN SHE AWOKE, DELILAH FELT like something the cat dragged in and then threw back out. She looked in the mirror and didn't like what she saw. Nevertheless, she forced herself to shower and threw on an outfit that she had run over quickly with a warm iron. The panic attack that had gripped her for the past few days had subsided enough for her to function, but she still had no answers. On her way down the hallway, Delilah quietly turned the doorknob to the spare bedroom, peering into the dimly lit room with hope. But she knew that Frank was already gone.

She stepped inside for a few moments and took a deep breath. She could smell that he had been there. Her eyes stung with tears. She willed them away.

She forced a piece of toast and a glass of juice down her throat. Grabbing her handbag, she headed off to work.

Chapter Twenty

Frank stumbled out of bed, stubbing his toe in the process and cursing up a blue streak. After conducting his business in the bathroom, he made his way back to bed and picked up the phone where he had left it while talking to Andy moments before. "I'm back," he mumbled.

"Great. How was the conference?"

"It was fine." He clenched his fist. "Listen, Andy, let me hit you back, okay?" Blood was hammering inside his brain, and he needed aspirin in the worst way.

Andy brought it down a notch. "You all right, man? You don't sound too good—"

Exasperated, Frank said, "Look Andy, I am fine. I just have a hangover. You know I hate flying."

"All right. You don't have to jump down my throat, man. Damn. Twyla says hi. Later."

It took Frank every ounce of reserved strength to shuttle back to the bathroom for the aspirin and a paper cup with which to toss the water down his throat. He debated inwardly for several minutes whether to make breakfast. When his stomach lurched in reply, he thought the better of it.

He returned to the comfort of his bed, pulling the luxurious Egyptian-cotton sheet over his head. He stifled a groan. The feel of the sheets, still warm from his own body, reminded him of Delilah. Rain pattered against the windows. He was glad it was Saturday, and he had no pressing issues or errands to contend with that day.

Sharp pains traveled intermittently from his head, to his heart, to his stomach, and back again. Two were as a result of the alcohol he had consumed on the plane Thursday night and once he arrived home. The other one would not be healed by aspirin.

Delilah.

Damn.

The pain of her not wanting to see him did not surpass the larger hurt—that of her not standing with him, of not standing up for their love.

Their love, which up until that point had withstood so much:

Racism.

Illness.

Long-distance.

Her supervisor.

Divergent upbringing.

Damn, Delilah.

Why?

He alternately understood and was enraged by her decision. She was making herself sick and depressed with her conflicting loyalties. Somehow he had hoped their love would win out.

It hadn't.

As the three pains continued their war with one another, the rhythmic sound of the rain won out, slowly ceasing the echoing battle in his mind, and allowing him to sleep.

"HEY, MAN, I WANT A rematch!"

"Andy, what the hell are you talking about?" Frank gulped a glass of orange juice, which burned in his stomach. "Maybe I should eat something. But I'm not really hungry," he said to himself as he and Andy talked on the phone the next day.

"What the hell are you *mumbling* about?" his friend demanded. "As for me, I want to play chess. You owe me a rematch!"

"All right, all right, man, don't get so excited." Frank's stomach was now bellowing in a major way. He grabbed a handful of crackers from the cupboard. "When?"

"Today."

"What?"

"I said today. I'll be over in about an hour," Andy replied and hung up, leaving Frank staring at the phone and listening to a dial tone.

"*Buenas tardes.*" Andy strolled into Frank's place later that afternoon, leaving Frank staring after him.

"Yeah, well, good afternoon to you too. I'd like to know why you're in such an all-fired hurry to play a game of chess." He headed for the kitchen.

Andy took off his jacket, draping it on the doorknob of the coat closet. It was raining cats and dogs outside. "That heat feels good. You got the fireplace on for me? I didn't know you cared."

Frank returned to the room with two beers, at which Andy shook his head. "Funny. All right, Andy, what is this about?"

"Ahh, you've got the board set up. Great." Andy grabbed a chair from the dining room and settled himself down on one side of the coffee table.

"C'mon, Andy."

Andy fixed a direct gaze at his best friend. "You tell me. But let me guess—you had a fight with Dee, right?" The stumble Frank made on his way to the sofa told him he was correct.

"You trying to channel your Jewish grandmama now?"

"Nope. Just want a straight answer, Frank."

"All right, I guess you could call it a fight but not in the way you think." Cracking open his bottle, Frank took a swig and sat down on the sofa side of the chessboard.

"How do you know *what* I think?" Andy made his first move. "Okay, so what happened?"

"She just can't hack the flak from her father, her job, and being involved with me." He emitted a quiet burp.

"You can't hold in those things, or your head will explode," Andy joked. "You two have been tight for what—almost a year now? *Now* she can't hack it?"

Frank pondered the board for a while and then made a move of his own. "It can get harder as you go along. But you didn't have that problem. Twyla's mother loved you." Try as he might to tamp it down, bitterness burned in his gut, along with the beer.

"I know, bro. I've been lucky. Her family's been great and so has mine. Well, damn, you two can work that out."

Frank looked up and gazed toward the bank of rain-splattered balcony windows behind Andy.

The weather is gloomy, a perfect metaphor for the way I feel, he thought. Aloud, he said, "It takes two to tango. She wants to sit this one out."

Andy made another move. "For how long?"

"How the hell do I know?" he snapped. "She didn't say." As if on cue, his insides writhed.

The two men played in silence. After a while, Andy said, "I know you're hurting, man. But I know you two will work it out. You two are a perfect match."

"Her father choked on some food, and I did the Heimlich on him. The man acted like he performed it on himself. Like I wasn't even there." Frank made a move.

"Wow."

"I wasn't really looking for thanks." Frank stared at the chess piece, the knight he held in his hand, "but he never even looked back. I couldn't believe it. He never looked back."

"Aw, fuggitabouthim. She'll figure it out." Andy grinned. "Checkmate."

Chapter Twenty-One

"Hon, you look like hell on wheels!" Vivian exclaimed as she and Delilah sat down to lunch.

Delilah picked at her salad and gave her a wry smile. "Thanks. I don't mind that comment coming from you, but you weren't the only one who said it." She nodded her head in the direction for Vivian to look.

Vivian obliged, just in time to see Agnes and another woman walking through the outdoor café several yards away. "And what did you say?"

"I told her to stick it where the sun don't shine."

They both laughed. They both knew that Agnes was a perpetual gossiper. Due to their adjoining cubicles, Delilah had the misfortune to having to contend with Agnes butting in on her telephone conversations or visits with customers at her desk on a minute-by-minute, hour-by-hour basis, sometimes with embarrassing consequences.

The weather was beautiful, sunny and warm, with a light breeze. It did not match Delilah's mood, however. The laughter was an aberration, a too-brief respite in what had been another long week. She forced herself to eat, although she hadn't had an appetite since she told Frank that she needed some space.

Frank.

She fought with herself, alternating between agreeing with her attempt to be humane by curtailing his being a receptacle for her father's behavior and berating herself for not allowing him to make the choice.

Vivian broke into her thoughts. "Let me guess: boyfriend trouble?"

"More like daddy trouble. It's a long story, Viv." Delilah launched into what had transpired over the past few weeks. She had been private about her private life with her other coworkers. Vivian was a good friend, and although she knew that Vivian's boyfriend was Japanese and Korean,

205

Delilah still had not been sure of how she would react to her dating an African American man.

"I can see where you were coming from in trying to spare Frank grief, but I think you were wrong," Vivian replied before she took a sip of her iced tea.

Delilah's eyes widened. "Really? Why?"

"At some point, you're going to have to draw a line in the sand. You are an adult. You no longer live with your daddy, and so you are no longer subject to his rules. Sure, if Frank was a bank robber or embezzler, you might want to take his advice." She patted Delilah's hand. "Ultimately, you have to make the choice of who you choose, or not choose, to love."

"But I don't want to forsake my dad," Delilah replied, fighting back tears. They seemed to appear as much as the spring rains.

Vivian handed her a napkin. "You don't have to forsake him as much as you simply distance yourself from any behavior you find objectionable. If you're at your parents' house and he starts his shenanigans, you simply excuse yourself and leave. He'll soon learn that you mean business." She looked her friend in the eye. "And if he doesn't, at least you'll know that you stood up for yourself and Frank, although he sounds like he can stand up for himself."

Delilah smiled through her tears. "Thanks."

"Sugar, I know. Xion and I went through the same thing with my mama. And to some degree, with his parents till we put our feet down." She laughed. "Now they all act like they've got some sense."

They laughed again.

"Now, what do I do about Mr. McDermott?"

In an instant, Vivian's mood became businesslike. "There's always the Equal Employment Opportunity office. That should throw cold water on his behind."

Delilah remained skeptical. "Maybe."

DELILAH FELT HER ANXIETY GROW every time she went to work, whether or not she actually had to face Mr. McDermott. Finally, at the behest of Vivian, she went to talk to a counselor at the Equal Employment Opportunity office, although she was still afraid of the possible repercussions once her visit came to light. She knew it would not remain anonymous for long.

AFTER WORK, DELILAH CHANGED INTO jeans and a blouse and went to work in her vegetable garden. She headed for the compost that had been percolating year-round in the compost bin. She smiled with satisfaction. Where else could one take scraps, vegetable peels, and other garbage and wind up with something valuable? She inhaled the earthy scent of the black gold. Scooping shovelfuls into a metal wheelbarrow, she rolled the contents to the plot and began enriching the soil with it.

The wheelbarrow, heavy with its contents and with one wheel that rolled in a reluctant manner, brought her thoughts again to her father. *He's just like this wheelbarrow,* she thought, the irony of it not lost on her. Patrick and her mother, Hazel, had given it to her as a housewarming gift when she purchased her home almost six years ago. One edge, where a bit of rust peeked through, also revealed the passage of time with it and with him. *He doesn't seem to be able or willing to let go of his racist upbringing,* she realized, tears falling from her eyes and sinking into the moist concoction. She took a shovel, breaking up the hard clay soil and mixing them together, barely able to see.

"Daddy, you were my hero," she sobbed, dropping to her knees and not caring if her neighbors might see. She clutched the shovel and allowed the tears to fall. She missed Frank terribly; their daily calls and text messages to each other. To abruptly stop communicating with each other was like a wet towel straight in the kisser, not to mention a dagger in her heart.

"I've got no one to blame but myself for sending him away," she replied, scolding herself. "He didn't want to go. Oh, Frank, I'm sorry!"

She knelt there, crying in the dirt, long after the sun began to set.

"SIR, DO YOU KNOW HOW fast you were going?" the Maryland state trooper, a stone-faced young black man inquired after Frank pulled over and pushed the lever to roll down the window. He resembled the Army sentinels who guarded the Tomb of the Unknowns at the Arlington National Cemetery.

No, but obviously you do or you wouldn't have stopped me, he thought to himself. *Why do they always ask that? Does it even matter?* Instead, he swallowed the retort and handed his license and registration out the window to the trooper without a word. After a small lecture on the hazards of exceeding the speed limit, the trooper let him off with a warning.

"Would rather have gotten a ticket," Frank mumbled to himself as he pulled out into the traffic. "I've probably been driving almost as long as he's been alive." His gut ached. He opened the glove compartment and rummaged through it as he kept his eyes on the road. Finally, his hand happened upon an old pack of cigarettes with two left in it.

He felt guilty, and his hand shook as he took out the lighter he still carried around with him like a pacifier and lit the cigarette he now held between his lips. He took a deep drag on it. His throat burned, and he grew dizzy. He was tempted to pull over to the shoulder as a result. He squinted through the smoke as he exhaled it slowly from his lungs. It wasn't as enjoyable as it used to be before he quit, but he needed something. He didn't know what to do with himself since his breakup or whatever it was with Delilah. His hands itched to call or text her. And although theirs was a long-distance relationship and they weren't together most nights, sleeping alone this way was infinitely worse. But this was what she wanted.

He selected another radio station and continued to smoke his cigarette as he rolled down the highway.

DELILAH CLICKED OFF HER HANDS-FREE device as she made her way through the streets of downtown Savannah on her way to her parents' house. Springtime was glorious in the city and in their backyard. They had done a fabulous job with the landscaping this year as they had in years past. Both retired, they shared green thumbs and employed no help with their massive front and backyards.

"This is our form of therapy," Hazel had pointed out to her more than once. "It's a hobby we enjoy together."

Delilah parked her car and walked down the gravel path that led directly to the backyard, her sandals making a pleasing crunching noise beneath them. She saw her father in the distance, deftly making his way along the back forty. After a few minutes, she caught his attention. He stopped and made his way through the golf course-like mowed portion of the lawn toward her.

"Why don't you put in a putting green?" she asked when he reached her side.

He was panting a little; otherwise, he appeared no worse for wear for wear for his near-death ordeal several weeks earlier. "I should, it looks good enough to be one. What are you doing here, doll baby?"

"I would like to talk to you. Can we sit down over there?" Delilah asked, indicating the nearby deck.

"Sure."

There was a pitcher of iced tea on the table, along with several glasses. She poured her father a glass, which he accepted, but she did not pour one for herself.

"Daddy, I stopped seeing Frank shortly after your ... uh, accident."

Patrick was visibly pleased although she could see him trying hard not to show it. "Oh, really?"

"Yes." She leveled her gaze at him. At his reaction, she felt both sadness and anger, which she pushed down inside. "But Daddy, I want you to know that it is only temporary. I love Frank, but I needed to get my head straight. I felt guilty; I felt stressed out. But I don't anymore."

At that, Patrick took a drink and then set his glass on the table. "Meaning?" His steely gaze met hers.

"Meaning that I am an adult, Daddy. I will see whom I choose, when I choose. I love you, but you will have to accept that fact from now on."

"Look, daughter, I—"

She held up her hand. "No, Daddy, you need to listen to me. I mean, really listen. I love you and Mama very much. But you two got to choose each other, and I should be allowed to do the same, whether it's Frank or someone else."

"So, will you or will you not continue to see him?" he asked, running a hand over his salt-and-pepper buzz cut.

"I don't know." She stood up and kissed his forehead. "But I need you to accept whatever I choose to do" She sighed. "I deserve to be happy, but I'm not. Between dealing with this and issues at work, I feel as if I'm turned inside out."

Patrick continued to sit. "I want you to be happy too, baby girl."

The green expanse of lawn seemed a peaceful oasis to Delilah. She understood why people chose to retire to the country or to a place on the beach. She tried to remember when she felt truly at peace. It hadn't been for a long time.

She left him sitting there to ponder what she said.

"WHAT THE HELL IS IT, Doc?" Frank asked, sitting on the table in the examination room.

Dr. Stewart gave him his scary undertaker stare before he turned to wash his hands. "You are well on your way to an ulcer, if you keep on the way you have been. And I thought you had stopped smoking."

"I did," Frank replied through gritted teeth. His abdominal pain had been unrelenting for weeks now.

"I smelled cigarette smoke when you came in here."

Frank smiled grimly. "I relapsed."

Dr. Stewart walked over to where Frank sat on the examination table and crossed his arms, shaking his head. "Mr. Ellis, you have had a few health challenges in the last year. You were progressing very well after your discharge. What happened?"

Frank looked away. "A personal setback."

"It happens." The doctor gave him a smile full of sympathy. He knew Frank Ellis had the stamina of two men, what with his hectic travel schedule and history of hard living on the insufficient sleep of an insomniac. "But you've got to try to kick that habit and not drink so much. Stress kills."

"Yeah, I know." Frank finished donning his shirt.

Clapping him on the shoulder as he headed for the door, the doctor said, "I'll give you a prescription for the pain. You know that the drinking is definitely not helping, and you've got to take better care of yourself. Maybe you can also learn to meditate."

Frank hopped off the table and followed the doctor. "I'll give it some serious thought."

Chapter Twenty-Two

The months of April and May crawled by, with both Frank and Delilah going about their separate lives, hating every minute of it. In late April, Frank and Andy conducted what they termed *The Disaster Preparedness Workshop for Life*. In it, they laid out the steps of what to do to prevent a financial disaster as well as how to be prepared in the event of a natural one. Enough people registered to conduct a second workshop, but Frank cautioned against them doing so until they saw how the first workshop was received by the public.

He need not have worried. Both he and Andy were in their respective elements, playing off one another as they turned what could be two grim endeavors into empowering opportunities. The workshop proved to be very productive and was well received by those who participated in it. That was some comfort to Frank but not much. He was the consummate professional and always attempted to keep his work separate from his private life. However, the private side of him ached day and night.

They walked down the street of Raleigh, North Carolina, on the last evening after the workshop. Frank pulled out a pack of cigarettes and lit up, taking a drag.

Andy stopped dead in his tracks. "Aw, c'mon! Not that again!"

Frank turned around. "What?"

"You're smoking again?"

"I thought you knew," Frank replied, in his best gangster imitation.

"I thought I smelled cigarette smoke earlier, but I thought it was one of the students." Andy caught up to him but kept shaking his head.

"What are you doing? I'll tell you what you're doing—you're overreacting," Frank laughed, attempting to make light of the situation.

Andy didn't. "I hate to see a guy self-destruct."

"You're too sensitive, man. It's not like I'm shooting up morphine or on methadone or something like that." He took another drag.

"Might as well be. Hey, I remember how you looked in the hospital."

This time Frank stopped. "Look Andy, I am a man. I've got faults, just like any other man. I admit it. It's a cigarette, dammit!" He exhaled. "Look man, I think I need to take a walk by myself. I'll see you tomorrow."

"All right."

Frank watched the friend he considered his brother leave as he stubbed out his cigarette. The enjoyment he derived from it was gone. He turned on his heel and walked in the other direction as night began to fall.

"HEY, STRANGER!"

Delilah's turn was slow and deliberate as she recognized the voice of her old boyfriend calling out to her one late-May afternoon. "Hey, yourself, Victor."

Victor Larsen cruised up in his car in the strip mall parking lot as she headed out of the cleaners toward her own vehicle. "I thought that was you."

"It's me." She did not attempt to conceal the sarcasm in her voice.

Victor swung his car into a parking space, conveniently cutting off the path to hers. He was an attractive man, the same age as Delilah. His thick locks of dark-brown hair gave him a boyish, star-quarterback-of-the-college-football-team look. It was ironic, since Victor had actually played the position of halfback but only in high school. Because of a nagging knee injury in his junior year that carried over into his senior year, Victor did not play football in college. During their three-year relationship, this wholesome yet sexy quality was one of the things that had made her pulse quicken about him.

He got out and sidestepped so as to stand directly in front of her, all one-hundred and ninety-five pounds of him. "Come on, Dee, don't be like that. It's been a long time."

"Not long enough, Vic," Delilah murmured, dismayed by the fact that he could still make her heart race. She sidestepped his sidestep and continued to her car, hanging her dry cleaning on the overhead hook above the rear passenger seat.

He took her arm and swung her to face him. "I mean it, Dee. I've missed you."

"Really?" Delilah looked up into his dark-blue eyes, eyes she used to get lost in. The expression there was one of sincerity, but she couldn't help herself. "What happened, Vic? Well run dry?"

"What well?" He appeared confused at first. It took a moment, but then it dawned on him. "You know I was never a player—"

"Maybe not, but you never could commit to me. We stayed on that perpetual dating track. Why go the next step, right?" Anger saturated her words, startling her and causing her to realize how hurt she had been when she broke up with him.

"I know, and you're right. I was scared." Victor's voice was soothing, and he loosened the grip on her arm. "But I mean it, Delilah, I've missed you. You've got to admit, we had some great times together."

Delilah did not speak. His touch and the scent of him brought back sweet but painful memories.

"I'm not trying to hold you up or anything but I … look, I'd like to take you to dinner, if that's okay with you. How about it?"

She took a deep breath. "I don't think that's a good idea, Vic."

"What could it hurt?" Victor smiled. "For old time's sake. Please, Dee Dee."

At his nickname for her, Delilah's heart thawed a bit, and she said, "Okay."

Since she still had the same cell phone number that she had when they broke up, and he still remembered it, they made a date for later that week, deciding to meet at a seafood restaurant on the edge of town.

He donned his shades and got back in his car. Delilah got in her car as well, watching in her rearview mirror as he backed up and drove away.

Twice Delilah thought to cancel her date with Victor as the day of their date drew closer.

"It's just a date," she scolded herself. It would help her to get out of the house and get her mind off her problems.

213

FRIDAY EVENING ARRIVED. DELILAH THREW on her thigh-high-length trench coat, grabbed her umbrella, and headed in the light rain to the restaurant and her date with Victor.

Victor was already seated when Delilah arrived. The host led her through the crowded restaurant to his table. He sprang to his feet to pull Delilah's chair out for her and help her off with her coat. She caught a whiff of the cologne that he wore. "Thanks, Vic," she said.

"Hi Dee Dee. You look great," he said as he settled back in his seat.

"Thanks. Look at you. You clean up good for a country boy," Delilah joked. He was dressed in a charcoal-gray suit and crisp white shirt and black tie. The combination, along with the lights that hung low over each table, brought out the intense blueness of his eyes. "What's this?" she asked, indicating a glass of wine beside her plate.

"I took the liberty of ordering a glass of wine for you," Victor replied, with a smile. "You still like rosé, don't you?" The restaurant, which used to be an old ship and was still owned by members of the captain's descendants, was full of nautical artifacts. It was one Delilah and Victor used to frequent when they were dating.

"Um, sure." Delilah picked up her menu and began to peruse it. "Have you been waiting long?"

"Oh, not long—about ten minutes." He shook out his napkin and laid it across his lap. Looking back up at her, he said, "You were worth waiting for."

At that remark, Delilah's thoughts floated back to a time when Frank had uttered those same words. She snatched up her glass of wine, almost spilling it upon herself in her haste. She took a sip.

"Did I say something wrong?" Victor's eyes probed hers, confused.

She closed her eyes for a moment, shutting out the memories. "No, of course not, Victor. Everything's fine."

After placing their orders, they caught up on events that had transpired since their breakup. Victor told her about his new job as manager at a local recreation center.

"Still keeping your hand in athletics, huh?" she teased.

"Well, you know. It's always been a part of my life. I even started coaching a Little League team about a year ago."

Delilah listened and mentally noted that he had indeed matured in the time they had been apart. She was glad.

The night was very enjoyable for both of them, with Delilah appreciating being able to get out of her own head for a while. Afterward, they walked in the rain for a little while, laughing because Victor's height and girth made it awkward for him to fit underneath the umbrella with her.

"That's okay—I can take a little rain," he laughed, struggling to avoid getting poked in the eye by the tip of her umbrella as he moved out from under it. They ran back in the direction of their cars as it began to rain harder. "Serves me right for opening my mouth!"

He closed her car door after Delilah was seated and gestured for her to roll down the window. "Hey, there's a Brad Paisley concert next Saturday in Macon. I know you used to love that guy. You wanna go?"

"Victor—"

"I can't hear you," Victor replied loudly as the steady rain became a downpour, "but I'll get some tickets for us. It'll be fun." Already soaked but appearing to not giving it a second thought, he leaned through the open window and kissed her.

His mouth was warm and determined as they kissed. Delilah found herself comparing it to Frank's. Her head swam with conflicting emotions as she pulled her lips from his. "Victor, you are going to drown out there! Get out of the rain, and I'll talk to you later!"

He waved to her, and then turned and began to run through the deluge. He sprinted effortlessly through the half-empty parking lot to his vehicle, displaying the talent he once had on the gridiron.

"You still got it," Delilah whispered.

"I can't believe you still have my number," Rita said as she looked Frank up and down as they sat on stools in the Mix Lounge atop THEhotel at Mandalay Bay in Las Vegas. She tossed her head to move an errant lock of blonde hair from her eyes and smiled a smile she no doubt used on a daily basis in her profession as a flight attendant. "I should be mad at you."

Frank sipped his club soda and gave her a look just as transparent. "Why should you? You wrote it on a napkin. I could've ended up throwing it away." He spread his hands and gave her a pseudo-helpless look. "Come on, Rita. You travel a lot, so you know how it is. You lose things—"

Her pretty eyes held a look of mild skepticism. "Uh-huh."

"Anyway, I'm here now." He touched her knee before he turned and motioned to the bartender. "Freshen your drink? What'll you have? Another autumn candy-apple martini?"

"Yes, please."

Frank held her gaze with his. "And after that, let's lose this place."

They had dinner at one of the hotel's restaurants and did a little gambling. Frank won a few rounds at the blackjack table as they conducted their foreplay on the floor of the Treasure Island casino. He then tried his luck at the craps table. He cupped the dice and swung them in Rita's direction. "Blow on these for me, baby," he ordered, in his most seductive voice.

She did as she was told. "Keep it up! Keep it up!" she yelled, joining in the whoops and excited cries of the onlookers. She hung onto his arm as she jumped up and down.

Rita's bouncing bosom in her low-cut dress was posing a bit of a distraction for Frank, so he concentrated on the shake of the dice before he threw it.

"We have a winner," the croupier announced to the jubilant crowd.

They left the table when Frank's luck began to cool. All told, he had won over thirty-seven hundred dollars. He handed Rita five hundred. "Buy yourself something pretty later. But right now, I can think of something else I'd like to do—"

"Like go to my place?" she asked, her barely covered breasts brushing up against his arm.

Frank quickly pulled on his suit jacket and took hold of her arm. "Like go to your place."

Once inside Rita's apartment, they grabbed each other, resembling a wrestling match more than an amorous encounter. Shedding their clothes and making it as far as the carpet in her bedroom, they kissed and groped their way around each other's bodies. Frank ripped open the condom package he had retrieved from inside his jacket pocket. He tried to slow it down. "C'mere, baby."

"Ooh, Frank—"

He kissed her and grabbed her hair as they caressed each other there on the floor. Then he grabbed her arms and pinned her to it. "Is this what you want, Rita? You want this?"

"You know what I want," Rita whispered as she kissed his chest and neck. "Come on."

He released her arms and raised himself. Still straddling her waist, Frank slid the condom onto himself and then slowly pushed himself inside her. As he did so, a patch of light from the moon outside illuminated Rita's face, and he gazed down at her.

The smell of her was different. The feel of her curves was different. The texture of her hair was different.

"Go 'head, baby! You know what to do!"

The sound of her voice, missing that familiar sexy southern accent, was like a bucket of cold water thrown on his private parts, and Frank felt himself lose his erection in a hurry.

"Damn!"

"What is it? What's wrong, Frank?" Rita pushed her hair from her eyes and stared up at him.

Frank lifted himself from her and lay there beside her as he struggled to compose himself and regain some of his dignity. "This has never happened before. I don't know—jetlag maybe?"

She leaned over and kissed him, stroking his chest. "Yes, maybe you're just tired."

Her tone, full of understanding, served to make Frank feel even more inadequate. He cupped her face and kissed her cheek as he said, "I'm sorry, Rita. Some other time?"

"Sure, sure." Her expression held the knowledge that she would not be getting another call from Frank Ellis anytime soon. "Call me."

They both stood up and put on their clothes. The moon was full, but with the draperies nearly closed, not much light peeked through them. Frank was glad of the darkness so that Rita couldn't see his face. "Thanks for understanding. You're a beautiful woman, Rita."

They walked to the front door, and she opened it for him. "Take care, Frank." The bright light from the hallway lit her face again. Despite what had happened, he knew she was being sincere.

"Goodbye."

"I can't, Victor."

Victor stood in the doorway of Delilah's house, dumbfounded. She had just finished telling him that she could not go to the Brad Paisley concert with him. "Why not?"

She held the door open wider. "Come inside."

He stepped in, and she closed the door behind him. He was dressed in faded blue jeans that fit him just right, a checkered shirt that showed off his muscular arms, a black cowboy hat, and black cowboy boots. He looked as much like a cowboy or country singer as Brad Paisley or any of the other country singers currently on the scene. Delilah wore white jeans, which hugged all of her curves, a pair of cute strappy sandals, and a black sleeveless silk blouse.

They stood in the foyer. Victor took her arm as he stood there looking down at her. "I don't get it, Dee Dee. You seemed to enjoy being with me at the restaurant last week. And when I kissed you, you didn't pull away in disgust or slap me, so I know that you liked it. What happened between then and now?"

"I did, Vic, and yes, I enjoy your company. Nothing happened, not really. I tried to call you every day since then. I don't know why I couldn't." She shook her head. "What I'm trying to say, and I've been too chicken to say since the night we went out, is that it's been three years and, well—"

He let go of her arm. "I guess I should've asked you then: is there someone else?"

"Yes, there is. The reason we're not together right now is because I needed a little time to figure some things out."

He laughed a sad sort of laugh and spread his large hands wide as he said, "I should've known you wouldn't be out there on the market that long."

Delilah pretended to be offended. "'On the market'? What am I, a side of beef?"

They laughed as Victor said, "No indeed, girl. You aren't a side of beef, that's for sure." The mood lightened, and both were relieved. "I thought I had gotten a second chance with you."

"Victor, look, when I went out with you, I realized that I still care about you. I care about you a lot." She sighed. "But this other man—I love him. Maybe I'm not making sense, but I love him and I want to be with him. I don't want to hurt you, so I knew that I needed to hurry up and tell you. I don't want you to end up thinking that I'm using you or trying to get back at you for when we broke up. I wanted to use this separation time to get myself together and try to simplify my life." She smiled. "If you had only come back into my life a year or so ago—"

"That's me, Dee, always a day late and a dollar short," he joked.

"Don't sell yourself short, honey." She tiptoed and kissed his cheek. "You're a very special man, and some woman's going to really appreciate that."

"But I already bought the tickets," Victor protested, pulling them out of his wallet and holding them up for Delilah to see.

"Tell you what, Vic, we can still go to the show but as friends." She wiped the lipstick from his cheek. "I'll even pay for my ticket. I just want you to know that that's all it can be. Okay?"

Victor's smile was wistful. "Okay, but you don't have to pay for your ticket. I even got you a cowgirl hat. It's in the car. Well, let's get going. We've got a long ride."

As they left the house, she locked up, and they headed to his car in the warm May sunshine.

"Andy!" Delilah exclaimed as she answered her cell phone. "Hi, honey. It's so nice to hear from you. How are you? And Twyla?"

He felt the tightness in his shoulders loosen a little as he listened to Delilah's sweet Georgia accent on the other end of the phone. It had been a while since they had talked or seen each other, and it was good to hear her voice. "Hey there, Missy. I'm fine, and Twyla's fine."

There was a pregnant pause. "I'm glad," she replied, avoiding the obvious question.

"Look, bright eyes, this has got to stop. I can't take it! Frank is miserable, and I'll bet you are too."

"He is?"

Andy heard the hopefulness in her voice. "Sure he is. Jumping down my throat every time I open my mouth, smoking—"

"Smoking?" She sounded shocked.

"*Smoking*, Dee. It's because he misses the hell out of you."

"I miss him too, Andy."

He didn't miss the catch in her voice. "Then do something about it! Don't let your father run your life!"

"I'm not!"

"Well, why are you two not talking?" Andy clicked on the television but turned the volume down low. He sprawled out onto the hotel bed.

Delilah took a long time to speak, and when she did, her voice was small. "I don't know how."

"How *what?*" He was becoming exasperated. The both of them were driving him crazy. "To call him? You just pick up the phone and dial!"

They both chuckled. "I'd rather slit my wrists," she said. "I'm too ashamed."

He groaned. "Okay, okay. Don't worry about it. Maybe I can think of something. You two are gonna send me to an early grave. Good night, Dee."

"Thank you, honey. You're so sweet. Good night."

FRANK BUSTLED ABOUT HIS KITCHEN, listening to *Anderson Cooper 360* on the television. His appetite was not what it should be and his stomach still bothered him, but he was taking his medication and attempting to abide by Dr. Stewart's advice.

The phone rang. A metal colander fell out of the cupboard he was opening as he answered it. "I'm sorry, Andy. How are you?"

"Geez! Hey, I'll let you know once I get my hearing back. What are you doing over there, anyway?"

"Making some rice for my lunch-slash-dinner, among other things."

"Yeah, man, you need to eat," Andy agreed. "And cut back on those cigarettes—"

Frank added rice, water, and a dash of salt to the rice cooker and stirred it. Then he placed it in the microwave and set the timer. "I'm trying. I can't get with having this stomach pain for much longer. Got the rice cooking and some salmon grilling. Hell, I should've invited you and the missus over."

"Yeah, you should've," Andy agreed with a laugh. "Why didn't you?"

He shrugged, even though his friend couldn't see him. "I just thought of it."

"I was kidding, anyway. But I did think you might still be pissed at me, riding you about smoking the other day," Andy replied, and his voice was somber.

"Nah." Frank looked for a plate on which to place his salmon. He fought the urge for a cigarette. Instead, he grabbed the tall glass of water on the counter and took several gulps. "I gave you a ride to the airport, didn't I? If I was still mad at you, I would've left you at the hotel." At that, they both laughed.

"That's hardly charitable, my friend," Andy chided him.

"You're right, Rabbi, I apologize." Frank walked to the balcony and took a peek at his salmon on the grill outside. He placed it on the plate and hurried inside. The sky was overcast, with the threat of rain and there was a steady breeze. He tossed the fish into the warmer while he waited for the rice to finish cooking. He opened a can of peas to go along with them. "What takes you away from your fine wife to spend time yakking with me?"

"A worthwhile cause." His friend cleared his throat.

"Yeah? What are you talking about now?" Frank asked. Once everything was cooked, he assembled his plate and sat down at the kitchen table to eat. "If you're going to start talking about UFOs or something like that, I'm going to hang up."

"Go ahead, Missy," said Andy.

"Hello, Frank," she said.

Frank took the receiver from his ear and stared at it. "Delilah?"

"It's me."

"Andy!" Frank didn't know whether to be shocked, angry, or happy. All three emotions fought for dominance. "You—"

"Gotta go, partner," Andy announced. "Stay sweet, bright eyes." He hung up, leaving Frank and Delilah to fend for themselves.

For a while, there was silence on both ends of the line. "Hey, baby. To what do I owe the pleasure? Andy?"

"You could say him. And me."

"Why not just you?" Anger was winning, although happiness was fighting hard against it. "Why did he have to run interference?"

"I deserve your anger," Delilah replied, "but don't be mad at Andy. I sort of asked him to."

"But *why?*" Frank forgot about the food in front of him.

She sighed. "I felt ashamed. I didn't know how to face you."

"Okay …"

"It's the truth! You've been right all the time. I felt kind of stupid. In fact, I still do."

His anger dissolved. "Don't, baby. He's your father. I know it's been hard for you."

"Very hard." Delilah's voice was almost a whisper. "I've missed you so much, sweetie."

"I've missed you too. I *miss* you."

"I love you, Frank."

"I love you too, Delilah." He laughed. Despite his stomach pain, he suddenly felt great. "So what are we going to do about it?"

"Love each other." Delilah replied. "I want to come see you."

"So, come see me." His voice was filled with promise. "On the first thing smokin'."

"Well, maybe the second thing. Mr. McDermott, you know."

"Oh yes. We mustn't forget Mr. McDermott. Look, I'm off for the next two weeks. Just let me know when and I'll make the arrangements. I hope that won't bother him too much."

"Frank, I can't wait. Oh, honey—"

"I know." All of a sudden, he was ravenous and began to eat with gusto, although his salmon had grown cold. "I know."

MISS CARPENTER, PLEASE COME TO *my office upon your return* was what was written on the note.

Delilah walked to Mr. McDermott's office when she returned to the office from lunch. She knocked on his closed office door.

"Come in, Miss Carpenter," was the muffled reply.

She felt fingers of uneasiness crawl along her spine, but she shook them off, suppressing a laugh. *The man's got X-ray eyes,* she thought. Just as quickly she added, *Don't be ridiculous.*

"Sit down, please," he commanded.

It always amazed her how quiet and serene his office seemed. It reminded her of convents and monasteries she had seen on television. Although it was located on the periphery of cubicles in the main office, it might as well have been a world away—away from the noise of numerous fingers tapping upon the keyboards of multiple laptops, away from the mechanical sounds spewing from the printers and fax machines, away from the chatter and gossip, and away from Agnes.

Delilah sat in one of the armchairs flanking the front of his desk and waited for him to speak. She had an idea of what he wanted.

He cleared his throat. "I was called into the EEO office today."

She met his eyes with calm directness. "Is that so?"

"You know, I—"

"Mr. McDermott, this last year I have felt as if I worked in a hostile work environment. First, you seemed to have it in for me, and then you did an about-face and started making unwelcome advances toward me. You know I have a boyfriend, and I've tried to give you hints that I'm not interested, which you ignore—"

"Well, you won't have to worry about that anymore, Miss Carpenter."

She sat there and waited for the other shoe to drop, wondering if he could hear the pounding of her heart where he sat. Would he attempt to retaliate against her? Only time would tell.

Mr. McDermott cleared his throat. "Although I don't consider what I did as 'sexual harassment,' I have been ... advised, shall we say, to keep my distance from you. Refrain from, uh, touching you. I didn't realize my touch was so repugnant, but I will do as advised." He rapidly tapped his ink pen upon the desk several times and glanced at the clock.

Before he did, she noticed a look of helplessness in his cold gray eyes. To Delilah, he resembled an animal caught in a trap. *A trap of your own making*, Delilah thought. She still didn't think he got the full message but hoped that he would be required to report to the EEO office for a while. At the very least, they had their eyes on him now. She felt a slight loosening of the grip of anxiety that had plagued her for many months, although she wasn't sure how it would reflect upon her next evaluation.

Aloud, she merely said, "I would appreciate that, Mr. McDermott."

He quickly looked away, shuffling some papers on his ornate desk. "You may go," he replied.

But she had risen from her seat and was already closing the door behind her, smiling a smug smile.

"You've been smiling like the cat that ate the canary," Vivian observed. "What's up?"

Delilah was about to burst with happiness since her conversation with Frank last Friday evening.

"You two made up?" Vivian guessed. She clapped her hands with glee. "I'm so happy for you!"

"So am I." Delilah jerked her head in the direction of Agnes' cubicle. She stood up and they left the office to get out of earshot of her nosy cubicle neighbor.

They rode a crowded elevator down to the lobby. "I saw you go into McDermott's office. Any news on that front?"

Delilah grinned. "I think he's shell-shocked that he was called into the EEO office, but he said that he will leave me alone. That's all I ever wanted. I just want to be treated like everyone else in the office. So we'll see."

"That's good," Vivian replied. "He knows now that he's been trying to get a little too familiar with you."

"Maybe. I hope so, because I'm getting sick of him riding me one minute and then trying to get close to me the next. I tried to make it known to him that I wasn't interested. But you know he still acts like he's clueless about why unwanted touching is considered sexual harassment. I'm happy that they're watching him now, and if he does it again, I'll just have to pay them another visit."

They walked outside into the warm fresh air. Delilah stretched out her arms and felt the sunlight envelop her. What a difference a day made! One day it felt like the end of the world, and the next day, it was sunshine and blue skies.

"You and Frank gonna make up for lost time, huh?" Her friend gave her a wink.

The smile Delilah gave her was demure. "Yes, ma'am. And I can't wait."

Chapter Twenty-Three

I *can't believe that I'm actually nervous,* Frank admitted to himself that early June day as he headed out of the parking lot of his condo complex toward the highway. *I wasn't even nervous the first time I spoke to her without any of the other seminar participants around.*

Maybe because you got a taste of what life would be like without her, he told himself, wiping out the ashtray he had forgotten to clean earlier with a wad of tissue as he drove. He crumpled the tissue and stuffed it in the door compartment next to him. At a red light, he extracted a new can of air freshener from the glove compartment: *Ocean Breeze.* After opening it, he stashed it in the floor under his seat.

Traffic was thin; the road projects were few for a change, so he sailed along and arrived at the entrance of the airport terminal in no time at all.

Finally, Delilah stepped out of the terminal as the glass doors parted, her reddish-blonde hair standing out among the other travelers. She wore a colorful blouse and a short tan skirt that barely skimmed her knees.

Frank pulled over to the curb, put the car in park, and headed toward her. They collided in an exuberant embrace.

"Who sat by you on the plane?" Frank whispered in her ear, after they kissed. "It had better been a nun, with that sexy, short skirt you have on."

"It was," Delilah murmured.

He released her quickly and grabbed her duffle bag. "C'mon, let's get out of here."

In the car, they talked nonstop, like birds chirping first thing in the morning. Frank ran his hand back and forth along her silky thigh and down to her kneecap. He hardly remembered driving.

Once inside his place, he yanked her to him and planted a kiss full of pent-up passion upon her lips, knocking her against the front door.

"Miss me?" she asked, her eyes half closed.

"What do *you* think?" He was about to envelop her in a bear hug when he doubled over in pain.

Delilah's eyes flew open. "Frank! What is it?"

Frank attempted to smile. "The pain of missing you." He suppressed a groan.

She batted his hands away as she said, "Come on, now. What is it?"

"The price we pay for love. Don't worry about it. I've got what I need now—you. So come here, woman." Taking her hand, they walked over and sat down on a sofa. He kissed her neck. "You know what to do. You always know just what to do."

"Well, you don't," Delilah replied as she tried to pull away from him. "Taking up that disgusting smoking habit again; working yourself to a frazzle—"

"So, what are you going to do about it, baby?" Frank asked, caressing her cheek.

She stopped. "Love you, I guess." She sighed, shaking her head in amusement. "You're a mess."

"You *guess?*" He lay back and pulled her down on top of him, running his hands down her back and to her curvaceous backside. Having her here with him after nearly three months was all that he needed. They lay entwined on the sofa, getting reacquainted for a while without words. He held her tightly in his arms and nuzzled her neck. "You *know.*"

She gave him a lingering kiss. "I know."

The weather was stormy the next morning, and Frank and Delilah spent most of it in bed, talking and making love until their stomachs finally forced them into the kitchen. There they feasted at the breakfast bar on cereal and then waffles and sausage.

Delilah watched with satisfaction as Frank downed his second glass of milk. "You just keep eating, honey. I'm gonna put some meat back on those bones."

He looked down at the sleeveless undershirt and checkered pajama pants he wore. He had lost weight since their separation, due mostly to his stomach ailment but also due to depression. He still had not gained back all of the weight he lost during his bout with pneumonia. "High metabolism, baby," he joked.

"Maybe." She reached over and pinched the nonexistent inch on his ribcage. "But I'm going to do my best with some good ole southern cooking."

"Feed me, baby!"

They laughed. It felt good to be laughing again. Although the weather outside was frightful, simply sitting beside Frank made Delilah feel that all was right with the world. She grabbed his free hand and held it in hers. Hers eyes began to burn, and she swiped the inevitable waterworks away.

He caught her as he polished off his last waffle square. "I didn't know you cared," he joked again, this time looking a little uncomfortable.

"Frank, I have probably cried enough in the last few months to fill that sink over there. I haven't been so miserable in my entire life. Except maybe when you had pneumonia."

He squeezed her hand. "I've caused you a lot of grief, haven't I?"

"Oh my gosh, no." Delilah reached for a paper napkin and dabbed her eyes and nose. "I've got you beat by a country mile, with my dad and my lack of faith in what we have. And I should've told you a long time ago about Mr. McDermott and how he was sexually harassing me."

"Although I would've wanted to go over there and kick his ass, I'm just glad that you finally told the authorities. You can't let that fool get away with it. No telling how many women he's probably done it to, and he should know better because he's in a position of authority. But I blame myself too. I should've been able to figure it out, although it still would've been your decision to make. Right now, I'm just glad that you're here. Now lean over and give me some sugar," Frank commanded.

She did not resist. Instead, she hopped off her stool and onto his lap, giving him a lip-smacking smooch. He tasted like maple syrup and link sausage, "Take all that you want, sweetie."

He groaned, his baritone voice cracking, sending them both into gales of laughter. "Maybe you'd better feed me. Help me keep up my strength."

"That and some good loving," Delilah replied, her fingers tracing the goatee that framed his lips. "Good loving for sure."

"Good loving for sure …"

BOTH ANDY AND TWYLA STOOD there, shocked, when Frank and Delilah appeared together to open the door at Frank's place.

"Welcome," Frank greeted in his most suave tone of voice. "Come in."

They obliged, but Andy didn't miss the bemused glance that passed between the reunited couple. "I did this," he remarked proudly to his wife.

"I know," Twyla beamed, touching his arm as they headed into the living room.

Frank pushed his friend, laughing. "All right, Rabbi. I'll give you your props, before you start crying—"

"Crying?" He laughed even harder. "Twyla, do you hear this? The man was about to head to a fortune-teller or somebody to read his palm or something! 'When will she come back to me?'"

"You two are silly," Twyla declared, shaking her head. "I should tell them what you did to me in the middle of the night—"

Andy whirled around. "C'mon, don't do that!"

"Go ahead." Frank grinned, his hands on his hips.

Twyla smiled but remained silent.

Delilah headed to the kitchen, laughing. She was enjoying the men's boyish kidding. They sounded exactly like brothers. She brought out the finger foods while the others continued talking.

The weather was not cooperating, and because it was being temperamental, Frank and Delilah decided to have their impromptu cookout indoors in the dining room.

They talked about a variety of topics, since the couples had not been together since Andy and Twyla's wedding. Frank braved the cool, windy weather to finish grilling the hamburgers and corn on the cob.

About a half hour later, Frank said that dinner was ready, and everyone took their drinks over to the table. Delilah had concocted several sinus-opening, heart-thumping, family drink specialties that nearly had them all passing out before they even got there. Twyla lost her voice for several minutes after her first sip.

"Old family recipe," Delilah announced, winking.

"You oughta bottle this stuff, girl!" Andy crowed. "This is great!"

They sat and enjoyed the meal. Twyla tapped Andy's leg with her shoe. "Nice dinner, you two. Kind of like you two live here together, all cozy and whatnot."

Neither of them spoke, although they did glance at each other and smile.

"I'm glad you like it, Twyla," Frank said, after a while.

Andy laughed. "Mr. Too-Smooth." This time, Twyla kicked him under the table. "Ouch!"

"There's cake for dessert." Delilah took her plate and Frank's and started for the kitchen. "Angel food, with strawberries."

Andy rubbed his hands together as Twyla rolled her eyes at him. "Mmm. Sounds good to me!"

Twyla picked up their plates and walked to the kitchen. As Delilah returned and placed smaller plates and forks around the table, Frank pulled her into his grasp.

"She's the best thing that's ever happened to me," he announced, an arm around her waist. He gazed up at her, almost as if he was looking at her for the first time.

"Y'all stop talking about me!" she protested, her face flushing.

Andy laughed again. "She's blushing!"

"Leave the girl alone," Twyla said good-naturedly as she returned with the cake. "Dee, don't pay them no mind. And Frank, I'm glad you've got sense enough to know when you've got a good thing."

Pulling Delilah onto his lap, he nestled his face against her breast. "That I do."

Chapter Twenty–Four

Frank and Andy both had long breaks between speaking engagements in the month of June. The second weekend of June, they coordinated their schedules with Delilah and Twyla, spending time at a timeshare Andy's parents owned in Virginia Beach. They lay around, sunning themselves and playing on the beach during the day and hitting the clubs at night. The weather was hot and a little muggy, making frequent dips in the ocean surf a welcome respite. They all got to relax.

"This is the life," Andy remarked one afternoon as both he and Frank lay on the sand on their respective blankets underneath large beach umbrellas, while the women frolicked in the frothy ocean waves, along with other beachgoers. "I could do this for the rest of my life and not have a problem with it." He adjusted the straw fedora to cover his sunglasses and then stretched his arms behind his head. "How 'bout you?"

Frank lay on his stomach, his face facing Andy, his eyes closed. The warm sun that managed to penetrate through the umbrella felt great on his back, and he hadn't felt this relaxed in a long time. "Brother, need you even ask? And I would too, if I had a trust fund I could draw from."

"Yeah, money always factors into it, doesn't it?" Andy agreed with a sigh. "But life is still good, isn't it?"

The sound of the waves was soothing to Frank, along with the mournful screeching of the seagulls overhead. "It is, indeed."

FATHER'S DAY ARRIVED. DELILAH SPENT time with her father and her family that Sunday. Frank had decided not to accompany her, and Delilah was okay with that, now that she had finally laid down the law with her father.

Delilah watched her father as he cast his line off a large rock at Tybee Island in the morning sunshine. Several men, young and old, stood among the rocks fishing as well, including her brother-in-law, Scott, and his father. Patrick hadn't caught any fish as of yet but just looking at the expression on his face, Delilah knew he was in his element.

"Having fun, Dad?" she asked although she already knew the answer. She smiled to herself as she noticed he was using the fishing rod she had bought him for his birthday. She was thankful that her relationship with her father had improved and that he had suffered no ill effects from the choking episode on his birthday months earlier.

"I'm havin' a ball, baby girl." He kissed her cheek. She squeezed his arm, then walked along the boards and over to the beach area where her mother, Hazel, and sister, Clementine, were sunning themselves on canvas chaise lounges. Delilah kneeled on a blanket beside them and reached into her tote bag for her sunscreen. She thought about Frank back at her house, mowing the lawn; he was spending the week with her in Savannah.

It would have been so nice if he were here, along with Daddy and Scotty, getting to know them better, especially Daddy, she thought with an air of wistfulness. *He doesn't even have a father to enjoy Father's Day with.* She slathered the lotion on her arms and legs, and then removed her shades and applied sunscreen to her face as well.

"Could you hand me a bottle of water, honey?" Hazel asked languidly.

"Sure, Mama." Delilah fished inside the ice of the nearby cooler and drew out bottles of water for the three of them. She handed them the bottles, and then lay back on the blanket and watched the blue-gray water as it crashed against the huge rocks. The sea breeze felt good against her face.

Maybe this is all I have a right to hope for, she thought, *just being able to celebrate Father's Day with Daddy.* But she knew that in her heart of hearts, she would never give up on trying to get her father to see how wrong he was about Frank.

THE WEEKEND AFTER FATHER'S DAY, Andy and Twyla hosted their belated wedding reception for their family and friends who could not attend their courthouse wedding in February. The beautifully decorated hall they rented vibrated with music by a DJ playing old-school and contemporary R&B music. He was joined by an old friend of Andy's who spun Hip-Hop, an Irish trio who played for the Irish contingent, and Jewish musicians who played for his mother's side of the family. They all took turns, playing music into the wee hours of the morning. The food and drink flowed freely, and although they closed the bar at midnight, they ate, danced, and celebrated to exhaustion.

"You've got it all covered," Delilah kidded, after she and Andy finished taking a spin around the dance floor.

"We tried," Andy declared with a laugh.

Throughout the night, one thought kept coming back to Frank. It did again as he stood near the crowded dance floor and overheard a snippet of Delilah's and Andy's conversation: *This is the way it should be.*

Chapter Twenty-Five

July arrived and the hot, sweaty days were upon them, but Frank was unable to spend the Fourth of July holiday with Delilah. He had a speaking engagement the day after in Vancouver, British Columbia, Canada. Although the flights were interminable for him, Frank was thankful for the trip to briefly escape from the sweltering cities he had been visiting of late. He had never been to Canada, but had always wanted to visit. He even squeezed in some time afterward to visit a few of the tourist attractions as well as a few of the nightclubs with the coordinator and some of her staff.

He basked in the warm reception he received from the Canadian audience as well as the coordinator and made notes to himself to forge stronger alliances with the United States' northern neighbor. He hadn't mined this promising possibility. Not only did the enormous nation provide the possibility of an endless income source, but he discovered that the two countries had a lot in common, and he wanted to explore that further. In his small way, he wanted to strengthen ties between the two countries.

Frank spent his last evening in Vancouver crafting an illustrious e-mail to the coordinator he had befriended over the past several weeks, thanking her for her hospitality and assistance as well as putting out feelers regarding whether she knew of other provinces that might be interested in his services. The next morning he would be returning to Washington, DC.

His text message notification buzzed. It was Delilah. *Asleep?* her text inquired.

He picked up his cell phone and hit her number. "Hi, baby." He completed the e-mail, sent it and then shut down his laptop. "As you can see, I'm not asleep. What are you doing awake this time of night?"

"I couldn't sleep."

"You sound nervous. What's going on in Savannah?"

She laughed, but it failed to convince him. "Come on, spit it out, Delilah."

"Okay, okay." She exhaled in a rush. "There are a lot of tornado watches and warning all over the state of Georgia and Alabama. Just all over the South, really. It just makes me nervous, that's all."

The thought hit him like a wall of bricks cascading upon him. Since arriving in Canada, he hadn't been keeping up with the news, let alone the weather reports, except to gaze in a distracted manner at the occasional news and weather alerts that hit his phone earlier in the day. A wave of guilty feelings washed over him. "Oh, wow, baby. I'm sorry to hear that. I've been so busy—how is it right now?"

"It's okay for the moment." Her voice shook. "I'm just so glad to hear your voice."

Frank attempted to put her mind at rest, and they talked until dawn broke. He stifled a yawn. "I'm sorry, Delilah, but I need to run to catch the shuttle to the airport."

"Oh, sweetie, I'm sorry. I kept you up all night!"

He smiled through his anxiety about the weather down south and her safety. He didn't want to hang up, as if his staying connected to her could keep her safe. But he had to grab a shower, among other things. He was cutting it beyond close. Curiously, he lost track of time whenever they talked. "That's the last thing I'm worrying about. But I do have to go."

"I know," she replied. Her voice was quiet. "Get going."

"I love you, baby. Stay safe." He forced himself to click off first and hurried to the bathroom to take his shower.

FRANK NAPPED ON THE PLANES. He already missed the cooler Canadian climate, particularly when he was smacked full in the face by the sticky mid-Atlantic humidity as he retrieved his car from the airport parking garage. He felt no air-conditioning there, but at least it wasn't hot enough to sustain a burn as it would have been if he had parked outside in the early-afternoon sun.

The thought once again brought images of Delilah and the dangerous weather she was facing down in Georgia. During the lag time in between the last leg of his flight, Frank glimpsed the weather report on CNN. It was not encouraging for the folks in many cities in the South.

Almost immediately upon arriving at his place, he called Delilah and spoke to her for a few minutes.

"Honey, let me call you back, my boss is on the other line," she said, fear still evident in her voice before she clicked off.

He turned on the television. The meteorologist on The Weather Channel was proclaiming tornado warnings for many cities in Georgia. They were extended into the overnight hours.

"Oh my Lord," he murmured.

Delilah had been on pins and needles for most of the last twenty-four hours. Her supervisor, Mr. McDermott, had been magnanimous for once in his life, allowing her and her coworkers not on vacation to work from home for the foreseeable future as long as the electricity was still operating at their residences. Hers was still working, but she was so jumpy that it was difficult for her to get much work done. She called her mother.

"No, we've had a little bit of rain off and on and some wind, but nothing serious yet," her mother replied.

"Same here," Delilah remarked, "although it's gotten awfully dark."

"I would tell you to come over to our house, but the weather's been so fickle lately, it's probably best for you to stay where you are. Sweetie, I worry about you sometimes, living alone."

Delilah made a half-hearted attempt to laugh. "Most of the time, I would say you have nothing to worry about. Unfortunately, this isn't one of those times."

They spoke a little while longer until she heard an ominous rumble of thunder so powerful that the windows rattled in the parlor where she sat. Her heart raced. "We'd better get off the phone, Mama. Give Daddy my love."

She hung up, and after peering out the window, she tried to get back to work.

That night, Frank awoke with a start and shot to his feet so fast that he became light-headed. It was now almost daybreak but still dark, and he almost broke his neck tripping on a stray shoe beside his bed. He fumbled on the nightstand for the television remote and the window shades. By the light of the television and the streetlights outside, he found his cell phone and Delilah's number.

No answer.

His fingers trembled as he composed a text to her. *Why do they make these damn letters so small?* he wondered, his impatience growing as he fingered the virtual keyboard. He grabbed his reading glasses from the nightstand and tried again.

He turned up the volume on the television as he awaited her reply.

"The southern states were pummeled with a barrage of tornadoes last night, the reporter on *The CBS Morning News* was saying. "The twisters, most of which forecasters believe to have been EF2s, zig-zagged through Alabama, Georgia, South Carolina—"

Georgia.

Frank glanced at his cell phone: *Undeliverable.*

What the—?

A trickle of sweat coursed down his face, yet he felt a chill creep up the base of his spine.

Delilah, why can't I reach you?

He spent the next hour flipping channels, devouring every morsel of information the reporters and weather personnel were giving out in piecemeal fashion. He gritted his teeth. *What was going on down there?*

To be fair to the reporters and meteorologists, Frank gleaned from his remote-control square dance through various channels that the reports were still sketchy because of the extensive damage.

It didn't look good.

The sun inched its way over the trees. Frank didn't notice.

Before sprinting to the bathroom, he turned up the volume in order to hear the news over the rushing water of the shower.

The phone rang. He almost broke his neck getting out of the shower to answer it. "Hello!" he barked.

"I just saw the news, bro," Andy replied. "You heard from Delilah?"

"No. I called and texted her. Nothing."

"Well, you know, even the news is having problems getting

information. Maybe it's just because there are just a lot of people trying to contact each other, and the cell towers and circuits are overloaded."

"Maybe."

"So what are—?"

"I'm going down there."

"No, Frank." Andy's voice was firm. "Don't go down there."

"What do you expect me to do?" Frank put Andy on speakerphone as he stalked to the bedroom and threw the phone down on the bed. He grabbed a pair of boxers and a sleeveless undershirt from the dresser in his walk-in closet. After that, he selected a pair of jeans and a short-sleeved shirt. When he returned, he began to dress and then picked up the phone again. "I'm sorry, man—"

"No need, buddy. I understand. But you need to wait for a minute; see what shakes out. Because frankly, you'll only be in the way of the authorities."

Frank stopped in the middle of dressing, the receiver to his ear as he listened to his best friend's advice. He was right, of course. He couldn't just fly down there willy-nilly. He needed more information concerning the damage in Georgia. For all he knew, the airport might not be accessible.

"Yeah, you're right. I'll wait for now. But not for long."

FRANK LEFT HIS PLACE AND drove down to Waldorf. It was rush hour and traffic moved at a crawl at times, but it gave him something to do while he waited for further news regarding the tornadoes down in the southern states. The old urge for a cigarette came roaring back. Taking a swig from his bottled water, he tried to drown it.

He ran a few errands and hours later, returned home. He worked out in the fitness center until he was ready to collapse, took a shower, and threw a load of clothes into the washer. After vacuuming his place and listening to more of the same on the news and weather reports, he threw up his hands and picked up his cell phone.

"Hello? Yes, I want to make a reservation," he announced.

"ARE YOU OKAY?" THE ELDERLY woman sitting next to Frank asked.

Her silvery hair was pulled back into a tight bun and her posture was stately.

"Huh? Y-yes, I'm okay," he replied, only just realizing that he had been gripping the armrests so tightly that one hand was cramped.

"Don't like flying, huh?" The woman's brown eyes were kind.

Frank forced himself to smile. The woman's voice and her kindly gaze gave him a bit of comfort. "Show's that much, huh?"

"If that's what it is," she replied, touching his hand for a moment.

Her candor left him at a loss for words. He fumbled with the magazine he had been attempting to read, until he dropped it.

"Call an old lady nosy if you want—"

"I would never do that, ma'am," he replied, trying to smile.

"But you look troubled, son."

He contorted his back and spine in various positions in the confined space as he finally retrieved the magazine. Her kindness was causing him to lose his cool. "I'm concerned about a loved one." He sighed. "I haven't heard from her since before the tornadoes down south—"

His throat tightened, and he closed his eyes for a moment, not allowing himself to think the worst. A moment later, he felt her warm hand on top of his. He did not flinch from her touch.

Over the roar of the plane's engines, the pressure in one of his ears, and the voices of the other passengers, her soft voice rang out as clear as a bell. "She will be okay; your young lady will be okay."

He swallowed hard. "I sure hope so, ma'am."

As he left the Florida International Airport and got on the shuttle bus to pick up his rental car, Frank's mind was abuzz with thoughts. He had gotten a variety of reports from airport staff and residents about the tornadoes. Thankfully, there was not much damage in the northern region of Florida where the airport was located.

Some infrastructure had sustained damage. Inspections as well as repairs were already underway throughout the state as well as in neighboring states. Trees and debris were being cleared away and roadways were being repaired. It would just take time, depending how severe the damage was. Unfortunately, he still didn't know about Savannah.

Frank attempted to contact Delilah's sister, Clementine, via

Facebook but got no response. He put out feelers on Facebook to two other contacts he had made during his numerous trips to Georgia in general and Savannah in particular, but the information served to be more confusing than helpful, except for one nugget of information he took as fact—and it was all he needed to know: Savannah had been hit.

His body shook whenever his mind wandered and he thought about Delilah. He kept the old woman's proclamation in mind whenever he felt himself sliding into thoughts of despair. As he drove away from the airport and into the outlying suburbs of south Georgia, he saw first-hand evidence of tornado damage. Uprooted trees and large limbs were scattered about, and people were using chainsaws to clear them from the roads. As he continued driving, he saw boarded-up windows and damaged siding.

His anxiety grew.

Stopping at a red light, he gripped the steering wheel until his knuckles grew pale.

"God, I need help," he prayed. "I'm about to go grab a drink somewhere just to calm my nerves. I need to prepare myself for whatever I find." He took a deep breath. At the same time, the driver behind him honked, and he resumed driving.

The damage seems to be so sporadic around here. I just need to stop thinking and get there. "Baby, I'm coming. I *will* find you."

On the highway, as he drove past neighborhood after neighborhood, Frank noticed the damage becoming more severe. A few electrical poles were being repaired by the power company crews and all manner of work crews were out in force.

"Oh, Lord," Frank whispered over and over. He hit Delilah's number again but to no avail.

As he entered the town of Savannah, Frank heard the buzz and hum of chainsaws everywhere. Quite a few houses had visible damage. Toppled trees made some roads impassable, and he had to take other streets. As he made the final turn into Delilah's neighborhood, Frank was nearly paralyzed by mind-numbing fear. He pulled over and stopped the car for a few minutes to calm himself.

He exhaled. "Okay."

As he approached Delilah's house, Frank could see damage from a large oak tree. A blue plastic tarp covered most of the roof, its vivid color stark against the sky that was bleached almost white by the heat. He parked the car, ran up the path to the porch, and banged on the front door. "Delilah!"

After a full five minutes of banging on the door, yelling, and trying to peer through the closed draperied windows, a neighbor from the house next door walked up to him.

"May I help you? A man of Asian descent about his age asked. He had a southern drawl. Frank did a double take.

"I'm—I'm looking for Delilah. Do you know where she is?"

The man's gaze behind rimless eyeglasses, was not suspicious, merely inquisitive. "And you are—"

"Frank Ellis," he replied, suppressing his impatience.

The man smiled. "Oh, yes. Delilah has spoken of you, but no, no one has seen her. The neighbors organized a search party, but we have been unable to find her. I saw a paramedic at the shopping center and told him about Dee. He told me that they are doing all they can, but the number of injury calls have outstripped their resources." He waved a hand in the direction of the roof. "My brother and I covered it with the tarp. We have no electricity yet. The phones aren't working, either."

"I know." Frank glanced at his watch.

"We have been hoping that she is staying with her parents because of the damage to the roof."

"I see." Frank wiped the sweat from his forehead with the back of his hand. "I'm sure she will be grateful."

The man indicated himself. "By the way, my name is Jei Rhee." His face brightened. "The paramedic said that they are calling in emergency personnel from Tennessee and North Carolina—"

"That's all well and good, but time is of the essence," Frank replied. He paced for a minute. "I know where her parents live. And you're right, she might've gone there. I'm going to head on over there."

"That's a good idea," Jei replied. "Can I help?"

Frank mustered a smile. "I can use all the help I can get." He turned and ran toward the rental car.

FRANK WAITED WHILE JEI WENT into the house and emerged after several minutes. He locked the door of his home and then ran to the car. In each hand, Jei carried a lantern-style flashlight. He placed them in the backseat and then jumped into the passenger seat next to Frank. "There's bottled water in the trunk," Frank announced. "I grabbed a couple of cases at the Walmart before I left Jacksonville."

Frank drove until he was able to get reception for his cell phone.

Andy picked up after the first ring. "What's up, Frank?"

"I need your help. Delilah's not at her house, and as far as we can tell, she hasn't been here since the tornado hit. The first responders are so busy that they haven't gotten to her neighborhood yet. So I'm not waiting. I'm looking for her; one of her neighbors is with me. I'm staying at the Hampton Inn in Savannah. I flew into Jacksonville. The tornadoes didn't do much damage down there."

"I'll see if I can get a guy I work with to handle my presentation tomorrow," Andy replied, "and let you know when I touch down at the airport. It should be sometime tonight."

"No, you don't have to do that. I'm going to Delilah's parents' house first," Frank announced as he stopped the car at a strip mall where the damage was minimal. He entered their address into the rental car's GPS, then swung away from the curb and began to head down the street according to its directions. "If she hasn't been there, I'll need you to tell me the best way to conduct a search, since you're the subject matter expert regarding disaster preparedness. But just sit tight for right now. Cell phone service is spotty, so if you can't get me, leave a message at the hotel. Their phones are working, at least for now, and I'll be checking in over there for any messages. But I'll let you know what I find out once I talk to Delilah's parents, okay?"

"Cool. You do that."

Frank made his way through the debris- and tree-littered neighborhood streets of suburban Savannah. On some blocks, the skeletonized remains of houses stood beside houses that were barely touched. Some people trudged through the devastation, while others picked through the rubble—for people or property, the pair did not know.

"It is incredible," Jei said softly, as if to himself, "the power of Mother Nature."

"Yes it is." Frank barely missed driving through shards of broken glass as he continued with single-minded determination toward a place he had visited only once before over a year ago. The GPS had ceased to navigate, due to the extensive damage in the area he was driving through. "Let's hope Mother Nature will supply us with a lot of luck and some miracles today."

With Jei's help, Frank found the Carpenter residence even without the aid of GPS. They stepped out of the car, the relentless heat assaulting them as soon as they did so. Both were glad that they had the presence of mind to wear baseball caps and sunglasses, as the summer sun burned into their flesh. Frank hurried toward the front door, his shoes crunching on the long gravel driveway. Jei followed.

He flew up the stairway and hammered down the nickel-plated knocker.

"What in the—" was the muffled inquiry before the front door swung open. It was Patrick. His eyes narrowed for a brief moment as his eyes adjusted to the laser-bright sunlight that pierced his gaze. "Frank?"

"Hello, Mr. Carpenter," Frank replied, a bit out of breath from the combination of exertion, hot weather, and trepidation. Had Delilah been injured during the storm? "I need to see Delilah. Is she here?"

Frank watched as a variety of emotions crossed the older man's sun-kissed features, finally settling on what looked like amazement. "No, she isn't. Come in."

They followed Patrick into the welcoming coolness of the foyer and through the parlor, the shades drawn most of the way down against the searing Georgia heat. Again, Frank swiped his sweaty forehead with the back of his hand.

He heard a familiar voice as they reached the sunroom. Twin white ceiling fans stood still. A woman sat in the room, manually fanning herself. The shades were pulled down in here as well, and the screen door was open. Even the insects were still and silent.

As their eyes adjusted to the shady semidarkness, Frank made out Hazel's silhouette.

"Frank?" Hazel called out as she stood up, uncertain, as if she couldn't believe her own eyes.

"Yes, Hazel, it's me, Frank. I was hoping I'd find Delilah here," he replied as he gave her a hug. Patrick and Jei stood beside them, watching.

"We haven't been able to get in touch with her either, but we thought she might show up here. As you can see, our electricity's out," Patrick announced. "Makes no sense to go to a hotel 'cause many of them are facing the same problems we're having. Anyway, the radio said it shouldn't be much longer." He turned to leave the room, mumbling, "Serves me right for never gettin' that generator—"

"That you meant to buy years ago," Hazel finished for him, with a laugh. "Oh, Frank, it's so good to see you. You want something to drink? Patrick ran down to the store earlier and managed to find some ice. We have water in the cooler here, and it still has some ice in it. You two look as if you could use a cold drink. I declare, Frank, you sound like you're about to pass out."

"No, thanks, keep it for you and Patrick." Frank turned to Jei. "Hazel, Patrick, this is Jei Rhee, Delilah's neighbor. He's going to help me look for her."

"So you think she's missing?" Hazel asked. Her hands flew to her mouth. Patrick, upon returning to the room, overheard his wife. He hurried over to put his arm around her and drew her to him in a one-armed embrace.

"I don't know for sure, Hazel, but I was at her house before I came here, and she wasn't there. Jei here covered her roof because it sustained some damage."

"Oh my gosh," she gasped. "Honey—"

"What are you gonna do?" Patrick asked.

Frank tried to think before he spoke, since he could plainly see that Hazel was upset and Patrick was also worried. "Well, Jei and I are going to attempt to retrace her steps. When did you last speak to her?"

"Yesterday afternoon, right before the tornado hit this area," Patrick replied. "I knew I should've gone over there—"

"It's probably better that you stayed here, in case she showed up, Patrick, so don't beat yourself up. The radio reception's been kind of bad, but the authorities want those people who don't need to be on the roads to stay off of them and just handle whatever cleanup you can do safely around your own homes." Frank gave Hazel a hug as said, "Don't worry, we'll catch up with her. Maybe she did go to her house, noticed that the roof was damaged but covered up by one of her neighbors, and went to stay at a hotel or something."

Patrick looked skeptical. "Did either of you see any fire department personnel or police? What are they doing?"

Jei nodded. "I did, but they're kind of overwhelmed right now—"

"Which is why we're going to go look on our own," said Frank. Both he and Jei turned to leave.

Patrick kissed his wife on the cheek and started after them. "We heard from Clemmie a few minutes ago, and Delilah's not over there. I figured if we hadn't heard from her in the next hour or so, I was gonna head over there. Wait. I'm goin' with you two."

Frank held up a hand as he said, "No, Patrick. I think it would be better for the two of you to stay here." He smiled although he felt the increasing weight of apprehension upon his shoulders. "You stay here and comfort your wife. She needs you right now."

Patrick nodded. "Okay, but you let us know if you find out anything, and I mean anything."

I will. Take care, you two." Frank gave them his cell phone number, along with the hotel's number. "If you can't reach me, leave a message at the hotel. Let's go, Jei."

After Frank called Andy back and relayed the latest information about Delilah's disappearance, Andy gave him tips on the most successful way to conduct a search. Frank clicked off and then said to Jei, "Let's check the area around here first and then slowly work our way from the Carpenter house back to Delilah's place."

The Carpenters were lucky that their property had not sustained much damage—only a few of the large trees had been downed in the front and back yards, and there was only minimal damage to some of their shrubs, so searching there did not take long. Frank and Jei got back in the car, and Frank drove until they reached the entrance to the subdivision. There he pulled over and approached a power company crew as they worked on moving an electrical pole that was partially blocking the entrance. They hadn't been there when Frank and Jei initially arrived.

A member of the crew held up her hand. "Sir, you can't come in this area," she shouted over the din of whining chainsaw motors. Many people in the subdivision were working on cutting down damaged trees, cutting up large limbs in their front and back yards, and cleaning up other debris. "There are live wires down—"

"I need to ask you a question." Frank pulled out his cell phone and showed her a picture of Delilah, taken during their vacation at the Maxwell timeshare at Virginia Beach. "Have you seen this woman or any emergency vehicles leave this subdivision in the last few minutes?" He swallowed to talk past the lump in his throat. "She's been missing since the tornado."

She shook her head. "No, there haven't been any vehicles or people in or out since we got here. Good luck with your search."

Frank called Andy and relayed to him what Delilah's parents had told him, and then Frank and Jei jumped back in the car. There were still a few hours of daylight left, and they wanted to utilize all of it.

Frank and Jei racked their brains to try to think of all of the other routes Delilah could have taken to her parents' house. The landscape had been altered considerably by the tornado, with authorities still attempting to classify whether it had been an EF2 or EF3 tornado that struck the region. Yet some streets suffered little more than a few limbs being stripped from trees or no damage at all. Neither Frank nor Jei could be 100 percent sure that the roads they were driving on were the same ones Delilah had taken.

"Well, now we know that she's not with her sister," Jei remarked as he wiped the sweat from his face and savored the car's air-conditioning, "so at least we don't have to go over there."

"Yep, we can concentrate on all routes leading from their parents' house back to Delilah's," Frank replied as he drove to a gas station. "I'm going to fill 'er up. Grab some of that water out of the trunk, will you?"

Night was approaching, and with it, Frank's concerns grew. He was glad it was summer, and it would not be cold during the night, but the summer heat presented its own problems. He called the hotel's voicemail and spoke to the front desk staff, but there were no messages except one from Andy, asking if he needed him to cancel any speaking engagements. He took Jei home to get a few hours of rest. "You need to rest too," Jei remarked.

Frank shook his head. "I'll rest when this thing is over."

He headed back out, stopping at a fast food restaurant that looked to be undamaged and open for a quick bite before he returned to Delilah's subdivision with one of Jei's flashlights. He searched around the back of her home again and peered into the windows of the bottom floor a second time. Frank's intuition told him that she was not inside, and he hoped he was right. Afterward, he drove slowly along a back road, stopping along the side of the road to look around fallen trees and tree limbs on foot.

At a loss at what to do after hours of searching, Frank drove along and listened to various all-news radio station reports. The wee hours of the next morning arrived. Every time his mind wandered to worst-case scenarios, he squelched the thoughts. "It's just a matter of time before I find you, baby," he whispered. "Just a matter of time."

Frank was relieved when the sun came up. Although he had searched throughout the night, because of the debris strewn everywhere in the region, he knew that it would be less hazardous during the light of day.

At the break of dawn, Frank climbed out of the car where he had parked on the shoulder only a few hours before, and he began walking down the street. It was a quiet, scenic two-lane country road that veered off of the main drag. Using the map he had gotten from the rental car agency, he had discovered the night before that it was also a shortcut to the Carpenter residence.

Frank rubbed the sleep from his eyes as he walked methodically, examining underneath fallen trees or any large debris along the way. Because he was walking, he came across a steep embankment hidden beneath a muddy ditch that extended along the tree-lined road to his left. Ahead of him, on the shoulder of the road, a lone car peeked from beneath a huge oak tree.

It was Delilah's car.

"Oh my God," Frank whispered, rooted to the spot. His blood froze, and he could hardly breathe. He shook it off and sprang into action, sprinting and hopping over branches until he reached the automobile. He aimed the flashlight's light beam through the window in an area of the vehicle not damaged by the tree, which wasn't much. He could see that it was totaled. But there was no sign of Delilah.

"Delilah!" he yelled.

Suddenly, he heard a roar of a motor and turned to see an extended-cab pickup truck swerve onto the shoulder. A husky man with red hair and most of his face covered with a reddish beard, jumped out and hurried over. He was dressed in faded jeans and plaid shirt, and he looked like a lumberjack. Frank was glad to see him.

"What happened?" the man called out.

Frank pointed. "That's my girlfriend's car, but she's not in it. She's got to be around here somewhere."

The man lost no time in joining Frank in the search.

The sun provided dappled light through the thick cover of trees as well as shade. The morning was already starting out sultry as a heavy curtain of fog fought the sunlight for dominance. Frank ran back-and-forth along the edge of the ditch. He cupped his hands around his mouth. "Delilah!

He heard his own voice as it bounced along the trees and down into a valley that was obscured by the woodlands. Birds chirped in response. "Delilah! Baby, where are you?"

Frank stood for a moment, listening for any sounds besides those of nature. He was about to start looking on the other side of the road when he heard a faint cry. "Frank! Frank, I'm down here!"

Frank walked closer to the ditch and nearly lost his footing. Further down past the trees and into the fog-shrouded valley, near a lone shrub, was Delilah. She lay sprawled upon the ground, weakly waving her arms. Frank thought he was staring at a ghost. When she tried to get up and her cry echoed in the distance, he knew that she was real. "Okay, Delilah, I'm coming to get you." He grabbed the man's arm. "My girl's down there."

Frank laid the flashlight upon the ground. He carefully made his way past the ditch and through the stand of trees and onto the grassy embankment, slippery with dew. He could hear the other man's footsteps and his heavy breathing behind him. He reached Delilah's side and kneeled down beside her as Delilah threw her arms around him. "Are you hurt anywhere, baby?"

"My ankle hurts, and I can't stand on it. I think it might be broken," she replied. "Oh, honey, I'm so glad you're here! Thank God you found me."

"You know I wouldn't stop until I found you, baby." Frank began to lift her into his arms, and then he stopped. He felt her ankle. "I'm sorry, I don't mean to hurt you—I think it is broken too. I know how to splint a leg, but it's going to be interesting splinting an ankle." He looked around. "I don't have anything with me."

The man held up his hand. "I have rope and duct tape in my truck. I'll go back and get them."

Frank patted the man on the back. "Yeah, that'll work. Thanks."

The man left and soon returned with a heavy coiled rope and a roll of duct tape.

Delilah sat as straight as possible while the man held her ankle still. Frank tried not to hurt her as he took off her tennis shoe. Her foot was swollen and discolored. He looked around for the flattest piece of wood he could find and then returned to her side. Delilah stifled a whimper as Frank broke the piece of wood in half. He placed a piece behind her ankle and wrapped it as tight as he could with the tape to immobilize it. Then Frank lifted her into his arms, and he and the man started back up the steep hill.

The man clambered up the hill first and then helped Frank as he handed Delilah to him and then scrambled up as well. By this time, an additional vehicle had stopped on the shoulder to investigate, and people from that car had gathered on the hill above them. They clapped as the trio emerged.

"Mister, where's the nearest hospital?" Frank asked the red-haired man as they carried Delilah to his rental vehicle and placed her in the backseat.

"Back in town. I can show you where it is," he said. "I'm heading that way. I work at a hardware store there."

Delilah was weak, dirty, and disheveled, but she was alive. Frank hurried to the trunk and emerged with several bottles of water. He opened one for Delilah and held it to her lips as she drank. As she attempted to hold the bottle herself, her arms and hands shook.

"Take it easy, baby. Sip it, don't gulp it."

After Frank had finished giving Delilah a drink, the men shook hands. Both were sweaty and had mud on their jeans and shoes. Delilah looked like a rag doll. "I … I know where it is," she said.

"You just sit back, little lady," the man replied. "I don't mind."

Frank handed him a bottle of water and then cracked open a bottle for himself and took a swig. "Thanks, man. I'll follow you."

Frank followed the man in his car to the hospital's emergency room entrance. While Delilah dozed, the man pulled over. Frank did the same and the man hopped out of his truck and approached Frank's car window.

"Thanks for your help … uh, I didn't get your name," Frank said.

"It's Robert. Hey, think nothing of it. Glad I could help. Let me know how it goes with the young lady, okay?" He handed Frank a business card. He was the manager for the hardware store where he worked.

"I sure will, and the name's Frank." Frank glanced in the rearview mirror at the still-sleeping Delilah and nodded his head toward the passenger seat where she lay. "Her name is Delilah."

"Well, you tell Miss Delilah that I wish her the best of luck."

Frank couldn't stop grinning. "I'll do that."

He carried Delilah inside to one of the few empty chairs in the crowded emergency room. While she was being triaged, he found out what happened. "It began to get really dark and there was a tornado watch for my area. I decided to go to my parents' house so I wouldn't be alone, and since it was a watch, I thought I still had time." She rubbed an eye wearily. "I took the shortcut, but halfway to their house, I saw a funnel cloud emerge from the clouds."

"Wow," Frank replied. He stood beside Delilah's chair, holding her other hand while the emergency room personnel took her information. He couldn't believe that she had survived the tornado and had been out in that field for two days, alone.

"I knew there were ditches on both sides of the road I took, so I jumped out of my car and headed for the closest ditch." Delilah chuckled ruefully and ran a hand through her hair. "The tornado rolled through, and I dug myself into the ditch with all my might. Afterward, I was terrified that it would come back, so I lay there for a few hours more."

"Aw, baby." He tightened his grip on her hand. She had been out there, alone and scared.

"When I finally got the courage to climb out of the ditch, I slipped and fell down the embankment. When I slipped, I heard a cracking sound in my ankle and felt pain, especially when I tried to stand up." She began to tremble uncontrollably. "After that, I waited for a car to come by, but nobody saw or heard me."

Frank kneeled down and held her tight. "Could someone get her a blanket or something?" he asked the nurse. "She's shivering."

Fearing that she might be going into shock, the nurse instructed a member of the emergency room staff to get Delilah a blanket while Frank continued to hold her, attempting to impart some of the warmth from his body into hers in the meantime. It was difficult since the hospital was air-conditioned and rather chilly. "Baby, I've been going out of my mind, I was so worried," he replied as he kissed her cheek. "But once we started looking for you, I could feel you. I could feel you within me, and I knew you were alive somewhere. I just had to find you."

Finally Delilah was taken back to one of the treatment rooms. "Can my boyfriend come with me?" Delilah asked the doctor as she wrapped the thin blanket tighter around her body.

The doctor nodded. "Sure."

Once inside the room, Frank helped her get up on the examination table while the doctor washed his hands. After drying them, he turned to them. Although he had been working long days since the tornado, he managed to laugh when he took a look at Delilah's duct-taped ankle, which was splinted with a piece of wood. "Quite a job," he remarked as he gently cut away and unwrapped the crudely wrapped splint.

"We had nothing else out there," Frank replied as he steadied Delilah against his chest while the doctor worked.

"You did a good job, considering. More importantly, you remembered to do it in the first place." Admiration was evident in his voice.

"Thanks, Doctor." Frank kissed the side of Delilah's smudged and sleepy face. "Take care of her, okay?"

Because Delilah had been outside for two days and nights with no food or water, had been bitten by insects and was dehydrated, the hospital decided to keep her overnight for observation and to administer IV fluids. As they prepared to admit her later that evening, Frank called her parents. Although he wasn't supposed to be on his cell phone in the hospital, he thought that this situation warranted a phone call.

"Hello? Who ... who is this?" Patrick asked, a little too loudly.

"Patrick, this is Frank. I found your daughter."

On Frank's end of the line, it sounded as if he dropped the phone, along with whooping in the background and other commotion. Frank smiled as he waited for Patrick to return to his senses and the phone.

"Is Delilah all right? Is she safe?" Now it was Hazel on the line.

"Yes, she's fine. She has a broken ankle and she suffered exposure, so they're keeping her in the hospital overnight for observation." Frank recounted in a concise manner what happened to Delilah over the past two and a half days. "Visiting hours are over, but I can give her the phone and let you speak to her before they admit her—"

"Yes, yes!" Hazel cried.

Frank handed Delilah his cell phone. "It's your mother."

She spoke for a moment to her parents and then handed it back to him. While the medical personnel finished assessing and treating Delilah, Frank left the room and walked around the emergency room for a while. He squelched the sudden urge to run to the nearest 7-Eleven or gas station and purchase a pack of cigarettes. Frank returned as Delilah was finishing the admittance paperwork and about to be taken to her room. Once she was settled in bed, he was allowed to visit with her—but only for a few minutes since visiting hours were over.

She was a bit cleaner and now and wearing a blue boot on her left foot. "I feel a little less grimy," Delilah remarked, "but I wonder how I'm supposed to take a shower wearing this contraption?"

Frank sat down on the bed, took her hand, and smiled. "You'll manage. I'll help you."

She chuckled. "You would help me do that, wouldn't you?"

"I'll help you with whatever you need, Delilah." With his hands, he attempted to comb her tangled curls. "The gift shop is closed; otherwise, I would've bought you a toothbrush and comb."

Delilah threw her arms around his neck and hugged him tight. "I still can't believe that you're here and you found me."

"Believe it, baby. I'll bring you some clothes and things tomorrow. Now you get some rest."

The nurse peeked inside.

"Don't worry, nurse, I'm leaving," Frank said, but not before giving Delilah a gentle kiss on the lips. "Get some rest now."

Frank got his parking permit validated before leaving the hospital, and he drove through the storm-littered streets toward the hotel. He was thankful that the hospital had only sustained a few broken windows.

As he arrived at the entrance of the hotel, he gave his car keys to the valet. "Is everything okay, Mr. Ellis? Any news on your girlfriend?"

"Yes, everything is fine now, thanks." He fished into the back pocket of his jeans for his wallet and handed him a tip.

Frank walked through the lobby and pressed the elevator button. When he got off the elevator and walked down the hallway to his room, he slid the key card into the slot of his door and unlocked it. He closed the door behind him, found the remote, and clicked on the television for background noise while he undressed. He padded to the bathroom, turned on the shower full force, and adjusted the water temperature. Snatching a fresh towel and washcloth from the shelf, he pulled back the shower curtain and stepped inside.

The beige-colored stone tiles grew blurry as Frank leaned against the cold, wet wall and allowed hard, racking sobs to take over.

"Thank you, God, for answering my prayers …"

THE NEXT DAY DELILAH WAS allowed to go home. Since her home was damaged to the extent that it was unsafe to inhabit, she would be staying with her parents until an insurance adjuster had inspected it and repairs had been made. Frank had taken her keys the night before, and contrary to common sense, he went inside and packed a suitcase with clothes, shoes, and toiletries from Delilah's bedroom. He shook his head in disbelief as he stared at the blue plastic tarp. It rustled in the breeze where it and a large portion of a tree poked through the attic ceiling. Again he said a prayer of thanks as he bounded down the stairs with the suitcase and out the front door.

Hazel and Patrick were just leaving Delilah's hospital room when Frank got off of the elevator down the hall. "Just call us when you're ready to leave, and we'll be back to pick you up," Hazel was saying.

As the door closed behind them, Frank was walking down the corridor toward them. "Hi, Frank," they greeted him in unison as Hazel and Frank embraced.

"You just missed Clemmie and Scott," Hazel said.

"I'll have to try to catch up with them," Frank replied. "You know, I can take Delilah to your house when she's released, if you want." He indicated the suitcase he rolled behind him. "I stopped by her house to pick up a few things."

"That's so thoughtful," she replied as they moved out of the way so that a nurse helping an elderly patient could pass.

"We drove past the house after you called us last night," Patrick said. He rocked back- and forth, as his emotions threatened to take over. "I'm just so glad she decided to leave the day of the tornado and not ride it out there."

Frank patted the older man on the back. "Me too."

At that moment, both men looked into the other's eyes and understood. "I'm glad you made it your business to come down here and look for her," Patrick said.

"I'm kind of stubborn," Frank admitted and grinned.

Patrick slapped him on the back and then pulled him into his arms for a quick embrace. "Thank you, son."

Astonished, Frank swiftly glanced over his shoulder in Hazel's direction.

She was beaming.

FRANK REMAINED IN SAVANNAH FOR a week to do some chores around the outside of Delilah's house. The second story was deemed unsafe to inhabit until the roof, walls, and ceiling of the attic were repaired. The insurance adjuster had inspected her home a few days after she was released from the hospital, but Delilah would remain at her parents' house until the repairs were made. Frank and Jei, the next door neighbor he met the day he arrived in Savannah, as well as Jei's wife, Susie, cleared away tree limbs and shrub damage. Later, Frank flagged down a tree-service company that was driving from the neighbor two doors down, and he hired them to remove, saw, and dispose of the huge oak tree that fell on Delilah's house.

Patrick had a good friend and neighbor who was a general contractor, and he was willing to get a crew together to replace the roof and repair the damage done to the attic and ceiling. The roof had been near the end of its life, so Delilah had been saving for its eventual replacement for over a year. She decided against submitting a claim to her insurance company.

"I think I can swing the cost of a new roof without using my homeowner's insurance," she announced.

"The tree's on me," Frank said.

Delilah shook her head and started to speak.

He held up a hand. "I don't want to hear it. You're going to have enough to handle with dealing with getting your car replaced."

"You're right about that," she admitted with a sigh as she leaned against the front of Frank's car while Frank held on to her crutches. She would have to wear the blue boot for a while. "Besides, the guy gave me a deal for throwing some unexpected business his way," Frank added.

"You're a silver-tongued devil," she cooed, pulling Frank close to her as they watched roofers begin tearing off the roof just a week later.

"You better know it, baby," he replied in his most seductive baritone against her ear. He smiled in a knowing way as he watched her give a little shiver. It was hot as Hell's pizza oven outside, but lately, he had hardly noticed. He was glad to help.

Her eyes sparkled. "You deserve a reward."

"Oh, you owe me, all right," he agreed as he gazed into them. "And I intend to collect when this work is done." He caressed her cheek. "You're coming to visit me."

She leaned closer. "Is that a promise?"

"Nope, a threat." His kiss sealed the deal.

Chapter Twenty-Six

————◆•◆•◆————

"Come with me. I'm going to pick Delilah up from BWI." Frank sat outside Andy's and Twyla's apartment, calling them from his car. It was a hot Friday evening in the middle of August, and he had the air-conditioning on, listening to music and chilling inside the vehicle. "You two aren't doing anything, are you?"

"No, not really, Andy said. "Just finished dinner."

"Good. Grab the missus and come on down."

About ten minutes later, the couple joined him.

"To the airport, Jeeves," Andy commanded with a jaunty wave of his hand as they climbed in the back seat.

"I got your Jeeves—"

"Hey, Frank," greeted Twyla.

"Hey, baby. How's this nut been treating you?"

Andy took her hand and pulled her against him.

"Like a queen," she replied, squeezing his hand.

They rode the rest of the way to the airport in spirited hijinks. Frank slid smoothly in and out of traffic with ease. There was the typical Friday night traffic but no accidents, so it moved without any impediments; they arrived about fifteen minutes after Delilah's plane landed.

"I want to go in," Frank announced, "so everybody out."

Andy and Twyla exchanged puzzled looks. Finally, Andy shrugged. "Okay. You're asking for a ticket, though."

Frank smiled. "I'll take my chances this time."

A few minutes later, they saw Delilah making her way down the aisle, pulling a small suitcase behind her. She was still wearing a blue boot on her foot, but she was now able to walk without crutches.

"Hi, everybody," she called out as she noticed the Maxwells flanking Frank.

In the midst of the people milling about as well as arriving and leaving the airport, Frank smiled and stopped when he reached her. There, he slowly dropped to one knee and simply said, "Delilah."

Delilah's shoulder bag slid off her shoulder and fell to the floor as realization set in. Her hands flew to her mouth. It fell open in shock.

Andy and Twyla stopped in their tracks not far behind Frank.

The people nearby who figured out what was about to happen stopped to watch. Those in a hurry continued on their way. Those in a hurry who noticed the scene unfolding before their eyes smiled knowingly or looked on with concern.

"Delilah, since you have come into my life, it hasn't been the same. You have illuminated it, and although you may not have known it, you shined a light on what was missing from it. And although I enjoyed my life, for a while now I realized there was a piece missing.

"You are that missing piece.

"Baby, we have had our ups and down, my health problems, family issues, living this long-distance situation—but we overcame them. We've handled them and still came out of it loving each other."

Tears began to slide down her cheeks as Delilah stood there, silent.

"But I'm tired of living without you on a daily basis. I want you with me every day, to share the rest of this journey with me. We'll figure out where; it doesn't matter. But I want you in my life, as my wife. Someday, to be the mother of my children.

"Marry me, Delilah."

Frank reached into the pocket of his jeans and pulled out a small, black velvet case. He opened it and then held out his other palm with the case inside of it. "This can never do you justice." He smiled shyly and his voice shook a little. "Delilah?"

"Oh, yes, Frank, honey, I'll marry you."

He slipped the ring on her finger, and they met together in a loving kiss.

The onlookers laughed and clapped and whistled. Some shook their heads with cynicism or amazement.

"Well done," Twyla said with a sniffle.

"Bravo, bro! I didn't know you had it in you. But I told you, Twyla, that he was the sensitive one," Andy said as they closed in around the newly engaged pair.

Frank stood up, feeling the waves of Delilah's and his best friends' love wash over him. "Time to take my fiancée home," he said as he took her hand.

And although he was a rambling man, endlessly traveling, now he had a home and, more importantly, someone to come home to.

THE END

About the Author

From the time she first held a pen, Pamela D. Beverly put it to paper—first drawing cartoons for her own amusement and later writing stories. A management analyst who works in Washington, DC, Ms. Beverly resides in Fort Washington, Maryland. This is her first published novel.

CPSIA information can be obtained at www.ICGtesting.com
Printed in the USA
LVOW13*1434100713

342267LV00002B/39/P